Out Of The

Stephanie M Turner

For Elaine

Stephanie M. Turner.

I dedicate this novel to my wonderful husband Stephen and our four children Jason, Damon, Holly and Harriet.

Chapter 1

One Grey Hair

Derby stirred as her iphone trilled out an unknown piece of guitar music, which she had randomly set as her alarm call months ago when her new phone had first arrived. Barely opening her eyes she reached for the phone and switched the alarm off. Opening her eyes fully, she didn't even look at the time, knowing it would be six thirty in the morning. For a minute she lay on her back looking at the white ceiling of her bedroom.

"No not my bedroom, our bedroom."

She whispered to herself, glancing sideways at her still sleeping husband David. Nothing short of an explosion woke David. Usually she would have to shake him awake or he simply would not get up for work, but this morning, Derby just didn't feel like the mundane routines the couple went through every day, had gone through every day for the last twenty four years.

"Twenty four years of married bliss"

Again Derby whispered to the room, a pink bedroom with pink flowered wallpaper and woodwork a shade pinker than the paper. A pink bedroom that had not been changed for ten years.

Sighing deeply, Derby quietly pulled off the duvet, and padded out of the room towards the bathroom. Closing the door and bolting it behind her, something else she had done for the whole of the twenty four years of marriage, she slipped out of her cotton pyjamas and cotton knickers, letting them fall to the floor in a heap. She plonked down onto the loo and rested her chin in her hands as she emptied her bladder, washed her hands and then brushed her teeth.

As she pulled the cord to warm up the shower, she looked deeply into the mirror over the basin. Looking back at her was someone she didn't fully recognise. Ok, the same small heart shaped face looked back at her, the same dark brown hair and blue eyes.

But everything about the image screamed dull, boring, lifeless, and then to top it all, a greyish white strand poked out of the middle of her head. It seemed to have a complete life of its own. Separate from the rest of her hair and somehow looking thicker and alien from the other normal strands of hair. Derby took hold of it and yanked, drawing a tear stinging pain from her scalp, and a yelp from her lips. But with it a small smile that she would defy time for a short while longer.

"Right on cue though."

She told her image, for today was her fortieth birthday.

The bathroom began to steam up from the nearly forgotten running shower, the mirror fogging and fading her reflection. Derby shrugged and stepped into the shower letting the hot water soothe shoulders and neck that she hadn't realised were so tense. She shampooed and conditioned her hair, scrubbed her body with silky smooth moisturising body wash, and stood for some time just letting the water run and rinse her off.

She felt quite lethargic and in no hurry to start the day. Besides, she had plenty of time to get ready for work. For as long as she could remember, well twenty odd years anyway, David had been a stickler for getting up at six thirty, actually she told herself silently, he had been a stickler for her getting up at six thirty, and relying on her to wake him too. So much so that even though she didn't need to be in work until eight and it only took ten minutes to walk to the nursery, she had long since got into the habit of the early morning alarm call.

Derby was brought out of her state of stupor by a tapping on the bathroom door.

"Derby, you finished in there? I need to pee."

With a huge sigh, Derby shut off the water and stepped out of the cubicle.

"Just a sec. How come you're awake?"

She called back. Drying off most of the excess water, Derby wrapped her huge bath sheet around her and unlocked the door. David bobbed in heading for the toilet.

"Just am I suppose."

Not wanting to watch her husband pee, Derby rapidly headed back to the bedroom. There she dried off thoroughly, slathered moisturiser over her face and body and donned her work clothes. Plain black trousers, a white school style cotton shirt and black cardigan, which she draped over her arm in case she got chilly later.

The teapot, cereal and toast were all laid out on the tiny kitchen table when David came down. Just another long term routine. Habitually, he was dressed the same as every day since he became store manager of the local supermarket twenty years previously, a plain suit, pale shirt and unassuming tie. His hair, what was left of it, had more streaks of grey than colour, and his pale blue eyes blended into his pale skin. Taking his usual seat opposite Derby, he waited for her to pour his tea, tip cereal into his bowl and pass the milk and sugar.

"Kid cereal."

Derby mumbled, practically under her breath.

"Mm what?"

David asked absently, spooning copious amounts of sugar onto the cereal.

"Oh nothing."

Derby replied, buttering her toast and taking a bite. David didn't respond. He was too involved with shovelling large spoonfuls of milk soaked cocoa pops into his mouth.

At exactly half past seven, David mumbled a hasty goodbye, and without even looking at Derby, picked up his keys from the hall table, grabbed his briefcase from the floor and headed out to his car. He could have walked to the supermarket it was that close to their home, but he preferred to give himself more 'Management Status' as he called it, by arriving by car and parking in the Manager elected parking space.

Derby, even after all the years still didn't see it that way. But David wouldn't listen to her protests over increased fuel costs, and how much healthier he would be if he walked, he was getting quite paunchy, no, his position at the supermarket required that he arrive by car to look like the boss. Nothing Derby said would change his mind. As she closed the door behind him, Derby suddenly realised that nothing she ever did or said made David change his mind about anything. Shrugging resolutely, she gathered her own bits and pieces and headed out for the nursery where she had worked for twenty years.

Derby was just finishing setting up the last of the rooms and organising the other nursery nurses, when the parents and carers began arriving to drop their children into their care. This was one of the best times of the day for Derby. She loved watching the little ones trot in, be carried in and sometimes lovingly dragged in, if a tot was being difficult, by the parents and childminders.

One mother especially, always made Derby smile. Twenty two year old Kelsey Jones, mother of three year old Chardonnay. Kelsey was a single mother, Chardonnay's father having left the two of them when she was barely two months old and had never shown his face again, balanced working as a teaching assistant whilst raising her little girl.

Kelsey was just a bottle of bubbles. She was like champagne about to force the cork. She always arrived bright and smiling when she dropped Chardonnay off and when she collected her. She always had time to have a little chat about her child, and let Derby know if there was anything amiss. Especially though, she always had time to ask Derby how she was, and had a knack of drawing out of Derby things she never divulged to anyone else. Things she would not even admit to herself.

This morning was just one of those times. Kelsey headed straight for Derby, Chardonnay on one hip, the child's bag of stuff bouncing against the other. Kelsey always made sure the nursery had several changes of clothes for her little girl, all washed, ironed and neatly folded. Also in the bag and as usual, was a pot of fruit and raisins, Chardonnay's favourite teddy and blanket, and a bottle of juice. Even though the nursery provided all food and drinks for the children, Kelsey lovingly provided extra in case her baby darling needed it.

"Derby, Chardonnay's a bit sneezy today."
Kelsey imparted to Derby.

"Can you keep an extra eye on her please. She's not poorly, no temp or anything, just a bit sneezy."
Derby held her arms out to the little girl who came willingly, wrapping her tiny fingers into Derby's hair and smiling brightly.

"Of course I will Kelsey."
She replied gently. Kelsey gave her a huge smile, and Derby felt her heart swell for the young mother and child. They could be her own daughter and granddaughter.

"Everything ok Derby?"

Kelsey asked intuitively. Realising she must have let some of her feelings show on her face, Derby beamed at her, giving Chardonnay a little tickle to cover up what was on her mind.

"I'm fine Kelsey. Thank you for asking. How is everything with you?"

This question was not just to swing the conversation away from herself but a genuine desire to check how the twenty two year old was coping. Recently she had told Derby that her landlord was putting up the rent, and the fuel bills were getting so hard to pay. She was looking for another job that she could do a couple of times a week in the evening, when her mum would be able to look after Chardonnay.

"Well I think I have something lined up. I just need to check a few things first. I'll let you know as soon as I know. Things will work out."

"You are always so optimistic Kelsey."

Derby replied with a little sadness in her voice that did not go undetected by Kelsey. She leaned a little closer to Derby, stroking her baby's face and whispering.

"What's wrong? I know something is up today."

Derby struggled with a sudden urge to burst into tears and managed a fake smile, forcing the moisture developing in the corners of her eyes back. Bobbing the little girl against her hip, she took a breath and replied.

"Nothing and everything Kelsey. I can't talk about it now, maybe at the end of the day when the children have gone home."

Kelsey nodded, a firm set to her face that told Derby she wouldn't let it go, gave Chardonnay a kiss and buzzed away to her own job.

By lunch time Derby had managed to push her strange mood to the back of her mind. Being with the children held her attention so fully, she rarely thought about things outside the nursery whilst she was at work. She loved her job passionately. Nothing gave her more pleasure than watching and helping the children develop. She adored holding and nursing the babies, changing their nappies, even the smelliest ones. She took great delight every time a toddler said a new word, took a more balanced step or put a wooden puzzle together. Each child, a unique little person was her entire world for the few hours they spent each day at the nursery.

So it was a bit of a shock to her when during the lunch break, Angela, a senior nursery nurse brought in a huge chocolate birthday cake lit with candles. The other nursery nurses encouraged the children to join in with a rendition of 'Happy Birthday' and this time Derby could not hold back the tears. Wiping at her eyes with her hands she blew out the candles, whilst whispering to Angela "Oh you" and smiling when a camera flashed as she sliced into the cake. Angela grinned and took the cake back into the kitchen to cut tiny slices for the children, and much bigger ones for the staff.

Derby followed and helped place the pieces of cake onto paper plates.

"How did you know?"

She asked Angela. Sliding cake onto the plates Derby held, Angela smiled sweetly.

"I have known you for fifteen years chick, and not once have I seen you ever celebrate your birthday, talk about David taking you out for a meal to celebrate, or mention any presents. But I have always known the date, and for that matter how old you are. I have never done anything before because you have never mentioned it, and some people just don't like their birthday. This year though, it is a special one, forty, you can't ignore that…"

Angela stopped when she saw the tears now pouring down Derby's face. She laid down the knife and carefully put her arms around her, trying to avoid covering her in chocolate.

"Derby what is it?"

Another nursery nurse ducked her head around the doorway, and seeing Derby's distressed state quickly took charge of the cake distribution without saying a word.

For a few minutes Derby just let the tears come, resting her head on Angela's shoulder. Never before had she let go to anyone, rarely even to herself. For some reason today was just different. Eventually the sobs subsided and grabbing a handful of tissues that were always on the counter, she wiped her face and looked up at Angela.

"I am so sorry."

Angela stood back and began pouring water from the kettle into two mugs, stirring milk and sugar into her own and handing Derby her regular black coffee.

"Derby, girl, there is nothing to apologise for. But just tell me, what is wrong?"

Derby sighed deeply and sipped her coffee. For a moment she said nothing, then.

"Today is also my wedding anniversary."

Angela waited, not sure what to say or what the connection was. For all the years she had known Derby, she knew very little about her, nobody did. What she did know was that Derby was a brilliant manager, a listener to all of her staff's concerns, home problems, relationships and just little every day niggles. She knew she adored children but had none of her own. She knew she was married to David, the local supermarket manager but that was it.

Derby was the most withdrawn and uncommunicative person she had ever met when it came to her own personal life, not in an unfriendly or hostile way. She just never talked to anyone about herself, and for some reason managed to get through life without anyone asking. Now Angela wondered for the first time ever, what made Derby tick.

"And?"

Angela carefully asked, wondering if she would be rebuffed. Derby shrugged her shoulders in a way that suggested despair and deep pain.

"That's it. I'm forty, I've been married for twenty four years, I have no babies of my own, and to top it all I found my first grey hair this morning."

The two women looked at each other, and for some reason the last part of Derby's sentence made them both laugh.

For Derby it was like a huge bubble had finally burst. Suddenly she saw Angela as a completely different person, a friend. Derby had no friends, never considered friends. She had been alone for so long, not physically, there was David, but mentally, inside, in her heart she was just plain lonely. Twice a year she would stand beside David at the Manager's Ball, an event organised by the supermarket chain in the summer and at Christmas, when all of the managers across the country would come together. They would have a fancy meal, some wine and chat to each other about stock and sales. Derby would smile and nod at the right times and then retreat into her own little world of running the nursery.

David would introduce her to new managers and their respective partners, and then mostly ignore her, as he did most of the time anyway. Derby didn't mind, she would mingle a little, talk about inconsequential things to the female partners of the managers, and wait until midnight when they would climb into a taxi and head for home, David always a little drunk. At home David would fall into bed and wait for Derby to lock up and join him.

Today for the first time, Derby saw another human being as a potential friend. Maybe she could actually go out for coffee or shopping with Angela, do stuff other women did naturally. Maybe, just maybe go out in the evening for a drink in a pub, or go for a meal in a restaurant with someone other than David, not that he ever took her out anyway.

Pushing aside these thoughts, Derby wiped away the last of the tears and smiled at Angela. She took a deep breath, ran her fingers through her hair and tested her voice.

"Are you free after work to go for a coffee?"

Taken aback, Angela tried unsuccessfully to disguise her surprise, and Derby immediately believed she had got it all wrong. She pressed her lips together tightly and was about to apologise when Angela spoke.

"Derby a coffee? Really, let's go get us a glass of wine. After all it is Friday."

Derby couldn't stop the grin that spread across her face as she nodded in agreement.

"Absolutely. Now chocolate cake I think."

Both women laughed together as they took large slabs of cake and ate them as fast as they could before going back to the main nursery room.

The rest of the day was the usual bustle of activities designed to entertain and educate the little ones in the nursery care. As the parents and childminders came to collect their children at various times, Derby felt a tiny tingle of anticipation for the evening with Angela. Kelsey arrived to collect Chardonnay, all smiles and excitement and typically headed towards Derby.

"Hey Derby." Then in a voice close to a whisper. "What was up first thing?"

Derby smiled back at the young woman, and as was the norm couldn't resist telling her.

"My fortieth birthday, first grey hair and nothing to look forward to."

She finished with a slight shrug. Kelsey put a caring arm around her shoulder.

"First, no one would guess you were anywhere near forty. Second, grey is so in now, all the celebs are wearing au naturel. Third, what are you doing tonight?"

Derby creased up with giggles as Chardonnay bobbled between her and Kelsey.

"First, you crack me up Kelsey. Second…hmmm…and last, I'm actually going for a drink with Angela."

"Well that is absolutely right. But, and you don't have to, but…you know I said I had something going to earn some extra cash, well I sort of need to do some practice on people I already know."

Kelsey replied, hesitantly, which was very unlike her. Derby gave her a small frown and chewing on the side of her lip tentatively asked.

"What are you up to?"

Kelsey grinned.

"Nothing dodgy. I'm going to be doing these parties and selling stuff, only I want to have a go with people I know first in case I, you know, cock it up."

Derby laughed at Kelsey's choice of words.

"Ok I give in. What do you want me to do?"

Kelsey beamed at her, the smile lighting up her eyes. Chardonnay joined in putting her tiny hands flat against her mother's face, and just for a moment Derby felt a pain so low and so deep it took her breath away. Shoving the feeling aside she gave her attention as Kelsey explained.

"When you and Angela have had your drink would you come to my house please. I have some wine and there will be a couple of other people I know there too. It has to be after seven thirty anyway 'cos I have to put Chardonnay to bed first."

"Did I hear my name mentioned?"

Angela appeared at Derby's side, tickling Chardonnay under the chin and making her wriggle and giggle.

"Yes you did, yes ok Kelsey, and Angela I will explain later."

Kelsey grinned.

"You are a star Derby, see you later, you know my address."

She twirled around with her toddler and bag and headed for the door.

"What have you got me into Derby?"

Angela asked curiously but without concern.

Derby began tidying the now empty nursery and explained whilst she worked. Angela collected toys and straightened infant size chairs and tables and listened without comment. Derby bent over and picked up a stray teddy bear from under a counter, hugging the soft toy to her chest for a minute. Angela noticed the pause and gently placed a hand on Derby's shoulder.

"Are you alright?"

Derby stood up still holding the bear and looked at her old colleague and newly found friend. She knew quite a lot about Angela, her family and her life. She had listened over the years and absorbed it all. Now she realised no one knew anything about her. It was like she had lived inside a grey cloud, barely visible. Swallowing the lump that threatened to choke her, Derby felt the weight of the cloud begin to lift. Light seemed to be seeping into her life from around the edges, bringing with it colour where there had been only grey. Finally she was coming out of the grey.

"Let's go and get that drink and maybe we can talk."

She said to Angela.

Chapter 2

Sharing

The bar Angela chose was ten minutes walk from the nursery, so close to Derby's own home, yet she didn't even know it existed. Walking in was quite nerve- racking for her, as she had never been into a bar before. When she and David were teenagers they didn't try to get into the pubs like their friends did. David would always tell her they didn't stand a chance of getting away with it, because she was so small no one would believe she was old enough. Then when she was old enough, they had already been married for two years and didn't have the money to go anywhere. A few more years and though money was no longer a problem, they just didn't go out.

Angela led the way to the bar and Derby followed closely. Couples, groups of men, groups of women, mixed groups all sat, stood and leaned holding glasses, smiling and chatting. The noise wasn't overpowering but it was noise Derby was not used to. The most noise in her life was the sound of children. These were adults, the tones and volume totally different. She felt alien, like she had just arrived from a different planet. Brushing a hand across her face she whispered to herself.

"How have I missed so much? I'm forty."

Angela turned to her offering her a glass of red wine.

"Isn't that what you are going to tell me."

She told Derby. Screwing her face up a little and taking a sip of wine Derby replied.

"I didn't realise I had said that out loud enough to be heard."

Angela giggled, taking a sip from her glass too.

"Let's get that table over there."

The two women sat at a tall round table on chrome and leather bar stools. Derby looked around the bar and absorbed everything. The clothes the women wore, the clothes the men worn, so completely different from the ones David wore, and from her own plain dull wardrobe. Thoughts of her husband made her start a little.

"Whoops, better text David. He'll be home soon and no dinner."

Angela cringed.

"God girl, what decade are you living in?"

Derby shrugged as she quickly tapped a message into her phone.

David one of the young mums needs some advice be late home best get a takeaway.

David wouldn't mind getting a Chinese or Indian, and he probably wouldn't even notice she wasn't there. Her phone chirped and she quickly read the message out to Angela.

"He says 'ok see you later' that about sums it up."

Then she picked up her glass and took a long swallow, wiping her mouth lightly with the back of her hand.

"My husband, Jake, he will get the children their tea, settle them in front of the TV and watch a movie or something with them until I get home. He will have a plate in the microwave waiting for me, and warm it when I get in. I texted him before we left work and told him where I was going and who with. He messaged me back with lots of love and kisses. I only have girlie drinks now and then, he's the same. Mostly we do this together or curl up at home with a bottle. We've been married for sixteen years and it's as good as it was at the beginning. Actually scratch that, it's better. We fit."

Angela told Derby. Holding her glass between both hands, Derby looked into the deep red liquid and then looked up moisture in her eyes.

"You are so very lucky. I have no family. My parents disowned me at fifteen when I thought I was pregnant, one month before my sixteenth birthday. Before chucking me out they made sure David married me, gave me their permission though it felt more like an order, and enough money for us to pay the first month's rent on a bedsit.

You see I started going out with David at school when I was thirteen. He was a year older than me. I fell for him, he was good looking and popular, and he seemed to feel the same way about me. At least that's what he told me, and we stayed together even though other girls wanted him, flirted with him, he didn't cheat.

Then the inevitable happened, like most teenagers we experimented. We touched a lot, snogged and finally in a field on his jacket we had sex. Both of us were virgins, it was a bit painful and very quick. I didn't feel much, just his breathing getting fast and his weight on me. He came, I didn't, I didn't really feel anything, except maybe a bit let down."

Derby stopped and emptied her wine glass.

"That first time, David told me he loved me. That meant more than the sex. So the second time I looked forward to it. Before, all the touching and stuff had been nice, I think I used to come, but well I didn't really know. I'd never touched myself or anything, my mother always told me it was dirty and bad. That girls simply did not, nor should not do that. Girl parts were for peeing and someday for having children, they weren't supposed to enjoy it. Men were different, it was their nature to find pleasure in sex, but for women it was un-lady like and sluttish."

Derby stopped talking, lifted the glass and finished her wine. She put the glass back on the table a little too forcefully, and looked at Angela for comments. Angela sat quiet for a moment, sipping from her glass and looking at Derby's miserable face.

"I didn't realise there were parents like that still. I suppose the years I've known you I have always thought something was not quite right, but I just kind of thought you were a very private person. Now I know different."

She paused and then hesitantly asked.

"Why didn't you have children later?"

Derby shrugged resignedly.

"Never happened. I mean at first I was on the pill, after the pregnancy scare and getting married. David was starting out, training, going up the ladder. He said he never regretted us getting married, but kids would have to come later, when we were more settled and money and stuff."

She looked down and saw her glass was empty. Angela reached for it, slid off her stool without a word and weaved her way to the bar. Derby propped her chin on one hand and scanned the crowd.

Everyone seemed to be with someone or in a group. They all looked happy and relaxed. They were all talking or listening, and a few were bobbing and swaying to music that Derby hadn't even realised was playing. She glanced at her watch and saw with surprise that they had been there an hour already. The atmosphere was a brand new experience to her.

The supermarket balls were dull compared to this. They always started out with the meal, the speeches then a disco. Most people stayed in their seats or milled about, mulling over the budgets and financial status of the chain. Some got overly drunk then bounced about on the dance floor, but that was about as exciting as it ever got. Here though the place had an electric feel about it, like the air before a huge storm, charged and powerful. Derby wondered if she really could fit in here, if she could change her life even at forty.

Angela returned with a fresh glass of wine, her own still half full. Derby sat up straight, thanked her and sipped. She then carefully placed the glass on the table and carried on the conversation as though there had been no break.

"Just about three years later, David got his assistant manager post and we had a mortgage and I was working at the nursery. Once I discovered I wasn't pregnant after we got married, I went to the College of Further Education and trained as a nursery nurse. I had always loved children anyway. So, we, well I suppose David decided we should start trying for a family. It was what I wanted more than anything, so I stopped taking my pill but nothing happened.

A year later I went to the doctor and they did loads of tests and checks and everything came back ok. David flat out refused to go near a doctor about his fertility, kept saying it would happen one day. But it never did, so I can only guess there's something wrong with him.

As the years went by, I stopped asking him to get checked and our sex life fizzled too. I mean, it had never been lively. He never seemed bothered, and I had never initiated it in all the time together. Another little piece of advice delivered by my mother. 'Women do not go to the man for it. They wait for him and then they do their duty. Those women who do are tarty and loose.'"

Derby mimicked her mother in a haughty voice, which Angela found both amusing and very sad at the same time.

"Derby darling, you sound like you have just stepped out of the Victorian era. Jake and me, we have a brilliant sex life. It has to fit around the kids and all that, but we always find time for us."

"Lucky you Angela. The last time I had sex was early December, after the supermarket Christmas Ball, and well I could have passed. As usual I didn't feel a thing."

Angela looked at her and then both women burst into giggles. Derby didn't even know she could giggle, it felt so good and so young.

"Is..is..is..that be…cause he's small?"

Angela asked, barely getting the words out because of the laughter. Derby, wiping tears from her eyes as a fresh wave of giggles took her tried to answer.

"Nnnnoooo…too qu..qu..quick."

Angela held her side, and had to grab the edge of the table to stop herself from falling off the stool she was laughing so much.

"One pump, a grunt and it's over."

Derby announced.

"Oh…oh God. Derby I can't breathe. I'm sorry it's really not funny."

Derby laughed with her friend, but realised even though it sounded hilarious, this was her life and that meant it was bloody depressing. The laughter subsided and Derby replied.

"Yeah, funny if it wasn't me. But it is and that's all I have."

She then downed the wine in one go, wiped her mouth with the back of her hand and shrugged. Angela finished her own drink and took hold of Derby's hand squeezing it gently.

"Plenty of time to change all that girl. Courage and confidence."

Derby nodded even though she didn't believe it.

"Come on let's go and see what Kelsey's up to."

Chapter 3

Kelsey

The two women arrived at Kelsey's house just after eight. They were led into a small sitting room. It was bright and cheerful, painted in soft pastels with a cream sofa and armchair, and a television in one corner. Along one wall was a bookshelf, the two bottom shelves lined with children's books, the top two bursting with paperbacks. Under the window were two large plastic tubs full of toys.

There were already three women sitting on the sofa, all in their early twenties and each had a glass of wine. Kelsey introduced everyone and disappeared to fetch Derby and Angela a glass of wine too. Derby felt a little awkward at first, not sure whether to sit in the armchair, leave it for Angela or if Kelsey had been sitting in it before. Angela decided against the chair and plonked down on the carpet near the toys. Kelsey returned with drinks and in her usual bubbly way chimed.

"Derby sit down. Go on have the chair. I need the floor anyway to show you what I have."

Derby quickly and feeling a little embarrassed, crossed the room and sat down, sinking a little into the cushion and almost spilling her drink. She glanced at Angela, who hid a giggle behind her hand. Derby felt a little hysterical burst of laughter bubble up, but managed to force it back with a sip of wine.

Kelsey settled herself on the floor in front of her guests and pulled a large plastic container in front of her. She took a breath and addressed the women in the room.

"Now you all know I'm trying to make some extra cash, and I thought I would give this a go. So, I'm going to show you some stuff, and then hopefully you might want to buy some. I have special order forms to keep it all private."

Derby frowned, unsure why this was important, but the younger women smiled and nudged each other as though they knew exactly what it meant. Kelsey lifted the lid from the box and put her hand inside ready to lift something out.

"First I have a couple of samples to show you, then in the dining room I have a rack and a table with the rest of the stuff laid out."

She pulled from the box a red silky thong with a fur waistband and sequins sewn onto the crotch

"This is part of our newest range."

Kelsey started but Derby put her hand up.

"Kelsey. Could you start from the beginning please?"

Kelsey looked around the room, realised she hadn't explained anything and grinned.

"God what an idiot I am. Lucky I decided on this trial run. Well, I'm going to have a go at selling sexy lingerie and adult toys. That's what I meant about the order forms and the display in the other room. You can choose the things you want, put it on your form which you put in a sealed envelope and give to me. I send it in and your stuff comes back in a plain sealed bag, with an invoice attached for the amount only. Inside your package is your stuff and a detailed invoice. So nobody knows what you're buying. You just give me the outside invoice and money and I send it in."

She stopped, beaming that she had finally explained it properly. Derby felt herself blush and sipped more wine to cover it up. She was saved by one of the younger women calling out.

"So get on with the demo Kelsey. What have you got in your box?"

Everyone laughed and Derby joined in, though she was still uncomfortable. It was so strange that she should be sitting in an armchair about to be shown what her mother had warned her against. More strange even, after the previous conversation with Angela. Kelsey began again.

"Well like I said, the thong. Then here we have the latest vibrator."

She switched it on and a soft humming came from the toy. She held it out.

"Go on have a hold and feel it's power." She giggled as she deepened her voice on the word 'power' "it's quite small to some of the others and comes (there were little squeals around the room) with it's own velvet case."

The vibrator was passed around the room and Derby once again blushed as it was handed to her. She saw Angela give her an encouraging smile as she held the sex toy, and felt it's soft rubbery head massage her palm. It gave her a tingly feeling especially when she moved the switch to high.

The next thing Kelsey took from her box was a full outfit made of black and red vinyl. There was a corset with laces and studs where the nipples would sit, and suspenders attached. A pair of crotchless knickers and long black gloves with studs in the palms completed the outfit.

Each item she showed them was passed around for them to examine and comment on. There were lots of giggles and whispered remarks, Derby catching the occasional "My Brad would love that." or "Gerry would explode if I wore that." Then when the box was empty Kelsey jumped to her feet and said.

"Just going to get the wine. Then I have some DVD samples to show you."

She trotted out of the room returning quickly with a tray with three bottles of wine, white, red and rosé. She put the tray on a small side table and filled everyone's glass. Then she closed the curtains, turned on the television and moved to the far corner of the room.

"Now I am going to show you some clips from various DVDs that we sell. They are all adult sex education films, so please don't think of them as porn."

Derby detected a rehearsed speech, as Kelsey didn't usually speak so formally. Feeling more relaxed, probably due to the wine, Derby settled into the chair and prepared herself for the show. She had never even looked at a top shelf magazine before let alone a sex movie.

The first clip introduced a whole variety of sex toys and a brief of how they could be used either individually or as a couple. At first Derby didn't find it too difficult to watch. But the second clip was a little more explicit because it showed the sex toys actually being used rather than just the explanation, but it was short and not too detailed.

Obviously the full versions would have more in them. The final clip was the most embarrassing for Derby, and she was glad the room was dimmed because the curtains were closed. This one was a DVD about how to get the most out of your sex life. It explained that each person should be comfortable with their own body to have a satisfying sex life. It briefed that the full version would show how to explore one's own body to achieve orgasm, and how to explore a partner's body too.

With the heat still tinting her cheeks, Derby gulped more of her wine as Kelsey switched off the TV and re-opened the curtains. The summer evening light flooded into the room, disguising her embarrassment as she scanned the faces of the other women to see if they had noticed. No one looked at her in a strange way or pointed or laughed. She took a deep breath and looked toward Angela. Her new friend intuitively looked back and smiled encouragingly. Derby felt herself relax, both mentally and physically, settling further into the cushion of the armchair.

"Now that's the end of the demo, but here are some catalogues (she handed round A5 size booklets) which have all of the products and their prices. Inside the back cover you will find an order form and envelope, and instructions on how to place your orders. Oh and of course, there's the other stuff to look at in the other room."

The three younger women all got up and headed out of the room. Angela scooted across the floor and kneeled up against the chair Derby sat in. She smiled at Derby cheekily.

"Seen anything you like?"
She asked openly. Derby clamped her lips together, unsure how to answer.

"I'm not sure I could buy any of these things."
Angela patted her hand.

"Have a close look at the catalogue."
She bit one side of her lip.

"Just as a suggestion…get that DVD about sexual gratification, you might discover something about yourself."

Derby knew her face had taken on a shade close to raspberry, and the heat had nothing to do with the summer warmth. Angela stood up ignoring her friend's embarrassment.

"I'm going to the loo. Just think about it."

Kelsey had taken herself off to the kitchen to fetch some nibbles, so Derby alone and in the quiet sitting room turned to the page in the catalogue that displayed the DVDs. There were several that hadn't been on the clip, but she quickly found the one Angela had referred to. Whilst no one else was with her and without thinking too hard about it, she quickly jotted down the details on the order form. She sealed the form in the envelope and held it tightly feeling like she was committing a crime of some sort.

The others, including Angela returned to the sitting room and Kelsey brought in bowls and plates of snacks. She went around filling wine glasses and chatting animatedly with her friends. She also passed around a box for the women to drop their orders into. When it came to Derby, she nearly baulked, but a nudge from Angela gave her the courage to deposit her envelope into the box. She was sure everyone would be pointing and staring, but no one was. Even Kelsey, she held the box out whilst still chatting, not taking any notice of who put anything in it.

As the evening wore on, Derby felt herself becoming more relaxed and comfortable than she could ever remember being before. The younger women included her in their conversations and she no longer felt embarrassed by anything anyone said. She saw Angela glance at her now and then and caught her little smiles and nods of encouragement. The wine had gone to her head a little so when Kelsey came to re-fill her glass, she covered it and refused. She most definitely didn't want to go home drunk, she was sure David would not approve of that.

By ten, Derby was ready to go home. She had thoroughly enjoyed the evening but was quite tired. She wasn't at all used to spending any evening drinking and socialising and this evening had completely drained her. Angela seemed to notice her flagging and stood up. She took Derby's hand and gently pulled her out of the chair.

"I think it's time we got going Kelsey."
She told their hostess. Kelsey bounced up off the floor and hugged first Derby and then Angela. She was still full of energy and Derby realised she had seen Kelsey drink just one glass of wine all evening. A little prick of pain cut through her, combined with a burst of pride at how Kelsey, alone and single, looked after herself and her daughter.

"Have a great weekend Derby."
Kelsey told her as she squeezed her.

"You too Kelsey. Have fun with Chardonnay."

"Think the car is staying here tonight Kelsey. Is that ok?"
Angela asked as they reached the door.

"Wouldn't let you drive it."
Kelsey replied, grinning and jangling Angela's car keys in front of her.

"Monkey."
Angela giggled back.

"I know and there's a taxi on the way, should be about five minutes."
Kelsey told them. Derby shook her head slightly, amazed at how organised the young mother was. She hadn't even thought about how they were getting home.

Kelsey waited at the door with them chatting about her plans for the weekend, and waved goodbye until the taxi turned the corner. They had decided that as Derby's house was closest she would be dropped off first, and as they neared her home she began to feel a tiny flutter inside at what she would say to David.

She had never been out this late on her own before. Even planning meetings at work never went on late. So by the time the taxi pulled up to the kerb outside her home her pulse was beating a little too fast. She kept her jitters to herself as she climbed out of the car and thanked Angela for the evening.

"Good to see you alive."
Angela told her as she closed the taxi door and waved. Derby waved back and turned towards her pathway. She walked steadily to the front door, took a deep breath and placed her key in the lock.

Chapter 4

David

The house was quiet. Nothing unusual about that, they rarely had the television on except when David wanted to watch some sport or the news. Mostly Derby would sit and read whilst David sat at the computer checking spread sheets and stock figures. But tonight it seemed even more quiet than usual.

Derby headed for the lounge sure David would be there, maybe even sulking because she was so late. However the lounge was empty and so was the kitchen. Frowning to herself, Derby dropped her bag onto the sofa and headed upstairs. The bathroom door was wide open so David wasn't in there and when she checked the bedroom, found that empty too. David was not home. This gave Derby a real pause for thought. She never went out alone but David didn't either. She had texted him to say she was going to be late and he had texted back ok. So why hadn't he messaged her that he was going out.

Derby sat on the very edge of their bed, the same bed they had when they first got married. They had replaced the mattress a few years ago.

"Not like it ever got much use"

She spoke to the empty room. She placed her hands palms down on the duvet close to her thighs and wondered again where her husband was. Obviously he hadn't thought about either her birthday or their anniversary either. Derby wasn't surprised and by now, so many years on, not bothered. David had never bought presents for either. Well, he had bought her a sixteenth birthday present which doubled as the 'something blue' for their wedding. It was a tiny sapphire set in a silver ring. Derby still wore it, the only sort of engagement ring she owned, next to her plain gold wedding band. David didn't wear a wedding ring. He declared that it was a waste of money and not really traditional.

Derby sat still and unthinking for several minutes before she gave herself a mental shake. She then looked around the familiar room and wondered exactly how it was that she had reached forty living this dull and inert life. How had she let herself and David become comfortable, habitual strangers. How had they both let it happen because she knew it wasn't just her doing.

The front door closing brought Derby out of her wonderings. She stood up, automatically straightening the duvet even though there was barely a ripple in the cover, and went out of the room to see her husband. From the top of the stairs she heard him moving about in the kitchen. She heard a cupboard open and a plate clanking onto the counter. She moved down the stairs, the carpet covering the sound of her footsteps even though she still wore her shoes and headed for the kitchen. Just inside the doorway she stopped.

"Hi."

David turned quickly, dropping a fork that he had taken from the drawer.

"Jesus Derby, you made me jump."

He bent and picked up the fork placing it into a tub of takeaway Chinese food.

"How come you are only just eating?"

Derby asked. She wasn't particularly interested, just a little curious. David usually followed a routine for his meals, rarely diverting from it. Actually she suddenly thought, it was mainly her routine of cooking. He never had to get his own meals. Just once, she remembered, when she had been in hospital with appendicitis years ago, and for only the one night because his mother had then come to stay and cooked for him. She left as soon as Derby had been discharged.

David's mother did not like her, always believing that she had trapped her son into marriage with a fake pregnancy. No matter what Derby said or tried to explain that she really had thought she was pregnant, missing two months periods, Irene, David's mother refused to believe her. So over the years David visited his family. They never came to visit him. At first it hurt Derby very much. Her own parents had rejected her and then David's family, for Irene convinced Brenda, David's big sister, that Derby had tricked him, also ostracised her. As the years wore on Derby pushed them all to the back of her mind and concentrated on her career. David still visited his mother and sister from time to time, but never talked about them. Derby knew he had a nephew and a niece but knew nothing about them and didn't ask.

"Well I was still at work when you texted me so I brought a whole load of files home and got into them and just forgot the time. It was my stomach that reminded me I hadn't eaten so I just popped out to China Kitchen."

He finished speaking, turned back to the counter and emptied a plastic tub onto the plate that already had a pile of rice on it.

"Oh ok. Sorry you had to get takeaway."

Holding the plate high near his mouth, David took a huge forkful of what looked like pork and beansprouts and shovelled it in.

"S'ok."

Was all he mumbled as he carried the plate into the lounge plonking down onto the sofa. Derby stayed where she was viewing the mess he had left behind. The plastic tubs, packet for the prawn crackers, and the bag the lot came in, were skewed across the counter. Some of the sauce and rice had dropped onto the work-surface and left a trail where David had taken a few mouthfuls, before putting the food on the plate. The sound of the news drifted into the kitchen from the lounge, and for a moment Derby just stood and leaned on the edge of the kitchen table, wondering why she had bothered coming home. She had never felt like this before.

She was so used to David's ways. She didn't expect a 'happy birthday' or 'darling happy anniversary, the last twenty four years have been wonderful. I love you' There were no surprises in anything David did. But today, for some unknown reason she just wished things could be that way. She closed her eyes, willing the tears that threatened to stay away, and wished just for once that things could be different, that David could be different.

Derby wiped at her eyes. They were dry as she knew they would be, she had shed a lifetime of tears today with Angela. She didn't think there were any left inside her. This was her lot. This was her life. Wishing wouldn't change it. Longing for a family, for David to be like Angela's Jake was a useless exercise in futility. She just had to get on with the way things were. She had her career and loved it passionately. She had David so she wasn't entirely alone. That thought stopped all of her thoughts like a bang to the head. Today she had realised that she actually was alone. Even though she was married to David, she had never been more alone than she felt at that moment.

A rustle behind her made her turn as David came into the kitchen with his empty plate. He put it in the sink and patted his stomach with one hand. His other hand he held across his mouth as he belched quietly. David always did that.

"Mmmm full up now. Well I'm going up."

Without waiting for her reply he turned and headed for the stairs, leaving Derby with the usual task of clearing up after him and locking up the house.

That night Derby lay for a long time awake and contemplative. Her mind churned, and though she was tired it would not shut down. The whole day played over and over like a movie on fast forward. She tried to shut off the thoughts of Kelsey's demonstration, but it kept flooding through her like a broken water mains. She tried to push aside the conversations with Angela by trying to think ahead to what she had to do the next day. That didn't work. Her weekends were always the same. Cleaning the house, doing the washing and then food shopping. Rarely did she divert from these activities, occasionally going into the town on the bus if she needed something from one of the big shops. Even then she tended to go only where she needed, and didn't stop to browse, or window shop, or even stop for a coffee.

Finally Derby drifted into a restless sleep. Images from the DVD clips invaded her dreams, and she awoke many times sweating and thirsty and hot with embarrassment. For in many of the dreams it was her that was on the screen taking part in the clips. Several times she got out of bed and wandered down to the kitchen to get a cool glass of water. Then she would drift back to sleep only for the pattern to repeat. By the morning she felt drained and dehydrated, realising this had a lot to do with the amount of wine she had drunk the night before.

After the usual morning routine, David left for the supermarket and Derby began her normal Saturday chores. Her head ached a little and she still felt very thirsty. She swallowed some paracetamol with two glasses of water and a cup of tea, and nibbled on toast whilst she loaded the washing machine.

Standing up, she looked around the kitchen and came to a sudden decision. Today she would leave the housework. She would go food shopping as usual but then she would go into town and have a look at the shops, maybe even stop for lunch at a café. Before she could change, her mind she grabbed her bag and headed out the door into bright hot sunshine.

Chapter 5

Big Shops

The town was busy, stifling and noisy but for once Derby did not care. She had all day. David would not be home until ten tonight as this was his Saturday where he had to stay late. He had to do this one Saturday in every month, designating to his assistant managers the remaining Saturdays. He wouldn't notice that she hadn't done any housework and she would probably be back anyway to catch up. The washing would go into the tumble dryer and be ready to be ironed tomorrow, so all his shirts and underwear would still be ready for Monday. She also had plenty of time to prepare his evening meal too, and for the first time wondered exactly how she managed to fill her weekend, it was so mundane.

At first Derby stayed in the main shopping centre just looking in the windows. Then she decided to actually go into the shops and wander about. The first one she ventured into was a huge multi-floor department store. She took the escalator down to the very bottom and found herself in the men's department. It was divided into sections displaying clothes by various designers and the variety was astounding.

She browsed as though she were seriously looking for something, giggling to herself as she imagined David in some of the fashions on display. But her thoughts were also very sad. David was a moderately handsome man, but he was regimental in his style. He had his hair cut exactly the same way all of the time, short and clipped though a lot of it was gone now. He wore the same suits, dark grey or blue. The same shoes, which he replaced every now and then and when he wasn't working, pale blue denim jeans and a polo shirt of some sort, either blue, green or brown.

She found it hard to picture her husband in anything that was hanging or folded in the store. Each time she tried, his face flickered away from her, and was replaced by one of the images dotted about the shop of male models showing off the clothes for sale.

The next floor Derby went to was full of everything you could possibly want for the home. She didn't spend a great deal of time there. She briefly looked at some tea towels and decorated mugs but decided she didn't find them very interesting. All of the things she had at home were still in good condition, and since they never had people round for anything, she didn't even contemplate dinner sets or fancy cutlery.

The third floor she stepped onto brought a huge lump to her throat. It was the children's department and was filled with clothes, nursery equipment and toys. With her eyes misted slightly, Derby strolled between the rows of little clothes and stroked soft teddy bears. She stopped in the toddler section and found a beautiful little outfit. It was a pink and white dress with a matching cardigan, and was perfect for Chardonnay. Without thinking too much she took the garment to the counter and bought it.

She would give it to Kelsey on Monday as a thank you gift for inviting her to the party. David would never know, probably wouldn't even care anyway, because the one thing she had always maintained, was her financial independence. Actually it was David that she had to thank for that. He had insisted from the beginning that she should have her own bank account for her salary to go into. That she would be responsible for shopping and household bills, but that it was his duty to pay the mortgage, insurance, utility bills and the like. So she actually had quite a bit of money of her own.

Over the years, even with increases in living costs, increases in her salary had allowed her to set up a savings account alongside her bank account which was now quite substantial. With the introduction of online banking, she could now transfer money rapidly between the two, but rarely needed to move any back into her current account. She hadn't ever really thought about her money, just monitoring her accounts regularly for security purposes. Now, once again she had a small epiphany, she could buy almost anything she wanted within reason.

The last department Derby visited was the women's floor and again she was bowled over by the variety on offer. Like her husband her own clothes were always the same. As she browsed she imagined herself in some of the clothes on offer, touching the fabric, and marvelling at how some of the garments felt between her fingers.

An assistant approached her and asked if she needed any help. At first Derby was shocked into silence, unable to respond. She had never been approached like this before, most of her clothes she bought from a mail order catalogue or from the online stores. Giving herself a little shake she managed to smile at the young woman, a sudden thought coming to mind.

"Actually, yes thank you. I'm looking for something to wear for a special meal out with my husband."
The assistant smiled and gave her a professional once over.

"Mmm yes, come with me please, I think I can show you something perfect."
Wondering for a moment what on earth she was doing, Derby hesitated then decided to go with the fantasy and followed her. The woman led Derby across the store to a small designer department. She headed straight for a rail of dresses and reached up removing one and draping it across her arms. Derby stopped and surprised herself by how much the dress jumped out at her. It really was very beautiful.

"I think if you put this with black heels and shrug you will have your outfit."
The assistant told her. Derby nodded as though she knew exactly what the woman was talking about. Seeming to understand her hesitancy the young woman offered the dress to her.

"Why don't you go and try it on. You'll get a better idea. I can get someone to fetch shoes and the shrug too, so you can see how it will look as a whole. What size are you?"
Derby took a breath and decided to take the plunge.

"I'm a five."
The woman spoke into a headset that Derby hadn't noticed, and then indicated she should follow her.

The changing room was a complete surprise to Derby. In the past, way back in the past when she had tried on clothes in shops, they had been small cubicles with a curtain that rarely closed properly. This changing room was completely different. It was a large room surrounded by large circular cubicles with heavy curtains. The assistant led her to an open cubicle hanging the dress on one of several hooks inside. There were tall mirrors showing every angle and a padded chair. Another assistant appeared holding black stiletto shoes and a black lacy shrug, which she placed in the cubicle too.

"Press that little button if you need any help, you know zip or anything."

The first assistant told her, pointing to a small box on the wall. Smiling brightly she then stepped out and pulled the curtain enclosing Derby in the small well lit room.

For a few seconds Derby stood and just looked at her surroundings. For a tiny moment she wondered exactly what she was doing there. Then she gave herself a mental shake and began removing her clothes. The dress slid over her head and seemed to know where to go by itself. She had never felt anything as lovely on her body before, not even her wedding dress. When she reached for the zip she realised she would need help and pressed the little button. Almost immediately the assistant was there slipping into the cubicle, barely making an opening in the curtain. She smiled as she saw straight away what Derby needed and quickly zipped the dress.

"It looks lovely."

The woman told her as she slipped out of the cubicle.

Derby straightened the dress, sliding her hands down the fabric and looked in one of the mirrors. The dress was cut low at the breast, nipped in at the waist and fell to the middle of her calves. It was an array of peacock colours and showed her figure off perfectly. Carefully she slipped on the shoes and the shrug, and turned to look in the different mirrors getting a full view of the dress from all angles of her body. She had no idea if this is what she should look like, but she was pleased. Shyly, she stepped out of the cubicle and tentatively moved towards the entrance. The assistant was there waiting, a genuine smile on her face.

"I knew it would be perfect."

She told Derby. Still unsure of how to react, Derby nodded.

"I think I will take the whole outfit."

She replied.

Walking out of the shop with her purchases, Derby felt like she was someone else. In less than twenty four hours she had done things she had never dreamed of doing in her entire life. It frightened her a little that she could suddenly become this other person. Rationally she knew that she was the same and was just thinking differently now, but it shook her to realise that for all these years, this other Derby had been trapped inside.

She stopped suddenly, angering another shopper, a chic looking woman carrying many bags who crashed into her. Frowning and tutting, the woman side stepped Derby who mumbled an apology. Ignoring her, the woman rushed on along the pavement. Derby moved nearer to a shop window so others didn't walk into her too. She pretended to scan the opposite side of the street as though looking for something in particular. She did actually focus in on a coffee shop, and taking care not to trip anyone else over, made her way across the road.

The coffee shop was busy. A well known chain full of busy shoppers queuing for hot drinks and cakes. Derby joined the queue, and gave her order to an harassed looking teenager who was already taking the next order as Derby took her change. The drink was dispensed quickly, and luckily for Derby a couple vacated a seat near the window just as she moved from the counter. Placing her shopping on the wide window sill she settled in the leather chair and sipped her coffee.

Staring out of the window at the busy street, Derby mused over her new self. How had she let her life become so completely dull? How had she let herself drift through a marriage that was empty and meaningless? She couldn't quite imagine life without David, but there had to be more. As she held her cup, her mind wandered and she imagined living alone, maybe in a city apartment, dressing fashionably, going out for drinks or to night clubs. This fantasy gripped her so tightly that for a moment she felt she couldn't breathe. Reality flooded back with a huge breath, and her cheeks warmed as she blushed, feeling so guilty. But she didn't want to feel guilty, she wanted to feel alive.

Grabbing her bags, Derby swallowed the rest of her coffee and headed back to the street. There seemed to be even more people around now, jostling for space on the pavement. She didn't know where to go now. The idea of more shopping had seeped away from her leaving her empty and lonely. She passed a bus stop, a poster on the side catching her eye. It showed a smiling young woman advertising a gym, where everyone was welcome. Never in her wildest dreams had she thought about going to a gym.

But being totally honest with herself, she hadn't ever thought about doing anything outside of work. Pulling her phone from her bag, she entered the number into her contacts. Maybe she would call later and find out more about it.

Deciding that she had spent enough time in the town, Derby headed for home. She found she was actually quite tired even though she hadn't really been out for long. But she thought, never mind, it was more than she had done in her lifetime and she had enjoyed the experience. She planned on many more. This thought brought to mind the DVD she had ordered, and she felt a rush of heat to her cheeks. It also brought another wave of excitement inside as she imagined watching the whole thing, and not just the less explicit scenes on the clip. For the first time ever, Derby felt anticipation.

At home she hung her new outfit in her wardrobe, leaving the shoes in their box stacked with other small storage boxes. She didn't consider David would find the clothes and shoes. He only ever went into his own wardrobe and drawers, never showing the slightest bit of interest in what Derby wore at any time. He had never commented or complimented her even when they went to the annual balls. Derby believed that he actually didn't realise that she existed. So long as his meals were ready, his clothes washed and ironed and the house clean, (though she suspected he didn't notice that either) he was happy to plod his way through life.

Derby set about doing her household chores that she had neglected due to her shopping trip. Her mind was not on the house though. It kept wandering of its own volition to the dress and shoes hanging in the wardrobe. Finally after hurriedly running the vacuum cleaner around, pegging some clothes on the line, and almost chucking the crockery and cutlery into the dishwasher, she gave up on the housework.

In her bedroom she lifted the dress from the rail and laid it across the bed. It seemed to shimmer against the dull off white, rose printed duvet cover. The colours filled the room and her senses, so much that she could almost imagine smelling tropical flowers and wild perfumes. Derby closed her eyes and breathed deeply. Pictures of Caribbean beaches and candle lit tables, deep blue sea and the sound of breaking waves, a man, muscular and tanned holding her hand, flashed through her mind flooding her body with heat and desire.

Sighing she opened her eyes and began removing her clothes to try on the dress again. This time she wiggled her arms around her back to zip it up by herself. She pulled the shoes and shrug from the wardrobe and slowly put on the whole outfit. One of the wardrobe doors doubled as a floor length mirror, and though she couldn't see herself from all sides of the room like in the shop cubicle, Derby could still see how well the dress fitted. The shoes and shrug accentuated it and for quite some time she pranced about the bedroom. Every now and then she would stop in front of the mirror and throw a hip out to one side, hand placed on her waist, imitating a model. She giggled at her image and flicked her hair about her face. She was thoroughly enjoying herself.

During one pass of the mirror, Derby stopped and checked the image looking back at her. A small frown creased her brow. At first she couldn't work out what was off about the outfit. Then she realised that it wasn't so much as what she could see, but what she couldn't. Her underwear was the problem. When she had been in town she hadn't thought at all about it. Now she imagined lace trimmed silk or satin in vibrant colours, not the plain cotton white or buff coloured knickers and bras that she owned. She envisioned sheer stockings and suspenders, corsets and bustiers in place of the dark twenty and thirty denier tights that she always wore.

"God I am just boring."

She told her image.

"Take off this outfit and wake up. Do something about your life now before it's too late."

She spoke sternly as though telling someone off. It almost felt like there were two people in the room, the Derby in the mirror and the physical Derby. Still watching her image she again twisted a little to reach the zip, lifting it over her head and placing it gently onto the bed. She treated it as though it were fragile china, re-hanging it and replacing the accessories too.

After closing the wardrobe door Derby went back to the mirror in just her underwear. Another out of the ordinary act, for she had never bothered to actually scrutinise herself before. Usually she gave a cursory look to check her hair was in place or that her skirt was not up at the back, then turned her back on the mirror. Today she looked, really looked. Most of what she saw was not a disappointment. Her figure was alright. She wasn't thin, but she didn't carry any excess fat either. She had large breasts and a neat waist, hips that were mostly in proportion giving her a more hour glass figure and shapely legs. All told she thought she looked ok, better than a lot of the women she had seen in the town that day.

"So what's wrong"
She asked her image. Turning sideways and back, she ran her hands over her body and cringed at the feel of the cotton underwear. It was old and bobbled from washing, and did nothing to enhance her figure. Tutting at herself she grabbed her normal clothes dragging them on and turning from the mirror and headed out of the bedroom.

In the kitchen, Derby turned the burner on under the kettle and spooned coffee into a mug. She leaned against the counter waiting for the kettle to boil, again letting her mind wander to sun-soaked beaches and gorgeous looking men. Her cheeks heated up again as the fantasy took her to lying next to one of these toned up guys, a delicate glass filled with some sort of cocktail in her hand, his fingers trailing a path up her thigh, feather light but electric.

The high pitched whistle of the boiling kettle brought her crashing back to her kitchen, the beach gone and more disappointingly, the man gone. She turned the cooker ring off and let the water settle before pouring it onto the coffee. She put both palms flat against her cheeks and took a steadying breath.

"Phew. You so need to get a grip girl."
She again spoke aloud to herself.

"At least try and control the blushing."
Then she burst into giggles.

She lifted the kettle, trembling a little as she continued to laugh at herself and poured hot water into the mug, spilling some on the counter. Pulling a sheet of Plenty from the roll she mopped up the water, tossing the sodden paper towel into the bin as she took her drink into the lounge.

Settling onto the sofa, coffee next to her on a side table, Derby booted up her laptop and sipped her drink as she waited. David mostly used the desk top tucked away on a desk in the corner of the dining room, a room that had a dining table that never got used, which was now mostly stacked with his paperwork from the supermarket.

Derby only touched any of it when she lifted it to dust underneath and couldn't remember the last time she had used the desk top computer, preferring the laptop as it was mobile. Quite often she would browse with it in the kitchen whilst waiting for something to cook, or on the sofa when David was ensconced in the dining room. Now sipping coffee she entered the web address for the shop she had bought her dress from and clicked onto the lingerie department.

She was amazed at the range on offer and found herself a bit overwhelmed by it all. Some of the items really stood out but she didn't buy. Looking at the photos of the models, she could see where her own underwear was wrong. She realised that her bras did not fit correctly. Opening another window she did a quick search and found a very informative website on correct bra fitting. So she decided that sooner rather than later, she would go back to the store and be measured for bras that would not only fit but look good too.

Something at the top of the window caught her eye. It was something she had seen before but never clicked on. A blue box with a white F in it. Without another thought she clicked on the box and a small pane opened asking her sign onto or sign up for Facebook. She had heard some of her co-workers and the parents talking about it, and knew it was a social networking site.

So she tapped the sign up for link and began entering her details. Shortly afterwards she had set up her profile but baulked at the idea of adding a photo. Rarely did she have recent pictures taken of herself and those she had were not good. All others were old ones which she wouldn't dream of scanning into her laptop to use.

So biting her lip she took out her phone and tried a few self-portrait shots. Viewing them, she was not happy that any did her justice, she just wasn't practised at taking photos of herself. She couldn't ask David, even though he probably wouldn't ask why, she did not want him to know about this new Derby. She resolved to ask Angela on Monday, knowing that she could tell her friend what she wanted it for, and that Angela would be chuffed to bits, and her reason.

Leaving the profile to complete later, Derby began to play around with finding friends. She was astounded when she entered names of people she knew and began clicking on the add friend button, hoping these people would recognise who she was and accept her. She hardly spoke to anyone outside of work so was afraid no one would want to be friends. However a few came back immediately accepting her, so her first experience of social networking began.

For some time Derby stared at the screen wondering what she should do now. So she clicked onto the page of one of her new friends and began reading posts and looking at photos. This at least gave her an idea of the sort of things people were talking about. However, she became a little upset when she thought about her own uninspiring life. She didn't think she would be able to write anything that others would want to read. Taking a very deep breath and letting it out slowly she tentatively tapped a few words into her status bar.

Bought a new outfit today.

She set aside the laptop and took her now empty mug into the kitchen to refill it. Returning with fresh hot coffee she glanced at the screen nervously. To her joy and surprise someone had commented on her post. They wanted to know what she had bought. So she settled herself back on the sofa and wrote more about the new clothes she had bought. Minutes went by and more comments were added. To Derby it was like being party to a conversation with people she didn't know. It was very exciting and she knew that this was an experience she could get used to and good at very quickly.

Time went by without her realising it. Even though she only had a few friends so far, she discovered it was easy to make general comments to what others had to say. Sometimes she read the other comments and looked at the profiles, sadness washing over her as she saw people had added pictures of their children and various family events. She had nothing she could share.

Finally realising exactly how long she had spent on the site, Derby logged off and put the laptop away. She felt edgy and frustrated. She had too much energy and didn't know how to get rid of it. Her life as it had been for all of these years felt like a volcano inside ready to erupt. She wanted it to spill from her, flow away and leave behind the new fresh and green Derby. A woman who she now believed could be like other women, like the girls at work, like the women in the town. All in control of their own lives and able to make their own choices.

Feeling the need to expel all of this pent up energy, she pulled her phone from her bag. She opened her contacts and found the number for the gym she had entered earlier. Without giving herself a chance to feel nervous or back out, she touched the screen and waited for it to connect. A business like female voice answered.

"Good afternoon this is Well Fit Gym, how can I help you?"

Derby hesitated just a fraction.

"I um, saw your add in town."

"Ok, would you like some information."

The woman answered, seeming to sense Derby was not sure what to ask.

"Yes please." She paused then plunged on "Actually, I have no idea what I need to know. I'm forty and have never been to a gym in my life. Never even thought about it actually."

She stopped herself as she felt she was beginning to babble. The woman didn't seem to notice.

"Oh that's alright. It's never too late to start a fitness program. I can send you out our brochure if that would help."

The way she was feeling at the moment, Derby didn't want to wait for anything.

"Could I come to the gym and speak to someone in person?"

"Of Course, do you know where we are?"

Derby acknowledged that she didn't and jotted down the directions the woman gave her.

Two bus rides later Derby nervously walked through double glass doors into an air conditioned foyer. Everywhere she looked was brightly lit. Large posters displayed beautifully toned bodies of men and women with gleaming pure white smiles. Beyond the huge circular desk in the middle of the foyer she could see a floor to ceiling glass wall. Behind this was every type of gym equipment imaginable, most being used.

Wanting to turn and run but forcing herself forward, Derby approached the desk. It was high with three young women sitting on swivel stools, all dressed in T-shirts displaying the gym logo. Each of them wore a headset, tapped at a computer and smiled dazzlingly. The young woman nearest to Derby spoke.

"Can I help you?"

She didn't stop tapping the computer but still gave her full attention to her.

"Umm, I phoned a little while ago for some details but decided to come here instead."

Derby answered shyly. The woman kept on smiling.

"Hi, that was me you spoke to. If you give me a moment I'll call one of the trainers to come and show you around."

She spoke into her headset quickly and professionally, the smile firmly fixed on her face. A sudden thought flashed across Derby's mind that the girl's face muscles must ache at the end of the day. Or maybe they had special equipment to exercise them too. A bubble of hysterical laughter tried to escape her lips, but she managed to stop it by nipping at her lower lip.

Almost no time passed when a huge man in shorts and the gym T-shirt came through part of the glass wall. He headed straight for her and at first Derby thought he must know her. However he stopped in front of her and held out his hand.

"Welcome. My name is Geoff. I'm one of the personal trainers here."

Derby had to look up and up before she could see his face. She felt like one of the children at her nursery, so small, next to this hunk of a man. Trying desperately to pull herself together, she held her own hand out and he shook it firmly but not overly hard. His hand was hard though, the muscles bulging on his biceps and his smile glowing white from tanned cheeks. Although the shorts and T-shirt he wore were loose, they did nothing to disguise the fact that underneath he would look just as beautiful, for that was exactly the word that came to her mind. It also brought a flush to her cheeks, and this she saw made his blue eyes twinkle, and his smile widen even more as though he could read her mind.

"Umm I...I my name is Derby."

She managed. Releasing her hand, (a wave of disappointment washed over her) he said.

"Don't be nervous Derby. None of us are ogres here. We don't go in for torture. We design a personal program that suits you."

Derby gave herself a mental shake. She wasn't the sort of person who got nervous easily, but then her life was so boring, so depressingly samey, day in day out that she had never encountered a time to be nervous.

She tried a smile and it fit nicely without trembling. She could, no she would do this. She had decided to change her life and she was not, absolutely not going to back out now. She forced to the front of her mind David's face, his voice and his complete lack of emotion towards her. Now was her time. God only knew she had wasted enough of her life. From today nothing would be the same again. She wasn't sure yet how she was going to accomplish it all, but she was intelligent and healthy and still young, so she would.

"Ok please give me the tour."
She told Geoff and was relieved her voice sounded normal.

Geoff stepped to her side and held his arm out indicating the way towards the glass wall.

"This is our main fitness suite."
Inside was noisy. Music played on large overhead flat screens and men and women puffed and panted as they worked on the equipment. There were many gym staff, all identically clad, moving around the room giving help and instruction to those exercising.

What did surprise Derby was the different shapes and sizes of the gym goers. She had expected all of them to look trim and muscly and super fit, but many of them looked just ordinary. Like people in the street. Some had floppy bellies, some were quite overweight, and puffed and sweated and struggled. Others were thin and wiry, but for Derby, all of the people looked like they were attempting to achieve something. They all had looks on their faces that told her they were there for a purpose, and this more than anything relaxed her.

Geoff looked down at her and smiled, seeming to sense the change in her demeanour

"We really do provide a service for everyone."

He told her. Derby, again having to look so far up to see his face, was a little taken aback. It felt like he had read her mind. Pulling on courage she didn't know she had she replied.

"Am I that transparent?"

He shook his head.

"No, it's just most people who have never been to a gym before react the same way. They all think everyone here will have perfect bodies. Mostly because of what they see in movies or TV, where the actors look terrific and never show any effort on the equipment. Really, it's like in the Bridget Jones film, hard work and determination."

Derby knew what he meant. She just hoped that she wouldn't be the one falling on her arse because her muscles couldn't take the strain.

"That will probably be me."

She told him.

"Don't worry. We wouldn't let you go hell-for-leather right away. We are professionally trained ourselves and your safety is our priority."

For some unknown reason Derby felt tears pricking her eyes. As irrational as it was, this stranger was making her feel more cared for than anyone had, since long before she had begun her relationship with her husband. Before, when she was little and had her Gran, who had loved and cared, where her parents hadn't. Before she had allowed teenage hormones to get the better of her. Sighing deeply she said.

"That's good to hear. So when can I begin?"

Geoff laughed and told her they should finish the tour first.

After having been shown various other suites, the pool, the tanning rooms and the sauna, Geoff led her into a personal planning room. It was like a little sitting room with a coffee machine and water cooler. She settled into a leather armchair and took the coffee he offered. Then from a cabinet he took some forms and a folder. He then began to ask her a series of questions, some that seemed very personal to her, like her weight, even though she knew she wasn't overweight, and if she had any medical conditions, or was taking any medication for anything.

"We have to ask because even a gentle program can put stress on the body's organs. So we need to know before we can

start that program. But I assure you your record is absolutely private"
He explained.

He then asked her questions about why she wanted to join the gym. These were a lot harder to reply to. She didn't want to lie, but she didn't want to tell him the truth either. That was just too personal. So she opted for somewhere in between.

"I just turned forty. I'm a nursery nurse, and most of my time is taken up at work or home. I just realised that I should probably do some exercise of some sort."
It was enough.

"I must say, you don't look forty. So whatever you are doing is working."
Geoff told her making her cheeks flush crimson. She thought it was probably just a line, but it made her feel good anyway. No one had ever said anything complimentary to her, so she lapped it up.

An hour and a half later, Geoff had completed her forms and created a beginners program for her. She had asked about what she should wear and he took her through to the gym shop where there was a range of sweats, shorts, T-shirts, shoes and swimwear. She was relieved, for she had no idea what to look for in the shops in town. Here was everything, and Geoff explained what would be best for her program.

It was seven o'clock by the time Derby got home. A copy of her program was in her new gym bag along with her new exercise attire. Everything was stored in her wardrobe. She then set about throwing together a hasty meal for when David came home from the supermarket. As she chopped tomatoes to add to pasta, she realised that she would have to tell David that she had joined the gym. She wasn't sure what his reaction would be but resolved not to care if he didn't like it.

Bang on time, David walked through the door placing his keys on the hall table and kicking his shoes in the corner. He headed straight upstairs and emerged a few minutes later out of his suit and dressed in his usual jeans and polo. Without a word to Derby, he flopped onto the sofa and turning on the tv promptly found some sport to watch. Derby was so used to this that she didn't even bother to go and greet her husband. Instead she completed the evening meal, put both plates on trays and took

David's into the lounge. He took the tray said a cursory thanks and without even looking at the food began forking it into his mouth. Derby went back to the kitchen and returned with her own tray.

"Had a good day?"

She asked.

"Mmm usual."

David said with a mouthful of pasta.

"I joined a gym today."

She told him.

"Ok."

Was his reply.

"Might mean I'm out a few evenings."

She tried again.

"Ok."

Was all she got back.

Realising she herself was very hungry she tucked into her food. With an inward grin, she thought, that was easy, and suddenly what she was eating tasted like ambrosia. As she had known, David did not care where she went so long as he got his meals. She resolved to make sure that never changed, thereby ensuring her new life, her new self would be kept completely separate. Almost giggling with joy she thought. I have a secret.

Chapter 6

New Beginning

The alarm went off as usual on Monday morning but Derby was ready for it. She reached for her phone and switched it off before it barely made a sound. Trying to move like a cat, she eased herself quietly out of bed and headed for the bathroom. Looking at herself in the mirror this morning was like looking at a completely different person. Gone was the frown and tiredness from her eyes. Gone was the dullness of her skin and hair. Or to Derby, that's how it seemed. She hadn't actually done anything physical to her face, but knew she did look different, and that was due to the last few days.

She showered quickly and returned to the bedroom glancing at her snoring sleeping husband. For a moment she felt like leaving him there to rouse himself from sleep. But the thought flitted out of her mind as quickly as it had entered. She wanted him awake and out of the house as usual. Mostly she didn't want him to notice anything different about her. This new beginning was hers.

Derby closed the front door behind David the same as she did every morning. She went into the kitchen and pulled vegetables and cubed beef from the fridge. Hastily she threw together a casserole and shoved it in the oven setting the timer, for she had no intention of coming straight home after work. She then went back upstairs and pulled her new gym bag from her wardrobe. She gathered her other things including the outfit for Chardonnay, and headed for the nursery. The gym bag was quite heavy but Derby felt like she was walking on air. By the time she reached the nursery, her arm was aching a little but she was smiling inside.

Angela noticed the difference immediately she walked in and saw Derby preparing the rooms humming to herself. She walked up to her and touched her shoulder making her jump.

"Whoa, Angela, you gave me a fright."
Derby exclaimed. Angela laughed.

"Someone's in a very good mood this morning."
Then she frowned a little.

"Or are you an alien that has abducted the real Derby?"
Both women giggled and Derby replied.

"Nope. It's me, human. At least that's how I actually feel today. I think maybe this is the real me and the one you knew last week was the alien."

"Mmmm think you lost me Derby."
Angela told her. Derby laughed placing some play dough and shape cutters on a table.

"Tell you all about it later."

Kelsey arrived with the other parents, Chardonnay as usual bouncing in with her mother. Derby gave the outfit to Kelsey who looked on the verge of tears when she saw it.

"Just to say thanks for Friday evening."
Derby told her.

"Oh you didn't have to do that."
Kelsey said quietly.

"Kelsey, you have no idea what you did for me inviting me to your party. It made me really look at myself over the weekend, and made me make changes to my life."
Derby told her sincerely. Kelsey beamed at her, threw her arms around her shoulders and gave her a breathtaking hug.

"Good on you."
She said. Then she hugged and kissed Chardonnay and waved as she headed for the door.

Throughout the day, even though all of the nursery routines were the same, Derby felt everything was different. She noticed the sunshine outside. Normally only to ensure all of the children wore hats and sun lotion. But today she saw the colours and shadows. She noticed the soft fluffy clouds and the shapes she could see in them. She smelt the summer air and breathed it deeply and enjoyed the warmth of the sun on her skin when she was outside with the little ones.

Most of all she was aware of the laughter, that of the children, the babies and the nursery nurses. She had always loved the sound of children's laughter, but today she really heard it. At first she felt the deep pangs of pain and regret that she would never hear the giggles of her own child. But then she pushed that out of the way and resolved to enjoy this fresh start to her life.

Derby sat with Angela monitoring the older toddlers as they ate their lunch. Each of the nursery nurses rotated the lunch breaks around the different age groups and Derby ensured each of them had time for a break too. She usually nibbled on something as she wandered around the rooms, but today she sat and ate and chatted with Angela.

"So what have you been up to Derby?"
Angela asked, a gleam in her eye. Before Derby answered Angela leaned close and whispered.

"Did you jump David and have really good sex?"
Derby held her hand over her mouth and laughed, nearly choking on her sandwich.

"Not likely." She grinned, then became serious again. "No, I just realised after Friday night that I had to do something with my life. You cannot imagine how boring my life is, was. Things are going to be different."
Angela patted her hand.

"Glad to hear it."
She looked at her slyly.

"I noticed a little profile and friend request on Facebook too."
Derby smiled.

"Mmmm. I need a little help with that actually."
She went on to explain the photo problem, and Angela agreed to take some pictures of her to add to her profile.

"Maybe a little makeup would be good."
Angela said to encourage her. Derby frowned thoughtfully, but agreed that it was a good idea. Makeup was another thing Derby had very little experience with, but knew it was something else to add to her new beginning.

"So, I think Kelsey mentioned our stuff should be here about the middle of the week."
Angela said. Derby felt her cheeks growing hot and continued nibbling her sandwich.

"I joined a gym."
She said, not wanting to talk about the 'stuff'. Angela didn't push the issue, realising it was still a topic of embarrassment to Derby. Instead she placed an arm around her shoulder and said.

"Bridget Jones, here you come."

Derby laughed.

"Hope not. My trainer said they don't push you like that. They start off gentle and build up. I'm going for my first session tonight"

"Well, however they go about it, just enjoy it. I tried a gym once but I just don't have the patience or will power to keep at it. Besides I get enough exercise, well me and Jake do."

Derby grinned and playfully slapped her hand.

"You are a devil Angela."

At the end of the nursery day, Derby stood outside with Angela and posed for some photos. Angela had taken her own makeup and lightly dusted Derby's face with powder and her eyes with eye-shadow and mascara. They had similar skin colouring, so the match was close. Derby tried smiling naturally but was very nervous. After many attempts, both women browsed the collection and found a few where Derby didn't look stiff and false. Angela then showed her how to add the Facebook application to her phone and upload the photos. Derby was pleased to see more friends had accepted her requests and some friend requests for her to accept.

Derby locked up the nursery and said goodbye to Angela thanking her again for her help. Angela waved as she headed for her car and Derby for the bus stop. The bus was crowded but she managed to find a seat, and squeezed next to a woman who took up most of the bench. Balancing her gym bag and handbag on her lap she pulled out her phone and tapped a message for David.

Going to the gym for my first session. Don't know how long I will be but there's a casserole in the oven on the timer. It will be ready when you get in.

She pressed send and held her phone, deciding it was too much trouble to try and negotiate her bag to put it away.

The bus bounced and Derby was jostled into the woman next to her. Then the bus stopped and the woman wanted to get off. So Derby stood up and inched into the aisle to give her room. Quite a few other people also disembarked leaving more room to move and breathe. As she sat back down again she sighed with relief, and since no one else seemed to need the seat next to her, she placed her gym bag on it, keeping her arm looped through the handle. She was about to return her phone to her handbag when it bleeped.

Ok.

One single word was David's reply. Derby felt her eyes tear up a little. Then she determinedly pushed them away. She would not cry over her loveless marriage. That thought shocked her for a moment. Up until then she hadn't given any consideration to how she and her husband felt about one another. Now she realised that love was definitely not a part of her life.

The gym was noisy and busy and Derby wondered what all the other members did with their lives. Maybe she would make some friends here and find out. One of the girls on the desk called for Geoff, and soon she saw him striding towards her smiling.

"Good to see you Derby."

She was surprised he remembered her name, but smiled back.

"I'll show you where you can change and then meet you in the main suite."

She nodded and followed him towards a door with 'Women' on it. The changing room was large with cubicles, lockers and showers very similar to a swimming pool. Derby was a little baffled, not sure of where to go. A gym assistant saw her looking a little lost and came straight over.

"First time?"

She asked in a friendly voice. Derby nodded and the assistant explained how the system worked. Some of the lockers had normal keys for people who came occasionally and paid on an hourly basis. The other lockers were designated for members who used their membership cards as card keys.

"Your card should be ready in a couple of days. So for now just use one of the regular lockers. Then after, you will have your own locker, so if you want to leave anything here, then you can."

The assistant told her. She also showed her that there was a door to the main suite and one to the swimming pool, something Derby was glad to know, imagining how embarrassed she would have been to wander into the wrong area wearing the wrong outfit.

Geoff was waiting for her when she emerged and smiled encouragingly. Her stomach did a flip and she wasn't sure if it was because she was nervous or his smile.

"This way."

He told her indicating a piece of exercise equipment. She noticed he held a folder and he saw her looking.

"Your program. Once I familiarise myself with it I won't need to bring it with me."

He told her, assuming she was looking only at the folder. Derby nodded, feeling stupid that she seemed to have lost the power of speech, because, yes she had wondered about the folder, but she was more interested in his huge tanned arms, the width of his chest and mostly his Adonis looks.

Geoff patiently explained and led her through her program making sure she took breaks and drank plenty of water. Derby put her all into it, determined to improve both her body and her mind. At the end of the session, she felt tired and her muscles knew they had been worked, but she felt alive. Geoff suggested they go to the juice bar and go through her program and chart her first day's progress. Derby was willing, not wanting to leave the gym yet, and especially not wanting to leave Geoff yet.

Sitting in comfortable chairs with tall glasses of fresh juice, Geoff talked her through her program and chart explaining where they could tweak it. She listened carefully. Then he closed the folder and she was sure he would finish his drink and leave her alone. However he sat back and relaxed.

"So what do you do Derby?"

He asked. Derby sipped her juice and replied

"I'm a nursery nurse."

"That's in your file. What I meant was, what do you do outside of work, you and your husband?"

Derby gulped.

"How...do you know I'm married?"

Geoff raised his glass and indicated towards her left hand and her wedding ring.

"Oh, yes I see."

She wasn't sure what to say, using the pause to take a sneaky look at his ring finger, where there was no ring.

"Umm, well...nothing actually. We umm...don't really do anything together. What about you? Wife, girlfriend, significant other?"

Geoff laughed, deep and softly.

"I'm not gay. I did have a wife once, she left. Most of my time is taken up here at the gym. Why don't you and your husband do anything together?"

Derby sighed. She really didn't want to get into this right now. Geoff sensed the change in her.

"Sorry. Shouldn't have asked. Not my business."

"No, no. It's not like that. I just don't want to talk about it now. For now, I just want to be me doing something new by myself for myself. Oh I'm probably making no sense at all."
She told him, feeling flustered. Geoff leaned forward a little holding his glass in both hands.

"Derby, it's ok. Whatever you do and why is up to you. But if you do want to talk anytime, well I'm a good listener."
Derby nodded not sure she wanted a listener. This thought brought a fresh blush and when Geoff grinned at her she felt sure he had read her mind.

The bus ride home was just as noisy and crowded. This was the only downside to going to the gym. It also took quite some time, as the bus stopped and started so frequently that Derby was sure it only ever moved a couple of metres at a time. By the time she got home, her head ached and she felt a bit sick. She unlocked the front door and went straight upstairs to put her gym bag away and go to the loo. She knew David was home, his shoes were in the hallway, but he didn't call out or say hello.

In the bathroom, she swallowed two paracetamol and rubbed her temples with her fingers trying to alleviate the pain. Looking in the mirror she eased her hands around the back of her neck and massaged. This gave her a little relief. She then turned and went downstairs. In the kitchen she found the casserole dish on the counter and David's plate next to it. The lid of the dish was askew and sauce from the food had smeared over the worktop. Sighing Derby rinsed the plate and put it in the dishwasher, then spooned some casserole onto a clean plate and popped it in the microwave.

Whilst she was waiting she thought about the journey to and from the gym, and decided she would buy a car as soon as possible. The microwave pinged making her jump. A car was not something she had ever thought she needed, she had taken her test at eighteen but rarely drove David's car. Now at forty, she knew owning her own car was another part of her new beginning. She ate her food standing in the kitchen, then went to find her husband.

David was sprawled across the sofa watching something on the TV that Derby didn't even bother looking at. She stood inside the doorway and quietly studied the man she had been married to for so long. He didn't notice her there, or if he did he didn't say. She watched him scratch his head, and then put his hand back down his jeans absentmindedly. She felt nothing. There was no stirring of desire, no pleasure in his looks. She had to force herself to speak when really she wanted to just turn around and go back out.

"I'm home."

David turned his head.

"Oh hi."

Was all he said and turned back to the programme.

"I'm going to buy a car. Getting to the gym on the bus was a real bitch."

She said.

"Mmhmm."

David replied. Derby turned away from the door and headed back to the kitchen. She was angry and frustrated at his attitude, but more angry at herself for allowing it to go on for so long. But she had no idea what to do about it.

Sitting down at the kitchen counter she opened her laptop and booted it up. She mulled over various solutions whilst she waited but everything pointed to leaving her husband. She didn't think she was ready for that. So many questions flew through her mind. Where would she go? What about the house? Could she contemplate divorce and all its complications? She didn't have any answers. So she decided for now she would stay where she was but live a very different life.

The laptop was ready, so Derby browsed websites advertising cars for sale. She had no idea what to look for and there was so much choice. Again feeling frustrated, she closed the lid of the computer and decided it was something else she would ask Angela about. With her hands propping up her chin, Derby sat and stared around her kitchen. It was clean and tidy, not special in anyway, just like herself, she thought. Pressing her lips tight together she sat up straight, angry at that thought. She seemed to be getting angry about a lot of things and resolved to stop feeling sorry for herself, beginning right now.

Opening up the laptop again Derby entered one word in the search bar, 'sex' and was not prepared for the millions of results. Most of the top websites were pornographic sites, which even Derby, though naïve didn't want to go to because of the names. So she pondered and refined her search to 'sex and marriage'. The top sites looked more like she was hoping for and clicked on the first one. After reading the first few lines, Derby realised it was too clinical so she tried another one. Several attempts later she found a forum and was surprised to discover many people were in similar situations to herself. Knowing this made her feel a great deal better about herself, and by the time she closed down the laptop to go to bed, she had a much more positive outlook for her future and some very good ideas.

Chapter 7

Mirror Mirror

Tuesday Morning Derby got up and did all of the usual pre-work routines, saw David out of the door and headed to the nursery. Angela arrived at her regular time and saw at once a shine to Derby's face that had been missing before and smiled to herself, feeling quite proud that she had participated in the change.

"How was the gym?"
She asked as they arranged toys and tables. Derby kneeling at a toddler sized table, sat back on her heels holding a tub of foam letters and numbers, smiled at her friend.

"I'm sore in places I didn't know existed."
She told Angela who laughed.

"Going back?"
She questioned. Derby grinned and nodded.

"Just one thing though. The bus is hell, so I'm going to buy a car but I don't have a clue about cars."
Angela pointed a finger at her.

"You should get a flashy little sports car."
Derby stood up placing the tub on the table and frowned. A sports car sounded great, but she was worried about handling something she automatically assumed was very powerful. David's car was a medium sized one point two hatchback, only two years old, but hardly a beast.

"I haven't driven much over the years, only David's car now and then. He's always bought small practical cars. Nothing flash."
Derby explained. Angela, arranging another table, pressed her lips together.

"Well, you can go for a test drive at a car dealership. That way you will have some idea of what you want. There's a good place on the Abbotts Industrial Park, Jake has used them a couple of times and they are pretty good. Would you like me to come with you?"

Derby sighed with relief. Angela had said exactly what she had hoped she would say.

"Any chance we could go after work?"
She asked tentatively. Angela nodded.

"I think we could get there before they close."
The children arrived and the nursery became noisy and to Derby alive. Kelsey bustled in as usual, Chardonnay tugging her hand. The toddler broke free and headed for a round rug and a box of toys. Kelsey headed for Derby, leaned close and all but whispered.

"Orders will be here tomorrow. I'll bring them when I collect Chardonnay."
Derby felt her face begin to heat up and quickly looked around to see if anyone had noticed. Relief spread through her to see no one had. Toddlers and babies were being handed over to nursery nurses, and adults were saying their goodbyes, all too busy to notice Derby's blush.

Throughout the day, Derby chatted to Angela and the other nursery nurses asking them about their choice of cars. Most of the younger members of staff had small, old run abouts. This was mainly due to the cost of insurance for younger drivers and not because they favoured their car's make and model. Derby, though never having had her own insurance, knew her finances wouldn't be a restriction to her choice. So she listened carefully to the wish lists of her staff, but by the end of the day was no nearer to knowing what she wanted. She hoped the car dealer would give her lots of help.

After locking up the nursery, Angela drove Derby to the car dealer. The industrial estate situated on the outskirts of the town was about half an hour away and Angela took the opportunity to ask Derby more about the gym. The nursery was not really the place to have an in-depth conversation, the children needing far too much of their attention.

"So what did you do there?"
Angela asked. Derby gave her a detailed account of her first gym experience, and felt herself getting redder and redder when she spoke about Geoff. Angela laughed openly, but not at all mocking her friend.

"Mmmm maybe I should join too."

She told Derby giving her a quick side glance. Derby huffed back.

"You have your own hunky husband."

Angela nodded.

"I have. I definitely have. But maybe I need to keep an eye on you."

Derby looked at Angela and saw the grin, realising she was being teased. But she replied in a more serious tone.

"It would be nice to have someone to go with...but..."

She didn't know how to finish, afraid she would offend Angela. However her friend seemed to know exactly what she was trying to say.

"But, you need to get out there by yourself. This is something for you, something new and you need to do it independently."

Angela replied, now serious too. Derby sighed and lightly patted Angela's hand on the steering wheel.

"Thank you. I didn't want to say it, I thought it would make me sound like a right bitch."

Angela briefly took one hand off the wheel and gently squeezed Derby's hand.

"Derby, I understand this is a huge step for you. I'm here for you to help any way I can."

Derby felt tears well up and blinked them back. Having a friend like Angela was new, unexpected, but a real joy.

The car dealership was a lot bigger than Derby had anticipated. As they pulled into the customer car park she could see cars for sale in row after row. Different makes, models and colours. She felt a little overwhelmed, not able to focus on any one car in particular.

Angela led the way into a large indoor show room with glass walls and doors. There were cars inside too on round plinths, rotating slowly. They were approached immediately by a young man in a suit with a big smile.

"Good evening ladies. My name is Liam how can I help you?"

Angela gave Derby a little nudge. Shyly Derby cleared her throat and spoke.

"Well, I'm looking for a car."

Liam smiled even more widely.

"Now that is something I can help you with. What do you have in mind?"

Derby shrugged lightly.

"To be honest, I haven't got a clue."

She replied feeling like the world's most clueless idiot. Liam's grin got even bigger and a gleam appeared in his eye. He could see he was probably going to get a huge commission out of this. Angela stepped forward just a tiny bit.

"Hi, my friend has only driven her husband's boring hatchback, but..." She paused for effect. "...don't get any ideas about making a mint out of her."

Derby felt gratitude and relief flood through her and was more than glad that Angela had come with her.

Liam barely paused, his smile firmly fixed on his face. He showed no signs of feeling intimidated by Angela, and Derby realised that this man, young as he was, was oozing a confidence she could only imagine.

"Ok, well do you think you would like something similar to your husband's car?"

He asked. Derby was nodding no before she realised she was doing it.

"Ok. Something a little more feminine then."

He stated. Derby had no idea what he meant but Angela seemed to understand what he was talking about.

"I reckon a nice little sports car."

Angela told him, all her earlier hostility towards the salesman gone.

"Oh but I don't know if I could handle one."

Derby gabbled. Angela put her arm around her friend's shoulder and squeezed gently.

"I told you, he" pointing to Liam "can give you a test drive. That way you can get the feel of the car and decide if it's too beastly for you."

Liam nodded in agreement.

"I have a lovely little Mazda MX-5 outside. Come with me and have a look."

Derby took a deep breath and agreed to look.

The car Liam took them to was indeed a lovely little sports car. It was red with a black soft top and seemed to Derby to be inviting her to drive it. She looked at Angela and beamed.

"It's gorgeous."

Was all she said. Angela smiled back, pleased that her friend was pleased but cautious too. She turned to Liam.

"Does it come with a warranty?"

Liam lightly ran his hand over the gleaming paintwork and for a brief moment, Derby imagined him running his hand over her skin. She immediately felt herself begin to blush and hoped he hadn't noticed. Luckily, he was busy replying to Angela's question.

"We give a three month warranty on all our cars. Plus, they are all HPI checked when they come in and fully MOTd before they leave here."

Derby, recovering from her blush, looked from Angela to Liam as though she were suddenly listening to a conversation in a foreign language.

"Whoa. Back up and tell me exactly what all that means please."

She interrupted. Liam turned to her.

"Your friend asked about warranty, well we sell our cars with three months. So, if it breaks down within that time, we will have it repaired at no cost to you. HPI means we check our cars with various agencies to see if they have outstanding finance, have been involved in a serious accident or have been stolen. The MOT.."

"I know what the MOT is."

Derby interrupted.

"I'm sorry."

Liam told her sounding sincere.

"So" He smiled straight at her. "Want to test drive it?"

Derby smiled back and feeling very nervous nodded.

Sitting in the small car, Derby felt very conscious of the young man beside her. He was tall and broad and filled the passenger side of the vehicle, whereas she felt small. She had slid the driver's seat forward to reach the pedals and looking through the windscreen, the bonnet appeared to stretch a long way away. Nervously she started the engine, and feeling like she was taking her driving test again, cautiously put the car in gear and pulled away. Following Liam's directions she eased the car out of the dealership's grounds and onto the road quickly gaining confidence.

Half an hour later, Derby steered back into the dealership and parked the car where Liam indicated. Angela had gone back inside the showroom and was flipping through a magazine sipping a cup of coffee. She looked up as Derby walked in chatting with Liam and saw excitement on her friend's face. Derby saw Angela, waved and headed towards her. Angela put the magazine down as Derby sat opposite her.

"Oh my God Angela. That was fantastic. I had no idea a car could be so so so…bloody awesome."
Derby exclaimed bringing her hands up to her face, palms together and finger tips pressed to her lips. Angela leaned forward.

"You're going to buy it then?"
She asked. Derby nodded the affirmative.

"Sure you don't want to browse others?"
Angela questioned. Derby shook her head.

"Can't see the point. I have fallen for this one."
Angela grinned.

"And the car."
She all but whispered. Derby looked up hurriedly, relaxing when she saw Liam was not within hearing distance.

"Shush."
She said with a giggle.

"He is cute though."
She whispered back and both women laughed. Liam returned carrying a folder and looked from one woman to the other, sure he had missed something and guessing it was about him. However, he didn't comment but sat next to Derby and began going through the relevant paperwork.

"When can I have the car?"
Derby asked after going through everything.

"We will need to make sure everything is fine. Get our mechanics to go over it and Mot it, so Friday?"
Derby clapped her hands like a child full of excitement and anticipation.

"You will have to arrange insurance to start Friday too."
Liam told her. Derby chewed on the corner of her lip and feeling nervous and naïve again asked.

"Where do I begin?"

"Try the comparison websites, you'll get the best deals then."

Liam replied. Angela patted Derby's hand.

"I'll show you tomorrow."

She told her.

Angela dropped Derby off at her home much later than she had thought. David's car was in the driveway and for the first time ever, wondered what he would say about her coming in after him without prior warning. Angela sensed her nerves.

"You ok?"

She asked as Derby unsnapped her seatbelt. Derby nodded.

"Mmmm. Just, I'm usually home before David, or have let him know in advance."

She let the sentence trail off.

"Is he going to be angry?"

Angela asked gently, afraid for her friend. Derby turned in her seat, realised what Angela was thinking and smiled.

"Oh, no Angela. Don't worry, he might be some things but aggressive is not one of them. Believe me, I'm not scared of him. He's more likely to just sulk, properly irritating but that's all."

Angela sighed, reassured.

"Ok Derby, see you tomorrow."

Derby walked into the house and headed for the sitting room. David was hunched over the desk tapping away on the computer keyboard. He didn't turn and Derby was sure he hadn't heard her come in.

"Hi. Sorry I'm late."

She said. David stopped tapping and looked over his shoulder.

"Mmmm, how long will dinner be?"

Was his response.

Derby felt a bubble of anger but held it back. She was late home, no dinner prepared, completely out of routine, yet here he was totally unconcerned. What if she had been involved in an accident she thought. How long would he sit doing his own stuff before he realised she wasn't there, when his stomach growled so much? Holding onto all of these thoughts she replied.

"As quickly as I can."

Without waiting for his reply she walked to the kitchen and decided she wouldn't even broach the subject of the car.

Pulling a pizza out of the freezer and slamming it onto a tray, Derby flicked the oven switch and leaned back against the worktop whilst waiting for it to reach its temperature. She realised she was still wearing her shoes and slipped them off leaving them where she stepped out of them. As the oven hummed, she mulled over David's reaction and decided that she really shouldn't have expected anything different. So, she simply would not tell him about her car. No, she would bring it home on Friday and leave it outside the house and see if he noticed.

He always put his car on the driveway, and as it was only big enough for one car, she wouldn't take his place. She would park it on the road outside the house. All of their neighbours who owned two cars did that. It was a nice neighbourhood, quiet and without trouble, so her lovely shiny car would be safe.

The oven clicked, indicating it was hot enough and Derby all but threw the pizza in. She remembered garlic bread and snatched that from the freezer too. She shoved it in the oven alongside the pizza, not caring if it cooked first. Tonight she just wasn't in the mood for being careful or caring.

That night in bed, Derby lay awake again unable to sleep. David, flat on his back was snoring loudly. Most nights she would give him a gentle nudge and he would turn over and go quiet for a while. Tonight, still feeling riled over his lack of concern, Derby huffed and whispered to herself "Shut the fuck up" as she gave her husband a less than gentle shove. David rolled onto his side, gave a big grunt and then went quiet. Derby felt a giggle bubble up, and decided to go down stairs and make a cup of tea since sleep was so far out of the question.

Sitting at the kitchen table, a mug of tea nestled in her hands, Derby thought about her reaction to her husband's snoring. As she sipped her drink she felt her cheeks begin to heat up, partly because of the hot drink, but partly due to the way she had reacted. Firstly, David's snoring only ever gave her mild annoyance. Tonight it had completely aggravated her. Secondly, she had shocked herself using such a strong expletive, even though it was whispered. She rarely swore and when she did it was very mild. Her use of the 'fuck' word was totally out of character. Pushing the mug aside, Derby laid her hands flat on the table. Then she was grinning to herself, imagining what David would do if her heard her. He didn't like women swearing, thought it made them appear coarse and uncouth.

"Fuck you. Fuck you. Fuck you."
She said to no one but herself, then giggled, enjoying the moment and holding inside another little bit of the new Derby.

For a while Derby just sat and held her now empty mug. She didn't feel tired or anywhere near ready for bed. So taking her laptop, she booted it up and logged onto her Facebook. She was surprised to see a lot of comments from her friends and many friend requests. Quite a few of these were from people she didn't know. She remembered Angela explaining about privacy settings and quickly found this in the drop down menu.

She noticed that hers was set to public and guessed this was why she had so many requests from strangers. However she decided to leave it as it was. After all, she wanted to find as many new friends as possible and she hadn't included many personal details on her profile, so wasn't worried about giving too much information away. Opening her friend requests, Derby quickly confirmed each one without looking very closely.

Feeling like she had achieved something, Derby logged out of Facebook and was about to shut the computer down. But a sudden and somewhat exciting thought came to her. Before she could put it out of her mind she tapped a name into the search bar, ' Geoff Stone' and hit enter. There were many results and she had no idea if any of them were the Geoff she was looking for. So she clicked on images and a page of photos came up. It didn't take her long to find the right one. A black and white photo of Geoff from the gym, his chest naked and his jeans unbuttoned, looking like the perfect male model.

Expanding the photo, she found a website and clicked on it. More model photos of Geoff in various poses, all barely clothed. There was also a brief bio about him which Derby read with increasing interest. He had been a marine, and the model photos had been taken as part of a charity drive to raise money for wounded marines. Derby's insides fluttered the more she discovered about her new gym coach, and decided that she would be returning to the gym very soon.

Returning to bed, Derby tried to force her mind to switch off. This was a lot harder than she expected. She had hoped spending some time on the internet would make her tired enough to sleep. But it had had the opposite effect. Now she lay and tried concentrating on things that did not include gorgeous young car salesman, or hunky gym coaches. Eventually she drifted into yet another restless night of dreams, intermingling men in various states of undress, and David in progressively old fashioned and frumpy pyjamas.

When Derby woke up she was relieved to start the day. She arrived at the nursery, and as the children began to file in she remembered that Kelsey was bringing her order from the party. A little buzz of excited anticipation skittered through her veins, quickly replaced with concern over exactly how she was going to view the DVD with David around. He never went anywhere except work and the occasional visit to his family. However, luck was on Derby's side this day because mid-morning she got a text from her husband.

Got two managers off with a sickness bug probably be off for the rest of the week going to have to cover so will be late every night.

No kisses, or I love you and no mention of meals, so Derby keyed a quick reply.

Will you need food when you get in?

She wouldn't add any loving endearments either, she just couldn't be bothered. David replied immediately.

No will get some from staff canteen.

Derby was ecstatic. Not only was her husband going to be out of the house until at least ten thirty every night until Sunday, she wouldn't have to cook and clear up after him either. The next few evenings were going to be hers.

That evening Derby all but jogged into the house, her DVD tucked in her bag still in its plain packaging. She was so excited about watching it that she didn't even bother with food. She kicked off her shoes in the hallway and headed straight for the lounge and the television. She inserted the disc into the machine and tucked her feet underneath her as she waited for it to load. The beginning was quite clinical, a sex therapist explaining what would be covered and introducing a couple who would show explicitly what was being taught. Derby felt her cheeks heat a little even though she was alone, but watched keenly.

When the DVD was finished Derby sat for a while pondering over its content. Most of it was very pertinent to her situation, especially the earlier stuff where the woman explored her own body. Derby had never done anything like that to herself, her upbringing too strict. Now she realised it wasn't dirty or evil, but natural. She felt confident enough and so frustrated with her own sex life to finally make some changes.

Up in her bedroom, Derby stood and looked out of the window. It was another hot evening, and the trees that bordered the garden gave the room complete privacy from the surrounding houses. She smiled to herself and moved away from the window to her chest of drawers that doubled as a dressing table. She took a small mirror and sat on the edge of the bed placing the mirror next to her. Without thinking too much about what she was doing, she removed all of her clothing and sat for a moment naked.

The summer air coming through the open window was lovely on her skin, and nervously she took one breast in her hand and looked at it. She felt its weight and rubbed her thumb around the nipple repeating the act on the other side. It felt very nice, giving her a tingling sensation between her legs. Then she took the mirror and settling her bottom right on the edge of the bed spread her legs wide. She leaned forward and placed the mirror close to her genitals. She moved the mirror back and forward a little just looking at the outside.

Then using her other hand she moved the labia aside visually examining her vagina. She located her clitoris and tentatively touched it with a finger. It felt very good, but having watched the DVD she didn't want to rush this. Derby then carefully inserted a finger into her vagina and wiggled it about. She swallowed, feeling a dryness in her throat and guessed it was nerves.

Derby pulled her finger out and went downstairs to get a glass of water. For the first time ever she was walking about her own house naked and it felt very good. Sipping cool water at the kitchen sink, she looked out at the garden and a little flush of excitement went through her. She opened the back door and stepped outside. The patio was hot underfoot and completely secluded. She turned back to the kitchen, trotted upstairs and grabbed the mirror and duvet from the bed.

Back out on the patio, Derby spread the duvet on the warm ground and sat down. She drew her knees up and opened her legs and again placed the mirror between them. Slowly she stroked her labia, and again inserted her finger into her vagina. She felt heat flood through her, and as the DVD had taught used her thumb on her clitoris. Watching in the mirror she slowly moved her finger in and out massaging her clitoris at the same time. Feeling aroused like never before, Derby again stopped and pulled her finger out, not wanting the sensation to end too soon. She put the mirror aside and touched her breasts. Her nipples were erect and hard, and rubbing her finger over them sent ripples of pure pleasure through her vagina.

Laying back on the duvet Derby ran her hands over her entire body. Each touch sending little sparks of sexual desire to every nerve ending. She turned over onto her tummy and raised her bottom in the air placing her hand flush against her pubic mound, tickling and stroking her hairs. Each stroke promised even more joy. Turning again onto her back, the mirror abandoned and now redundant, Derby used both hands to satisfy her increasing urge.

With the summer heat enveloping her body, she put a finger back inside her vagina and rotated it as she moved it in and out. She had never been so wet, even during the sexual fumblings with David as a teenager. But her thoughts were miles away from her husband. With her other hand she teased her clitoris, and as of its own volition the finger inside her began to move faster.

Her breathing increased and she felt a tension in her whole body. She moved her head from side to side, her eyes closed as she pushed her finger deeper and deeper inside herself. She felt something building deep within her, knew something amazing was about to happen. Then with one hand rubbing her clitoris, and the other moving inside her like a piston, an explosion of the purest pleasure gripped her and held her taut.

Her back arched against her own hands, her orgasm coming in jolts like electricity pumping through her. Her breath caught and held for seconds as though her heart had stopped beating. A feeling so intense and powerful engulfed her entire being, so strong she didn't want it to end. Then as the orgasm abated a sense of elation and peace took over.

She flopped to the duvet, her finger still inside herself and a huge smile spreading across her lips. She took a deep breath and let it out slowly, stretching her body and sliding her hands up and down the inside of her thighs. She felt completely satisfied and satiated, unlike anything she had ever experienced before.

For some time Derby just lay in the warm sunshine, exulted in this new found freedom and ability to give herself what David never had. She gazed up at the summer sky, occasionally closing her eyes and remembering what the orgasm had been like. To her, this was the next new chapter in her life, something that should be familiar at her age, but was as new as though she was a teenager.

A soft gentle breeze caressed her naked skin and whispered through her pubic hairs like the lightest of touches. It was enough to tease her into arousal again. This time she dared wander through the garden onto the little lawn, bending roses so the velvety petals stroked her labia. She broke a small branch from a tree and delighted at the feel of the leaves as she brushed them on the inside of her thighs and nipples.

She lay face down in the grass and rubbed her body into the lawn. Again pushing her bottom up a little, she placed her finger inside her vagina and quickly, but just as powerfully gave herself yet another orgasm. This time she had to stifle a squeal of delight. After, she buried her face in her arm and giggled silently, as she heard Bob Stockton next door talking to his wife about watering their lawn, as the heat was making it shrivel. She imagined what the older couple would do if they saw her at that moment, or earlier, and this made her giggle even more.

Reluctantly Derby raised herself from the lawn. He body still felt tingly and a fire smouldered deep inside. But time was going by and she still hadn't eaten. So without much enthusiasm she went inside and back upstairs. She put on a light cotton dressing gown, but without underwear she could feel a pleasant sensation between her legs as she moved. She took the DVD from the player and hid it away with her new dress, not at all worried that David would find it. Then in the kitchen she made herself an omelette, poured a glass of juice and took both out into the garden.

There was a patio table and chairs, rarely used, and for the first time Derby wondered why.

It hit her then that most of her life had been spent simply working, tending to chores and staying in the same house day after day. David mowed the little lawn when it needed it, and she weeded and tended the plants without thinking. Never had she looked at their garden as somewhere to sit and enjoy. They had never just sat out in a summer evening and had a glass of wine, a conversation. A few tears trickled down her cheeks but she brushed them aside, angry at herself. She had let this happen, she had let her life pass her by with no memories to speak of. Finishing her food she resolved that memories, good ones would begin right now, and giggled when she thought about the first of those memories, and the wonderful feelings they had given her, and the many more to come.

Chapter 8

Toys

Derby was still sitting on the patio when David came home from the supermarket. She had found some tea lights in the back of a kitchen cupboard and a bottle of red wine, a Christmas present left over from the previous year. She heard her husband close the front door, but made no move to greet him. Sipping her wine she thought she would wait to see if he noticed where she was.

A thudding on the stairs told her David assumed she was in bed and was going up too. She took a small breath and held it, waiting for him to come looking for her. Minutes passed, the toilet flushed, but David did not appear. She let out the breath and shrugged to herself. Sipping more wine she whispered to the air.

"Nothing changes."

Derby sat for another half hour barely touching the wine left in her glass. She thought about her husband's actions and realised none of it bothered her. In fact she felt quite relieved that he hadn't come to find her. What did worry her was knowing this. Marriage or any relationship should not be like this. Living together but not being together was wrong on so many levels, yet she now realised it suited her, was convenient. She knew she wanted more from life now, knew she wanted love and sex so, lifting the wine glass and draining it, she decided that she would have it all.

Quietly entering the bedroom, Derby felt a little irritated to see David curled under the duvet already snoring loudly. She collected her night wear and slipped silently out of the bedroom into the bathroom. She went through her normal night time routines, re-entered the bedroom, slid under the covers and managed to fall asleep quickly.

Angela cheerfully greeted Derby at the nursery the same as every other day. She was about to turn towards the kitchen but stopped suddenly, something in Derby's smile making her look directly into her friend's eyes.

"Has something happened?"

She asked. A surprised expression flitted across Derby's face.

"Umm…what do you mean?"

She asked Angela, her face heating a little. Angela grinned.

"It did! Was it the gym, Geoff?"

Derby blushed to the roots of her hair shaking her head at the same time.

"Shush. And no I didn't go to the gym last night. Look the children will be here in a minute. Can you hold off 'till we finish work?"

Derby implored. Angela, still grinning nodded.

"But you my girl will tell."

She told her pointing at her.

The day progressed as any day in the nursery. They had a couple of toddlers throw up and had to call parents to come and collect them, Derby praying there wasn't going to be an outbreak of a sickness bug. She wasn't over confident remembering that David's managers had already gone down with it. She reminded all of the staff to be extra vigilant with their own personal hygiene and that of the children, and double checked all of the sterilization and refrigeration systems.

At the end of the day she instructed the staff to speak to the parents and child minders explaining the possibilities of the bug, and to ask them all to use the anti-bacterial gel when they came in and left. Feeling confident that she had done everything in her power to minimise the spread of the bug, she locked up the nursery and made coffee for her and Angela.

The two women sat in the little nursery kitchen sipping hot coffee. At first they chatted about the day, the sick children and planned to come in early the next day to go over every surface with anti-bacterial spray.

"Just as an extra precaution."

Derby told Angela."

"So are you going to tell me?"

Angela asked in a soft voice. The teasing humour from earlier gone as she knew whatever her friend was going to tell her was an important step for her. Derby pondered for a moment, swirling the last of her coffee in its mug.

"I watched the DVD, you know from Kelsey's party."

Angela waited knowing there was more, but also knowing it was difficult for Derby to speak it out loud. With a big sigh, Derby plunged on.

"I…discovered…well…what it showed was…well…how to look at your own…umm…" She put the mug down and covered her very red face with her hands, " bits…and…and…how to…oh shit…touch yourself and make yourself come."

She finished quickly. Angela gently pulled Derby's hands away from her face and leaned forward.

"Chick, it's ok. Don't be embarrassed. You don't have to tell me in detail. It's natural and normal to masturbate. In fact it helps keep your libido going. And since you haven't had a normal sex life, I would think whatever you discovered about yourself was something of a revelation."

Derby, still blushing took a deep breath.

"Yeah it was. I did find out quite a lot. Stuff I had no idea about and…" she paused blushing even more deeply, "feelings I didn't know I could feel."

Angela patted her hand.

"About time girlie. I'm assuming you mean an orgasm."

Derby burst into giggles nodding. She didn't think her face could get any hotter so what did it matter if she told Angela what she did.

"Yes, and it was orgasms. In my garden."

Angela grinned back.

"Oh my God girl. You have gone from zero to a hundred in point five of a second."

Derby smiled back.

"Don't think I know what you mean by that, but it was very good."

"What it means is, a lot of people start with the sex outside as teenagers, then get back to it later on when they are more comfortable with their partner. You got straight down to it. But then I guess, it is sort of like teenage stuff with you isn't it."

Derby nodded in agreement.

"Do you and Jake do it outside?"

"When we get the chance. But with the children around most of the time, it's hard."

Both women laughed at the sexual intimation.

"Not something I know much about."

Derby replied wiggling her eyebrows.

"Well…" Angela paused chewing on her lip. "This is not something I would usually advocate…I mean I believe in being faithful and all that…but in your situation…maybe you need to have a fling."

"Already ahead of you there."
Derby told her. Angela grinned.

"You cheeky monkey you. Anyone in particular, Geoff?"
Derby grinned back.

"I wish. No, no one. Yet. I'll keep you posted."

"You better. In the meantime you should get some toys"
Angela replied, gathering up the mugs and washing them in the sink. Derby frowned.

"What do I need toys for. I don't have any children."
Angela burst out laughing.

"Sex toys. You know, like the stuff at Kelsey's."

"Oh, I get you now."
Derby replied thinking about the catalogue that came with the DVD.

"Time for home I think. All this talk of sex, well I think the children are going to have an early night."
Angela told her folding the tea towel and draping it over a rail. Derby smiled and followed Angela out of the nursery locking up behind her.

Once home, Derby headed upstairs and took out the package with the DVD and catalogue. Perched on the end of the bed, she flipped through, finding the section on sex toys. She folded the corner of the page and took the booklet downstairs. Without much thought, she threw some pasta in a pan and put it on the hob to cook. She then grabbed a can of Coke out of the fridge, and with the catalogue in the other hand went outside.

Turning straight to the folded page, Derby began to peruse the items on sale. Her eye was instantly caught on the range of vibrators. Some of them looked huge, and a shudder went through her at the thought of having something so large inside her. Then her fear was replaced with curiosity. Just because she had never experienced the pleasure of an enormous, hard pulsating penis, (David definitely did not come into that category) didn't mean it would be painful. In fact right then the thought made her feel quite warm and wet. Laying aside the booklet, Derby returned to the kitchen, noticed the pasta was about to boil over so turned it down, and retrieved a pen from a drawer.

Back outside, she chewed the end of the pen whilst mulling over the vibrators on the pages. She put a circle around three of them. A large transparent one, which had a protruding part from the lower half of the shaft ending in what looked like ears. One which had what appeared to be studs embedded in it, and another that was shaped like a spoon. She then turned the pages and found a selection of dildos and chose a flesh coloured eight inch one and finally chose two clitoral stimulators.

There was an order form attached to the catalogue which she then filled in, this time feeling no embarrassment. She could have ordered everything over the internet, but wanted to give Kelsey the commission by ordering through her. After all, it was Kelsey that had got her started on this in the first place, and the young woman really did need the money.

Derby returned to the kitchen and dug out a pasta sauce from the cupboard. She drained the pan and added the sauce, dumping the whole lot unceremoniously onto a plate. She took the meal outside, relishing in another hot evening and again wondered why it had taken her so long to realise how pleasant it was to sit outside. She didn't think she would want to spend another dry warm night indoors ever again, and hoped the summer would continue as it was, knowing it was probably unlikely.

This thought brought about another. What if it did rain? She suddenly imagined herself laying in wet grass, a storm raging around her, a dildo or vibrator pulsing deep inside her, coming to the crash of thunder. Pushing aside her partly eaten meal, Derby leaned back in the chair sliding her dress up her thighs. For a few minutes she caressed the insides of her legs, running her nails up and down delighting in the light scratching sensation. Slowly she began to move higher and nearer to her crotch, teasing herself by letting her thumb briefly rub over her now very wet undies.

She rested her head on the back of her chair, eyes closed letting the heat of the sun wash over her face. Her hands now found their way into her knickers and stroked and pressed her pubic mound and hair. Pushing her pelvis up to meet her hands she let her fingers find and part her labia. Then she inserted two fingers and began to move them in and out slowly and sensuously. Her other hand found her clitoris and tapped and rubbed as her fingers increased in speed. She now moved her pelvis to meet her fingers and plunged and pressed, nipping her lip between her teeth.

Her orgasm came as powerfully as the day before, shaking her body as though she were riding an earthquake. Her breath came in gasps and little murmurs of pleasure erupted from her lips as she came back down from the peak of her orgasm. Sighing with satisfaction, Derby let her hands rest where they were as her body began to relax. She opened her eyes and looked around the patio, just to be sure no one was watching. That would be something to tell Angela, she thought, but of course, her garden was still and quiet, empty but for herself.

Straightening her clothes, Derby took the remains of her dinner into the kitchen, emptied the plate into the bin and put it in the dishwasher. It barely had anything in it. Just the things from the night before and their breakfast cups and crockery. Still she set it anyway knowing it was a waste of everything and not caring one bit. She folded the order form into its envelope and tucked it in her bag to give to Kelsey the next day, hoping upon hope that Chardonnay hadn't got the sickness bug. Then she felt a little guilty for feeling so selfish. Of course she didn't want the child to get sick anyway, but she really wanted to see Kelsey tomorrow and give her the order.

For a moment Derby scanned the kitchen and quickly decided that she didn't want to be at home right now. She wanted to be near other people, so she trotted upstairs and grabbed her gym bag. The bus journey was as annoying as before, and Derby longed for tomorrow when she would get her new car and the independence it would give her. At the gym she signed it at the desk and was given her key card. She took it, smiling widely at the assistant, she was now officially a member.

Geoff was called and he came through the glass doors smiling and sending shivers down Derby's back. She felt just like the dizziest school girl with a crush, as she beamed back at him, instead of a forty year old woman. She realised that over the years she had been blinkered, never having taken any notice or shown any interest in men. Now with the covers removed from her eyes and mind, she looked and took pleasure in what she saw.

After changing, Geoff again took her through her routine, upping the pace a little to work her more. Between equipment she managed to ask him a little more about himself, not giving away the fact that she had Googled him and knew quite a bit. He told her about being a marine, but left out his charity work which told her that he was modest. He let out a little bit more about his failed marriage. After just four years his wife left him and found someone else. There were no children involved so the divorce wasn't as traumatic as it could have been. That had been six years ago and Geoff didn't seem to be suffering from it.

"It hurt like hell at the time, but, well now I see it was for the best."

He stated with a shrug. Derby was now too breathless from exercise to respond with anything more than a couple of words. This seemed to amuse Geoff.

"No more chat whilst working out. Let's save that for the juice bar after."

Derby smiled, but lit up inside. She was sure he didn't spend as much time on all of his members.

After showering and dressing, Derby met Geoff in the juice bar. He had already ordered drinks and stood up politely as she approached. That was a new thing for her too. Even at the annual balls, David never did that. He would just tuck straight into his food, barely noticing she was sitting next to him.

"So now you know more about me, what about you?"

Geoff asked sipping his juice. Derby gave a little shrug.

"Not much to tell."

Then with her eyes lowered she all but whispered.

"At least not yet."

"Mmm…what does that mean?"

Geoff asked with a cheeky grin on his face. Derby felt the blush begin at her neck and flood into her cheeks. But she ignored it and looked directly into his eyes.

"I'm sort of going through some stuff right now. I…I…can't really talk about it yet…"

She didn't know how to end the sentence but Geoff didn't seem put off by it. He covered her hand with his huge one, sending little electric shocks right through her, right to the heart of her womanhood. She didn't think he knew what he was doing to her, at least she hoped not and his reply seemed sincere.

"It's fine Derby. Just know I'm here whenever you do want to talk."

"Do you do this for everyone you train?"
Derby bravely asked. Geoff shook his head.

"No, just you."

She had no reply to that so simply lifted her glass and drank her juice. She heard Geoff laugh very softly and wasn't sure if he was mocking her, but when she glanced at is eyes, they looked so gentle she believed he wasn't.

Geoff's phone blipped and he connected to his headset. After listening for a minute he told the caller he would be right there.

"I'm sorry Derby. I have to go. Come back soon, ok."
She nodded.

"I will. Because I really do want to get fit and healthy."

"You are already fit and healthy."
He told her with a wide grin as he stood and made to depart. Derby wasn't sure exactly what he was saying, but hoped the 'fit' meant more than just her physical condition.

Back home Derby threw her gym clothes into the washing machine and wandered out to the garden. The evening was cooler than the last few had been, a few clouds blocking the late sunshine. Derby didn't care. As she strolled around, pulling the odd weed from amongst the roses, she thought about Geoff. Was she ready, even capable of having an affair. Could she really keep it from David? Yes that she could do she told herself, but what about other people? Someone could find out and tell David, what then? Shaking her head a little she realised the prospect of an affair raised many questions and was she reading the signs right? What if she just wanted to see the flirtations and hear the innuendoes so much, that it was all in her imagination. What if Geoff was just being her coach, a very kind and polite coach?

"No I won't accept that."
Derby quietly told the weed she held up in front of her.

"I might be inexperienced but he is definitely interested."
With that she stomped back to the kitchen casting the weed aside on the way.

Stripping her clothes as she walked, Derby headed for the bathroom. She didn't need a shower having had one at the gym. But she needed to do something. She felt jittery and unsettled. All the changes had happened so quickly and for a moment overloaded her body and brain. She turned on the water and set it to cool. Her skin felt hot and she prayed that she wasn't coming down with something. Standing under the fresh jets of water Derby closed her eyes and simply let the tension drain from her.

The water felt soothing and alleviated her fears of illness as she began to feel less stressed. More thoughts of Geoff intruded her peace. She had always believed in monogamy, frowning upon the women she overheard discussing affairs, belittling their husbands, because she had never looked deeply at her own relationship. However since her birthday, and she still didn't know why that was the turning point, she saw that life was not just black and white. Hers was many shades of grey and she was coming out on the bright side, changing the grey to colour.

Without thinking Derby squeezed shower gel into her hand and began to lather her body. At first it was a normal and mundane act, one she performed every time she bathed. Suddenly her body reacted to her own touch, as she imagined what Geoff would look like naked and wet. Suddenly she wasn't just wet from the water. She spread her legs wide and let her hands wander all over her body. She tickled her erect nipples and massaged her breasts. Wanting more, she lifted the shower head from its bracket and turned the dial so the water came with force.

She held it close to her nipples and delighted in the slight stinging sensation. She then turned it upside down between her open legs, holding it close to, but not touching her vulva. She moved it about, her breath coming in short bursts as the warm jets jolted her clitoris. Wanting to delay coming she moved the head away and threaded the hose back and forth, sliding it between her labia giving herself more pleasure.

She licked her lips as her need to reach orgasm increased so she put a finger inside her vagina. She squeezed her muscles against her finger enthralled in the feeling, and directed the head of the shower back to her clitoris. Her hips moved naturally and pushed against her finger as the water sent thrilling little stabs at her clitoris. Then she came, fast and furious, a squeal of pleasure erupting from her lips, the shower head pressed against her pubic mound her finger deep inside herself. She took a deep breath and slumped forward slightly as the orgasm abated, her body awash with satisfaction and no longer tense and stressed.

Derby spent the rest of the evening watching television. She flipped through channels and finally settled on a drama that she actually found very interesting. Usually David hogged the TV when he wasn't on the computer, so the news was what Derby mainly watched. Now she found it quite enjoyable just sitting and watching actors and actresses deal with life issues. She didn't wait up for David, and so by the time he flopped into bed beside her, she was already asleep.

In the morning Derby double checked her order was still tucked into her bag and headed for work. She hoped Kelsey would arrive as normal and sighed with relief when she came in hand in hand with little Chardonnay. As bubbly as usual Kelsey headed for Derby and engaged her in chat about her daughter. Derby smiled and told her she was so glad Chardonnay was well and hadn't come down with the sickness bug.

"Oh I know. Loads of the children at school are off and a couple of teachers. God I really hope neither of us get it."
She replied. Derby gently eased her to one side and whispered.

"I have an order."
Kelsey edged closer and took the little envelope, quickly stuffing it into the huge bag draped over her shoulder.

"Good on you. I'll get this sorted as soon as I can. And thanks Derby, you could have ordered on line."

"I know, but…you well, you don't know what this has done for me. And, you started it so you should get the commission."
Derby told her sincerely. Kelsey smiled warmly, unusually a little embarrassed.

"Well, thanks again. If you want the order really quickly I can phone it in, but it means opening the envelope."
She all but whispered. At first Derby was horrified and her blush told Kelsey so.

"Oh but I don't have to. It will just take a little longer."
Derby swallowed and weighed up the wait or the embarrassment, deciding the latter was less important.

"Go for it."

She told Kelsey.

"Ok, in my lunch break. And of course everything is kept completely confidential. The stuff will most likely be here tomorrow, if you are really lucky a rep might be able to drop it round tonight."

Derby could barely keep the smile from spreading across her lips.

Angela noticed the hushed conversation going on between Derby and Kelsey and approached Derby after all the children had been dropped off. Before she had the chance to ask though Derby blurted it out.

"I've ordered toys."

Angela waggled her eyebrows.

"Toys. As in the plural?"

Derby nodded, a flushed smile on her face.

"Oh yes. Well I don't know what is best so thought I'd try a few."

"Good on you. When do they arrive?"

Angela replied.

"Kelsey said could be as soon as tonight, or tomorrow."

"What about David?"

Angela asked.

"He's still tied up with sick managers."

She giggled and Angela joined in.

"That would sound rather perverted if you were talking about anyone else."

Angela told her making her laugh even more.

As the work day drew to a close Derby sighed deeply. Three more children had gone home sick and one nursery nurse was complaining of feeling nauseous. At least it was the weekend, so Derby hoped by Monday she would have got over it. On the bright side, she was collecting her car, Angela going with her, and Kelsey had told her a rep would be able to bring part of the order round later. So feeling cheerful, she locked up the nursery and headed towards Angela's car.

The young car dealer Liam greeted the two women as they walked into the showroom. He offered them coffee and showed them to his desk asking them to sit down. On the desk was a folder which he opened as they sat. Derby could see various pieces of paper and had no idea what any of it meant. Liam seemed to sense her lack of knowledge and smiled his very charming cheeky smile.

"Don't look so nervous. It's really quite straight forward."
He told her, making her blush, much to her chagrin. Trying to hide her embarrassment Derby sipped her coffee.

"Did you sort your insurance out?"
He asked. Derby nodded and pulled a document from her bag handing it to him.

"Good. Now this is the V5, which shows the registered keeper of the car. You have to sign it here." He indicated boxes and Derby quickly scrawled her signature. "Then we send this bit off and you keep this bit. In a couple of weeks the DVLA will send you a new one with your name on it."
He tore off a section and put it to one side next to her insurance document.

"Next is the MOT certificate. You don't have to do anything except keep it safe."
He grinned and Derby began to feel like a child, angry with herself for never having done this before.

"Ok. What next?"
She asked, aiming for enquiring instead of naïve, and hoping she had pulled it off.

"We have the warranty certificate and finally the sales paperwork. You're not financing the car, am I right?"
Liam asked.

"No I will be paying for it on my debit card. Is that alright?"
Liam smiled kindly this time.

"That's perfectly ok. If you would just like to read through this and sign where the crosses are."
He said handing her the paperwork.

"Would either of you like more coffee?"
He asked as Derby read. Angela accepted but Derby declined.

A short time later Liam was showing Derby how to put the top down on her shiny red sports car, and explaining the various dials and buttons on the dashboard. Angela stood to one side, proud that her friend was taking her life into her own hands. Finally, Liam stood back after handing Derby his business card, holding onto it a little longer than necessary so Derby's fingers touched his, so Angela noticed. She smiled to herself, Derby definitely was attracting male attention without really noticing.

"I'll follow you Angela."

Derby said, breaking into her friend's thoughts.

"Ok. Do you want me to lead you back to yours?"

"Mmm, thanks. I'm sure I'll soon get used to it all."

She replied, settling herself in the driving seat and revving the engine a little. She enjoyed the sound and the feeling of power, but knew she had to take it steady at first and get the feel of the car.

Angela pulled up outside Derby's house and Derby pulled up behind her. The car handled beautifully and already she felt completely at home driving it. A few neighbours, enjoying the evening outside looked up but nobody made any comments. Derby stepped out and all but skipped over to Angela who had her window down waiting.

"Well?"

Was all she had to say. Derby beamed holding her hands together like one of the toddlers at the nursery.

"Wow. It is absolutely terrific. I love it. I want to get back in and just keep on driving."

"Don't you go disappearing on me now."

Angela told her jokingly.

"Mmmm nice thought, but no I won't. I do have to call Kelsey though and see if my stuff has come."

Angela waggled her eyebrows.

"Very appropriate word."

"Oh you. Get on home to your hunk."

Derby told her waving a hand at her. Angela grinned and pulled away from the kerb, waving out of the open window as she drove up the road.

A quick phone call later and Derby was back in her car heading for Kelsey's. She was excited about driving and about what she was about to collect. But, she had also decided to go to the gym, delaying experimenting with her new toys. The evening was again hot and with the top down her hair was blowing around her face. She felt alive and free and full of colour.

Finding directions on her phone, she pulled into the gym car park, amazed at how quickly she had got there compared to the bus ride. She locked her car and bounced into the gym.

The workout that evening was definitely easier on her body and she topped it off with a swim, enjoying the cool water on her sweating body. Geoff had again asked her to join him in the juice bar, and so once changed went to meet him. At first he was talking to two other members of staff, but when he saw her he broke off and came right over. Ordering their drinks he openly looked her up and down.

"Exercise must be good for you. There's a definite difference."
He told her, handing her a juice cocktail. Derby lowered her lashes and smiled shyly.

"It's not just the exercise."
She told him.

"Oh. What else then?"
He asked cheekily. Derby's cheeks heated up and Geoff grinned.

"You are so delightful when you blush."
He said. Derby couldn't believe what she was hearing. No one had ever said anything like that to her and she wasn't sure how to respond.

"I got my car."
She blurted out, just for something to say. Geoff laughed, a deep very enjoyable sound, and at first Derby thought he was mocking her. But when she looked into his eyes, she saw something that was most definitely not mockery.

"Do you have it here?"
He asked. It took a moment for Derby to register that he was asking about the car.

"Umm…yes. I drove it here tonight." She paused. "Want to come and have a look."
She asked, excitement at showing off her car evident on her face.

"Yes, I would. In fact I'm finished for the evening, so you could take me for a spin in it."
Derby was so surprised that she couldn't catch her breath for a moment. The thought of having this gorgeous man sitting close to her in the confines of her small car sent shivers of delight down her back. Giving herself a mental shake and afraid Geoff might think she was putting him off by not replying, she took a breath, smiled and said.

"Ok. I hope I don't scare you."

"I think I'll be alright."
He told her finishing his drink. Derby emptied her glass too and the two left the gym.

Derby nervously buckled her seat belt. Geoff seemed to fill the small space of the car even with the top down, but sat back looking relaxed and comfortable. Starting the engine and putting the car into gear, Derby took a breath and said.

"Well here we go. Anywhere in particular?"
Geoff grinned and shook his head. So Derby pulled out of the car park turning right, but having no idea exactly where that would take them.

"You know, I don't know where I'm going."
She told Geoff as she drove through fairly heavy traffic.

"This will take us through town. If you want a quieter road take the next left."
Geoff responded. Without replying Derby made the turn and immediately found fewer vehicles. She felt foolish not knowing her way round a town she had lived in all her life.

"I...I...don't...well...go anywhere. I had to use my phone just to get me to the gym."
She told him feeling like the world's most stupidest person.

"Derby, it's fine. I know quite a few people who don't or can't drive, and never venture far from home."
He replied, briefly covering her hand on the steering wheel. She glanced at him quickly.

"Well I am going to discover all the roads round town and further afield. I really am not going to let myself drift along in a bubble anymore."
She told him quite forcefully.

"Whatever happened to you Derby?"
He asked. Again she glanced at him.

"I woke up. At least that's what it feels like. I'll tell you about it sometime, but for now, I think I need to concentrate on my driving, and where are we going?"
They were now on an open road with green hedges on either side. Geoff laughed.

"I didn't think we were going anywhere, just driving. But if you take the next left, there's a park if you would like to go there."

Derby nodded and followed his directions, soon pulling into the car park of a park she had no idea existed. It was busy and Derby felt a very small tinge of relief.

"What now?"

She asked Geoff. He laughed.

"There's a café."

"Sounds good."

She replied exiting the car and straightening her dress. Geoff unfolded himself from the passenger seat, seeming very tall next to the little car. Derby locked up and waited for Geoff to show her the way.

The café was busy too, but they managed to find a table outside and ordered coffees. The evening was warm, and to Derby the air felt charged as though a storm was impending. Looking up at the clear blue summer sky she thought the feeling must be inside her because there was certainly no signs of a storm coming. As the waitress laid their coffees in front of them, Derby glanced at the other clientele.

Most of them seemed to be chatting, sipping drinks and enjoying their company. One couple looked like they might be arguing quietly, frowning and gesticulating at each other, Derby didn't linger on these two. There were families eating snacks, the children giggling and running around playing, which sent little pangs of envy through her.

"Are you ok?"

Geoff asked, touching her hand lightly. Derby turned to him and smiled.

"Yes, I'm fine."

She picked up her cup and sipped, suddenly a little nervous and also a little afraid that someone would spot her with Geoff. However, no one seemed to be taking any notice of them, so she relaxed just a little.

"Derby, where's your husband?"

Geoff asked, startling her.

"He...he's at work. He's a supermarket manager with people off sick, so he has to cover."

She replied, blushing. Geoff looked at her quizzically.

"Look, something is obviously not right at home. Would you like to tell me about it?"

Derby looked away again at the families and sighed.

"Before I do, why do you want to know?"

It was Geoff's turn to think about her question. For a moment he stared into his cup, swirling the coffee.

"I like you."

He stated. Derby waited, sure there was more to come.

"Well actually, more than like you. There's something I see in you that I've never seen in a woman before." He laughed. "God that sounds like the corniest chat up line ever."

Derby looked at him seriously.

"Actually, I wouldn't know if it is or not."

She said tears prickling the corners of her eyes. Geoff immediately saw her distress and covered her small hand with his large one.

"Hey, it's ok. You don't have to say anything. We can just have our coffee and chat about nothing in particular." Then he grinned. "But I have to say, I've never made a woman cry before by paying her a compliment."

Derby's eyes dried up quickly as she giggled.

"Well I don't get compliments."

She stated matter-of-factly. Geoff was about to tell her he doubted that, but saw from her eyes that she was being serious.

Derby leaned back in her chair holding her cup in both hands even though it was now empty. The café had thinned out considerably, most of the families having finished and taken their children off around the park. A few couples lingered, but the arguing couple had gone. Derby hoped together and in a happier mood. They had looked young and she couldn't bear the thought of the row being serious, even though she knew nothing about them. A tiny breeze whispered across her cheeks lifting a wisp of hair from her face. It smelt of trees and green leaves and brought a small smile to her lips.

"What are you smiling about?"

Geoff asked. He had been staring at her, watching the emotions on her face change as she studied her surroundings.

"Just enjoying the summer air."

She replied. A waiter came over and nervously told them the café was about to close. Derby smiled at him and handed him her empty cup. Geoff stood up and offered his hand.

"Want to walk through the park?"

Derby nodded and took his hand which he held onto as he led her along the pathways.

"I have an empty marriage."
Derby blurted out as they skirted the duck pond. Geoff squeezed her hand gently.

"What do you mean?"

"David, my husband of twenty four years doesn't take any notice of me. We barely speak, don't do anything together, go anywhere together. We…we…sleep in the same bed, but…nothing ever happens there either."

Geoff stopped walking, Derby having to as well as he was still holding her hand. A few ducks milled around them thinking they had food, retreating when no bread was given. Tugging her hand gently, Geoff pulled her a little closer. He looked down into her eyes, she having to look up.

"Crikey, you must have been a very young bride."
Was the first thing he said making her laugh but feel a little sad at the same time.

"Just sixteen. Actually on my birthday. Thought I was pregnant and…well…parents forced the issue."
She told him looking away and blushing.

"But you weren't."
It wasn't a question, Derby shaking her head in reply as she gazed out over the water.

"We stayed together. I thought I loved him, suppose I did back then and we drifted along. Never did have any children. Qualified as a nursery nurse and until a few days ago didn't really think anything of it. Then on my birthday, I…well…I don't know what triggered it…but…I suddenly realised there had to be more to my life, and here I am."
Geoff smiled.

"And here you are. And here am I. So what next?"
Derby sighed deeply.

"Geoff, I really don't know. All this, it's new and strange. I'm finding things out about myself that I had no idea about. Finding out things most women my age are experienced about. Stuff I'm not ready to talk about. Does that bother you?"
Geoff shook his head.

"Just so long as you let me keep getting to know you."

He told her sincerely. Derby smiled in return.

"I'd like that. I can't promise anything, but well…"

She didn't know quite what to say. She felt her face begin to heat up as she imagined what she would like to do with him, what she would like him to do to her. The smile on his lips told her he had guessed some of what she was thinking.

"I can live with that."

Derby dropped Geoff back at the gym. He had given her his mobile number and told her to call him anytime, that she didn't have to wait until she came to the gym to see him. Driving away, Derby felt a fresh wave of excitement, a thrill of fear that she was doing something naughty behind her husband's back. She felt a heat begin to build deep within her as she imagined Geoff's hands on her and in her. She glanced at the dashboard and was surprised to see it was nearly ten.

The sun had already set but because the night was so clear there was still a glimmer of light on the horizon. David would be home but she didn't care, thought he probably wouldn't even realise she wasn't. She didn't want to go home. It was Friday night, summertime, warm and dry. She felt alive and not one bit lonely even though she was alone. The streets she drove along were busy, people out for the evening, enjoying the summer. She had no destination in mind, just stayed with the flow of the traffic feeling a power that was more than the car's engine. It was her power, she was in control, she was free.

Finally Derby found her way home and parked outside her house. David's car was in the driveway but she felt no guilt. She left her gym bag in the car, locked up and went into the house. All was quiet and there were no lights on. She took off her shoes, and with barely a sound went upstairs. Gently pushing open the bedroom door, she saw a lump under the duvet and heard the familiar grunts of David's snores. Even on such a hot night, he had the cover pulled up to his chin. Derby turned back towards tha landing and just as quietly went back downstairs without disturbing her husband.

Unlocking the back door, she stepped out onto the patio and sat at the table. She thought she should feel angry about David's lack of concern over her, but felt nothing. Her thoughts were with Geoff and the time they had spent together. She remembered the feel of his fingers and his large hand holding hers. She closed her eyes and saw his smile and his muscular body sitting close to her in the car. In her imagination she could feel him touching her, his hands stroking the inside of her thighs.

She let her own hand wander to her now very wet knickers. With her eyes still closed, she licked her lips, Geoff's face very clear in her mind. Slowly she began to stroke her clitoris leaning back in the chair. Enjoying the sensations she was giving herself, she was startled when her mobile rang. Jumping out of the chair, Derby trotted into the kitchen grabbing the phone from her bag. She didn't recognise the number on the screen and answered as she went back outside. A deep familiar voice replied to her hello, it was Geoff. Taking a quick glance at the phone, she wondered why his name hadn't come up, she had put his number in her contacts just a little while ago.

"Hi."
She said after he had said his hello.

"You sound surprised and a little out of breath."
He told her.

"I think I must have put your number in wrong 'cos your name didn't come up on my screen."
She replied, her face heating up as she remembered why she was breathless.

"As for being breathless... I um...was outside and my phone was in the kitchen."
She lied, her face getting hotter. She heard him laugh lightly, deep and wonderful and oh so sexy. She didn't think he believed her, but couldn't fathom how he would know she wasn't telling the truth. She settled herself back in her chair, the warm night engulfing her. Leaning back she lifted her dress high up her thighs and stretched her legs open.

"I just wanted to be sure you got home safely."
Geoff told her.

"Thank you. I did. I did drive around for a while, in fact I've only just got back in."

"Wasn't your husband worried?"
He asked gently.

"Oh he's tucked up in bed snoring. Don't think he even noticed I wasn't here."

She replied, a flatness to her voice. There was a short pause from his end.

"Derby, if I came home and you weren't there and I didn't know where you were, I would be worried out of my mind."

Tears pricked at the corner of her eyes. No one had ever said anything so nice to her. Even when she was a little girl parental concern hadn't come with hugs and kisses.

"That is so lovely. Nobody has ever worried about me."

She all but whispered back, struggling to keep the tears at bay.

"Have I upset you?"

Geoff asked. Derby was surprised that he could tell her mood over the phone. David never cared if she was upset. The few times she had cried in his presence over the years he had simply told her to 'Get over it'

"No of course not. I just got a little emotional over your concern. How could you tell?"

"I heard it in your voice."

He told her softly.

"I'll be ok. I'm tough."

She told him.

"Yes I know you are. You are also incredibly beautiful and very very sexy."

His voice had changed. He now sounded flirtatious and teasing. Derby took a deep breath before she replied.

"I'm not sure how to reply to that. Except…um…you are too."

She felt herself blush again, glad he couldn't see her face, but sure he knew exactly what was happening to her.

"Thank you Derby. You know, it's so refreshing to meet a woman who isn't vain."

"I don't know how to be."

Derby told him honestly. He laughed again, a deep sexy laugh that set her pulse beating hard and her body on fire.

"You also don't know what you are doing to me with that sexy voice of yours."

He said, his voice husky, sending spikes of desire through her like little electric shocks. Without even thinking, her free hand traced a track down from her breasts to her inner thigh and came to rest against her wet undies.

"What am I doing to you?"

She asked cheekily, suddenly feeling confident. Again he laughed.

"Making me want to hold you."

He paused and her hand began to stroke, lightly and teasingly.

"Go on."

She said, again a little breathless.

"Making me want to kiss you all over."

Her hand delved inside her knickers plucking her clitoris.

"Anything else?"

She whispered. His deep voice whispered back.

"Oh yes Derby. Much much more. I want to see you naked and in pleasure."

That tipped her over the edge. She climaxed, her body going taut, biting her lip so she wouldn't make a sound over the phone which she still pressed to her ear. For a brief moment she couldn't hear anything, couldn't think of anything, couldn't speak.

"Derby…Derby…have I said too much? Are you ok?"

Geoff asked worriedly. Letting out a deep sigh Derby got herself together.

"No…no."

Her voice didn't quite have the volume she had hoped for. So licking her lips she tried again.

"Geoff."

It worked, her voice sounded normal.

"I'm fine…you…umm…I…just…you made me feel…good."

She finished the last word quickly. There was a pause from the other end.

"I'm glad about that."

Geoff told her softly, and for a moment Derby was sure he knew just how good his words had made her feel. She felt fresh heat in her cheeks but kept her voice level as she replied.

"So am I."

"Derby I want to see you."

"Now?"

She heard him laugh.

"Well yes actually. But I didn't mean that. What I mean is I want to see you, not at the gym but a date."

Before she could absorb his words he continued.

"Look I know you're married and it's probably too soon, but I get the feeling there's something between us. I think...you maybe...feel it too. I heard something in your voice just now."

Derby took a deep breath of warm summer air, sure that whatever he heard in her voice was definitely not what was actually in her voice. Suddenly not at all sure how to respond Derby felt in over her head.

"Geoff...I do feel that way too. I don't think it's too soon, but I do need to think about it. I'll call you tomorrow. Tonight has been strange for me, in lots of ways, I need to adjust quite a bit. Is that alright?"

She was afraid she had said the wrong thing, that he would now run a mile. But was pleased by his reply.

"Derby, I very much look forward to your call. Don't forget to make sure my number in your phone book is the right one."

She giggled.

"Oh definitely."

"Well, goodnight Derby. Sleep well, have nice dreams."

Again feeling that he knew how he made her body react she said goodnight and hung up. She checked her contacts and under his name discovered she had entered a digit the wrong way round. She corrected it and saved it, hugging her phone to her breast and feeling more alive than ever before.

Chapter 9

The Apartment

Derby awoke to the sound of birds tweeting. Glancing at the clock she saw it was very early, not quite half past five. Quietly and slowly she pushed back the duvet stopping for a moment when David turned and grunted. Barely breathing she waited but he didn't wake, so she continued out of bed and tiptoed out of the bedroom closing the door behind her. Once out of the bedroom she moved about more naturally heading for the bathroom.

As she ran the shower she felt wide awake and fully rested. She realised this was the first time she had felt this way. She also realised that usually on a Saturday she felt drained and low. For so many years she had not known how miserable she had really been. Now as the warm water gushed over her skin, she resolved that she would never feel that way again. She would be happy and damn David, she would find that happiness any way she chose.

Stepping out of the shower she wrapped a bath sheet around her, towel dried her hair and headed downstairs. She hadn't thought to collect clothes from the bedroom, and didn't want to risk waking David by going back. In the kitchen she put the kettle on the hob, unlocked the back door and stepped out onto the patio. It was already warm outside and by the look of the clear blue sky, promised to be another brilliant hot day.

She wandered onto the lawn and breathed in the deep scent of the roses, startling the birds pecking around. Everything was fresh and alive, just as she felt. She heard the whistle of the kettle and quickly returned to the kitchen turning it off before it got louder. She dropped a teabag into a mug, poured on the water, squeezed the teabag out and took her drink into the garden.

Settling herself at the patio table thoughts of the previous evening and her conversation with Geoff came back to her as did the memory of the orgasm she had whilst talking to him on the phone. This brought heat both to her face and deep within her body, but she didn't want to do anything at that moment except enjoy the early morning. Besides, it wouldn't be too long before David would be awake, that thought damping down her desire.

As she sipped her tea she remembered thinking yesterday about how she would manage an affair, if it happened. She was almost sure that it would. Geoff had made it quite clear that he was interested. Exactly how interested was a bit of an enigma to her just now, and how far did he want to go, she asked herself. She herself wasn't sure how far she wanted to go.

He was gorgeous, sexy and extremely masculine. Was it just sex that she wanted, or for that matter what he wanted, or was she looking for a new relationship. Holding her mug in both hands, she knew she didn't know. Was she prepared to swap one man for another, or was she looking for more in her life. After all, she felt like Sleeping Beauty, having awoken from a very long sleep, the world passing her by, oblivious to everything around her.

Finishing her tea, Derby took the mug back to the kitchen and mindlessly laid the table ready for David's breakfast. So many thoughts and questions buzzed inside her mind, but no answers emerged. She looked at the kitchen clock and saw the time had flown by, her phone alarm would be going off soon. Reluctantly she went back upstairs and walked into the bedroom just as the alarm began. As usual David did not stir. She switched off the alarm and gave her husband a nudge.

"David, time to get up."

She shook him lightly. She could barely see his face as like always he had the duvet wrapped around him despite the summer warmth. She could just see the stubble on his chin, and noticed for the first time the traces of grey in his sideburns. Immediately she felt herself comparing him to Geoff, whose light streaks of grey in his hair enhanced his looks. Staring at her husband, all she could see was the beginnings of an old man. He did nothing to look after himself. His skin looked rough and dry and there were more than just a few crows feet around his closed eyes.

"Come on David. Time to get up."

She shook him a little harder and this time he opened his eyes and groaned.

"Can't be. I'm knackered."

He mumbled. Derby stood up, went to the window and opened the curtains.

"Why'd you do that?"

David moaned.

"Because it's light outside and it's time for you to be up."
She replied.

"Fine."

David said, sounding like the worst recalcitrant teenager ever. Derby actually felt a giggle bubble up inside her which disappeared as soon as she turned to look at him. He was standing by the bed stretching. His belly was just beginning to hang over the bottoms of his pyjamas which he rubbed as he yawned widely. His face was scrunched up against the sunlight and Derby could see more grey in what was left of his hair.

"Got to pee."

He mumbled heading for the bathroom. Derby turned up her nose, glad that he would soon be heading off to work and out of her way.

With David in the bathroom, Derby moisturised her skin, combed her almost dry hair and dressed. Looking at herself in the mirror she decided that today she would go and buy some new summer clothes, modern ones. The dresses she owned for summer had been around for quite some time. Even her summer work clothes were just a lighter version of her winter ones. So once David was at work she gave the house a cursory going over, chucked the washing in the machine and decided she would once again venture into town, and this time she would have more confidence.

Driving into town was rather daunting as was locating the car park, but once again her iphone came in handy. However, eventually Derby strolled out of a multi-storey car park straight into the main shopping centre. It was busy and hot but immediately she felt joy and excitement at the prospect of new clothes. She decided the first thing on her list was underwear. Now she knew what she wanted she had no trouble in finding the right shop. Inside, she browsed the rows of bras and knickers, delighted at the choice. An assistant strolled over and asked if she needed help. She felt a little embarrassed but took the plunge.

"Yes I actually need a lot of help."

The assistant smiled professionally and Derby instantly felt at ease.

"Are you looking for something specific?"

The assistant asked. Derby shook her head.

"No. I need…"

She wasn't sure what to say.

"Umm…first…I need measuring, then…well….I want to get rid of all my old stuff and have everything new."

The assistant looked pleased without looking condescending.

"Come with me and we can get you sized. Then you can see what takes your fancy."

"Everything."

Derby replied as she followed the young woman making her laugh.

After being measured and suffering the embarrassment of discovering she had been wearing the totally wrong size bra for ever, the assistant reassured her that many many women were in the same boat.

"It really is so very common. I see young girls right through to very old ladies wear what they think is right. More often than not women wear a bra too big around the back and too small in the cup. That's what you have been doing. You will feel and look so much better when it's the right fit."

She then led Derby to the various rows of lingerie that had bras in her size. Derby was astounded at the choice.

"Try on as many as you want. Even though we measure, some bras are slightly different in their sizes according to style."

She then left her to browse through the selection.

After an hour, Derby left the shop very pleased with herself. She had a large bag full of bras, knickers, thongs, strings and matching sets. At first she had baulked at the thought of thongs and strings, but pushed aside the old Derby and ended up buying several. She imagined undressing in front of Geoff and watching his reaction to seeing the tiny garments. That thought brought a flush to her cheeks and dampness to her old cotton knickers she was intending to bin the moment she got home.

Her next stop was a large well known store full of fashionable clothes and accessories. He nerves almost stopped her from entering, but then she saw women of all ages flipping through the racks of clothing. Immediately, her confidence returned and she strolled in looking everywhere at once. She joined the throng of other shoppers and held various items up to get a better look.

Derby chose so many things, the shop assistant had to hang them on a rail outside the dressing room as shop policy only allowed so many items at a time. Most of the things she tried on she decided to buy. There were a few things that were obvious mistakes, but Derby thought she was quite good considering she had never shopped like this before. The counter girl practically gasped when she rang the whole lot up, especially since Derby had bought shoes and bags too.

Loaded down with her bags of new clothes Derby headed for the coffee shop she had previously been to. She was hungry and thirsty but not stressed. Now she understood the term 'retail therapy'. It really did boost her mood. The coffee shop was crowded and noisy, but this time Derby joined the queue feeling young and light hearted. She placed her order with a brightly smiling boy who looked no older than eighteen, and waited for her drink and muffin. It didn't take long. The problem was that she had so many shopping bags she had no idea how she was going to carry her order, the bags, and navigate the busy shop to an empty table. As she attempted to balance her coffee and muffin, another young man who had been clearing tables came to her aid.

"Let me carry that for you. Do you want the window table?"
He said, taking the small tray and giving her a huge grin.

"Thank you. I was wondering how I would get over there."
She replied. Leading the way to the table the assistant glanced over his shoulder.

"Looks like a productive shopping session."
He said, his eyes sparkling mischievously as they briefly settled on the bag with the lingerie shop logo. Derby blushed as she reached the table, looked at him and replied cheekily but quietly so only he could hear.

"Oh yes. Every item in my undies drawer is going in the bin and being replaced with what's in this bag."
She lifted the bag a little higher than the rest and gave it a small shake. It was the man's turn to blush, but being young and confident he took it in his stride and laughed as he pulled her chair out, indicating elaborately with his hand that she should sit.

"Enjoy your coffee and muffin madam."
He told her still smiling. Derby thanked him and with a grin he sauntered off to clear more tables.

As she sipped her coffee and nibbled her cake, Derby let her eyes wander around the café. There were quite a few other women shopping alone and carrying many bags, but not once did she see the young assistant offer his help to them. She pondered over this wondering why he had singled her out. Maybe, just maybe she was more attractive than she had ever thought. She mentally shook the notion from her mind, sure there must be some other reason for his attention but unable to fathom what it was.

She finished her muffin and leaned back in the chair holding her cup. Outside, people streamed past the window, some rushing, some strolling. Most were wearing light summer clothes, T-shirts, shorts, mini skirts, dresses and sandals or flip-flops. Some wore tailored suits in pale colours, the women with high heels and looking flushed and uncomfortable, the men just hot and stressed.

But one old lady interested Derby and she watched her until she couldn't see her anymore. She was tiny and hunched. She looked very old, very wrinkled. She wore a huge coat that came almost to her ankles and boots. She was all but dragging a shopping trolley that bulged with shopping and bumped over the paving. She walked very slowly, a purposeful expression on her face and took no notice of anyone else.

Other shoppers had to stop behind her and let others pass or step off the pavement and walk around her. She seemed oblivious to the heat and in no hurry to get anywhere. Derby could see the irritation on the faces of the passersby who were hurrying about, and found herself championing the little old lady for not letting the bustle of modern day life impact on her.

Thoughts of the old lady and what her life might be like made Derby again reflect on her own life. Mostly it brought back the idea of an affair and if she really wanted to go down that track. What she did think about seriously again was how to keep it from David. The town was large and most likely she could go to places where she wouldn't be known. She could go to Geoff's own place, at least she assumed he lived alone, she hadn't asked.

But there was always the chance someone she did know would see her, people David worked with mostly, since socially it was unlikely anyone would know what her husband looked like. For a moment she had a little daydream. She was in a posh restaurant with Geoff, an acquaintance saw them and came over to speak, someone she knew by sight, knew she was married but had never met her husband. She would introduce the sexy man with her as 'my husband' and watch the acquaintance, it would be a woman, gasp at how lucky she was to have such a man. Geoff would smile and hold out his hand to the woman, never once denying the lie.

Derby came back to reality when the young man asked her if she had finished with her plate. She smiled and nodded and he cleared the table. She still held her cup in her hand, the remains of the coffee now cold so she handed it over to him. But she didn't want to leave yet, so with a cheeky smile she said.

"I know I shouldn't ask, but could you just watch my bags whilst I get another cup?"

The young man agreed with a smile.

"I'll just take a little longer wiping your table. The queue's died down now so you should get served quickly."

"Thanks. I'll be quick."

She slid off the chair and headed for the counter. He was right and in no time she returned with a fresh cup of coffee. He gave her a little salute when she thanked him and went back to his work.

Leaning back in her chair, watching the people outside, Derby let her mind wander again to the practicalities of an affair. If only she had somewhere of her own to go to. Then she wouldn't have to worry about being seen. Her imagination was in full swing today, in her mind she saw herself gliding around a chic apartment dressed in a silk gown. She carried two glasses of wine, one which she handed to Geoff who was waiting for her on a soft leather sofa. He took the glass in one hand and pulled her onto his lap with the other. Giggling she snuggled into his neck, nipping at his throat, then he was taking her mouth with his, kissing her deeply as fire swept through her body.

Derby was brought back to reality as someone bumped into her table. A couple carrying even more bags than she had squeezed past, apologising on the way to a table in the corner. Derby acknowledged their apology with a smile and sipped her now cool coffee. Even though her imaginary apartment had disappeared, the idea of it was firmly planted in her mind. As she finished her drink, it grew and blossomed into a definite plan.

Leaving the coffee shop, Derby joined the crowd on the street. She now had a purpose in mind that did not involve shopping. Instead she headed back to her car and loaded some of her bags in the small boot space and the rest in the passenger foot well. Lowering the top she drove out of the car park and turned south. She was heading for the city twenty miles away. For a second she had a nervous blip for she couldn't remember the last time she had been in the city. Certainly she had never been there alone. Also, she had no idea where the place was she wanted to go. So at the first lay-by she pulled over.

She reached for her bag and rummaged for her phone. Laughing at herself and mumbling that she was an idiot, she opened the internet on the phone, thankful that she had a strong signal. She did a quick search for what she was looking for, found the address and entered it into the phone's built in SatNav. She had used her phone to find directions before, but had forgotten it had the SatNav feature. She pressed start and rested the phone in the centre console, checked the traffic and pulled out. The voice directions gave her a start, but only briefly, then she was cruising along towards her destination.

Entering the city was very daunting, but her trusty phone directed her well. The streets were very busy, as were the roads, some areas closed to traffic. Derby expected these to be the main shopping areas and was thankful where she wanted to go wasn't there. She followed her SatNav and found the place she was looking for had street parking. Sighing with relief at not having to find a car park too, she eased the little car into an empty space.

The office of Robertson's Estate Agents was two cars away as she stepped out of the Mazda. Straightening her dress and smoothing her hair, she took a deep breath and headed for the door, hoping she looked far more sure of herself than she felt. The door dinged on opening and a woman about her own age looked up as she walked in smiling a greeting.

"Good afternoon. Can I help you."
She asked standing up from her desk. She was the only person in the office and her smile instantly put Derby at ease.

"I hope so."
Derby replied moving towards the chair the woman indicated.

"Please sit down. My name is Caroline."

Derby sat and leaned forward slightly.

"I'm looking for a flat."

She didn't know what else to add so left it at that, sure she was going to be bombarded with questions. Caroline smiled.

"I think you might be new to this."

She said. Derby leaned back in the chair and sighed, afraid this was going to be a lot more complicated than she had thought.

"Yes I am and I haven't a clue what else I should say."

"Buy or rent?"

Caroline asked.

"Rent."

Derby replied. Caroline turned to her computer and tapped a few commands. She then moved the screen so Derby could see it. There was a list of flats, all with thumbnail pictures.

"Ok, first, where would you like to live?"

Caroline asked. Derby gave a little start, obviously the woman would think she wanted to live in it, and yes she supposed part of the time she would. However, she had no intention of telling her the real reason she wanted a place of her own.

"Umm…somewhere in the city."

She said chewing on her lip.

"Ok. What level of rent do you want to pay?"

This completely stumped Derby. She had no idea how much flats cost to rent, so she gave Caroline an apologetic look with a little shrug.

"Maybe you should tell me what sort of place you have in mind and I will find a match. Then we can look at the rents. How's that?"

Derby relaxed, smiled and nodded.

"First though, how about some coffee?"

Caroline asked.

"Please."

Derby replied.

A few minutes later the two women were settled at the desk with hot mugs of coffee. Derby leaned with both hands wrapped around the mug, the heat of the summer kept out of the office by cool air conditioning.

"Well…I sort of imagined a chic place, not big or anything, but modern and well….I suppose…upmarket."

She blushed a little, certain Caroline would think her a snob. But the estate agent clicked on something on the computer and the screen changed. She pointed at the screen and spoke.

"Here we are. We have several flats that fit your requirements. It just depends now on where and how much."

"What are the going rates?"

Derby enquired. Caroline clicked again and brought up a larger picture of one of the flats. Derby leaned forward to see better.

"Well, for example, this one is a one bedroom in a secure building right in the city centre. As you can see it's eight hundred a month. That does include service charge and security though."

The main picture showed a brick and glass building. Caroline clicked on a small row of thumbnails and these enlarged to show the interior. First the kitchen, modern, bright and white. The bathroom with separate walk in shower cubicle. The lounge with a huge glass wall looking out over the city, and finally the bedroom. It was roomy with built in wardrobes, an en-suite shower room and another large glass wall. Just looking at it made Derby blush, her mind racing, imagining Geoff and herself in the room. Caroline looked at her curiously but the only comment she made was.

"Like it?"

Derby nodded.

"Here's another one, not quite so high in price because it's not in the city centre, but I think better quality."

She paged back and went to another thumbnail. Again the flat was in a newly built brick building, but it overlooked the river and marina. Derby saw the rent was seven hundred a month. Caroline brought up the other pictures and instantly Derby could see what she had meant about being better. From the photos it looked beautiful.

The kitchen was similar to the previous one but had black glossy work services against white glossy cabinets. The lounge was spacious and looked directly out onto the boats in the marina. But it was the bedroom that caught Derby's eye. It too looked out over the boats, but it was much bigger than the previous flat, had a walk in wardrobe and en-suite bathroom with a whirlpool bath and double shower. Derby fell in love with it and Caroline could see she didn't need to show her any more at that point.

"Would you like to go and view it?"
She asked.

"Yes please. When can that be arranged?"

"This flat is unoccupied at the moment so whenever you like. At least in about half an hour when my colleague comes back from lunch. I can't leave the office empty."
Derby was so excited she felt like clapping her hands like little Chardonnay did when she was pleased.

Whilst they waited Caroline went through the finer details of renting. She explained about the searches and administrative charges involved, deposits and up front rent and the six months short let contract. Even though it was all new to Derby, it wasn't complicated. Then Caroline asked a question that she had to think about before answering.

"So I can see you're married, are you separating, is that why you want your own place, and what about your present home?"
After pondering the question, Derby decided to tell part of the truth.

"Yes, I am married. We own our own home, the mortgage will be paid off in a couple of years. No we are not separated, but things are not going so well. Taking on my own place for a little while will give us some space to sort things out."

Caroline gave her a quizzical look and Derby felt the blush begin again. She had the feeling that the estate agent didn't quite believe her. For a moment she thought maybe Caroline had some sort of psychic power and could read her mind. However all she said was.

"Ok, not a problem I was just curious. These things happen."
From her tone, Derby guessed Caroline might have or had her own marital issues but she didn't say anything. To change the subject Derby asked.

"Would it be alright to pay the whole six months in advance?"
A surprised look from Caroline replaced the curiosity.

"If that's what you want to do. It's unusual but perfectly ok."
Derby leaned back in her chair even more excited.

Forty five minutes later Derby was following Caroline's car towards the marina and her potential new flat. The traffic was easier in this part of the city until they neared the complex but not congested. Caroline stopped at a barrier and spoke to a security officer. He glanced at Derby and then raised the arm to give them both access to the car park. Derby stepped out of her car and smiled at Caroline.

"I forgot to mention. All the tenants have card key access to the car park and have two designated spaces. Access to the building is by pin number and of course buzzers in the flats to notify you when you have a visitor. Security in the lobby will let us in today."

A hulk of man in his fifties let the two women into the building. He was obviously acquainted with Caroline speaking to her by name. He seemed very friendly but Derby was sure no one would get past him easily. Caroline led Derby to a lift and whilst they waited said.

"The flat is on the top floor. I don't think I told you that. It also has a large private balcony. Didn't tell you that either. I don't think I'm doing my job very well today."
She gave a little giggle. Derby replied.

"Don't worry, you're doing fine. I probably put you off getting all excited over the first photos."

The lift arrived and both women stepped in, Caroline pressing the top floor button. It wasn't a high building, just four floors. In no time the lift stopped and Caroline led the way to the door of the flat. She turned the key and stepped back to allow Derby to enter first and peruse her surroundings.

The hallway was wide and had a thick neutral coloured carpet. Derby immediately slipped out of her flip flops and scrunched her toes into the pile. It felt wonderful. All the carpets at home were old, flat and dull. She moved slowly, not wanting to miss a thing, absorbing everything she saw and loving it all.

The lounge took her breath away. It was modern and fresh, decorated in soft creams and browns. The floor was covered in a deep shag pile cream carpet which gave the room a never ending look. The large sliding patio doors drew her to the view of the marina. She stepped onto the balcony and saw that the flat was actually positioned on the corner of the building, so only one side of the balcony was walled high giving privacy to both sides. She walked to the railing and looked out over the river. Glancing back she saw a second set of glass doors and realised they gave access to the bedroom.

Back inside, Caroline showed her the way to the bedroom and it was more impressive than the photos. She simply fell in love with it. She felt like a very young woman, no where near her forties. She felt like this was the first time she had seen the world beyond her closeted one and in reality it was. She had no idea places like this existed.

"How come the rent is so much lower than the other flat?" She asked. The first words she had spoken since entering.

"A few years ago, this part of the city alongside the river was run down, a handful of small businesses fringing the bank, a lot more closed and boarded up. A developer saw the potential of the site, built the marina and got planning for the flats. But the property crash came and the flats just didn't sell.

The marina was successful, great access to the sea, but most of the boat owners already had nice homes. So the flats were sold on to a company that specialised in rentals, they contracted out to local estate agents and slowly they began to fill. But most of the tenants were up and coming business types, so turn over was quite rapid. Now some have been sold privately and some are sitting empty. Access to the city is not great on week days so a lot of people choose to live nearer. Because of that, rents are not as high. Does any of that put you off?"

Derby turned a full slow circle around the bedroom. Her face was glowing with the pleasure of her surroundings. She stopped and looked at Caroline smiling brightly, her eyes sparkling.

"Not at all. Everything about the place and location is perfect. I want it."
Caroline stepped forward and held out her hand. Instead of shaking it, Derby held it in both her hands.

"You have no idea what this means to me."
She told Caroline.

Back at the estate agents office Caroline pulled forms from her desk and Derby sat and filled them in. She was buzzing, on a high.

"How soon can I have the flat?"

She asked, completing another page.

"Well since you want to pay the whole six months up front I can waiver the credit search. If you pay by cash or debit card we can go back today, do meter readings and hand over the keys. If you pay by cheque, when that clears."

Derby bounced in her chair like a child.

"I'm paying by card."

She all but squealed. She pulled her phone from her bag logged straight onto her mobile banking application and said.

"How much all together?"

Caroline smiled.

"Four thousand nine hundred for the rent and deposit and I will only charge fifty for admin since I didn't need to do the credit search."

Derby tapped her phone and transferred the amount from her savings to her current account, inwardly praising the technology that allowed her to do it.

"All done."

She said to no one.

Late afternoon Derby stood on the balcony of her new 'apartment'. That was the word she used in her mind as the image she had earlier was exactly what she had in real life. On her way back to the flat she had stopped by a supermarket and bought a pack of wine glasses and a bottle of Merlot, which she now sipped from one of her new glasses.

Of course, for now there wasn't any furniture in the place, but she already had that resolved. She had asked Caroline where to go and again the estate agent had given her a curious look, but this time with sympathy too.

"I know you must think I'm totally dumb not knowing this stuff, but really I'm learning fast."

She told Caroline.

"I'm sorry. I didn't mean to make you feel uncomfortable. Maybe someday you will tell me what it's all about. I'd like to think we could be friends."

Caroline replied. Derby grinned, liking that idea.

"Don't be sorry. I have been naïve about a lot of stuff for years. Not any more. And friends are what I could do with, so when the flat's all sorted you will have to come round for a drink." Now looking out over the water and admiring the boats, she reflected on the choices she had made at the furniture store Caroline had suggested.

She had chosen a deep red leather corner sofa with two matching footstools and a glass coffee table for the lounge. A king-size bed with white leather curving edges with a deep quilted mattress, two bedside tables and a tiny dining table for two. She knew there was a lot more to get, but for now was satisfied with the start she had made. Two weeks seemed a long time to have to wait for everything to be delivered, but she was patient, needed to be in her line of work. So for now she would visit the flat as often as she could, and buy the various things she needed that could easily be carried.

A noise from below alerted her. She glanced in the direction it came from and saw two men on the deck of one of the boats. They wore shorts only and seemed to be trying to get the boat started.

"Go again!"

She heard one call to the other. Derby knew nothing about boats, but this one did look very nice. She watched as the man pressed something and suddenly the engine roared to life.

"Hey. Yes yes!"

The first man yelled, obviously very excited at the result. He revved the engine, joined the other man by the outboard and gave an air punch, seemingly pleased that the boat continued running.

Derby felt some of their excitement and smiled to herself. Then a little bubble of confidence burst from her.

"Well done!"

She shouted down to the men. She followed this with a giggle as both men looked about for the source of the praise. Finally one looked up and saw her, grinned, waved and said.

"Thank you. It's only taken four long weeks to get this baby running!"

"Great success then!"

She returned holding her glass up in salute.

"Going to share that?"

The other man said cheekily. Derby laughed joyfully, she was flirting with strangers and loved it.

"Well I could, but I think it might end up in the water first!"

She teased. Both men laughed.

"Bring the bottle down instead!"

The cheeky one replied. Realising she had backed herself into a corner and not ready for such interactions she quickly made an excuse.

"Sorry none left!"

"Ah never mind. We're here a lot, so plenty of time!"

He told her, still with the very mischievous smile.

"Good to know!"

She called back. The men seemed to sense the banter was over as they both returned to tending to the boat. Derby stayed where she was, sipping her wine and taking in her surroundings.

Below her balcony was a path of blocked paving that edged the marina. It was quite wide and there were several people strolling along, some using the gateways to access their berths. On the other two sides were more blocks of flats with small shops and cafés facing the walkways, but Derby could see her building on the corner was where the entrance and exit to the river and sea was. Her view offered the way to the sea with an expanse of fields on the other side of the river.

Derby stood just looking out at her surroundings sipping her wine. She had only poured a very small glass as she knew she had to drive home later. How much later yet, she hadn't decided. Pondering this she didn't hear her phone when it first rang. Realising someone was calling her, she quickly went inside and retrieved her phone from her bag. It was Geoff, her pulse already racing just by seeing his name on the screen. A little breathless she answered.

"Hi."

Was all she could manage.

"Did I catch you at a bad time."

He asked, humour in his voice. Derby realised she was shaking her head before she replied verbally.

"No...no not at all. It's lovely to hear from you."

She felt the embarrassment in her cheeks as she silently berated herself for feeling so flustered.

"It's really nice hearing your voice."
Geoff told her, and instantly like the click of fingers her embarrassment turned to desire. She waited, sure he would say more and he did.

"You didn't call so I took a chance and rang you instead. I wondered if you would like to go out for dinner tonight?"
Her heart thumped against her chest as she tried to contain her excitement.

"Oh I'm so sorry…"
She didn't get any further.

"It's ok. I shouldn't have called, been pushy…"
This time she interrupted.

"Geoff, I meant sorry for not calling. Yes, I would like that. Do you want to meet up or…what?"
She had no idea how to arrange a date so left it up to him to tell her. She heard him breathe a sigh of relief and felt a tingle of excitement that she could make a man feel unsure of himself.

"That's probably best. I know it might be difficult for you, so perhaps meeting would make it easier. Do you know Chiquito's on the edge of town?"
She didn't but told him she would find it.

"Great, seven thirty ok for you?"
Derby paused, took a quick glance at her phone, saw it was already near to six and mentally tried to calculate how long it would take to get home.

"Umm…I'm not at home just now. Could you make it eight."
She asked, so giving herself more time. Geoff agreed and with excited anticipation she ended the call.

Quickly emptying the remainder of the wine and rinsing the glass, Derby locked up the flat and with a spring in her step, headed for her car. She was a little reluctant to leave, but the thought of dinner with Geoff far outweighed that. Before exiting the car park, Derby re-set her SatNav for home, she definitely didn't want to get lost. Surprisingly it took less time than she expected and although unconcerned, was a little relieved to find

David was not home, he probably still had to cover sick staff. As she pulled up to the kerb she said to herself out loud.

"Going to have to fend for yourself again tonight David."

For a brief moment she wondered how he would manage and if he would notice the changes that had taken place. But she brushed this off immediately, David probably wouldn't notice if she wasn't there at all.

After a quick shower, Derby pulled a matching set of lingerie from the bag shoving it and the rest of her shopping into the bottom of her wardrobe. She would sort it all tomorrow. She then donned the dress she had previously bought and slipped into the shoes. Her make-up was light and fresh, how Angela had shown her and with a new bag and the shrug she made her way downstairs. Before leaving the house she tapped a quick message to David.

Going out with girls from work. Sorry means takeaway or there's stuff in the freezer.

She didn't wait for a reply as she pulled the front door closed and headed for her car.

Chapter 10

Geoff

After a quick internet search, Derby found the postcode for Chiquito's and entered it into her SatNav. She giggled to herself. She had owned the phone for nearly six months but had only just begun to use all of its features. The voice began the directions and she pulled away from the kerb, anticipation for the evening ahead making her skin tingle.

After a short drive, Derby pulled into a business park. Another place she had no idea existed. There were several restaurants, a bowling alley and a cinema. It was modern but didn't look new. Derby sighed as she parked, angry at herself for letting the town she had known all her life grow around her without noticing. For a few minutes she just sat in her car watching the world go by.

She saw families with children of varying ages. Couples, groups, some teenagers, some adults. All looked relaxed and free. All enjoying the company they were with, the summer evening and whatever plans they had. The cinema and bowling complex had a steady stream of visitors going in and out. One group of men and women exiting the bowling, Derby guessed were in their twenties, seemed to be jovially arguing about the game. One young man had his arm slung over another's and through her open window, Derby heard part of the conversation.

"Got you this time."

"Fluke, pure fluke. Will never ever happen again."

As the group disappeared around the corner of the complex Derby felt a tiny tear prickle the corner of her eye. She blinked it back, determined not to feel sorry for herself and to not spoil her makeup. That would look fabulous, to meet Geoff with smudged black eyes.

Giving herself a mental shake and a firm set to her shoulders, she stepped out of the car. The evening was still hot so she threw the shrug back onto the passenger seat. She wouldn't be needing it. She pulled her phone from her bag and checked the tine. She was early, it was only ten to eight. That gave her pause for thought. What should she do, stand and wait, head for the restaurant or call him? A loud wolf whistle made her jump. A group of teenage boys were coming out of the cinema laughing and nudging each other.

"How about taking me for a ride?"
One called out to her.

The others laughed uncontrollably like only teen boys can, completely unabashed by the double meaning of their friend's words. Derby felt a little thrill at the comment, even while knowing the boy wasn't serious. Still she got a buzz out of giving him a reply.

"Come back when you hit your twenties."
She called back with a cheeky smile. The other boys whooped and oohed, giving their mate not so gentle slaps on the back.

"Teasing the teens now are you?"
A deep gentle voice said close by. Startled, Derby swung round and saw Geoff standing nearby, a grin on his face.

Derby stepped towards him. His voice, his body his whole aura sending signals through her, she instantly forgot the teens. She stopped just in front of him, her cheeks beginning to flush as always when she was near him. He leaned towards her and gave her an innocent peck on the cheek. His lips felt like fire and she had to force herself to stay put, when all she wanted to do was turn into him and kiss him deeply. He stood back and again Derby had the uncanny feeling that he could read her mind.

"Hello."
Was all she could manage. Geoff laughed.

"Hello back. Just as well I got here when I did, or you might have run off with them."
He lightly indicated the now retreating boys.

"No…no…they…I….joking."
Derby stammered, afraid he would think she was being tarty. Geoff laughed, softly and alluringly and took her hand, squeezing it gently.

"Derby. It's ok, I'm not being serious. Come on relax, let's go into the restaurant."
Derby did relax especially since Geoff showed no sign of letting her hand go as he led her towards the entrance to Chiquito's.

Inside the restaurant was cool and busy. The décor was stunning. Earthy coloured walls combined with rustic tables with painted tiles in the centre, paired with wood and leather chairs. The floor was tiled and the walls were decorated with painted plates and statues nestled in niches and on shelves. The atmosphere exuded passion and joy, and Derby soaked up this latest new experience.

A smiling waitress showed them to their table and gave them food and drink menus. A long list of alcoholic and non-alcoholic drinks was on offer, many Derby had never heard of. These included an array of cocktails with descriptions. Derby chose a mixed fruit cocktail as she had already drunk a half glass of wine at the flat. The waitress asked if they would be wanting wine with their meal, but Geoff declined. He then looked to Derby for affirmation.

"Oh yes, that's fine."
She hastily agreed.

"Both driving."
Geoff told the waitress, even though Derby was sure he didn't need to justify the decision.

"Good idea."
The waitress replied in a friendly manner.

Shortly after, Derby sat opposite Geoff sipping through a straw a delicious beverage in a tall glass decorated with slices of fruit. Geoff had a similar drink too. For a moment she felt a little awkward. Then Geoff spoke, immediately putting her at ease.

"Have you had Mexican food before?"
Derby shook her head.

"Not Mexican, Italian, well except pizza and pasta, but not from a restaurant, French, Spanish…oh the list goes on."
She told him. Then she sighed, deep and wistfully. Geoff reached across the table and took her free hand.

"Don't be sad little Derby. We can change all of that, starting right now. Let's look at this amazing menu."

Derby did look and everything looked wonderful. So much so she had no idea what to order. Not wanting to appear indecisive or safe, she opted for what appeared to her the most Mexican. She was ready to try anything different.

Whilst they waited for their starter Geoff asked how her day had been. For now she didn't want to tell him about her new flat. She wanted it to be ready when she took him there, for she had no doubt that she would be taking him there and soon. So keeping that part of her day to herself she replied.

"I spent the day in town shopping."

From the look in her eyes, he sensed this was not something she did frequently.

"You don't shop often?"

He asked. Derby shook her head.

"Only food shopping and occasionally clothes when needed. Most of those though I get mail order. Boring aren't I?"

She told him dismally. Geoff stroked the back of her hand.

"Not in the least. Most women I know or known, spend half their life shopping and think about nothing or no one else."

She sensed something more from his tone but didn't want to pry. She didn't have to.

"My ex-wife. When I was in the Navy and away, she spent every penny we had on stuff we didn't need. When I was on leave, all she wanted to do was go out and have fun. When I came out she hated me being around, went off with another marine, did the same to him. Finally she found a guy with plenty of money. As far as I know she's still with him. After the divorce, there was no need to keep in touch, no children you see."

Derby could feel a sadness in him and a loneliness similar to her own.

"What about girlfriends since?"

She hated herself for asking but it just popped out. He grinned and Derby had an instant suspicion that there would be a long list. But when he spoke again he surprised her.

"Just two. One lasted six weeks the other two months."

Again she waited hoping he would elaborate. When he didn't she took the plunge and prompted him.

"And?"

She said. At first she didn't think he was going to answer. He looked into his glass a little frown on his face which Derby hoped was not anger. Then he looked up, took a sip of his drink and spoke.

"Fiona was the first. I sort of knew her anyway. She was Navy too, never married, had loads of previous boyfriends, some married. Anyway, after the divorce, she looked me up, offered to 'make everything better'. I went along, it was a relief to just have someone. Of course it was never going to last. I mean Fiona is, well, she's nice and pretty, but it was all about sex for her."

Derby took a little breath and Geoff noticed.

"Sorry does that embarrass you?"

He asked. She shook her head honestly. But she couldn't tell him what she was really thinking, he would bolt for the door. Sex was exactly what she wanted and lots of it, but she wasn't sure she wanted a relationship.

The waitress arrived with their starters giving Derby the perfect chance to avoid saying anything. Geoff looked at her quizzically but didn't question her further. Besides the food looked so tempting that Derby just wanted to concentrate on it for a while. Tentatively, she raised her fork and took a small bite. It was delicious but quite spicy. Geoff, knowing what he was eating showed no trepidation.

"Good?"

He asked. Derby nodded.

"A little hot, but tasty."

She told him. He smiled and said cheekily.

"Mmmm like you."

Derby blushed pleased with the compliment.

"So are you."

She told him with a gleam in her eyes. Much to Derby's surprise she saw him blush too.

"You're blushing. Surely women tell you that all of the time."

She teased.

"Not really. I mean sometimes down the gym a few hit on me, but that's part of my job. I don't meet many women outside of my work."

Derby was discovering that this man was not at all what she had first thought. She expected him to have beautiful women falling at his feet. Imagined him walking around with one on each arm. All of them tall and slender in designer clothes and heels. But from what he was telling her, that wasn't the case.

"Tell me about the other girlfriend."
She said.

Geoff put down his fork and sipped his drink. Again he paused, this time looking around the restaurant. Derby waited sure he would tell her. She tapped her finger lightly against her own glass in time to the music, enjoying the smells and sounds around her. Geoff turned back to her.

"I realised very quickly that I didn't want to carry things on with Fiona. She was fine about it when I told her. Her actual words were, 'Geoff I'm not looking for a ring. You're a great guy, fab in bed, but for me it is all about the sex. Keep in touch, don't be a stranger, and if you find you need a little under the covers therapy, you have my number."

Derby giggled thinking how much she would like Fiona, at the same time feeling a little jealous that she could be so out-going. Geoff nodded his head.

"That's the sort of girl she is. Anyway, I stayed away from women for quite some time after that. Gave myself a mental talking to. Looked at what and where I wanted my life to go. I did some charity work for a while." He paused seeing something on Derby's face. "What?"

He asked. Derby looked down at her now empty plate.

"Derby, you're going very red in the cheeks and I don't think it's the spices."

Fiddling with her napkin she screwed up her face a little.

"I know."

She stated.

"Know what?"

He asked.

"About the charity stuff."

Geoff leaned back in his chair.

"How? That was ages ago."

Derby cringed, sure he was going to be very mad at her. So with a deep breath she said in a tiny voice.

"I…sort of….Googled you."

She couldn't look at him but she felt him. He placed his hand over hers, putting a stop to her fidgeting and she heard him too, laughing very softly.

"You little minx."

He told her. She looked up into the most beautiful sparkling blue eyes she had ever seen.

"You're not angry?"

He stroked her hand with a single finger sending tingles pulsating through her body.

"Of course not. But why didn't you say?"

His voice melted her, was like a caress from the summer breeze.

"Thought you would think I was some crazy old woman."

She all but mumbled.

"Little Derby, for one you are definitely not old."

This made her laugh with some relief.

"And two, I happen to love crazy, it's a life saver, and I think that what ever has happened to you, crazy has given you the chance to overcome it."

Derby looked intensely into his gleaming eyes. She was shocked a man could see so deeply into her soul, could sense how she was feeling. David barely spoke to her, let alone understood her. Her husband was like a shop window mannequin compared to this warm hearted man before her. David was cold and lifeless. He had no passion for anything. His job was just that, he gave it all it needed to get him where he was and wanted to stay, but that was all. He had no interests outside the supermarket except the odd television programme. He visited his mother and sister a couple of times a month but Derby had no idea what they talked about. She suspected they did little talking, imagined her husband sitting on his mother's sofa being fed copious amounts of cake. She could almost see the woman stroking the remains of his hair as though he were still a little boy. She shuddered.

"Are you ok?"

Geoff asked, concern in his voice. Derby shoved aside her imaginings.

"Sorry. Yes I'm fine."

The main course arrived hot and sizzling on a platter. Derby closed her eyes and breathed in the aroma. Emotion nearly swamped her as she thought of all of the wasted years, the things she had allowed herself to miss. A soft stroke on her cheek made her open her eyes. Geoff was looking at her with an intensity that set her skin alight and her body throbbing.

"Derby, what is it?"

He asked so gently she nearly cried. She brushed the tips of her fingers against the corners of her eyes, even though there were no tears and took a very deep breath, determined to eliminate the self-pity. Putting on a smile, she spoke.

"I won't let myself wallow."

She stated.

"Is that what you're doing?"

He asked with a laugh. Derby sat up straight in her chair.

"Not any more."

Then she lifted her glass and in a mock dramatic voice declared.

"From this night forward I will no longer be a boring, sexless old fashioned idiot. I will be passionate and modern, totally in control of my own destiny."

A table nearby, seated with a large group of young people clapped and whooped, holding up their glasses in her direction and clinking them together. Geoff laughed joyfully, deep and delicious. Derby felt her cheeks flame. She hadn't realised she had spoken loud enough to be heard, thinking the music would cover her voice. So determined not to shrink back into her old self, she tilted her own glass in the direction of the table and grinned.

Feeling a buzz of confidence, Derby tucked into her platter, and though again found the food far more spicy than she had ever had, enjoyed the taste immensely. She openly watched Geoff eating his meal. He ate almost delicately but not effeminately. Each mouthful taken almost sensuously, unlike David who chopped everything on his plate into small pieces, and then shovelled it in huge amounts into his mouth, chewing and chomping with his mouth open. Derby pushed that image completely away and concentrated on Geoff. For a moment she imagined laying on a rug in a field in the sun, Geoff holding a juicy red strawberry close to her lips, teasing her, waiting for her to take the fruit.

"What are you thinking about?"

Geoff said bringing her out of her fantasy. She jumped, dropping her fork onto the plate.

"Oops. Sorry. Was miles away for a minute."

Then to disguise the fact that she was fantasising.

"This is so tasty."

She told him with a smile.

"Mmmm...I don't think it was the food that had you elsewhere."

He told her with humour in his voice. She feigned shock.

"I'm sure I have no idea what you mean."

He laughed.

"No of course you don't little Miss Innocent."

They laughed together and Derby couldn't believe how relaxed she could be around someone she barely knew. Yet it felt like she had known him forever, it was that comfortable.

After the main course, Derby felt too full for dessert but didn't want the time in the restaurant to end. One reason, she was enjoying herself so much, the other she was nervous about what would come next. Geoff seemed to sense the change in her mood.

"Something bothering you?"

He asked lightly.

"No...no definitely not. It's just nice in here, and I am having such a good time it seems a shame to leave."

She told him not wanting to tell the whole truth.

"We don't have to leave yet. We can just have another drink or coffee and talk, get to know each other a bit more."

Derby was surprised. She had no experience of sitting in a restaurant leisurely chatting. At the supermarket annual balls each course was hurriedly placed and removed. As soon as the meal was over, the tables were cleared and people either left or had the odd dance. David always headed off to meet other managers and she was usually expected to tag along. There was never any true socialising, friendship or even friendliness. Most times she simply stood around waiting for it to end, occasionally having the odd short conversation with other wives or girlfriends about trivial subjects.

"I'd like that. Besides, you still have to tell me about girlfriend number two."

The waitress brought them coffees and cleared their table. The restaurant was even more busy but no one seemed to be in a hurry. The staff smiled brightly toing and froing between tables, the bar and the kitchen. All looking like they were enjoying their work. Some of the tables had large parties, people laughing and eating heartily. Others were families and some like their own, couples and more intimate.

One old couple caught Derby's eye. They looked to be in their eighties, sitting opposite each other and chatting animatedly to one another. They ate as they talked and looked so comfortable together. Derby sensed they had spent many years at each other's side. She longed for that feeling, had no idea if her own parents were still together, alive even. But she wouldn't dwell on any of it. The here and now was what was important, Geoff was important.

Again Geoff watched and waited for Derby to come back to him. He saw in her eyes the sadness and loneliness that washed over her as she took in her surroundings. For a moment he felt anger at the husband who had ignored and mentally abandoned her for so many years. What sort of man could, or for that matter want to ignore such a beautiful woman. His own wife had been beautiful, on the outside. Inside she was a cold materialistic bitch, yet he felt no bitterness towards her. But he did feel that way about David.

"Derby."

He spoke softly. She looked at him.

"Oh I'm so sorry. I was watching the old couple over there. They look so happy together."

Geoff smiled and reached for her hand.

"Yes they do."

He agreed. Derby saw something in his eyes which startled her. It was not just passion, it was more and she didn't know how she was going to handle that. So to ease the tension which she suddenly felt she said.

"So girlfriend number two."

Geoff laughed.

"Ok, girlfriend number two. Her name was Eve. She was a few years younger than me."

"How old are you?"

Derby interrupted.

"I'm forty two."

He told her.

"How much younger was Eve?"

"Not much really. Thirty four when I met her. That was four years ago."

At first Derby felt a little pang of jealousy towards the younger woman, even though she had never met her. That was quickly replaced with astonishment. Geoff had been divorced for six years and yet he had only been with two women in that time, the last four years ago. Guessing what she was thinking from her expression, he went on.

"I told you only two girlfriends."

"I know. I just didn't think about the time frame."

Geoff laughed.

"Well… Eve and I met at a charity function. She was one of the organisers. We had a drink and liked each other. We dated a few times before anything serious happened. It all started off good enough but she wanted it to move a lot faster. She wanted us to live together, I wasn't ready for that. Then she dropped a bombshell. She wanted to go to Africa to do aid work, and she expected me to give up everything here to go too. I knew then she wasn't right for me, so I finished it. She wasn't impressed, screamed and shouted quite a bit. Lucky escape for me I think."

"And me."

Derby said. Geoff smiled and stroked her palm.

"I like that you think so."

Derby gasped. She couldn't believe she had actually said that out loud. To her it was in her mind.

"Oh. I said that out loud didn't I."

"Don't you mean it?"

Geoff asked seriously. She blushed and wished she didn't keep doing it.

"Yes I do…"

Her phone chirped indicating an incoming text.

"Oh excuse me."

She reached into her bag wondering who would be texting her. It was David.

Got the bloody bug myself now. going to mums.

A small smile formed on her lips without her even realising it.

"Anything important?"

Geoff asked.

"It's David. He's come down with the tummy bug half his staff has. Says he's going to his mother's."

She quickly tapped a reply as she spoke.

Ok get well soon why your mums?

She pressed send and laid the phone next to her, turning her concentration back to Geoff.

"From the look on your face, you seem rather pleased that he's sick and not coming home."
Geoff stated.

"Well at least I don't have to put up with his complaining."
She giggled.

"You really are a little demon."
He teased. Derby drew her eyebrows together as tight as they would go.

"So watch out Mr Gym Coach."

Her phone chirped again. She picked it up and opened the message, pressing her lips together and frowning for real. Geoff immediately saw the change and with concern asked.

"Derby, are you alright?"
She looked up at him as she not so gently dropped the phone to the table.

"Bloody cheek."
She said quietly. Geoff waited without saying a word.

"His mother sent a reply. She says…" Roughly she picked up the phone again and re-opened the message. Then with indignation read it out. "Says…I told him to come home so he can be properly looked after…like I haven't been doing that for the last twenty four bloody years. Poor little spoilt David needs mummy to take care of his bad tummy."
She gripped her phone and Geoff covered her small hand with his large one.

"Hey. This is not going to spoil our evening."
He told her gently. She looked at him, a fierceness in her eyes that Geoff felt compelling.

"Not a chance. At least I won't have to put up with is moaning and groaning all night. I wouldn't be surprised if he's just got indigestion and is playing on it. He would do that."
Suddenly she relaxed and giggled.

"You know one time, about five years ago he came in from work saying he had chest pains, rubbing his arm and saying it hurt and please Derby get an ambulance, something's seriously wrong. First thing I thought was heart attack. So there I was phone in hand about to dial nine nine nine when behind me I hear an enormous belch, then another. I turned around and he's standing there rubbing his belly and smiling. Goes 'that's better, must've been that burger on the way home'. I didn't know whether to be relieved or throw the phone at him."

Geoff stroked her hand and laughed with her.

"Sounds like a real jerk."

He said.

"Oh that and more. So now where were we?"

Geoff leaned closer across the table taking her other hand too. He held them lightly, his thumb stroking her fingers. She felt the gentleness of his touch and wished at that moment that they were not sitting in a crowded restaurant. She wished there was no table between them, or for that matter, no clothes. All thoughts of her husband disappeared in that one moment. Geoff's deep blue eyes penetrated her and sent fiery shivers through the lower part of her body. Sensations like tiny electric shocks tingled deep within her. For a moment she imagined she was Meg Ryan in the movie When Harry Met Sally she was that close to an orgasm. Geoff seemed to sense her feelings, for he glanced around and quickly caught the attention of the waitress.

"Could we have the bill please?"

Whilst they waited, Derby had a moment of nervousness. Somehow she had communicated her arousal to Geoff without saying or doing anything. What did he expect when they left. What was she prepared to give. She didn't even know if she should offer to pay her share of the meal. That dilemma was quickly eliminated when Geoff settled it and offered his hand as she stood. They thanked the waitress and headed for the door.

The evening sun hit them as they exited, but the heat within Derby's body had nothing to do with the summer. As Geoff placed a hand on the small of her back she felt her insides were in turmoil. A storm was building within, so powerful she didn't know how to control it. She was sure it must be visible to everyone around her and especially to Geoff. Her cheeks heated with embarrassment. She was going to make a fool of herself right in the car park. People would see her displaying the most intimate moment of her life.

"Derby, are you ok?"

Geoff's warm voice asked close to her ear. She jumped slightly.

"Umm…oh….yes."

She said looking around to make sure no one was watching. No one was. People were going about, doing their own thing. She sighed with relief.

"Derby you look terrified."

Geoff said, again almost whispering. She tried a laugh and found it worked quite well. So taking a deep breath she replied.

"I got a little over heated in the restaurant. But I'm alright now."

She wasn't sure how he would interpret that. He didn't make any comment but gently pushed a small strand of hair away from her cheek. His touch was like a flame and Derby just wanted to melt into him, but she didn't move, afraid of giving out too many signals.

"Do you want to go somewhere else now or do you need to go home?"

He asked. Derby desperately wanted to go somewhere else, but she also knew she wasn't ready for what she wanted. She thought that maybe she could just have a little bit of in-between.

"I don't have to get home…and I would like to spend a bit more time with you…but…"

She didn't have a clue how to express what she wanted. Geoff helped her out.

"Derby…I don't expect you to jump into bed with me tonight. It hasn't been about that. How about we drive to the park we went to and just enjoy each other's company?"

Derby gave him a huge smile and agreed.

They pulled into the park's car parking area which was not as busy as Derby expected. She stepped out of her car and locked it. Geoff had the boot up on his car so Derby went over to see what he was doing. He was just closing the lid as she got there and saw he held a soft tartan rug in his hands. He took her hand in his and led her into the park.

The pathways were lit with street lamps but the grass areas were dark. The night sky was clear and a half moon shone brightly casting shadows all around. It was still very warm and balmy. Other couples strolled along too, and there were also still some groups of teenagers scattered about. It was a new environment for Derby, one which she embraced nervously.

She held Geoff's hand tightly, afraid she would trip as she was not used to walking in heels. Geoff glanced down at her and she saw his beautiful smile shine through the darkness. The lake came into view and Derby could just make out a few ducks still swimming near the edge. Geoff led them to a grassy area under a clump of trees overlooking the water. It was quiet. He laid the rug on the grass and sat down gently pulling her down next to him. She went willingly, settling herself on the ground and slipping her shoes from her feet.

"It's beautiful here."

She whispered, afraid to speak louder in case her voice carried to the others in the park. Geoff placed his palm on her cheek.

"Not nearly as beautiful as you little Derby."

Instantly her body reacted to his touch and she took in a breath. She leaned her head into his hand, and let him stroke her skin so softly it was like a feather brushing against her. He moved his hand and with one finger traced a path down her throat. She swallowed, terrified she would be consumed by the intensity of her feelings. He placed his other hand on the back of her neck and threaded his fingers through her hair, gently kneading her scalp. She felt herself melt, and with a sigh brought her own hands around his neck. His mouth hovered so close to hers she could feel his warm breath on her lips. They parted involuntarily, inviting him in. He took the invitation closing his mouth over hers.

With his lips nipping at hers, Geoff gently pushed her back onto the rug and splayed one large hand over the small of her back, the other hand still entwined in her hair. Derby had her hands on the back of his neck and in his hair twisting and pulling, desperate to bring his mouth even closer. Geoff gave her what she demanded, his tongue probing. Even though she had no experience of kissing this deeply, instinct took over, and she hungrily probed his mouth back with her tongue. He moved closer and pressed against her side, his body hard and rigid. Derby moved one hand down his back, pleased she could make a man so aroused, and let her fingers wander under his shirt to his hot skin. She heard him gasp as she gently raked her nails against his wide back and his kiss deepened. Her own body was throbbing and burning as she pressed against his erection, turning her own body into him. He moved his hand to her buttocks and pulled her tight against him, a groan coming from his throat as she wriggled to get closer.

She had never felt anything so wondrously pleasurable even though their clothes were still between them. She wished they were naked and that he was deep within her, but she also knew she didn't want that to happen here by the lake. Geoff didn't seem to either. His hands stayed on top of her clothes, still stroking and massaging but going no further. He eased back on the kiss and spoke softly.

"I want to go so much further right now, but I don't want to push you."

Derby sighed, wanting his lips back but answering him instead.

"I want to as well, but not here and probably not now."

Geoff stroked her hair and looked into her eyes.

"You are so tempting."

She giggled.

"Kiss me again, please."

He lowered his head and took her mouth more gently this time. She kissed him back deeply, and the barely damping fire inside her ignited again. One more time she pressed into him, his erection still very apparent. Again he groaned but this time pulled away.

"I can only take so much little Derby."

He said with a smile. She grinned up at him, desperately wanting more but knowing not now.

"Ok. Me too I think. Perhaps it's best if the evening stops here."

Geoff stood up awkwardly, pulling her up too. He winced as he bent over to pick up the rug. Derby tried not to look, but couldn't resist glancing at the bulge in his jeans. She was ecstatic that she was the cause of it, and very nearly gave in to her own desire to push him back onto the grass and take him inside her.

Hand in hand they strolled to the edge of the lake and stood gazing at the water. The ducks were all quiet now and there was no one else around. A few wispy clouds glided across the sky, barely making an impact on the brightness of the moon. To Derby it was the most romantic setting she had ever encountered and a small gasp escaped her lips.

"Derby, are you ok?"

Geoff asked with concern. She looked up at him, tears in her eyes.

"I'm fine. It's just...just...I've never seen or felt anything like I have tonight."

The tears overflowed and Geoff pulled her to him and held her tight. There was no sexual intent in his hold, just comfort. He stroked her back and neck for a while and let her cling to him and sob. Slowly her tears subsided and she wiped them away with her hand, no longer worrying about smudged makeup. With a tremor in her voice she said.

"Oh God. I'm so sorry. You must be wanting to run a mile."

"No Derby, not at all. I just hope I haven't caused this."
He replied sincerely.

"Sort of."
She told him with a little giggle. He leaned back and looked into her eyes, a small frown across his brows.

"Oh not in a horrible way."
She quickly reassured him.

"I mean the whole evening is a first experience for me. The way I felt, feel, back there on the rug, what we did, what I want to do. All of it stuff, that I as a forty year old woman should be used, to but have let myself miss out on. It's you who have showed me that."
Geoff rested both palms against her cheeks cupping her face and kissed her chastely on the lips.

"Glad to help. I want to show you and give you much more. Will you let me?"
Derby nodded, covering his hands with her own.

They slowly wandered back to their cars still hand in hand. The park was practically empty now as was the car park. Geoff waited until Derby was seated in her car with the top, down before leaning in and giving her a gentle kiss goodnight. He made her promise to phone him once she was home, so he would know she was safe. That brought a small lump to her throat, for David had never been concerned about her welfare.

Derby drove out of the car park with Geoff close behind. She had no idea where he lived, and when they reached a junction, he pulled up to the side of her car ready to turn in the opposite direction to her. He put his hand out of the window and so did she, their fingers just touching as he said bye bye. He let her turn first, and she watched in her mirror as his tail lights faded into the distance.

Derby went straight home and parked outside her house even though the driveway was clear of David's car. She didn't want to park in his spot, the kerb was now her own parking place, not owned in any part by her husband. It was such a little thing, but gave her more of a sense of independence. She locked up the Mazda and strolled up the path to her door. David had stayed at his mother's house many times in the past, but tonight it felt so different coming home to an empty house.

She placed the key in the lock, and as she turned it an emptiness washed over her. She didn't feel the loneliness that had dominated her life for so long, just a gap. She didn't feel sad that she was entering a dark empty home, but a sense of relief that she was alone.

Inside the hallway she left the lights off, made her way through the lounge closing the curtains, left her bag in the kitchen and then headed upstairs. She had no intention of going to bed, but didn't want the lights to intrude on her feelings. In her bedroom she left the curtains open, enough light coming from the moon to see what she was doing. She stepped out of her shoes and lifted her dress over her head, dropping it to the bed.

She stood in front of the mirror looking at her body. She turned side to side, running her hands down the silkiness of the lingerie set she had chosen earlier. She thought it was a great pity that Geoff hadn't got to see what it looked like, but knew he would and soon. Those thoughts brought back her arousal that had been hovering near the surface since the park. She placed both hands between her thighs and felt dampness and heat. She wasn't ready for Geoff to pleasure her, but she was ready.

Dipping into her gym bag, Derby pulled out her package of sex toys. It was the first time she had looked at them, and was a little daunted by the size of one of the vibrators and the dildo. Unwrapping both she decided she didn't want to stay in the bedroom. There was something about the room that made her shudder. Maybe it was because it was the one place that should hold within its walls years of passion and love, when in reality all it gave was an aura of coldness. So still in her underwear she took the toys downstairs and out into the garden.

Once again the night garden enthralled her. The grass was ever so slightly damp, with a light covering of dew which felt warm under her feet. She scrunched her toes into the lawn, then wandered around the garden letting her mind dwell on the sex toys she carried. She was in no hurry. She had all night if she wished, there was no one to disturb her.

She heard her phone ring inside the house, and gently dropping the toys onto the lawn went in to answer it. It was Geoff, and realised she hadn't rung him as promised.

"Derby. You didn't call."

He admonished. Glad of his concern she replied.

"Geoff I'm so sorry. I should have remembered."

"Just glad you're home safe."

He told her.

"I came in and…" she paused then plunged on. "and…went straight upstairs and undressed."

She heard a small gasp from the other end. His voice changed, became softer and even more sexy.

"So little Derby. What are you wearing now?"

She covered her mouth and giggled to herself.

"Just my underwear."

She replied. Before he could respond she went on.

"And I'm outside in the garden."

To stay truthful she went back outside and sat at the patio table.

"Derby you have no idea what image that conjures up for me."

Geoff told her.

"Then tell me."

She all but whispered.

"If I do. I'm going to bed tonight very uncomfortable."

She giggled out loud that time.

"But I really would like to know."

She told him teasingly.

"Derby I can see you, smell you and feel you here by my side. I can see every curve of your delicious body. All I want to do is touch you."

"I want you to touch me."

She let her hands wander over her own body delighting in the feel.

"Derby you are driving me crazy."

He gasped, his voice husky.

"Mmmm."

She replied, almost to herself, still stroking her own warm skin and tickling herself along the edge of her panties.

"Derby…oh…damn…Derby,… phone's….go….ing…flat. Good…night."

Even though she was very disappointed that she could no longer talk to him her body burned, reminding her that she had left her toys on the lawn. She left her phone on the patio and returned to the damp grass. Kneeling down she picked up the vibrator and pressed the button, realising quickly it had no batteries in it. Cursing to herself she swept back to the kitchen and rummaged in a drawer. She found a packet of batteries and clipped them into the holder on the vibrator. She then tried the switch again and delighted when it began to buzz. Still in the kitchen she played around with the buttons until she knew what each did, then returned to her spot in the garden.

A little noise came across the high fence from her next door neighbour's garden but she ignored it. The grass was still warm but more damp. She didn't mind. She settled herself on her back and lay the vibrator next to her. She tilted her head back and gazed at the stars, letting one finger trail down her own throat. From there she softly stroked her cleavage, and with her other hand massaged her breasts through the silky feel of her bra. Light voices drifted across from the neighbour's garden, but she didn't let them interrupt the exploration of her body. She had no idea what they were saying and didn't care. Her mind was centred exclusively on her own pleasure.

Arching away from the warm wet grass, Derby trailed her hands down her stomach stroking and tickling and teasing. She stopped at the waistband of her knickers and flicked the elastic gently against herself. Then she slipped both hands inside and slid them down over her pubis to the wetness that waited. She flicked her clitoris and eased a finger inside herself, biting her lip lightly and letting out a soft sigh. In and out she moved her finger, her pelvis rising to meet her own finger. She felt the tension building within her, but determined to delay the orgasm she took her finger out.

Without looking she reached for the vibrator and switched it on, the soft buzzing loud in the still night. She pressed it against her undies and felt the vibrations deep inside. Raising her knees she pushed her knickers down, opened her legs wider and tentatively pushed the head of the toy into her body. She took it willingly, her muscles tightening around the shaft. She increased the speed and rotation and felt its power. Rapidly she was bucking to meet the mechanical penis, her breath coming in gasps and pants as she rose towards climax. She very nearly let go of it as she came, clenching her teeth and almost squealing with delight. She held on and felt the orgasm pound through her, making her jerk as though electrified.

She slumped back to the grass, the vibrator still inside her. Breathing deeply she eased it out and let it lay across her thighs. Never had she felt anything like it. Even the orgasms she had recently given herself were nowhere as powerful as that had been. As she lay with her eyes closed, she wondered then what a man like Geoff could do for her.

"Bob can you hear a funny kind of buzzing?"
Came Fiona's voice from next door.
Derby curled up in the grass and stifled a giggle. She imagined what her elderly neighbours would make of their nice respectable 'teacher' next door, for that's what they thought she was, laying half naked in the wet grass sexing herself up.

"Sounds like it's coming from near the fence."
Bob replied. Derby crossed her arms across her stomach and laughed silently, desperately trying not to make a sound. She heard a rustling of bushes on the other side of the fence, and barely breathing managed to flick the switch of the vibrator to off.

"Nothing here. Seems to have stopped."
Bob called to his wife.

"Funny that. Never mind, come and have a cuppa."
Derby heard Bob retreating, then the garden was again silent. She rolled onto her back and let out a deep breath, her ribs a little sore from holding in the laughter. Slowly her body relaxed and she closed her eyes. Another rustle, this time from her own garden startled her. She glanced sideways and in the moonlight

saw a little hedgehog trotting across the lawn. She smiled to herself as the little creature stopped and sniffed the air. She didn't move, afraid she would spook it. For a few seconds the hedgehog snuffled at the blades of grass. It then hurried off towards the fence and the plants in the border. Derby watched the space it had headed to, and for a while heard the animal scuffling around looking for food, but it didn't appear again.

Reluctantly, Derby stood and picked up the vibrator and dildo, heading back to the kitchen, collecting her phone on the way. Inside she just stood and looked about the room. It was clean but not fresh. Her appliances were old except for the dishwasher. She had indulged herself in that piece of equipment two years ago, not really needing it, but glad she had decided to buy it. Everything else looked worn and dull. Suddenly she didn't want to be in the house at all. She trotted upstairs and pulled on one of her new sets of track suits, grabbed her keys, phone and bag and headed for the door.

The drive to the flat was a little difficult in the dark, but again she followed her SatNav, and all too soon she was pulling into the car park. There was a different security guard on, a younger man who politely acknowledged her but asked no questions. As she placed her key in the door to the flat, she paused, took a breath and then opened it. A feeling of pure pleasure enveloped her as she stepped over the threshold. She closed the door behind her, flicked on the lights and just stood absorbing her surroundings.

Everything was the same as she left it, but it was still so new and fresh. She headed for the kitchen, and lifted the glass from the sink that she had rinsed earlier. She poured wine and sipped as she studied her kitchen. Her very own kitchen. Even though she always thought of the house kitchen as hers, because David never did anything in it for himself, it was still their house.

This place was totally and absolutely hers alone. She squealed in excitement. It was like time had been turned back. Like she was a young woman venturing into the big world, leaving home and living by herself for the first time. She had a tiny daydream. She had graduated from university. She was the teacher her neighbours believed her to be, and her parents were oh so proud of her. They had helped her find the flat, excited for her, but nervous about their little girl managing on her own.

Without realising, Derby felt tears on her cheeks as she raised her glass to sip her wine. She brushed them away with force, determined not to wallow in what could never be. Topping up her glass she carried it into the bathroom and set it on the side next to the basin. She then turned on the shower and stripped off her clothes. Stepping into the cubicle she felt the force of the water on her skin and turned her face up. She had no toiletries with her, so just let the warm water wash away her tears. She turned a full circle delighting in the space and reached for the opposite shower unit and turned that on too. She gasped at the jet of cold water that came out first, but it quickly warmed up. The force of the water from both sides was exquisite, like being outside in a summer storm. It soothed and eased her tension as she simply stood and let the water flood across her body.

Reluctantly Derby switched off the water and stepped out of the shower. She had no towels to dry herself with, and was very glad the night was still so warm. Careful not to slip on the now wet floor, she picked up her glass of wine and went into the bedroom, heading for the patio doors. Sliding them open she stepped onto the balcony letting the water drip from her body. There was a light breeze coming from the river, tinged with a slight tang of salt from the sea, which gently dried her skin. Another revelation hit her. All these years and she hadn't noticed how close to the sea she lived. She resolved to take a trip there very soon, maybe with Geoff.

Still sipping her wine, Derby eased to the edge of the balcony. It was late but she didn't know the exact time, and she also didn't know how busy the marina would be on a Saturday night. She giggled to herself at the thought of weekend revellers glancing up and observing a naked wine drinking woman standing on her balcony. But as she peeked over the railing she saw the cafés were closed, and the walkways silent and empty.

The boats bobbed and gently nudged one another in the marina, a few of them with lights on. It was so peaceful and relaxing, warm and bright, that Derby began to feel sleepy. She turned back to the bedroom, and with the doors still open, settled herself on the deep soft carpet. She drained her glass and put it to one side, lay down and turned on her side. Through the open doors she could see the moon and the stars in the clear velvet sky twinkling hypnotically. Her eyes began to close and soon she drifted into a deep and peaceful sleep.

Derby woke stretching and yawning. She felt a little cold, and at first was uncertain why. Then realisation came as a breeze filtered through the open patio doors over her naked body. From her position on the floor she could see thick clouds swirling across the sky, and noticed the temperature was considerably cooler than it had been. Thinking that was what had awoken her, she sat up and rubbed her arms. Remembering she had left her clothes in the bathroom, she stood up and quickly retrieved them, feeling warmth spread through her once she was covered up. Then she heard her phone chirp and realised it was the text alert that had in fact woken her.

The message indicated it was from David. At first she thought he must have returned home and found the house empty. However when she opened the message it was from David's mother. She had written it like writing on paper.

To Derby.

David is very unwell. He will not be going to work for several days. I am keeping him here so I know he will be properly cared for. I will be around to collect some clothes and personals at ten this morning.

Irene.

Derby glanced at the time on her phone.

"Oh yikes. It's just gone nine. Better get myself back there and quick."

She told herself.

Derby arrived home with ten minutes to spare. She dived into the house and was about to run upstairs and change, when she remembered the sex toys were still on display in the kitchen. She giggled as she ducked into the kitchen to grab them, imagining her mother-in-law's expression if she saw them. In the bedroom she quickly shoved them into her wardrobe, pulled off her track suit, and donned one of her old cotton dresses. She had just straightened her clothes when the doorbell rang.

Derby opened the door to David's mother, who without even a hello, swept past and into the lounge. She stopped and swung around, as usual glaring at her son's wife. She looked haughtily at Derby, who being so used to the look ignored it and smiled.

"Irene. How are you?"

She asked politely. Irene pursed her lips.

"I am in perfect health. Unlike my poor boy. He's at home drained from being sick all through the night. I didn't want to leave him alone to come here, so Brenda is sitting with him. You don't seem too concerned."

Derby sighed. She didn't want to get into an argument with David's mother, and she knew that whatever she said would result in just that. Even after all of these, years being an attentive if not exactly loving wife, Irene still disliked her.

"I'll go and get some things for him."

She decided to say, keeping it neutral.

"Hmmmph...." Then barely audible "Could have married a nice girl."

Derby snatched items of clothing out of David's drawers and all but threw them into a bag. Mumbling angrily to herself, she grabbed his toiletries and dumped them on top of the clothes. She yanked the zip closed and stomped back downstairs, dropping the bag on the hallway floor. Irene was still standing in the lounge in the same spot, but Derby could see her scanning her frowning eyes around the room. She was always critical of Derby's housekeeping, never once taking into consideration that she worked full time, and that David didn't lift a finger.

"Everything he needs is in the bag. Let me know if I've missed something."

Derby told the older woman. Irene jumped slightly, she obviously hadn't heard Derby come back down. This gave Derby a pleasant little feeling inside, childish she knew, but still one up for her.

Irene swung around haughtily, and lifted the bag from the floor. Derby could see she was dying to open it and make sure everything was clean, ironed and neatly packed, but didn't dare. Derby smiled at her, mentally challenging her to do just that. Irene looked at her as she opened the door and frowned as she saw the smile on Derby's face. Determined not to cover it up, Derby added a note of sarcasm to her voice.

"Bye Irene. Tell David to get well soon, and give my regards to Brenda."

"You should be telling him yourself. A proper wife would. And his sister really won't care if you sent her love and kisses."

Derby gritted her teeth but didn't reply, knowing it just wasn't worth it.

After she had closed the door on the retreating Irene, Derby leaned against it for a moment. She felt sad but didn't cry. She had no tears for David, his family's attitude, or her twenty four year marriage. Her sadness was about the waste. She wondered for the first time what David thought about it. He wasn't one to talk about feelings, or anything really. Occasionally, he would tell her about new products or ideas for the supermarket, but in such a way he could be discussing these things with a colleague.

Derby pushed away from the door with a sigh. She went into the kitchen and absentmindedly emptied the washing machine. She took the load outside and began pegging it on the line. The breeze had picked up and the clouds swirled across the sky. It was warm and she wondered if a storm was brewing. There had been wall to wall sunshine for days now, so rain would be no surprise. She only hoped the washing would dry first. Still with mundane thoughts on her mind, Derby went back into the house and pulled the vacuum cleaner from the cupboard. She ran it around the house, followed by dusting, and finished off her housework by cleaning the bathroom.

The weather hadn't changed by the time she poured herself a cup of coffee and made a sandwich, so she took both outside to the patio. She was hot and sweaty from her housework, and the breeze cooled her skin. She relaxed in the chair nibbling her sandwich and sipping from her mug. With the clouds and the wind the garden looked different. She gave herself a silent telling off for all of the years not noticing her very own surroundings. She heard voices from next door.

"This little lot should dry nicely today if the rain holds off." Fiona said to her husband. Bob replied.

"Hmmm, think I'll give the lawn a going over. If it does rain it's going to grow like mad."

"Have another look in those bushes to see if you can find whatever was making that funny noise last night. I'll go and get us some lunch."

"Ok, probably won't find anything our side, maybe someone's got one of those cat things, you know to keep them off the garden."

Derby couldn't help but giggle as she heard Bob pushing plants aside on the other side of the fence, searching for the source of the buzzing. She also felt a little envious of her neighbours. They had lived there when she and David bought their house, so must have been married a long time.

Her sandwich finished, Derby had no desire to go back inside, so stayed and listened to Bob start up his lawn mower. It was such a simple sound, one which she heard a lot. Most of the neighbouring residents looked after their gardens, a few too diligently, Karen and Keith being one of those couples. They had lived on the other side of Derby for two years and kept mostly to themselves. What Derby did know was that they were younger than her, and tended both front and back gardens like they were constantly entering a competition. Not a plant was out of place, and no weed would dare poke up through the ornamental gravel surrounding the flowers and shrubs. To Derby it was far too ostentatious. She didn't know much about gardening and her own was kept just tidy, but she did like a more natural look.

She remembered the garden at home when she was a little girl. Her dad mowed the lawns regularly, and her mum would spend hours on her knees weeding and planting. There were two apple trees, a bird table and bird bath, and thinking back now, Derby believed her mum gave more attention to those than she did to her daughter. She was never allowed to get dirty in the garden. Never allowed to dig and make mud pies. She was allowed to sit on a rug with her dolls and toy tea set and play by herself. She had no siblings and her mother never sat with her. Her father barely spoke to her, and many times over the years wondered if it was because she was a girl. Believing that to be so, she now thought that her mum too was disappointed that she hadn't given her husband a son either before she was born or after. That because she was the only child they would ever have, she was simply not enough.

The sound of the lawn mower next door brought so many memories to the fore of her mind. One in particular brought tears to her eyes and spilled over onto her cheeks. Her Grandmother, who had given her the love her mother had not. She only had one Gran, the other Grandparents having died when she was very little. But Gran was there for her until she was twelve. When she was small, Gran would come around and sit with her whilst her mum went shopping. She hated taking Derby with her, claiming she couldn't behave herself and was whiny and annoying. Gran would say nothing to her daughter, Derby not wondering about it until she was grown. At the age of eight, Derby took herself to her Gran's instead, she only lived ten minutes away.

Gran would always welcome her with a hug and a smile. She would take Derby into the kitchen and show her how to bake pies and cakes. She would sit and read with her, and let her paint pictures and get dirty in the garden. Gran had bought a few clothes for her to keep there, so she never returned home with any splash of paint, dusting of flour or smudge of dirt on any part of her. They would sit eating the cake they had made, and drink tea from china cups, and Gran would talk to her and ask questions.

For four years, Derby began to develop like any other girl, and cherished every moment she spent with her Gran. It got so that she would pop in on the way home from school and stay for her dinner, doing her homework with Gran there to help. Her parents didn't show any signs of minding, and Derby seriously began to think about asking Gran if she could live with her.

Then one cold winter's day, Derby arrived at Gran's house and her mother was there. She opened the door to Derby when she knocked but didn't speak. Instead she just turned and walked into the lounge, leaving Derby to follow and wonder what was going on. For a moment she thought she was in trouble, that she had done something wrong. But she couldn't fathom what that could be. Her mother sat down on the edge of an armchair. Derby hovered in the doorway. The room was silent and for the first time a tiny thread of fear tugged at her heart.

"Where's Gran?"
She had asked. Her mother looked at her.

"She's dead."
It was said with no emotion. Derby stood rigid, unable to comprehend what her mum was telling her.

"Wh…wh…what."

Was all she could mutter. Her mum looked away, dry eyed and still as a statue.

"I said, she's dead."

"How…when?"

Derby could barely breathe.

"The postman had a package for her, knocked and got no answer. He tried knocking on the window and saw her sitting in the chair not moving. The police came, found her, called me. They said she had been dead for about two hours. That's it. Now go home, I have stuff to do here."

Derby had remained frozen in the doorway. She couldn't take in what she was being told. Her Gran could not be dead. She had seen her just yesterday, they had made an apple pie. Her mother glanced up with a frown.

"I told you to go home."

"But where….where have they taken her. What happened?" She tried again.

"None of that is your concern. Now go I won't tell you again."

Derby had turned from the house too shocked to even cry. She couldn't comprehend what was happening. Without thinking, she found the path to home and arrived not even sure how she had managed it. The key was under the back door mat as usual and mechanically she let herself in. She went up to her room and simply sat on her bed, numb and cold. She pulled her eiderdown from her bed and wrapped it around her, but even that couldn't warm her. So many questions began to invade her mind but no answers were forthcoming. Her mother's attitude and reaction was alien to her but not really surprising.

She remained on her bed without moving for a time she could not calculate. Eventually she heard a door close downstairs and ventured onto the landing. With a deep breath she went downstairs, determined to find out what had happened. However it was her dad, not her mum. He was in the kitchen putting the kettle on. She stopped in the doorway and watched him for a moment. He hadn't changed much over the years. His hair was still thick and dark, just a few grey strands poking through. He had put on a little weight but nothing significant, and his eyes, as always looked as though he was far away.

"Dad."

Derby said. He jumped a little.

"Derby, you made me jump. What are you doing standing there?"

"Have you spoken to mum?"

She asked, barely above a whisper. He shook his head as he spooned coffee into a mug.

"No why?"

"Dad…" Tears began to trickle down her cheek. "Dad…Gran's dead."

Her father stopped, the spoon in mid air. He frowned at her.

"I didn't know. When did this happen?"

He didn't move, didn't offer his open arms.

"I don't know. I went round, mum was there. She told me to come home."

Derby was crying fully now. Heart wrenching sobs tearing her apart, yet still her father stood holding a teaspoon.

Chapter 11

Silk And Satin

Moisture against her cheeks brought Derby out of her awful memories. Raindrops mingling with tears slid down her face, salty as they touched her lips. She sat up quickly and saw the sky was much darker as fat drops of rain plopped onto the patio table. Pushing up and out of the chair, she trotted over to the washing line and hurriedly dragged the clothes down. She managed to dive into the kitchen with her arms loaded just as the heavens opened. A loud rumble of thunder vibrated through the house as a quick flash of lightening lit up the room.

Derby piled the laundry onto the work service, and stood looking out of the kitchen window as the storm transformed the garden. The wind had picked up and the plants were bent almost to the ground with the force. Small puddles began to grow into larger ones on the lawn, rose petals floating on top like lilies on a miniature pond.

Derby stood for some time just watching the storm, memories of the day she had lost her Gran as tumultuous as the weather outside. After that day everything changed for her. Her phone trilled, bringing her out of her reverie and she scanned the kitchen, not sure for a moment where she had put it. Finally she located it under the pile of laundry and saw it was Geoff.

"Hi."

Her voice was barely above a whisper. She swallowed and tried again.

"Hi."

"Derby. Are you ok? you sound…strange."

Geoff asked. Derby put a false lightness into her voice.

"I'm fine. I…umm…was just bringing the laundry in, then couldn't find my phone because I dumped the whole pile on top of it, so, a little out of breath."

She finished with a little giggle and hoped her voice sounded natural. There was a silence on the other end, and at first Derby thought that maybe she hadn't got away with it. Then he spoke.

"Ok. I thought for a moment something had happened, you know, maybe with your husband."

Derby felt the tension slipping from her. When she answered it was with a true naturalness to her voice.

"Oh no. David's mother came round and collected some things for him. He's going to stay there until he's better, so yes a bit uncomfortable, but that's usual when we see each other. I'm not bothered, used to her attitude."

She laughed.

"Going to let me in on the joke?"

Geoff asked warmly. Derby giggled.

"It's a bit childish really. But well, I sort of like to wind her up a bit, be a bit sarcastic. She doesn't really get it and tries to give me this I'm so much better than you look. I have to bite my tongue so as not to laugh in her face."

She heard Geoff laugh.

"Told you you're a little demon. So, what are you doing today? I wondered if you wanted to meet up."

Derby looked around the kitchen, out at the storm and came to a very quick decision.

"I've done all I need to so where?"

She really hoped she didn't sound too eager.

"How about our park then go from there."

Excited, she agreed and they arranged to meet an hour later.

After a quick shower, Derby pulled on a lemon silky bra and thong. She snipped the tags from one of her new dresses, and slipped it over her head, delighting in the feel of the soft material against her skin. She applied a light layer of makeup and left her hair to dry naturally. By the time she was ready to leave, the storm had blown over and sunshine peeked through the dissipating clouds. The temperature was lower than previous days but still warm enough not to need a jacket or cardigan.

Derby pulled into the park and saw Geoff already waiting. He strolled over to her car looking handsome in jeans and T-shirt. and bent to the edge of her open window. She had left the top up in case it rained again, so he leaned in and kissed her on her lips.

"Hello little Derby."

She smiled at him, full of joy at his greeting.

"Hello back."

She told him. Resting casually against her open window Geoff smiled warmly.

"You look stunning."

He told her. She felt her cheeks fill with heat, unused to compliments. His smile widened.

"You also look so very lovely when you blush."

This made her cheeks redden even more.

"I'm sorry. So I thought maybe you might like to come to my place."

Derby looked up quickly, nervous but very excited at the prospect of seeing his home.

"That would be very nice."

"Ok. Do you want to leave your car here and let me drive, or follow me?"

He asked.

"I'll follow you."

She told him. He leaned in again and kissed her then turned back to his own car.

Derby had a lot to think about whilst she drove keeping Geoff's car in sight. She was nervous but excited, her mind wandering in many directions. Would this be the right time to finally experience real lovemaking. She asked herself. Would Geoff expect it or leave it to her make the move. She knew she could do that. Knew it wouldn't take much, his innocent kiss of hello had set her pulse racing. But she didn't want him to think she was easy. He might have sex with her and then tell her that was it, done and dusted. He was after all a very handsome man. Any woman would want him in her bed. He had told her about the two girlfriends, but that didn't mean there wasn't a long list of sex partners. Some women could do that, some even initiated it themselves, could quite happily flit from man to man just for sex. Could she?

By the time she saw Geoff turn into the gated driveway of a very large detached house, Derby was virtually shaking from nerves. She slowed to the kerb and waited. Geoff stepped out of his car and indicated that she put her car next to his. As soon as she had turned off the engine, Geoff opened her door and offered his hand. She took it and he gently pulled her from the car.

"Welcome to my home."

He told her smiling.

Derby looked up at the house. It was very impressive. Old with wisteria growing up the walls and beautiful ornate sash bay windows. The gates they had driven through were tall wrought iron, and trees and shrubs grew against a high stone wall surrounding the property. She couldn't see the houses on either side. Geoff waited patiently still holding her hand.

"Do you like it?"

He asked. Derby looked up into eyes that showed pride but no sign of smugness.

"It's beautiful."

She told him.

Geoff led her to the front door tucked into a porch. He unlocked it and stood back to let her enter first. She hesitated for a moment, suddenly very aware that she was with a man who was virtually a stranger, in a place that was all but isolated from the rest of the world. Geoff sensed her hesitation and placed a gentle hand on her arm

"We don't have to stay."

He said very softly. Derby turned to him her eyes giving away her concern.

"It's just…."

She didn't know how to finish.

"Derby, it's fine. I don't want you to feel afraid, or worried that I'm some weirdo or monster that has lured you to my den." She giggled beginning to feel more relaxed. "I just want to show you my home, cook you something nice and enjoy your company." She breathed deeply realising that had he wanted to hurt her, the night before in a virtually empty park would have been the perfect opportunity, given the height of arousal they had both felt.

She stepped over the threshold and pulled on his hand. He followed and closed the door behind them. The hall was wide and Derby had no idea which way to go, so she let Geoff go ahead of her. He led her towards the back of the house showing her a large sitting room, library and dining room on the way. The kitchen was big and airy with an old fashioned wooden table and cupboards. There was a back door that he unlocked, which opened onto a large tiled patio. A glass topped rectangular garden table with padded chairs and parasol sat in the middle of the patio looking modern and new, unlike her own little old plastic set.

Green lawns surrounded by old trees and shrubs spread before her, with stepping stone paths leading into a small wooded area. Derby had never seen a home like it. Actually she had seen so very few homes other than her own, that she felt quite overwhelmed.

"Geoff this house, garden…it's amazing."

She told him as she stepped out and turned a full circle taking it all in. He followed, stood behind her and put his arms around her, giving her a little hug.

"I've done a lot of work on it. I bought it a year ago. It needed quite a bit of renovation and a great deal of tender loving care. There's still some to do, but I'm not in a hurry."

Derby wrapped her own arms around his and leaned back against him. She could smell the trees and the scent of roses, and breathed them deeply. She felt his breath in her hair and closed her eyes enjoying every moment. They stood unmoving for some time. Then Geoff murmured in her ear.

"Would you like to see the rest of the house?"

She nodded and let him turn her back to the door.

Back inside, Geoff showed her in more detail the downstairs rooms and then led her up the wide curving staircase to the upper floor. There were four bedrooms, all large with wide windows which let in a lot of light. Two faced the front, one completely refurbished in soft pastels, the other obviously still needing some work. There was a vast bathroom with a huge deep claw footed tub in the middle, and separate shower cubicle, all with Victorian fittings. The first of the back bedrooms was smaller than the front two, and looked to be where Geoff stored all of his decorating materials. It too needed work and looked as though it hadn't had anything done to it. Finally, with a sigh of anticipation, Geoff led her to what she guessed must be his own room.

The door was ajar when they reached it, and Geoff stood aside indicating that she open it herself and enter first. She glanced at him shyly as she did and stepped into the room. Her first impression was that it was big and perfectly masculine. One wall was a deep rustic red, the others a neutral hessian colour. The woodwork was cream and the ceiling was just beautiful, white with original Victorian coving and ceiling rose. There were two windows, and in the middle a high antique bed in dark wood.

Geoff stood in the doorway letting Derby explore the room on her own. She saw another door and opened it to reveal an en-suite shower room, again with Victorian fittings. She opened his wardrobe and looked at him watching her in the full length mirror. She turned as he came closer and smiled at him.

"This is perfect. Did you do all of the work yourself?"
He stopped close to her but didn't touch her.

"Mmm…most of it. I had a couple of mates help with the bathrooms and kitchen, you know the plumbing, and the electrics and gas, all of that has to be professionally certificated, otherwise yes, by myself. It's relaxing and I enjoy it."

"I should find something else to do with my time."
Derby said wistfully. Geoff gently touched her arm and stroked her skin with the back of a finger. It was comforting rather than sexual, and for a brief moment Derby wanted to cry. This man before her had shown her more care in the short time she had known him than anyone had in her entire life.

"Help me with the house."
He said lightly. Derby looked at him thinking how wonderful that would be.

"Mmmm…never done any DIY, so would probably make a right hash of it."
She giggled. Geoff took her wrist and gently tugged her towards him.

"Doubt that." He planted a light kiss on her lips. "Now how about some food. I thought I would barbeque."

The sky had cleared to leave a warm afternoon, cooler and fresher from the storm. Derby was nestled on a comfortable wicker sun lounger as Geoff stood turning steaks on the barbeque. She watched him deftly flip the meat, impressed. She had already observed him tossing a salad and cook minted baby potatoes. He was obviously a dab hand in the kitchen. She was fully responsible for all of the cooking at home, and it felt very good to have someone else treat her for a change. Leaving the barbeque for a moment, Geoff came over to her and leaning down brushed a soft kiss against her lips.

"Would you like another drink?"

He offered. Derby nodded.

"More wine, or a soft drink?"

She came to an instant decision. She would not be driving home tonight. She held her glass out to him and he smiled as he lifted the bottle of wine from the patio table. She thought he sensed her decision, but made no comment as he poured wine into her glass. She leaned her head back, his body shielding her eyes from the sun and sighed.

"This is the most relaxed I have felt in...oh for ever."

She told him. Geoff grinned.

"Good to know. But please don't go falling asleep on me, the steaks will spoil."

She giggled, still surprised at herself that she could sound so giddy and feel so young.

"Oh I won't. Having someone cook for me is such a treat I wouldn't miss it for the world."

She stretched, her breasts lifting and pushing against the buttoned bodice of her dress, and watched Geoff's eyes darken with desire. A hissing sound came from the barbeque and he quickly turned away.

"Ooops...can't let them burn."

He said with laughter in his voice. Derby watched him tend to the meat and sipped her wine, excited by what she was sure would happen later.

Geoff had laid the table with a bowl of floating candles, the salad and potatoes in dishes which matched the plates. It was all far more presentable than any of the tables at the annual balls, and of course so was the company. The beef was perfect, tender and full of flavour. As they ate they chatted about inconsequential things, the work he had done on the house and what yet had to be done. Derby listened and even offered some suggestions, which he accepted with nods and smiles.

"So when I phoned you sounded....well I'm not sure how you sounded...just not right."

Geoff asked as he laid his knife and fork on his empty plate. Derby laid her own cutlery down and lifted her wine glass taking a sip. She felt no embarrassment as she spoke.

"I was in the garden having some lunch. I could hear my neighbours talking about their garden and I thought about my childhood. More than that, my Gran."

She stopped for a moment, again going back to the day she had re-lived a few hours before. Geoff placed his hand over hers and gently squeezed.

"Go on."

He said tenderly.

"My parents didn't take much notice of me. But Gran did. Where mum never played with me Gran did. She gave me love where my mother and father didn't. Then when I was twelve she died."

Derby stopped and took a large mouthful of wine.

"There's more to it isn't there?"

Geoff prompted.

Derby nodded and tiny tears pricked at her eyes. She then went on to tell him about that awful day so long ago, but still so painfully fresh. By the time she had finished, Geoff was kneeling next to her chair and she was sobbing in his arms. He held her and rubbed her back, and let her tears soak his T-shirt.

Eventually her tears eased as Geoff brushed her hair away from her face. He dabbed at her cheeks with a napkin, and cupped her face in his big hands. She sat up straighter covering his hands with her own.

"I'm sorry."

She mumbled. He smiled.

"Don't be. It's fine. I think that's been coming for some time."

Derby realised he was right. She couldn't remember letting out her emotions for that event, since the day she had cried and her father had done nothing.

"God I must look a right mess."

She said, her nose blocked from crying and her face feeling hot.

"No you don't Derby. You look like a woman who has let something out that's been bottled up for a long time."

She started to protest.

"But…if you want to go and splash some water on your face…well…I'll get dessert."

She couldn't help but giggle. Geoff seemed to be able to soothe her by doing very little. He stood up and taking her hands pulled her to her feet.

Derby stood in the big bathroom running cold water over her hands and face. She looked in the mirror and saw red blotches on her cheeks and around her eyes. After drying her skin, she smoothed a light foundation on her face and gloss on her lips. Her eyes felt a little puffy, but otherwise she thought she didn't look too bad. She went back downstairs and out into the garden. Geoff was spooning ice-cream and fresh strawberries into bowls, looking up and smiling when she approached.

"Better?"

He asked. Derby nodded and sat back at the table.

"Hope you like strawberries."

He said handing her a spoon.

"Oh I love them. Gran used to grow them and she would let me eat them straight from the plant."

Geoff sat down and began to eat his own dessert. Derby took a mouthful and sighed. It was delicious and flooded her with memories. But this time she felt no tears.

"We used to do so much together. Mum and dad didn't care that when school finished I would go straight round to Gran's. She was more of a mother than mum was. So that day, when she died a part of me did too. Only I was still so young and I didn't understand what was going on. I mean I knew she was dead, but no one would explain how or why. When I asked I got told 'You don't need to know. You're too young.'

I wasn't too young and kept on trying to get answers. In the end mum yelled at me and dad ignored me. I wasn't allowed to go to the funeral either, had to go to school that day. My teacher didn't even know, mum didn't bother to tell her. It was like she…well Gran had told me mum doted on her father…didn't like cuddles or attention from her…and when she got to her teens barely spoke to her."

Derby stopped talking and concentrated on her melting ice-cream for a while. Geoff spooning his own dessert, waited silently for her to continue.

"Then, after mum and dad got married, mum would visit but only if her dad was home. Granddad died about a year after I was born. Gran said that mum would take me to see him before that, but after only bothered with Gran when she wanted her to come and look after me. Gran said she didn't mind because at least she got to spend time with me, that I loved being hugged and played with and read to."

Derby finished her dessert and leaned back in her chair. Geoff had already emptied his bowl and sat swirling his wine in his glass, taking in everything she told him. Holding her wine glass in both hands Derby sat silently for a while, just remembering the good times she had spent with Gran. The garden was so quiet except for a few birds singing and the soft rustle of leaves swaying in the early evening breeze. She jumped very slightly when Geoff spoke.

"It explains why you got married so young."
He said. Derby leaned forward and drained her glass.

"You know, I've never thought about that."
She reached for the wine and refilled her glass, rubbing her thumb up and down the stem.

"David was in the year above me. He was mates with my then best friend's brother. I used to see him at her house after school. I spent a lot of time there after Gran died, didn't like being at home. Anyway at first he used to ignore me. Then I got boobs."
Derby giggled at some long ago memory. She looked at Geoff, a gleam in her eyes.

"Me and Annie, that was my friend, we would stuff tissue down our tops and pretend they were real. Then mine grew for real, Annie's took a bit longer to catch up. One day we sat in her garden, it was summer and David and Brad, Annie's brother, crept up on us with a hose pipe. They soaked us and poor Annie had soggy wet tissue sliding out from under her top, but me, well the water was cold and you can guess what that meant."
Derby waggled her eyebrows at Geoff as he nodded.

"Yep. Little hard nipples poking through my top. I mean my boobs had grown but weren't that big, still a bit out of shape too. Anyway, David spotted them and he went bright red. He was good looking and quite a few girls fancied him but was a bit shy. Anyway being a bit more forward than him, I sort of stuck them out and he couldn't take his eyes off them. I made a show of it too."

Derby sipped her wine and looked at Geoff through lowered lashed.

"Little minx."

Geoff said with humour in his voice. Derby laughed, not in the least embarrassed at telling him stories she had never shared with anyone else.

"Annie had run inside trying to disguise the wet tissue, and Brad was still messing with the hose. Anyway I lifted my wet hair and shook the water out, you know like you see in the movies. Then I really laid it on. I tugged at my top pulling it away from my body and squeezing some of the water out. As I let it spring back it clung to me and of course turned almost see through.

I could see David was watching and I wanted him to. I was thirteen and hormonal, craving some sort of attention. Well of course nothing happened that day. But David did start speaking to me, in school too. He started walking home with me and then he asked me to go to the cinema. I didn't bother asking permission I just went. My mum found out from a neighbour. She didn't have a go at me or anything, just said, and I remember her exact words. 'Don't forget what I've told. Keep your clothes on, girls don't let boys come near them. Not until they're properly married."

Derby tilted her glass from side to side, the red wine forming tiny waves with the movement. She heard rather than saw Geoff stand up and come towards her. Just as his hand touched her shoulder they heard the telephone ring inside the house.

"Damn."

He exclaimed.

He jogged into the kitchen, Derby watching him as he went. She then stood up, and taking her glass with her wandered across the lawn and followed the path into the trees. It was much cooler and darker under the canopy of lush green leaves. Birds flitted from branch to branch, and Derby noticed several nesting boxes hooked on the trunks of the trees. It was so different from her own garden and those of her neighbours. Her home was one of many of the same on a flat estate, purpose built with no real character. This house and garden was unique and she loved it.

Strolling along the path she came across a circular clearing. It was small but sunlight shone down through the gap above. There was a patch of perfect grass edged with decorative stone slabs and a curved stone bench. She sat on the bench and found the stone was warm from the sun. She slipped her sandals from her feet and felt warmth on her toes too. It was blissfully peaceful. She leaned back and closed her eyes. She couldn't believe she was in such a wonderful place, feeling so completely at ease.

"Found my little sanctuary."

A deep voice all but whispered close to her. She opened her eyes and sat up quickly almost spilling her drink. She placed her empty hand over her heart and gasped.

"Oh you made me jump. I didn't hear you."

Geoff laughed and sat next to her.

"I'm sorry. I thought you would hear me coming."

He brushed a stray strand of hair form her face settling himself more fully onto the bench.

"No I was miles away. This is so perfect and peaceful."

She leaned back again turning her face up to the sun.

"Sorry about the interruption. It was the gym, nothing important though."

Derby looked at him. She had virtually forgotten the phone call.

"It's fine. Actually I didn't even think about it. I wandered here and everything else went from my mind."

"Even me?"

He whispered as he leaned in closer. Derby looked into eyes so blue and gleaming she felt herself melt. She raised a hand and placed her palm against his cheek. And whispered back.

"No, not you. I could never forget you."

Geoff took the glass from her fingers and stood it on the ground. He then took both her hands and placed them around his neck. He put his arms around her and drew her close to him.

"I've wanted to do this all day."

His lips hovered for a moment close to hers then he took her mouth and kissed her passionately. She felt the fire deep within her body and kissed him back, straining to get more from him. His tongue swept the inside of her mouth and tickled her own. She gripped the hair at the base of his neck with one hand, and let the fingers of her other hand find their way under his T-shirt where she gently scraped her nails against his skin.

His kiss deepened and every fibre of her being tingled, charged with desire. More than anything she wanted his hands between her thighs, wanted him between her thighs. As though communicating this wish through her touch, she heard him groan as she plunged her own tongue into his mouth. Inexperienced as she was, she knew she had him as aroused as she was herself.

Geoff pulled her closer still, one hand tangled in her hair. With his other hand he cupped a breast, and even through her clothes she could feel sensations she had never felt before. His thumb teased her nipple, and more than anything she wanted to feel his large hand stroking her naked skin. Kissing him deeply she strained against the cloth of her bra and dress. His hand moved away from her breast, and for a moment she wanted to grab it and push it back. But then he slid it down her side, stroked the dip of her waist, and squeezed the curve of her hip. Gently he lifted the edge of her dress and Derby almost stopped breathing. She heard herself moan, a tiny sound in her throat. Geoff responded, moving his lips from hers, raining light kisses against her throat and nipping at her neck.

Derby tugged his hair and pulled his lips back to her mouth. He came willingly as his hand traced a path up the inside of her thigh. She lifted her pelvis to meet his hand, as he touched the now very wet tiny piece of silk of her thong. She heard him groan against her lips. He pulled back just enough to murmur.

"God you're so wet."

"Don't stop, please."

She whispered back.

Taking her mouth again Geoff tweaked the side of the thong and let his fingers explore the soft wetness. She twisted towards him to get closer as he stroked her labia, and pressed a thumb against her clitoris. She gasped against his lips, a deep but sensuous tension building inside. He placed two fingers inside her, pushing up and then sliding down. Her muscles clenched and relaxed, clenched again as he began to move more quickly.

Derby leaned her head back, forgetting his lips, forcing her pelvis hard against his fingers. Geoff nipped and kissed her throat and neck, all the while moving his fingers deep and quickly in and out as she raised her hips to meet him. As the feelings intensified towards climax, Derby grabbed his arms and clung to him, every part of her body taut and tense.

Then she came, a squeal of pleasure erupting from her throat. Her body froze, suspended in time for the briefest of moments. Her heart beat fast and deep, within, every nerve ending twitched and tingled. Coming out of the orgasm was just as pleasurable. Geoff's fingers still inside her slowed to a gentle stroke, as her body began to relax against him bit by tiny bit. His kisses softened and when she opened her eyes and looked at him he was smiling. She smiled back, feeling pure delight and no embarrassment.

"Did you enjoy that?"

He asked softly. She nestled into his shoulder.

"Mmmm…it was….wonderful."

Then she looked up at him.

"I'm sorry I didn't do anything for you." Then a little shyly. "I…I…still could."

Geoff planted a light kiss on her lips.

"Little Derby. I can't say I'm not aroused, but I can wait. That was your moment."

She sighed.

"You know…nothing like that has ever happened to me before."

She told him honestly, for even the recent orgasms she had given herself were nowhere near as intense as that had been. She blushed a little.

"Don't be embarrassed Derby."

He said. She giggled.

"I'm not. I was just wondering what it would be like if….we….when we…"

"When I make love to you."

Geoff finished for her. She nodded feeling her cheeks heat even more.

Geoff quietly rearranged her clothes and brought his arms up and around her. She leaned into him feeling so comfortable and for the first time in her life secure. She had no idea what the time was and didn't care. The sun filtered into the clearing still providing warmth, and for a while they simply sat, quiet and motionless listening to the birds in the trees. After a few minutes Geoff let his hand wander to her hair and he ever so softly twisted the ends between his fingers.

"So what happened after the cinema?"

It took a moment for Derby to understand what he was saying. Then it came back to her, their conversation before the telephone interruption.

"Oh yes, I was telling you about David wasn't I."

Geoff laughed.

"Glad to know I can make you forget some things."

"Cheeky. But well yes you can."

She looked at him through lowered lashes.

"Keep giving me that look and I will make you forget again."

He told her, his voice sexy.

"Mmmm…promise?"

Geoff tickled her ribs making her wriggle.

"Little Demon Derby."

They laughed together. Then Geoff said in a more serious tone.

"Really, I would like to know."

Derby sighed but snuggled into his arms.

"Well there was a school disco and me and Annie were going. It was the end of term, summer holidays. I got ready at Annie's house. Even though my parents mostly ignored me, mum still bought all my clothes, and none of them were very…well…sexy. So Annie let me borrow some of hers. Even though my boobs were bigger, we still wore the same size. So David went with Brad and we sort of met up when we got there. This was about two weeks after the cinema and we hadn't been out again. I was a bit…put out…by that, so played it cool. David came over and started chatting. I did think he was good looking, so acting like I didn't care didn't last long."

Derby paused and shifted against Geoff getting more comfortable. He moved his arm along the back of the bench to accommodate her, and she drew her feet up under her as though she were sitting on a sofa. She laid her hand flat on his chest as she continued with her story.

"The disco was pretty good. Annie and I danced a lot, the boys didn't. Brad tended to watch over his sister quite closely, but she was having none of it. There was a boy called Ian she fancied and so we kept dancing near him. Brad and David sort of kept inching closer too. Anyway a slow record came on and Ian asked

Annie to dance. She glared at her brother, daring him to object, he didn't. David saw me step to the side of the dance floor and came over. He asked me to dance and that's when we had our first kiss. It wasn't anything special, no tongues or anything. I didn't think anything of it, we were both young and inexperienced."

Derby let her hand smooth his T-shirt in a small circular motion. Geoff stroked her hair in return.

"After the disco David asked me to go out with him. I fancied him so I said I would. We spent quite a bit of the summer holidays together, went swimming, the park and so on. Annie had started going out with Ian, and Brad a girl we knew and liked. So the six of us used to just hang out, quite often at Annie's and Brad's. We never went to mine or David's. He said his mum was strict, that even his sister who was three years older wasn't allowed to bring boys home."

Derby stopped talking, leaned her head against Geoff's shoulder and closed her eyes for a while. Geoff waited, gently massaging her scalp, sensing she was reflecting on her teen years and knowing more was to come. She shifted position slightly settling more comfortably in his arms. Then with a little sigh she continued as though there hadn't been a pause.

"Of course going to my house was completely out of the question. It's like, as long as I was out of the way, and they didn't know what I was doing then I wasn't doing anything I shouldn't. Do you get that?"

She looked up at Geoff and he nodded.

"Not like I was doing anything I shouldn't, not then. I mean, we were just kids hanging around. I was the youngest out of all of us, just being part of something, a group, friends, was enough. I mean, David and me used to snog a bit, but it was never proper kissing. It was more like pecking really. Neither of us knew what we were doing."

Geoff gave her a little poke in the side making her giggle.

"Well you certainly know what you're doing now."

He told her, amusement in his voice.

"Mmmm…"

She looked at him seriously.

"Only because of you."

Geoff placed a finger under her chin tilting it upwards. He laid a very soft kiss on her lips and smiled as he drew back to study her face.

"So much wasted beauty."

He told her. Derby blushed with joy, suddenly feeling a little shy. Geoff stroked her cheek.

"I mean it Derby."

She nodded.

"I know. It's…well…no one has ever said…it was lovely to hear."

Geoff looked up at the gap between the trees. Clouds were beginning to build up again and the clearing was a lot cooler. The stone bench had lost some of its warmth too. Taking her hand in his, he stood up and gently pulled her up with him. Though a little puzzled, she didn't protest. He bent and picked up her sandals and without speaking began to lead her out of the clearing back towards the house. Just as they reached the patio a few drops of rain splashed onto the tiles, so they stopped at the table and sheltered under the parasol.

"How did you know it was going to rain?"

She asked.

"Oh just one of the things I picked up when I was in the Navy."

He glanced up at the sky.

"Wouldn't be surprised if we get another storm."

For a few seconds Derby fantasised. The storm was overhead and they were laying naked on Geoff's lush lawn. As thunder and lightening crashed and flashed around them, Geoff made passionate love to her.

"Derby?"

She came back to reality and her face flamed.

"Share them?"

He asked. She giggled, wondering if she dared. Then decided to tell him part of the truth.

"Just wondering what it would be like to stand naked in a storm."

She heard him gasp and looked at him quickly thinking she had said something wrong. But what she saw set her heart racing. His eyes were full of fire and she wanted him, right then and right there.

They moved together in silent communication. Geoff pulled her down to the lawn and wrapped his arms around her. The grass was soft and wet the rain coming more heavily. Hungrily, he took her mouth as the first flash of lightening lit up the darkening sky. She lifted her head and met his kiss full on, pushing her delicate tongue into his mouth. He groaned as the kiss deepened, rolling her to her back and laying on top of her. She could feel his hardness pressing against her pubis and wriggled against him. His hands moved up and down her body over her dress. She desperately wanted to feel his hands and lips on her skin. Pulling away from the kiss she murmured.

"Take it off, please, all of it."

Geoff lifted his weight from hers and looked into her eyes.

"Are you sure?"

He asked huskily. She nodded. Kneeling back on his heels he pulled her into a sitting position.

Her eyes dropped to his jeans and saw the bulge straining to be released. Her body burned with desire and anticipation, impatience too. Geoff deftly unbuttoned the bodice of her dress and trailed a finger down her throat into her cleavage. She took a breath, pushing her breasts towards him. Quickly he undid the rest of the buttons and pushed the dress from her shoulders where it floated to the ground. Still sitting on his heels he looked at her.

"My God, you are stunning."

He whispered. Derby leaned forward taking his T-shirt in both hands and tugged it over his head. He lifted his arms to accommodate, and she threw it to the ground. She traced a line down his chest towards his waistband with one nail and heard him gasp.

She seemed to know what to do even though she had never done this to any man before. She stopped when she got to the top of his jeans, hovering for a moment. Then she slid the tip of her finger inside the waistband and slowly trailed it from side to side. Geoff groaned but didn't move. Derby then unbuttoned his fly, relishing the thought of releasing his hard penis. She pushed the denim down his thighs, and Geoff lifted up to make it easier for her. For a moment, his huge protrusion straining against his pants hovered close to her mouth making it water. She knew nothing about oral sex, but had an almost overwhelming desire to wrap her tongue around him.

Geoff flipped to his feet and Derby felt bereft. However, he quickly let his jeans fall around his feet stepping out of them. The rain came in sheets soaking them both and making his skin gleam. He then kneeled back in front of her twisting his hands in her wet hair. This time she reached her hand out and stroked his shaft through his trunks, which had become translucent with the rain. She heard him take a breath in and felt his fingers tighten. Feeling empowered, she slipped his pants down and released him. He was big, and as she stroked the length of his erection she heard him inhale sharply, heard him moan deep within his throat.

She took him in both hands, sliding them up and down squeezing gently. Nervously she leaned forward and flicked the end of his penis with her tongue. She had no idea if what she was doing was right, but the sound that emerged from above her indicated she was. Still very unsure of her actions, Derby placed her mouth over him and tentatively sucked. He bucked and she knew she was giving him pleasure. Slowly and gently she dragged her teeth along his shaft, cupping his balls and stroking them sensuously.

"Stop! Oh God Derby stop!"

She moved back afraid she had hurt him. But he took her shoulders and pushed her back onto the soaking grass. His hands unclasped her bra and her breasts tumbled into them, her nipples hard as tiny pebbles. He lowered his mouth and nipped at one whilst massaging the other. Then he let his tongue slide across her nipple giving it little flicks. He moved onto the other one sucking and pulling with his teeth. Derby arched, desperate to get more from his mouth. Her insides had turned to liquid and she felt on the brink of orgasm, even though he had barely touched her. She threaded her fingers in his hair pulling him closer murmuring "more" which he gave.

Geoff took one hand from her breasts and ran it down the side of her body. She strained against him as he found the juncture between her thighs. Again she moaned and murmured.

"You are so wet."

He whispered between kisses to her throat and neck. He tweaked at her thong, sliding it down her legs. She lifted her legs so he could remove the tiny garment, then she was naked in his arms. He stroked her soft hairs and thumbed her clitoris and she cried out with pleasure.

"Please."

She said.

"What do you want little Derby?"

He asked.

"You inside me."

Geoff covered her mouth with his own and kissed her deeply. He shifted his body over her and she opened her legs wider. He settled between her thighs and eased inside her. She gasped. He was even bigger than the vibrator. He stopped, afraid he had hurt her, but she grabbed his buttocks and pushed him fully into her. Slowly at first, he slid in and out, her muscles clenching and relaxing around him as she met him stroke for stroke. Automatically she raised her knees allowing him to penetrate deeper. His rhythm increased as she lifted her pelvis to meet him. His kiss deepened too, his tongue probing and poking, finding hers.

The storm raged around them, thunder roaring in her ears as Geoff pounded and plunged. Every thrust she met with mounting desire, dragging her nails across his wide back. She arched even more towards him as his mouth lifted from hers and he leaned up on his arms, deepening each thrust. As she felt her orgasm build, she wrapped her feet around the back of his thighs forcing him even deeper, and truly believed she would explode it was so powerful. She came around him, muscles tight, a scream erupting from her throat. Her whole body juddered and jerked, her knees clasped tightly around his hips as he continued to thrust faster and faster.

She felt his whole body go taut and opened her eyes. She watched in pure delight and wonder as his jaw tightened and his lips opened, his breath suspended. Then he let his breath out a soft "ahh" with it as his shoulders shuddered and his hips bucked. She felt a wet warmth flood through her, and though he had come he still thrust sending her over the edge again. This time her orgasm felt like it would never end. She leaned back in the grass, her arms spread wide, her pelvis pressed to him as hard as she could, eyes closed again.

Eventually and it felt like forever, she came down from her peak as Geoff slowed. He lowered himself to his elbows and stroked her sodden hair. She opened her eyes and felt tears mingling with the rain. He placed tiny kisses all over her face and took her tears with his tongue. Inside she felt complete satisfaction. Never had she known anything could be so wonderful. Every part of her now felt totally relaxed. Despite the storm and wet grass it was like she was floating on a bed of feathers.

Geoff smiled down at her. He was still inside her and neither moved both prolonging the pleasure. He kissed her lips and she put her palms either side of his face and kissed him back. The rain still came heavily but they ignored it.

"Thank you Derby."
Geoff said surprising her.

"What for?"
She asked puzzled.

"No one has ever given me an orgasm like that before."
He told her. She was amazed.

"I…I…don't know what to say. I mean that's great. I mean…oh I thought…well the same…well that I've never come like that before either."

Geoff pressed his face into her neck and nuzzled. It was intimate but not sexual and Derby felt tears begin again. How could she have let so many years go by without love and affection. She was angry with herself, but more so, angry with David. He must know there was nothing between them, hadn't been since they got married. But for all of their married life he had used her as a replacement mother. That thought gave her a physical jolt. Geoff leaned up again on his elbows a little frown on his face.

"Are you ok. Did I hurt you?"

"No…I just had…"

"An orgasm…"
He interrupted her with a cheeky smile. She giggled and poked him in the side.

"Well yes, that too…but what I was going to say was an epiphany."

Geoff kneeled back on his heels, sliding out of her and brought her to a sitting position too. They were drenched, Derby's hair clinging to her face and back untidily. Her dress was soaked and lay in a heap where Geoff had discarded it, his clothes in a similar state. In one movement he stood up and pulled her up with him. The rain came down more lightly now, the storm blown over as they stood holding hands. Derby looked into his eyes, and then slowly trained her own down his body. She felt no sense of embarrassment or self-consciousness at their nakedness, and Geoff certainly didn't show any signs of that either.

Without speaking, he bent and collected their clothes with one hand, still holding Derby's hand with the other. Then he led them back to the patio and beyond to the kitchen. Once inside he reached into a cupboard, took a towel and gently rubbed her hair. He then towelled his own which left it tousled making him look young and boyish.

"So this epiphany."
He said with a grin. Derby took the towel from his hand and patted his chest and shoulders with it.

"David has never needed or wanted a wife, just a replacement mother."
Geoff leaned his head back and laughed. Derby gripped the towel and felt laughter bubble up inside her too. It broke the surface of her lips and burst from her. Together, standing naked and wet in Geoff's kitchen they shared the humour.

Eventually they calmed as the laughter subsided. A small puddle had appeared on the floor where they had dripped onto it. Geoff took the damp towel from her fingers and knelt in front of her to mop it up. Derby threaded her fingers in his wet hair smoothing it back into place. Leaving the towel to soak up the water, Geoff put his hands on her waist and stood back up. As he did she let her hands slide over his shoulders and down his back. His skin was smooth like satin, his muscles hard. He stroked her waist and then wrapped his arms around her drawing her to him.

He took her mouth in a warm kiss and she pulled him tight against her. Her breasts still sensitive were tickled by his chest hair, and she rubbed lightly enjoying the sensation she achieved. Instantly she felt his erection pushing between her naked thighs and spread her legs slightly. She heard herself moan a little, her insides more than ready for him again. He pulled back and looked into her eyes smoky with desire. He hesitated a moment then spoke.

"Derby...I didn't use any protection. I'm sorry I should have thought."

Derby frowned at first then realisation hit her.

"Oh...um...look so should I have. It's...um...I've never had to, you know, David and not getting pregnant and all that. I mean...no one else."

Derby lowered her head. She didn't quite know what to say or think. Geoff tilted her chin with a finger and bent his knees to level with her face. He stroked her cheek and smiled at her.

"I can promise you I'm clean."

Derby gasped. He wasn't worried he might have made her pregnant, he was worried she would be concerned about him passing something on to her.

"Geoff...that never even crossed my mind. I thought...maybe you meant...you know...getting pregnant."

Geoff smoothed her face with his thumb.

"Is that likely?"

He asked. Derby pondered for a moment.

"Well...probably unlikely by my dates but like I told you...why I got married. I never got pregnant and it's not me, but David would never get checked. And like I said we don't have an active sex life, well dead in the water I'd say. I've never needed contraception."

She finished hurriedly a tiny sob escaping her lips.

Geoff stood up straight and again pulled her to him wrapping his arms around her tightly. Despite their nakedness there was no longer any sexual suggestion in his hold, just pure comfort. He stroked her back and smoothed her hair whilst her sobs increased. She clung to him, sadness for a loss of years of love deep within her. As she cried she shivered slightly and Geoff must have noticed because he moved his hands to her shoulders and began to rub them briskly.

"Derby you're cold. Come on."

He led her, tears still falling, to the staircase. Up in the bathroom he turned on the shower, and whilst they waited for it to warm, he brushed away her tears with light kisses. Then he took her into the large curved shower and stood with her under the water. At first it stung her skin a little but then began to soothe. Geoff tipped shampoo into his large palms and began to gently wash her hair. Then he smothered her in scented soft body wash and massaged it into her shoulders and back. She stood with her hands at her side, completely absorbed in the attention.

As the hot water rinsed her body, she lifted her hands and pressed them against his chest twiddling her fingers into his hair. She squeezed his pecs ever so lightly digging in her nails. His wet skin gleamed, golden from a natural tan, firm to the touch. She moved to his arms and slid her wet hands up and down his biceps feeling the strength within. She stepped closer as the water hot and sensual sprayed over them. She traced a pattern with her hands down his body and to his back, coming to rest against his hard strong buttocks. She grasped one in each hand and squeezed, scraping his skin with her nails. Geoff stepped forward and took her face in his hands, plunging his tongue into her mouth. She opened her lips to him and let his kiss deepen.

Pressing against him under the steamy water she again felt his erection push between her thighs. She lifted onto her toes wriggling into him and felt him jolt. Wanting to give as much as she could she spread her legs still on tiptoe and pressed. She could feel her own arousal and slid back and forth against his rigid shaft, teasing her own clitoris as water flooded around them. She could feel herself peaking but wanted to prolong the wondrous feeling longer. Geoff pushed his pelvis towards her, but she couldn't get enough height even on her toes to allow him entry.

Geoff realising their predicament stepped back and pulled her out of the shower. She didn't hesitate. Still wet he took her to his bedroom and gently pushed her to the bed. She dug her heels into the covers and inched her way up until her head rested on the pillows. He kneeled over her dripping water, his protruding manhood alluring. She sat up and took it in both hands running her thumbs up and down the length. He was hot and she looked up into his eyes. He looked down at her biting his lip a little.

"I'm just holding on."
He told her through partially gritted teeth.

She grinned pleased with herself, desperate to feel him inside her but excited at the prospect of seeing what she could do to him. She flipped to a kneeling position too and he took her breasts in his hands, stroking her nipples in a circular motion. She took a deep breath but held her hands wrapped around him.

"Do you know what you do to me?"

He gasped. She giggled.

"No but I'm learning."

Geoff groaned and leaned his head back. The bed gave a little under their weight but Derby shifted nearer. She had given herself pleasure on her own and Geoff had given her pleasure. Together they had given each other amazing orgasms. Now despite her own intense desire, she wanted to make him come, and she wanted to watch it happen. So, she lowered her head and gently bit around the head whilst sliding her hands up and down, all the while keeping her eyes open. She watched as his penis twitched beneath her touch. She pulled back his skin and flicked her tongue around the ridge, heard him inhale sharply. He put his hands on her head and twisted his fingers in her hair and heard him whisper.

"So close."

She leaned back a little to see more clearly, increased the pressure from her hands and slid them up and down more quickly. His pelvis met her hands as he began to pump, pushing hard into her palms. She saw and felt him get bigger and even harder, then he went rigid, throwing back his head as wet warmth flew from him across her hands and neck and chest, a loud release of pleasure coming from deep within his throat.

Still sliding her hands up and down, his whole body twitched and then slumped. The pressure in her hair eased as he settled back on his feet and he sighed with satisfaction. Derby let go of him, kneeled up and kissed him. He wrapped his arms around her and kissed her back holding her tightly. He then pushed her to her back and lay over her.

She wrapped both her arms around him too. His penis was just beginning the soften but the wet stickiness against her thighs was just as arousing and she rubbed against him. He let her, taking a still hard nipple in his mouth and sucking. She squealed with joy and writhed into him moving her pelvis from side to side, feeling her desire mount. Geoff sucked and nipped at her nipples, massaging her breasts as she felt her orgasm begin and rise. She rubbed hard enjoying the feel of his semi-hard penis and came quickly. He held her whilst she climaxed and came down, feeling her rapid breath on his face.

"Derby that was amazing."

He whispered.

"Sure? I've never done that to anyone before."

She asked shyly. Geoff planted a kiss on her cheek.

"More than sure."

Geoff rolled them to their sides and cradled her in his arms. The storm had passed, the rain had stopped, and the sun was just beginning to set, a glowing ball of fire in the now clear sky. Derby snuggled into Geoff, relaxed and comforted beyond anything she had ever known. A warm gentle breeze drifted through the open window soft as silk against her skin. She closed her eyes and a peace settled over her as she slipped into sleep.

A movement next to her roused Derby and she opened her eyes. Geoff stood up quietly, unaware he had woken her. She watched him as he stretched, his muscles taut in his shoulders, chest and thighs. Moonlight flooded the room turning his skin ivory, a stone God standing before her. She took in a breath. He looked down.

"I didn't mean to wake you."

He told her in a gentle voice.

"It's ok."

She replied leaning up on one elbow and openly admiring his form.

"Enjoying the view."

She said cheekily. Geoff laughed, deep and husky.

"A true little devil."

He told her as he turned towards the bathroom. Derby watched him go delighting in the shape of his rear end, and the muscles in his back as they rippled with his movement.

As he closed the bathroom door Derby flipped over and looked about the room. She saw an old fashioned clock on the bedside table, the moon giving enough light to read the dial. It was nearly one in the morning. She had no idea how long they had slept, since it had still been light when they entered the bedroom, but she felt awake and rested. She pushed against the pillows and stretched her entire body, feeling the pull of muscles she didn't know she had. However, smiling to herself she thought she would gladly contend with the soreness if it meant more of what Geoff gave her.

Sitting up she swung her legs over the side of the bed and realised the antique was so high she couldn't reach the floor. She pushed off and a little jump brought her to the floor. She wandered to the window and looked out over the garden. It was even bigger than she had first thought. She could make out the stone wall that surrounded the house, the woodland at the bottom. She couldn't see any other houses, just tall trees and assumed the properties either side must have similar perimeters.

The bathroom door opened behind her, electric light competing with the moon. She turned and saw Geoff coming towards her. He stood behind her and wrapped his arms about her.

"Your home is beautiful Geoff."

She whispered.

"Not as beautiful as you."

He replied kissing her bare shoulder. She leaned back into him.

"Mmmm…that's nice. But…I…have to use the bathroom."

He let her go. She closed the door behind her and quickly emptied her bladder. She washed her hands and looked in the mirror above the basin. Her hair was all over the place and looked tangled. She ran her fingers through it loosening it a little. She felt something on her neck and chest and examined it in the mirror, realising quickly what it was. She touched it with her fingers, and it peeled off like a face mask. She was awed at the feel of a man's most intimate fluid dry on her skin. Even when David and her had sex she had never felt his come. It made her wonder then if he ever actually did. Could her husband of twenty four years and partner of twenty seven have faked it for all this time? It was a question she would never get an answer to, for she had no intention of ever asking him, no interest in knowing. No, to her it was just another little revelation into her husband's life.

Derby found a tube of toothpaste and used her finger to rub a blob across her teeth. She then splashed some warm water on her face and feeling refreshed went back to the bedroom. Geoff wasn't there but the bedroom door was open. She found a thick masculine robe hanging on the back of the bedroom door and wrapped it around her. It was far too big. Then she followed the light down the stairs and wandered down to find him.

Geoff was in the kitchen a pair of jog pants his only attire. She watched him silently from the doorway as he gathered their wet clothes and took them into the utility room. He saw her when he came out and stood for a moment looking at her.

"I've put your dress and underwear in the dryer. I checked the labels first."

He told her, a smile lighting his face. Derby felt a tiny lump in her throat and swallowed back tears. Such a small act of consideration, but one she had never experienced.

"Are you alright?"

He asked, concern in his voice. They moved together, closing the distance between them as he took her in his arms and held her close against him. She nodded into his chest.

"I'm just being silly. It's just…I've had to look after myself for such a long time."

She didn't get the chance to expand on that statement as Geoff took her face in his hands and kissed her tenderly. Then he leaned back and said.

"Maybe you'll let me change that."

Derby looked into his deep blue eyes, uncertain of how to reply. Geoff sensed her hesitation.

"Too soon?"

He asked. Derby nodded.

"I'm sorry, I think so."

Taking her hand, Geoff led her across the kitchen and flipped the switch on the kettle. With his free hand he lifted mugs from a cupboard and held up a jar of coffee.

"Please."

She said. He had to let her go to spoon coffee into the mugs. As they waited for the water he leaned against the worktop.

"No, I'm sorry for trying to push you too fast."

He told her.

"Look, the call I had from the gym earlier, I have to go to Sheffield in the morning." He glanced at the clock on the cooker. "Actually later today. It's just for four days training newbie gym coaches. It will give you a bit of time. I will call you if that's ok, but I don't want to make you feel like I'm muscling in on you. From what you've told me, I get the feeling that though you have been sort of independent, you haven't had much of a life, seen much of life."

The kettle flicked off, and Geoff poured water into the mugs offering milk and sugar which she declined. He handed her one of the mugs and sipped from the other watching her intently.

"You know, I think you know me better than my own husband."
She told him.

"I take notice Derby."
He replied sincerely. She nodded holding the drink in two hands and turned towards the door to the garden.

She stepped out onto the patio and stood looking at the clear sky and the moonlight filtering through the trees. She heard Geoff behind her and looked at him over her shoulder.

"It's so peaceful here."
She told him.

"That's why I bought it. The navy was hectic, so was my marriage. The gym is a very noisy place, so coming home to this house, getting on with the renovations and doing the garden, it's relaxing."

Derby walked over to the table and chairs and sat down cradling her mug. She leaned her head back and breathed in the scents of the summer night. She could detect roses and honeysuckle, both gentle reminders of her Gran. She heard a chair being pulled out and the slight creak of wicker as Geoff sat near her. Without opening her eyes she said.

"I do need some time to find myself. I mean, what we did today, yesterday, I....don't feel guilty. I know that's bad, but I don't. I haven't had...sex...like that ever before. It's new and I need to know what it means for me."
She sighed and sat up opening her eyes.

"I don't think I'm making much sense."
Geoff leaned on the table towards her.

"Derby, I'm glad that I was the one who showed you how to enjoy being a woman. What you said makes a lot of sense, and I realise that maybe you need to explore your new found, I won't say freedom, because it's not quite that, but it is a sort of liberation. I want to be part of your life, but I don't want you to feel that you are jumping from the frying pan into the fire."

She giggled, David couldn't be compared to Geoff in any way. He was more like a pot roast that needed hours to cook, only he never ever tenderised.

"My husband is no frying pan. He has no heat in him whatsoever."

Geoff smiled.

"You know what I mean."

He told her laughing. Derby laughed with him.

For some time they sat sipping their coffee in a comfortable silence. A tiny breeze lifted the leaves on the shrubs and rustled the treetops, mingling the scents from the plants in the beds. An owl hooted somewhere in the woodland, a sound Derby had never heard. Even though she had followed Geoff home, she didn't really know where they were, but she guessed they must be nearer to countryside than town. She hoped her now trusty SatNav on her phone would show her the way home.

"We should probably get some rest."

Geoff interrupted her thoughts.

"I have to leave before six."

He continued.

Derby drained her mug and placed it on the table. She shifted in the chair relaxed, comfortable and reluctant to move. But she also had a vision of returning to Geoff's huge bed, his hands on her body as he took her to sexual heights again then sleeping snuggled close to him. As though he could read her thoughts, he took her hand and pulled her from the chair leading her back through the kitchen, up the stairs and into his bedroom.

Slowly he eased the robe from her shoulders and let it fall to the floor. He pushed his jog pants down, stepped out of them and moved closer to her naked body. He slid his hands down her neck, across her shoulders, down her arms and settled on her waist. He spread his fingers and rolled his thumbs across the soft skin of her belly. She stood motionless enjoying the feel of his hands and the heat that was building inside her.

His hands moved down to her hips and around to her buttocks and squeezed each one gently. She brought her hands up to his chest, tangling in his hair. She let one finger trail a path down to his stomach and heard him inhale. She stepped a fraction closer, still not touching but feeling the heat from his body. She looked up at him and saw he was looking at her. They moved together, her hands coming up around his neck, his hands holding her face.

His lips pressed against hers, his tongue finding the gap between them. She opened her mouth wider and the kiss deepened. He moved his hands back to her buttocks and pulled her tight to him. She felt his hard erection pressing into the juncture between her thighs and opened her legs giving him more access. As before she raised onto her tiptoes to get closer and felt frustration when she couldn't.

Geoff walked her backwards to the bed and lifted her onto it. She dug her heels against the mattress and pushed back. He came with her and they tumbled onto the already untidy covers. His hands stroked and squeezed every inch of her. He took his mouth from hers and she wanted to drag him back, but when he trailed his tongue down her throat to her cleavage, she took his head and guided his mouth to her waiting breasts. He nipped at her nipples and flicked them with his wet tongue. She thought she couldn't feel anything more sensuous.

Geoff then took her breasts in his hands and rubbed the nipples with his thumbs as his tongue made a path down her body. She took in a deep breath as his mouth closed on the wet softness between her legs. She lifted her pelvis as his tongue licked and pressed into her. She grabbed his hair and pushed his head hard against her, wriggling her hips to heighten the pleasure. She could feel her orgasm building and hovering close to edge. Then he took away his tongue and she moaned. But quickly it was replaced with his hard penis, and as he pushed into her she came with a scream of delight, bucking to meet his thrusts. Then he froze and again she felt warmth flood her insides.

After, they lay with his arms wrapped around her gently stroking her back. Her breathing began to settle and she could feel his heartbeat returning to normal.

"Sorry Derby"

She heard him mumble against her hair. She looked up at him a little thread of fear inside her.

"What for?"

She asked in a small voice.

"I didn't use a condom…again."

He said. Derby let out a breath she hadn't realised she was holding.

"God I wondered what you were going to say."

Geoff tilted her chin and planted a little kiss on her lips.

"I won't hurt you Derby."

She sighed.

"I just didn't know what you were apologising for…and…I should be just as responsible too, so I'm sorry as well. Like I said, by my dates I think we are ok."

Geoff hugged her.

"Ok, we're both idiots."

He said laughing. She laughed with him then they settled back and gently stroking each other, they slipped into sleep.

Chapter 12

Cocktails And Chocolates

Derby awoke to the sound of running water, rolled over and looked at the clock. It was four thirty and the morning dawn was just beginning to lighten the sky. She stretched like a cat, arching her back, arms over her head and toes pointing to the end of the bed. The bathroom door opened and Geoff stepped out, a towel wrapped around his waist, another in his hands rubbing his wet hair. He saw her and smiled.

"Morning."

She sat up pooling the covers around her.

"Morning to you."

She replied smiling too.

"Sorry it's so early. But you don't have to leave when I do. Just be sure to pull the door closed when you do."

He told her. Derby threw back the covers and hopped off the bed.

"It's fine Geoff, honestly. I should get home and start getting ready for work too."

She slid past him towards the bathroom and lightly touched his shoulder on the way. She heard a little groan come from his throat.

"Mmmm….Derby you don't know what you do to me. If I didn't have to get going, I'd follow you straight into the shower."

Derby giggled.

"Down boy."

She said flipping her hair over her shoulder and entering the bathroom.

Whilst the water heated Derby looked in the mirror above the basin. It was circular with lights all around the edge which kept the steam from it. Her hair was all over the place, but there was a glow to her face that she had never seen before. She blew a little kiss to herself, giggled silently and stepped into the shower. She shampooed her hair and lathered herself in body wash, then stood with her face raised to the water as she rinsed off. Stepping out, she found a huge fluffy bath sheet folded over the towel radiator and smiled, knowing Geoff had put it there especially for her.

Still drying her body, Derby walked into the bedroom. Geoff was not there but her clothes were. He had laid her dress over a chair, her bra and thong folded on top. Her breath hitched a little, such a small thing, but the consideration was so immense. Keeping the tears at bay she dressed quickly and headed downstairs. She heard Geoff in the kitchen and made her way there.

The door to the garden was open and the sound of birdsong flooded the kitchen. Geoff was pouring water into an old fashioned teapot softly whistling along with the birds. He turned and grinned.

"Black like you like your coffee?."

He asked with a smile.

"Thanks…you remembered."

She replied.

"I remember everything about you Derby."

He told her a more serious note to his voice. She lowered her lashes and smiled shyly.

"Breakfast?"

He asked. At first she thought about refusing, a sudden image of the morning routine at home with David. Then she brushed that aside and nodded.

"Good because I've already made it."

He told her confidently. Derby felt she should be annoyed that he had made the assumption that she would eat breakfast with him, but inside she was delighted. This was another first, someone making her breakfast. No one had, except for Gran, since she was old enough to tip cereal and milk into a bowl.

Geoff glanced at her, watching the change of expressions on her face but said nothing. Instead he held out a hand and led her to the patio carrying the teapot. The table was laid with patterned delicate china that matched the teapot. He had put cereal, milk, toast, jam and fresh fruit out, all arranged in serving bowls. It looked like something from a scene from the nineteenth century and Derby loved it.

Geoff pulled a chair out for her and she sat down. He handed her a linen napkin and stood by her side pouring golden tea into a china teacup. He then sat beside her.

"Help yourself."

He said and waited until she had taken a slice of toast before he spooned cereal into a bowl for himself. Feeling completely at ease, Derby buttered her toast and spread strawberry jam on top. She sipped her tea and felt like a Lady.

The drive home was very pleasant. The roads were quiet and the air was fresh. She had the top down and delighted in the feel of the warm wind blowing her hair about. Geoff had kissed and held her by the side of her car, promised to phone later and told her he was going to miss her. She had never been missed before and inside she felt like she was full of bubbles.

As Derby pulled up outside her home she saw Fiona, her elderly next door neighbour snapping the gone over roses from her bushes. She watched Derby as she lifted the roof up on the car, and when Derby stepped out she called to her.

"Morning. You're up and about early."
Derby turned and smiled.

"Stayed at a friend's house last night."
She said trying for innocence and hoping she wasn't about to blush. Fiona opened he gate.

"Come and have a cuppa."
Derby would have liked to refuse but Fiona was smiling, holding the garden gate open. So she nodded and went with her neighbour.

Derby had never been inside Fiona and Bob's house before, but it was exactly as she expected. The hallway, like her own had stairs on one side, the lounge on the other and the kitchen at the back. The walls were covered in rose patterned paper with white woodwork, and the kitchen had tile patterned paper and oak cabinets. It was neat and clean and fitted the elderly couple perfectly.

Bob was sitting at a small kitchen table reading a newspaper which he lowered when they walked in.

"Bob look who's here."
Fiona said to her husband gleefully. Bob took off his glasses and stood up.

"My my what a pretty sight first thing."
He said grinning, the wrinkles on his face deepening. Derby couldn't help but smile back. Before she could reply Fiona had pulled a chair out.

"Sit down dear. How do you like your tea?"

"Black please."

Derby replied as she settled into the chair.

Bob sat back down and folded the newspaper, laying it to one side. Fiona placed a pretty mug in front of her, and stood behind her husband resting her hands on his shoulders. He covered one hand with his own, and Derby felt an almost overwhelming desire to burst into tears. To cover up she took a sip of tea, it was hot and stung, making her eyes water. Bob noticed.

"Oh dear be careful."

He said sincerely. Derby put the mug down and smiled.

"Ouch..."

The old couple laughed and she joined in.

"So did you go out last night then?"

Fiona asked taking Derby completely by surprise.

"Um...no...just went to a friend's for a barbeque, and because I had a couple of glasses of wine, thought it best to stay over."

Fiona nodded, and Derby was certain she knew she wasn't quite telling the whole truth.

"So...where was your...husband?"

Fiona asked, and Derby could see she had pursed her lips slightly when she said 'husband' and got the impression she didn't approve of David.

"He's at his mother's. Picked up that bug that's going round, so she's looking after him."

She saw the corners of Bob's lips twitch, and felt sure he was on the brink of laughter.

"Humph, a grown man needing his mother to pander to him, just because he's got a little tummy bug."

Fiona stated openly. Derby felt her jaw drop open, and quickly lifted her mug to disguise her shock.

"Now now love, it's none of our business."

Bob told his wife patting her hand.

"Hmmm...well."

Then she beamed at Derby.

"So how is your job going dear?"

She asked, rapidly changing the subject.

Derby gave a little laugh thinking how like Gran Fiona was. She had barely spoken to this couple in all the years she had lived next door to them, yet suddenly found she had warmed to them.

"It's going very well thank you. In fact I really should be getting ready to go there. We had a few staff off last week, same bug, hopefully they will all have recovered over the weekend."

She lifted her now cooling tea and drained the mug. Fiona stepped away from her husband, Bob stood up and so did Derby. The couple followed her to the front door and when she turned to thank them, first Fiona gave her a hug and then Bob. Again she was surprised and stiffened slightly at their show of affection. She saw a tiny frown cross Bob's face and hoped she hadn't offended him. But then he spoke.

"Derby, you come over for tea any time you want. We have lived here for a very long time, and in all the years we have known you, well not known you I should say, this morning is the first time we have seen you look happy."

Derby felt her eyes well but bit back the tears. More lost years, more waste. She could have been friends with this lovely couple, but had let herself be swallowed up by David's neediness. Mentally she slapped herself, and turned on the brightest smile she could.

"Thank you Bob. I will come and see you both soon, and I'm sorry I haven't been a very good neighbour. I promise to be better."

She held up the Girl Guide finger sign and gave a little giggle.

Fiona stepped forward and laid an old hand on Derby's shoulder. She placed a soft kiss on her cheek and stepped back.

"My dear. I might be getting on but I'm still sharp. Come and see us soon, our old ears still listen well, we won't judge."

Derby gave them both hugs.

"I will."

She told them and meant it. Then she headed back down the path to her own gate. The old couple watched her go up her path and waved as she went into her own house.

Derby closed the front door and leaned back on it for a few seconds. The familiar smells of the home invaded her nostrils but in no way felt homely. A shadow of depressing silence seemed to waft towards her like fog, and she did not want to be there. The whole place was David. It was her house too and she had been the one who had painted and put up wallpaper. But it was David who had decided on the furnishings and colour scheme. Her choices ranged only so far as the small things like towels and bedding. David had even been responsible for choosing curtains and kitchen appliances, except the dishwasher, which she had bought online and which she didn't think David even realised was there. Almost everything in the house came from his decisions. Then everything was left for her to arrange, and since the rooms were not large, there were not many ways any of it would fit.

Derby pushed away from the door, determined not to let the house and her husband spoil a promising week. She headed for the kitchen and checked the kettle for water. She put it on the hob and left it to go upstairs to change. She stripped and dropped her dress and underwear into the empty washing basket, turning to her drawer for fresh underwear. Automatically she lifted out cotton knickers and bra, and was about to put them on when she realised what she was doing. Huffing to herself, she threw the old underwear onto the bed and took out new ones. She slipped into them, and then glanced at the bedside clock. She had plenty of time.

Ten minutes later, Derby descended the stairs with an armful of clothes. She was still only dressed in bra and panties but didn't care. She went into the kitchen where the kettle was whistling away to itself, completely forgotten.

"Ooops."

She said out loud, and quickly dropped the pile of clothes and turned off the hob. She pulled a roll of bin bags from under the sink and began stuffing them with clothes. She returned to the bedroom and collected the rest of her old attire, a feeling of pure satisfaction when the last of it went into a bin bag. She tied the tops of the bags and dumped them all in the wheelie bin. With a sigh of pleasure she rubbed her hands together and trotted back to her bedroom to dress, donning new and more modern work clothes. The trousers were still black but more shapely, and the blouse soft and feminine.

Derby arrived at the nursery at the usual time and set about her normal routines for the day. Angela came in and came to a halt when she saw Derby. Theatrically she stared and opened a few cupboard doors.

"Where's Derby gone?"

She said to no one. Derby, on her knees rested back on her heels and laughed.

"Here."

She said. Angela made of show of being startled, came to her friend's side and touched her shoulder, squeezing slightly. Then she gave herself a tiny pinch.

"Hmmm…not dreaming."

She giggled.

"What happened to you over the weekend?"

Derby looked over her shoulder to check they were out of hearing distance. She held one finger up and indicated that Angela should kneel down beside her. Then in a lowered voice she said.

"Geoff."

Angela opened her eyes wide and gave a little gasp.

"You and he…"

She nodded her head and waved her hand in a circular motion. Derby grinned.

"Yep."

Angela shifted until she was sitting sideways on the carpet. She put a hand against her heart, and wafted her face with the other one.

"Wow…well you look like it did you the world of good."

"It did. Look it's a little difficult to tell you all about it now. Any chance we could chat after work?"

Derby asked. Pushing to her feet Angela grinned.

"You bet."

Nursery life progressed normally. All of the staff were back fit and healthy as were the children. Kelsey breezed in with Chardonnay and as usual headed straight for Derby, and as usual gave her a run down of Chardonnay's weekend. Then after explaining a bruise the toddler had received from a fall in the garden, she stopped and looked Derby full in the face.

"Something's different."

She mused. Then she smiled.

"New outfit?"

Derby nodded, but Kelsey gave a little frown pressing her lips together.

"Hmm…not just that. You look…well…new too."

Derby laughed.

"I'm not sure what that means, but I think it's a compliment."

Kelsey nodded enthusiastically.

"I can't really explain what I mean, but yes it is."

Derby lifted Chardonnay and briefly hugged her.

"Just had a good weekend."

Was all she said as she lowered the toddler to the ground.

Chardonnay waddled over to a box of toys and plonked down pulling out a doll and teddy. Kelsey gave Derby a quizzical look but didn't say any more. She knelt next to her daughter, hugged her and gave her a kiss.

"Bye bye angel. Be good, see you later."

She told her. Then as she passed Derby on the way to the door she winked.

"Toys."

Was all she said and Derby burst out laughing.

During the lunchtime Derby spent a few minutes in the tiny office opening mail. One letter gave her a brief heart stopping moment. It was from Ofsted, the nursery was to be inspected. Even though Derby knew the standards were very high, and all of the policies were up to date and practised, she still got nervous at being inspected. The nursery had never failed, or even had elements of unsatisfactory, but Derby believed there was always a first, and would take nothing for granted.

Throughout the day, Derby passed the news on to the staff and asked them to all come in twenty minutes earlier the next day for a staff meeting. Those who had experienced inspections before knew what to expect, but Derby had two fairly new staff who had come from college, so she especially wanted to prepare them. They had a week and a half to get ready, and in the back of her mind she was relieved Geoff was away. He would be too much of a distraction.

At the end of the day, Derby and Angela walked to Derby's house. It would have been easy to invite Angela in for their chat, but Derby just didn't want to be home.

"Fancy a drive in the car?"

She asked Angela who nodded enthusiastically.

"Ok, I'll just drop my bits inside."

Hurriedly, Derby opened the front door, ignored the mail on the floor, dumped her work bag on top of it and slammed the door behind her. She trotted back down the path pressing the remote to unlock the car.

The two women settled in the little car, the top down. Derby pulled away from the kerb, already feeling the buzz of driving, and the excitement of being away from the house. She headed in the direction of the park that Geoff had called 'theirs'. She didn't really know where else to go, still being unfamiliar with most of the town, and since she knew Angela would not want to be out too late, the park was quite close. They didn't talk as they drove. The wind whipped their hair about their faces and made it difficult to hear each other.

Quite soon Derby pulled into the now very familiar car park and pulled up into a vacant space. She turned off the engine and pushed her hair away from her eyes, combing it through with her fingers. She glanced at Angela and saw her doing the same.

"How was my driving?"
She asked her friend. Angela turned slightly sideways, patting her own arms and face.

"I'm still in one piece."
She told her jokingly. Derby laughed.

"Oh you…"
After raising the roof and locking up, they strolled through the park to the café. There were plenty of seats, so they took one on the edge of the café perimeter. A teenage girl came and took their orders, and they chatted about the nursery and upcoming inspection whilst they waited for their drinks. But once their coffees were placed in front of them and the waitress was out of earshot, Angela leaned forward.

"So…give."
Derby waited, taking a sip from her cup, keeping her on suspense. Then with a grin that stretched from ear to ear, she put her coffee down, leaned forward and launched into an account of her visit to Geoff's.

At first Derby thought to edit some of the time she had spent with him. But she had never had anyone to confide in before, and she knew instinctively she could trust Angela. So she gave her friend all of the details, and especially how Geoff had made her feel. By the time she finished, her coffee was lukewarm, so she drained the cup in one go, then sat back for Angela's reaction.

"Wow."

Was all she could say at first. Then she smiled warmly.

"He's good for you Derby. Wherever this goes, wherever you want it to go, it's set you on a new path. Kelsey was right this morning, you do look new like…like…oh I know this might sound wrong…but like a snake shedding its old skin, a fresh bright one replacing it."

"Mmmm…not sure about the analogy."

Derby told her friend, but not unkindly. Angela laughed.

"Sorry…no…no, I've got it. A butterfly emerging from a caterpillar that's been trapped in its cocoon for years."

"Now that description I do like."

Derby replied.

The waitress came near to their table and asked if they would like fresh drinks. Derby looked at Angela, letting her make the decision. After all she had a family to get home to, unlike Derby. All that waited for her was an empty depressing house. Angela nodded to the girl and held out her empty cup.

"Please."

She said. As the waitress turned away, Derby gave Angela a tiny frown.

"You sure?"

Angela said.

"Of course. It's ok. I texted Jake earlier and told him I would be a little late."

She hesitated slightly.

"I hope you don't mind, but I explained a bit of this to him. I mean, not about your, you know, sex stuff, just about you and David and that."

Derby reached across the table and covered Angela's hand.

"Angela, it's fine. I don't mind what you tell Jake. I know I can trust you, so, I can trust Jake too. He's the love of your life, I'm glad you share things with him. That's how it's supposed to be."

Angela grinned.

"So, sex in a storm. That's one Jake and me haven't done."

The two women laughed as the waitress brought more coffees.

Derby dropped Angela off outside her house, declining the invitation to come in. She didn't want to intrude on her friend's family life. Angela protested that she would be doing no such thing, but Derby wouldn't be swayed. As she said goodbye she did promise that she would visit soon, meet Jake and their children. Angela told her to make it sooner rather than later and stood on the pavement waving her off.

At first, Derby didn't really have a destination in mind beyond the end of Angela's road. She didn't want to go back to her empty house, there was nothing there. So as the crossroads approached, she made a hasty decision. She turned in the direction of the city and her flat. She tried to find the route unaided, but found she needed her SatNav still. She knew she would get used to it soon, the more she drove it. But starting from Angela's was different from her house.

More quickly than she anticipated, Derby pulled into the car park of the flats. She hopped excitedly from her car and jogged up to the main entrance. The older security officer was at the desk when she entered. She smiled shyly, not sure if she should address him or not. He made the decision for her.

"Evening. Nice to see you again."

He gave her a huge warm smile.

"Uh…evening."

She replied nervously, feeling like she shouldn't be there.

"I'm George. I'm on shift tonight."

He told her in a friendly manner that settled her nerves. Derby held her hand out.

"I'm Derby."

He took her small hand in his large one and gave a firm but not hard handshake.

"Pleased to meet you Derby."

She smiled.

"You too."

He let her go and she headed for the lift.

Derby paused for a moment outside the flat door, just breathing in the scents of the hallway. It was clean and fresh, the management of the building obviously diligent. As she opened the door, she took a deep breath and stepped over the threshold, a feeling of intense contentment washing over her. She moved slowly, running her hand along the wall of the hallway, peeking into the bathroom and stopping in the lounge. She turned a full circle clasping her hands to her chest like an excited child. She gave a little squeal of delight and a tiny on the spot jump. She opened the patio doors and stepped out.

The early evening was again cloudless and warm. A light breeze drifted towards her, a slight sea tang on it. Her curiosity spiked and she took out her phone. She opened the maps and saw her location pinned. She zoomed in a little, and followed the line of the river from the marina to the sea. It really was very close. She also saw a footpath that zigzagged from a corner of her car park to the beach. Excitement bubbled inside her. She had a little fantasy of her and Geoff in the sand dunes, hidden by grasses, naked in each other's arms. Her phone rang, the sound like that of an old phone. It was the ringtone she had set for Geoff, and she almost believed thoughts of him had actually conjured him up. She answered.

"Hi."

She said, enthusiasm evident in her voice.

"Hi too. You sound happy."

Geoff replied. She gave a little laugh.

"I am. I really am."

"Me phoning?"

He asked. She could visualise the cheeky grin on his face.

"Yes definitely."

"That's what I like to hear. How's your day been?"

They chatted for quite some time. Derby told him about tea with her neighbours, coffee with Angela and the impending inspection. He described his day as 'tough'. The newbies needed a lot of work. The boys more so than the girls. He told her the lads had an arrogant attitude, believing that because they were males, would have an easier understanding of the demands of the gym equipment. When in fact the young women were far more astute, listening and following instruction studiously. He assured her he would 'whip' the boys into shape before the end of the week. Any of them that didn't come up to standard would be put back, given another opportunity on a later course. It all sounded very interesting to Derby.

The conversation finally ended with Geoff telling her he already missed her. She said she missed him too. She had wanted to tell him about the flat, but decided to keep it a secret for a bit longer. Maybe at least until the furniture arrived, and it looked a bit more like a proper home. It already felt like that to her, much more so than her actual house.

Hugging her phone to her, she leaned against the balcony railing and looked down onto the walkways. A few people were busy on their boats, and the cafés and shops were still open. She saw people strolling along or sitting at the outside tables with friends and children. It all looked so different from the street where she lived. It was busy, but not noisy.

The road she lived on was always quiet. She rarely saw any of the neighbours children out playing. Sighing, she assumed it was a sign of the times. Parents were reluctant to let their offspring play out, even on summer nights when it was light. She also knew that many just didn't want that responsibility, preferring to plonk their children in front of a television or computer. Even some of the little ones at the nursery already had their own phones and laptops. Sadness enveloped her, as she imagined how she would have raised a child of her own.

Resolutely deciding to stop feeling sorry for herself, Derby turned and went back inside the flat. She closed and locked the patio doors, took a look in the kitchen and bedroom and headed for the front door. She didn't want to leave, but this was a work night. She had nothing with her, and nothing to sleep on. She would have to be a bit patient, wait until the furniture arrived, then she could stay anytime she wanted, Geoff too, she thought.

The drive home was even easier this time, and Derby felt comfortable behind the wheel of her car. She was beginning to recognise the route, and relied less on her SatNav. Just as she made the turn into her road, she noticed an orange light on the dashboard, and was sure it hadn't been there before. Pulling up to the kerb, she sighed, hoping there was nothing wrong with the car. She would have to phone the dealership in the morning.

Derby unlocked her house front door and stepped into the hall. Immediately she felt a heaviness hang over her. She pushed it aside and headed straight for the kitchen. She unlocked and opened the back door letting in the evening. She then went round and opened all of the other windows except the lounge. She intended to leave the windows open all night, and didn't want to risk uninvited visitors. The street had never had problems with crime, but she wasn't taking any chances.

Back in the kitchen, she put together a hasty meal. She then took it and her laptop out onto the patio and ate whilst she checked emails and banking. She then pulled up the website of the car dealership, but the only number was for main enquiries. She remembered Liam, the salesman had given her a card with a direct number on it. So, taking her empty plate into the kitchen, she headed upstairs and lifted the folder with all the paperwork for her car from the drawer.

Back out on the patio she found Liam's card slotted into the edge of the folder. She laid it to one side, intending to put it her bag later. She found the paperwork that referred to the warranty, and read through it, checking that she was covered. When she finished reading she gave a little sigh of relief, and relaxed shoulders that she hadn't realised were tensed. If there was a problem they would fix it. She had dreaded the warranty wouldn't cover the light, worrying that she would have to find a garage, and knowing nothing about them.

Derby spent the rest of the evening on her laptop. She updated her Facebook and read what others had to say. She had a few more friend requests and accepted them eagerly. Anything that gave her wider access to the world was welcome. She found the message button and typed a quick few lines to Angela, telling her about the light on her car. Then she brought up maps and once again zoomed in on the area where her flat was.

It was a lot easier to see on the bigger screen as she navigated around the marina. What she hadn't noticed before, was that because the maps had been done a while ago, the marina wasn't quite complete. She could see some of the buildings were still surrounded by machinery and building materials.

She moved the map around and zoomed in on the river as it wound its way to the sea. The estuary wasn't wide, and along its banks she could make out anchored boats, mostly fishing boats, but a few small yachts. Using the buttons on her laptop, she followed the river out to the sea. She could see beaches on either side of the estuary.

One stretched along the coastline, towards her home town. Fields and farms separated the town from the sea, it was more inland than the city, but still she felt cheated. Maybe when she was little, someone, perhaps Gran, had told her about the sea, but she couldn't remember. Then after Gran died, there was no one at home to talk to her at all. Her and Annie, then David and the others mostly hung out close to where they lived. They didn't mix with any of the other teen groups, and for the first time, Derby wondered why, but knew she would never know the answer.

Leaning back in the patio chair, Derby looked up at a sky that was beginning to cloud over. The temperature had dropped since she came home, but it wasn't cold. She wondered if the summer was breaking and hoped not. This was the first summer for a few years where it had stayed hot and dry. It would be lovely if it could last, at least throughout August. Then she would be ready for the Autumn, could look forward to it. As she closed the lid of her laptop, she smiled to herself. She had quite a lot to look forward to.

Derby had a very restless night. Even though David wasn't there to keep her awake with his snoring, the oppressiveness of the bedroom did. The room was in semi-darkness, light from the sprawl of houses on the estate invading the room. Geoff's house had very little light pollution, being on the edge of town, and the size of the property. At the flat, a few street lights bordered the marina, but went off at midnight, leaving the stars to shine down over the ever moving water.

Derby had never noticed the street lights filtering into the bedroom before. She had simply accepted them as part of where she lived. Now they were annoying, especially as her mind was churning. She drifted in and out of a light sleep as the hours ticked by. Occasional dreams took her deeper, Geoff's arms around her, his kisses on her body. But too many times she came out of them from some disturbance of the night. She stretched across the whole bed, but still felt uncomfortable and restless. At one point she got up and made tea, but even that didn't settle her.

Her phone alarm sounded and Derby dragged herself from bed. She remembered the last time she looked at the clock it read five past four. So she assumed that she had at least got a couple of hours proper sleep. She showered and dressed, drank a hasty cup of tea, munched two slices of toast and headed for work. She knew she would be very early, but being at the nursery was better than staying at the house.

The staff arrived early as she had asked, and Derby quickly went through her tried and tested routine for the inspection. She focused on the two younger nursery nurses, as it would be their first inspection, and she wanted to be sure they knew what was at stake. She had no real worries about the impending visit, but she was also taking nothing for granted.

After the children arrived and parents and minders had left, Derby popped into the office to phone Liam. She got through straight away, and began explaining what her concern was. She could here in his voice the cheeky confidence she had seen when she bought her car.

"Mrs Waite, Derby isn't it? I can assure you we will sort out whatever the problem is. Is there any chance you can bring it in today?"

Derby pondered for a minute.

"Umm…just a sec…I need to check."

She laid the phone on the desk and ducked out of the office. Angela was with a group of children at the messy play table, her hands covered in paint.

"Angela, would you lock up tonight. I need to take the car back. There's a light on the dash that's not right."

"Course."

She replied with a smile, never taking her eyes off the tray of paint and printing objects.

Derby returned to the office and told Liam she could come by at about four. He accepted that and they said their goodbyes.

Derby made sure everything at the nursery was in order before she left it in Angela's capable hands. She then entered the dealership details into her phone and set it to route. She didn't think she would find the place without the SatNav, as she had been with Angela on the previous visits. She found some of the roads familiar, but still didn't have full confidence in herself to get there completely by memory. Soon, she was turning into the car park and slotting the car into a vacant spot. She left the hood down and trotted up to the path to the showroom.

Liam was at his desk. He stood up, smiled and offered his hand to shake. She took it and smiled back.

"So, best go straight out and have a look at this light then."
He told her exuding confidence. As Derby turned she noticed his
eyes wander over her figure, making her smile to herself, and
lapping up the attention.

Derby led Liam over to her car, put the key in the ignition
and turned it on. Instantly the orange light came on. Liam leaned
into the little car to get a better look.

"Hmmm…engine management light."
He said. Derby frowned.

"And that is?"
She enquired. Liam stood up and looked down at her frowning
face.

"It's the computer that pretty much runs the car. When the
light comes on, it's indicating a fault somewhere."
Derby puffed out her cheeks.

"Wonderful. Is it serious?"
Liam laughed lightly.

"Probably not. But Derby, don't worry. We'll get it over to
the garage. One of our mechanics will plug it into the diagnostics
computer and it will tell him exactly what's wrong. Mostly it's
something very simple. It's just these systems pick up everything."
Derby sighed.

"Will it take long?"
She asked. Liam shook his head.

"Probably not. But let's go and ask."
He opened the passenger door and she got in. He then went round
to the drivers side and slipped into the seat.

Liam drove them over to the other side of the dealership,
through huge open doors, into what looked to Derby like a
warehouse. It was clean, something she didn't imagine a garage to
be, and the mechanics milling about were all in smart overalls with
the dealership logo on. Liam parked the Mazda in a numbered bay
and got out. He came round to her side and opened her door. He
then led her into a air conditioned waiting room and went to the
desk.

After speaking to one of the men at the desk, he came over
to her and sat on the seat adjacent to hers.

"They're not going to be able to do a diagnostic on the car
until the morning."

Derby folded her hands in her lap and felt miserable. She didn't want to leave her precious little car, but knew it was necessary.

"It will be fine."

Liam told her, patting her hand. She looked up and felt tears threaten. She swallowed them back.

"I know I'm being over-emotional. It's just…"

She had no idea how to finish. She couldn't explain how she felt to this young man. Couldn't tell him why the car meant so much, what being without it would do. Liam squeezed her hand gently.

"It will just be one day. They'll get onto it first thing and fix it. Is there someone who can pick you up now?"

Derby thought. If Geoff wasn't away. Then there was Angela, but she didn't want to have to disturb her evening again. David's mother. She shuddered at that thought, and was shaking her head to Liam before she realised it.

"Uh…no. Umm…is there a taxi service nearby?"

She asked. Liam stood up.

"How about I run you home?"

Derby gulped. Liam was a virtual stranger, but inside she felt a little spark of excitement at the thought of being in a closed car with this young man.

Before she could find any reason to say no, Derby was smiling and agreeing. So Liam led them back round to the showroom, collected his jacket and keys and guided her to his own car. It was a very smart modern car, and from the shiny polished paint work, she got the impression it was his pride and joy. He saw her looking and grinned, making him look more boyish than ever.

"Like it?"

He asked as he unlocked the car.

"It's lovely."

She replied as she climbed in.

"Very fast."

He said as he started the engine which practically roared to life.

"But I won't go mad. I promise."

He said as he backed out of the parking space and headed for the entrance. At the end of the road to the dealership, Liam stopped. He looked at Derby.

"Which way?"

He asked. Derby pointed, but he didn't make the turn.

"Or I could take you for a drink."
He stated.

Derby assessed the situation in seconds. He would want more than just a drink, that she was sure of. Geoff's face came to mind, but she shoved back the twinge of guilt. Here was the chance to discover a bit more about herself. Geoff was a wonderful lover, and she knew she had feelings for him. But could she really gauge the importance of those feelings without knowing more about herself. So she smiled at Liam and nodded.

"I know the perfect little place."
He told her as he made the turn.

Twenty minutes later, Liam pulled into the car park of a cosy thatched pub. It was very quiet, only one other car in sight. Liam jumped out and opened her door, just as she had her hand on the handle. He smiled and stood back as she stepped out. She looked at the pub sign, Cock And Chocs, which had a picture of a Cockerel, his tail feathers spread dipping his beak into a box of chocolates.

"Strange name for a pub."
She said. Liam laughed leading her towards the entrance.

"I know. The couple who bought it didn't want a regular name, it used to be called The Plough. They wanted it to stand out, there's a website. They do great food, but what makes it special are the cocktails. They both trained in London, you know, making them properly, and they certainly know how to do it. All the shaking and throwing stuff."
He moved his hands up and down as though juggling, and Derby laughed.

Liam draped an arm over Derby's shoulder as they crossed the threshold into the bar. The interior took Derby completely by surprise. She expected old beams, wooden tables and an open fire. The beams were there, but the tables and chairs were glass and chrome. There was no traditional open fire, instead where it had once been was a sleek, white, circular designer fire with real flames. The bar was shiny and lit from above with small coloured lights. It reminded Derby of the bar Angela took her to, but that place fit with its location. This pub was completely removed from anything anyone would expect to find in the middle of the country, and they were the only customers.

Liam led her to a table near the window and held out the cocktail menu for her. She had no idea what to order. If she had been with Geoff, she wouldn't have hesitated to ask him about the drinks. But Liam was young and she didn't want to appear unsophisticated for a woman her age. So she studied the ingredients in each drink, and finally ordered a Pina Colada.

An uncomfortable silence ensued as they waited for their drinks. Liam tapped the table lightly and Derby looked out of the window.

"So…what do you do?"

He asked, breaking the silence. Derby smiled.

"I run a nursery."

She told him.

"What like plants and garden stuff?"

He said. She shook her head.

"No, children."

The light coming through the windows showed the blush on his cheeks.

"Oh…didn't think of that."

At that moment their drinks arrived, saving him from further embarrassment. They came on little glass saucers with a chocolate on the side. Derby picked up her drink, and sipped it through a straw, deciding it was very nice. She smiled over the top of her glass, thinking that the young man in front of her wasn't as confident as he appeared to be.

"What are you smiling about?"

He asked with a grin.

"Just thinking how nice this cocktail is."

She replied. When really she was wondering what sex was going to be like with him. For she had decided that they would have sex. There was now no doubt about it. She felt a warmth low inside her, and shifted her body, leaning back so her breasts were pushed forward. She watched Liam's eyes move to them. She took the straw in her mouth and sucked. Then she pinched her chocolate between thumb and finger and popped it into her mouth, pushing it in with one finger, which she then let slide down her throat, and tweak the top button of her shirt open. She saw his eyes widen as he looked into her slightly exposed cleavage, the lace from her bra just peeking out.

Liam tried not to show that he was gulping his drink down, obviously anxious to get out of the Cock And Chocs pub. Derby sipped her drink, but didn't linger either. She was fired up and ready, excited. In front of her was a very hot young man, who by the look in his eyes, was just as excited.

As soon as she emptied her glass, Liam stood up. Derby followed and thought it was lucky the pub was empty, as Liam's desire for her was quite obvious. Outside he quickly unlocked the car, again opening her door for her. He all but ran around to his side, and practically leapt into his seat. The engine roared to life and with a quick turn of the steering wheel, they left the car park. Liam seemed to know exactly where to go, and in no time, he turned the car into an open field.

The field was deserted and completely quiet. He drove a short way in and parked along the edge of what looked like wheat, the hedge on the roadside thick and concealing. Before he had turned the engine off, Derby leaned across and kissed him. He wrapped his arms around her, and plunged his tongue into her hot open mouth. She gave him her tongue back, and his hands moved to the front and cupped her breasts. She let her hands scrape down his shirted back until she found the edge. She lifted it and trailed her nails across his skin. His kiss deepened and one hand moved to her inner thigh. She pushed into him, and felt his fingers fumble over her zip and buttons.

Derby moved back for a moment, undoing her own trousers and wriggling her hips until they slipped off. Liam was busy with his own clothes. Derby stretched out her hand and took hold of him through his boxers, kneading his erection lightly. Even though she was inexperienced, she knew a man as young as him wouldn't be able to hold back for long. She didn't want to wait either, didn't want this to be 'lovemaking'. This was pure sex, and she wanted him inside her instantly.

Liam dragged his boxers down and reached under the steering wheel. There was a tiny slot which Derby hadn't noticed. From it, he took a small package, a condom, which even though she hadn't thought of herself, was now very relieved that he had. Expertly he ripped the cover and sheathed himself. Then he leaned across her and pressed something on the side of her seat, making the back move. Derby shifted, pulling him over to her side of the car. He came willingly. Even in the confined space, she managed to manoeuvre him until he was laying back in the passenger seat. She wiggled out of her undies and straddled him, digging her nails into his shoulders. He lifted towards her and kissed her deeply as she lowered herself onto him.

He pushed his pelvis up and she pressed down squeezing her internal muscles against his hardness. Using her knees, she moved up and down, feeling her orgasm mounting each time she pushed herself down hard onto him. His tongue was flicking hers and she leaned forward pressing him into the back of the seat. She came quickly and felt him go taut as he climaxed too. Then it was over. She was sexually satisfied and he seemed to be too, as he relaxed against the leather of the seat.

"That was fantastic."
He mumbled with eyes closed.

Still straddling him, Derby looked at his young face. He had a tiny smile on his lips and looked as though he was about to fall asleep. She knew she should give him some verbal response, he would expect it.

"I enjoyed it as well."
She told him. He opened his eyes and looked into her face. She was flushed.

"You certainly look like you did. I have been told I'm good."
Derby giggled at his youthful arrogance. She didn't have the heart to tell him that it was mostly the heat inside the car making her cheeks flame. Saying nothing, she lifted off him and slid into the drivers seat, so he could sort himself out. Whilst he did, she scooped up her clothes and put them on.

When they were both dressed, they stepped out of the car and swapped seats. Liam smiled at her as he started the engine and backed the car out of the field. There was no awkwardness between them as he asked her where she lived. She told him and as she rolled down her window, Derby thought it was like nothing intimate had just happened. She didn't feel anything emotional about the sex, just a sense of relief, like finally being able to eliminate an itch that's hard to reach.

When they arrived at her house, she opened the car door, putting a hand on his knee as he began to open his door. She shook her head a little, indicating that he didn't have to get out and open her door for her.

"Thanks for the drink…the umm….and the lift. Should I come by the dealership tomorrow for my car?"
She said as she stepped out and leaned down to talk to him. Liam, with one arm resting on the steering wheel, and his other hand leaning on the passenger seat smiled.

"Thank you too. It was fun. I can pick you up if you like."
He said with a wink. Derby didn't want a repeat performance, but she also didn't want to offend his masculinity either. He was far too young for a knockback, but she also knew that his being so young, he would get over it if she handled it the right way.

"That's good of you, but I'm not sure what time I'll get finished. So I think I'll just ask my friend to run me over, the one who came with me when I bought the car. We have a lot on at the nursery, an upcoming inspection, so we will have to shoot over, collect the car and then get back. The inspection's mid next week, so all fun time is suspended until then"
She giggled, making light of it, and the smile she got back assured her she had pulled it off.

"Ok Mrs Waite…I'll see you tomorrow when you collect your car."
Derby closed the passenger door and waved as he drove from the kerb, giving her a wave back.

Derby unlocked her front door and stepped inside a house she once thought of as home, but now just seemed like a place she had to be in. Once again the silence that greeted her gave her an immense feeling of loneliness. Unlike the quietness of the flat, or Geoff's house, both of which gave her a sense of peace. She had a tiny pang of guilt when she thought of Geoff, but refused to let it surface.

Dropping her bag in the hallway, Derby trotted upstairs to the bathroom. She was hot and sweaty from the heat of the car and from the sex. She could feel dampness in her underwear, but not the stickiness that she had felt with Geoff. The condom had done its job. She was relieved about that, not so much because of the risks, but because she didn't want any other man's sex fluid inside her. It seemed like such a silly thing really, but in her mind, Geoff's fluid represented more than just sex, it involved emotions and intimacy. Feeling his come flow into her brought a closeness she had never felt before. Whereas, sex with Liam was just physical, more like a human form of vibrator.

Stepping into the shower which she had set on cool, Derby turned her face into the water and analysed her own feelings. Sex with Liam had been good. She had felt satisfied sexually, but without any emotional connection. His youthful eagerness gave her quick release, whereas sex with Geoff was totally different. He filled her completely. Every nerve, every limb, her whole heart and soul was touched by him. It wasn't hurried, there was no rush to reach the peak, each kiss and stroke having its own special meaning. Just being with him, talking to him gave her joy, not just the sex. There was something special about their relationship, much more than just the physical. As the water cooled her skin, she realised it was love, but was still afraid to admit that, it was still too soon.

Stepping out of the shower feeling refreshed, Derby wrapped herself in a towel and went downstairs to the kitchen. She was hungry. She opened the fridge and pulled out cold chicken and salad and plonked it on a plate. As she turned to put the packets back in the fridge, she stopped, a thought racing through he mind. The person she hadn't considered, the one she should have, was David. Yet the only guilt she felt was for Geoff, not her husband.

Leaving her plate on the side, Derby went into the hallway and retrieved her bag. She took it back to the kitchen, and as she forked chicken into her mouth, she dug out her phone. There was one message, which was from Geoff. But before she opened it she quickly tapped a message to David's phone.

How are you feeling?
It was more a sense of duty than care, that she sent the message. She then opened the message from Geoff, feeling excited.

Hi hope you're having a good day mine's been hard.
She giggled to herself then read on.

Missing you can't wait 'til thursday xxxx.
Derby hugged the phone to herself, all thoughts of David and Liam gone from her mind. She took her plate and phone out onto the patio, and still wrapped in a towel messaged Geoff back.

Day's been ok. Car had to go back, a warning light came on. Should be fixed by tomorrow. Missing you a lot.

She paused and ate some of her dinner, thinking about what she wanted to add to the message. She typed a few words.

Especially your body.

Then deleted that part of the message, thinking it sounded too flippant. She missed everything about him.

Missing everything about you.

She added and pressed send before she could change her mind.

She laid the phone on the table and tucked into the rest of her meal. It chirped, but the tone wasn't Geoff, the message was from David. She opened it and found that again her mother-in-law had replied.

To Derby

David is still rather unwell. He has stopped being sick, but is drained. He will be here for the rest of the week. Thank you for your concern, although as today is Tuesday and you have not been in touch, concern actually seems lacking.

Yours

Irene.

Derby huffed to herself, plonking her phone down. Finishing her dinner, she refused to be baited by Irene, even though she was longing to send a caustic reply. However, the frown that had appeared across her forehead soon disappeared when her phone again chirped, it was Geoff this time.

That makes me feel very good more than anyone ever has.

Derby held the phone in both hands close to her heart. Then she tapped a reply.

Tell me that when you come home. Please.

She wrote pressing send. Geoff's reply came immediately.

I will little Derby. Dinner is here will text later.

Derby wished she was eating dinner with him. She wondered who, if anyone he was eating with, and felt an overwhelming sense of jealousy. She knew she had no right, especially after what she had done with Liam, but her mind wasn't working rationally right then.

Taking her plate into the kitchen, Derby decided to go to the gym. Thoughts of Geoff sitting with another woman invaded her, creating pent up energy. She needed to do something, get out of the house, and the gym was the obvious place. She ran upstairs and threw the towel into the bathroom. She grabbed underwear and a jog set, and dragged them on. Then she stopped, a little breathless. How was she going to get there? her car was in the garage. The bus would take forever, especially this time in the evening, it was nearly eight o'clock.

Feeling dejected, Derby plodded back downstairs unsure of what to do. In the kitchen she saw a small pile of leaflets on the side, the day's mail. Absentmindedly, she flipped through them. One practically leapt at her. It was an advertisement for a new local taxi service. She grinned, here was the solution to her problem. She grabbed her phone and tapped the number. It rang once and a female announced the name of the firm. Derby asked for a taxi as soon as possible and gave her address and destination. She asked if she could also book a return and was delighted when it was arranged.

Fifteen minutes later, Derby sat in the back of the taxi heading for the gym. The driver was a large man in his fifties with grey thinning hair. He was chatty and friendly, asking harmless everyday questions. Derby answered politely and before she realised, they were turning into the gym car park. She paid the driver and he confirmed her return car was booked.

"Probably be me anyway."
He told her as she stepped out of the car. She smiled and thanked him, then headed for the entrance.

Derby went to the desk, and handed her membership card to the receptionist to be scanned. The girl smiled and spoke into her headset. Then she turned to Derby.

"Geoff's not here tonight. Molly will coach you instead."
Derby didn't let on that she knew exactly where Geoff was. She had no idea what the gym policy was for sleeping with your coach.

A young lithe woman came through the glass doors and headed for the desk. She stopped in front of Derby holding out her hand.

"Hi, I'm Molly. Geoff asked me to take you through your routine if you came in."
Derby smiled and took her hand.

"Thank you. It's still a bit new to me."
Molly smiled back.

"Are you going straight into the main suite?"

Derby nodded, and Molly told her she would wait inside until she had put her things in the changing room.

Derby found Molly next to a tread machine chatting to one of the other coaches. They both looked at her as she approached, but their smiles were friendly. Molly then took her through her routine, encouraging and praising her. It was different to Geoff's coaching but still she enjoyed the workout. At the end of the session, Molly made a few notes on her chart.

"You're doing very well. Geoff will be pleased."
Derby wasn't sure what that meant, but decided to wait until she saw Geoff to ask. So she just thanked her.

"Geoff said to tell you, drinks are on the house if you want to go to the juice bar."
Molly said. Derby glanced up into the young woman's face. She was smiling, with no trace of snideness.

"That's....very good of him."
Derby said, a trace of hesitancy in her voice.

"Well he's the boss."
Molly said, closing her file. Derby inhaled, and tried not to appear as though this was a complete surprise to her.

In the changing room, Derby pondered over Molly's words. Geoff was the boss. Well, she thought, that could mean he was the gym manager. She took a quick shower, dressed, and checked the time on her phone. She had twenty minutes before the taxi arrived, plenty of time for a drink. So she headed to the juice bar and slid onto a high stool. The bar tender took her order and placed a tall glass of freshly squeezed mixed juices in front of her. He seemed to know who she was, as he didn't ask for payment. Derby felt rather conspicuous as she sipped the drink. The bar was busy, other members enjoying refreshments, but there were some like her, alone, which made her feel a little more relaxed.

Just before the taxi was due, Derby went to the desk and signed out. The receptionist smiled as she handed back her card, said "Goodnight" and "Come back soon."

She had the same driver on the return journey. He was just as friendly, and just as chatty. She found she liked him. He seemed fatherly, although she didn't really know what that meant. Her own had been far from what the word suggested. She settled into the back seat of the car, her muscles telling her she had worked them, but they weren't as uncomfortable as when she first started.

"Good workout?"

The driver asked.

"Mmmm, yes, it was thank you."

"Not my cup of tea. I'm more of a, sit and watch others sort, football mainly."

He said with a deep laugh. Derby smiled.

"Although I think my Mrs would like me to do something. She says I've got a belly, driving all day doesn't help."

Derby nodded, even though he couldn't see her.

"Maybe you should try something together."

She suggested. He laughed again.

"Probably should, but probably won't. Nah, we're sort of comfortable as we are, well thirty five years of marriage, gotta be doing something right."

Another deep laugh. Derby felt a tiny pang of jealousy. She couldn't speak so fondly of her own long marriage.

The taxi stopped outside her house. She paid the driver and gave him a tip. He grinned and thanked her as she alighted. She dreaded going into the house but knew she had to. She just couldn't wait for the flat furniture to arrive. She didn't think how she would work it once David was back home, but right then she didn't care.

In the kitchen she loaded the washing machine with her gym gear. Then she stood gazing out of the window sipping a glass of water. The summer sky was beginning to darken, wispy clouds transforming from pink to purple. It was beautiful to watch. Derby put her glass down and wrapped her arms around her middle, a deep sadness penetrating deep within. She longed for Geoff to be with her, sharing the wonder of evening, and imagined him standing behind her, his arms wrapped around, her instead of her own. She sighed, watching stars appearing like tiny pins of light being switched on from above, as the sky became a cushion of velvet.

Suddenly feeling tired and drained, Derby decided to have an early night. She locked up the house and headed upstairs. As she brushed her teeth she thought how hectic the past week and a bit had been. Climbing into bed, she checked her phone, but there were no messages from anyone. Feeling disappointed, she stretched out across the whole bed, enjoying the space, but not the aloneness. She wasn't missing David. It was Geoff she missed, even though he had never been in this bed. She closed her eyes and images of him came to mind. Just one week and a bit. That was all the time it took to fall in love. She drifted into a deep sleep, a little smile on her lips at the realisation that she did indeed love Geoff.

Chapter 13

Furniture And Fur

Derby awoke to the sound of heavy rain. She looked at the clock and saw it was just ten minutes before the alarm was to go off. She groaned, but threw back the duvet and sat up. The rain was pounding against one window, the curtain on the side of the open one, flapping soggily. She jumped out of bed and pulled the window shut. The curtain dripped onto the floor, so she trotted out to the landing and grabbed a towel from the airing cupboard. She returned to the bedroom and laid the towel on the floor, soaking up the rainwater. For a moment she watched the weather. The rain was coming in sheets, being swept against the windows by a brisk wind. She hoped it would ease off before she set out for work.

The rain did ease, just as Derby locked the front door. She put up her umbrella, but as she reached the end of the road, it stopped, the sun beating the rain to a retreat, shining hot and bright. She folded the umbrella and turned her face to the sun, soaking up its warmth. Derby felt joy spread through her. It looked like it was going to be another beautiful day.

Kelsey arrived with Chardonnay at the usual time. She headed for Derby and as usual went through the routine of her child's needs. The little girl put her arms out and Derby took her from her mother and gave her a hug. Chardonnay hugged her back, then wriggled to be set down. Once on the floor, she waddled off to find toys. Derby watched her with a smile.

"I can't get enough of watching her."
Kelsey said quietly to Derby. Derby turned to the young mother.

"I know what you mean Kelsey, she's adorable."
Kelsey looked at Derby knowingly.

"You would like one of your own, wouldn't you?"
Unusually, she was speaking in a low soft voice. Derby felt a tiny prick of tears and didn't know why, so she nodded, not trusting her voice. Kelsey patted her arm.

"There's still time."

She said gently. Derby didn't reply, couldn't reply. It would never happen, she would have to settle for looking after other people's children.

Angela came over, breaking the intensity of the conversation, much to Derby's relief. She greeted Kelsey and the three chatted for a few minutes about everyday matters. The parents and childminders left, and the nursery day got underway. Mid morning Derby got a call. It was Liam telling her the car was fine and she could collect it anytime. He sounded relaxed and polite with no awkwardness. Derby was relieved, she had dreaded seeing him, but the call set her mind at ease.

Early afternoon, Derby got another phone call. This one filled her with excitement. It was from the furniture store. They told her everything was ready, sooner than expected so would she like to arrange delivery. Of course, she thought, but didn't say, and even more exciting was that they could deliver on Saturday. They offered her time slots, and she accepted the morning one, even though she would have to be there at nine thirty. She didn't mind at all. Her flat would be liveable and that was more important than anything.

Angela noticed her obvious excitement after the phone conversation, but Derby managed to brush it off with.

"Oh just some stuff I ordered will be here Saturday."

She still didn't want anyone to know about the flat. She had shared a lot with Angela, but for some reason she couldn't fathom herself, she wanted to keep the flat apart from her normal life. Geoff though, well he wasn't part of her normal life anyway.

After work, Angela drove Derby to the dealership. She kept glancing at Derby on the way, sure there was something on her mind.

"Ok…give."

She finally said. Derby jumped a little. Telling herself Liam's phone call had been ok was one thing, actually seeing him was another. But she hadn't realised Angela had noticed anything.

"What?…ummm."

She mumbled. Angela laughed.

"Come on Derby. You've barely said a word since we got in the car. You've been miles away."

Derby sighed.

"Can you pull over for a minute?"

Angela complied, pulling into a supermarket car park. She switched off the engine and turned to her friend, waiting for her to speak. Derby leaned back in the seat and closed her eyes.

"You're going to think really badly of me."

She said, opening her eyes and looking sideways at Angela.

"Why?"

Angela asked. Derby took a deep breath.

"'Cos I had sex with Liam, the car guy."

She squeezed her eyes shut and lifted her shoulders, expecting a verbal blow. Instead, Angela covered her hand with her own.

"Derby, open your eyes and look at me."

Derby did. Angela wasn't frowning, or giving her a disapproving look. She looked sympathetic.

"Derby, love. You have only just discovered what sex is. A little exploration is fine. Don't be harsh on yourself. I mean, you had a great time with Geoff, but it's like he was practically your first. Liam, well he's a hot lad, any woman would like a piece of that. Not me, I've got my Jake. But anyone who's had a life like yours would be mad not to try it."

Derby sighed again.

"Should I feel guilty, because I don't."

Angela looked at her.

"For Geoff or David?"

She said. Derby answered immediately.

"Geoff. No not David."

Angela turned in her seat facing Derby. She took her hand and squeezed it gently.

"Derby there's nothing to be guilty for. Geoff has no claim on you and neither does Liam. Are you going to, you know again with him?"

Derby shook her head.

"Oh no. I mean it was good, satisfying, but well, not Geoff. He's something else."

Then hurriedly.

"Angela I think I've fallen for him."

Angela took a deep breath and let it out through puffed cheeks.

"Wow…he has made an impression. Just be careful love. I mean I hope he feels the same. I'd hate for you to get hurt just as you turn a corner in your life."
Derby nodded feeling miserable.

"I know. Suppose it's a risk I have to take."
Angela squeezed her hand again.

"Life's all about risks. About time you took some."

She re-started the car and pulled back onto the road. Derby sat quietly, pondering her friend's words. Yes she was taking risks, and she knew the possible consequences to her heart. If things went cock-a-hoop with Geoff then she would deal with it. What she wouldn't do is let her life go back to what it was. After all, she had begun to make the changes before she met either Geoff or Liam.

Derby and Angela walked into the showroom and saw Liam sitting at his desk. He stood up when he saw them and held out his hand. Both women shook it and sat in the chairs he indicated. He gave Derby a broad smile and a tiny wink, making her blush rapidly, but made no comment. He opened a folder in front of him and began to explain what the problem was.

"As I thought. Just a small thing. One of your sensors wasn't working. It's all fixed now."
He looked up and smiled brightly at Derby. She sighed, pleased the problem was solved and that Liam didn't show any signs of discomfort.

Liam then led them both over to the garage, where Derby's precious little sports car was waiting in a parking bay. It was gleaming, the red paint shining in the bright evening sun. Liam handed her the keys, and she unlocked the door, heat flooding out, the leather seats hot to the touch. She turned to the young salesman and held out her hand.

"Thank you."
Liam held her fingers a moment longer than necessary.

"That's quite alright Mrs Waite. Call me anytime, even if there isn't a problem with the car."
Angela stood behind him, a wide grin on her face as Derby nodded and slipped into the seat of her car.

Angela trotted around to the passenger side and got in too. Derby would drop her off at the main car park for her own car.

Liam waited until they moved off, gave a wave and headed into the garage.

"See, not awkward at all."

Angela said. Derby giggled.

"Nope, not at all. And if I'm not mistaken, I could easily have a repeat performance....if I wanted to that is....which I don't."

Angela laughed, throwing her head back.

"Naughty."

Was all she said as they arrived at her car.

Derby drove home leisurely. She had waited until she was around the corner from the dealership, pulled over and then slid the roof down. The morning rain had not returned, and again the evening promised to be hot and dry. She pulled up outside her house and saw Fiona and Bob in their front garden. She stepped over to the fence and said hello. The old couple, both kneeling on gardening pads looked up as she spoke.

"Hello dear."

Fiona said.

"You ok?"

Bob asked. Derby nodded. Bob pushed himself to his feet.

"Come on in."

He said. Derby pushed the gate open. The garden looked fresh and bright, the earlier rain a welcome to the plants and grass.

"That rain we had was needed."

Bob said, holding a few dead stems in his hand. Fiona held out her hand and her husband helped her up.

"Want a cold drink?"

She said to Bob and Derby. Both nodded and she turned towards the house, rubbing her back a little on the way.

"She gets a bit of arthritis in her hips."

Bob told Derby, looking lovingly at his wife.

"But she doesn't let it stop her doing the things she loves."

He said as he dumped the stems into the recycling bin.

Fiona soon returned with a tray of glasses. She handed one to Derby who hadn't realised until then that she was thirsty. She sipped the beverage, homemade lemonade and felt it rehydrating her. It was delicious, not too sweet and still very lemony.

"Mmmm that's lovely."

She told Fiona warmly. The old woman smiled and nodded.

"Gives you a right proper boost."

Bob said, draining his glass.

"So how's the day been then. Kiddies behave?"

Fiona asked Derby. Realising the couple still thought she was a teacher, Derby decided to gently put them right.

"The children at the nursery I run are still small enough to do as they're told. You get the odd one whose parents have spoilt them rotten, but not very often."

"Oh…so you're not a teacher then?"

Fiona said. Bob nudged her gently.

"Don't know where you got that idea from in the first place."

He mocked, but in a kindly way. Derby then quickly added.

"Lots of people get us muddled up because we do teach the children in many ways. It's just not as formal as school."

"Well I admire you anyway. Looking after children any age can be tough."

Fiona added.

Derby looked at the old couple and wondered for the first time if they had any children. In all the years she had lived there, she couldn't remember seeing any family visit, couldn't recall hearing the sound of any grandchildren. Not wanting to upset them, but being curious, she decided to ask.

"Do you two have any children?"

Bob put a protective arm around his wife as sadness crossed both their faces.

"We do….did."

Fiona began. Derby immediately regretted asking, it was obvious something awful had happened. Bob pulled Fiona close to him.

"We had two boys, Jasper and Arnold. Jasper got killed in a car crash when he was eighteen, just a baby really. Arnold, he got married to a lovely New Zealand girl, she was studying here, that's how they met. They've got two girls, but they live out there. So, well the last time we saw them was four years ago. We managed a trip out there. They never come to England. Zoe, that's our daughter-in-law, is terrified of flying. The grandchildren have never been here."

Derby felt so sorry for the couple. She longed to have a set of parents that cared. A little spike of anger dug at her heart towards the daughter-in-law that they spoke fondly of, but who wouldn't make an effort to come and see them. There was plenty that could be done about flying phobia, and she must have flown some time in the past to have met their son. Derby secretly believed the woman just didn't want to put herself out.

"Do either of you know how to use a computer?" She asked, a sudden thought coming to mind. Bob laughed and Fiona grinned self-consciously.

"We had a go a while back. Arnold wrote and told us to get a computer so we could communicate more easily. So we did, but neither of us could work it out. We asked at the library, but they didn't seem to have much patience with us. So it's sitting on the sideboard, been about a month now."

Derby knew then that she would help this lovely couple out. Even though she was new to the whole social networking, she was very computer literate. Her own laptop had Skype, but she had never had a need to use it. If Fiona and Bob's computer was that new, it would have it too. She would show them how it all worked and give them the chance to see and talk to their family.

"How long ago did you buy the computer?" She asked.

"Oh about two months ago. It's one of those thin ones, lap something." Bob told her. Derby smiled.

"Brilliant. Look it's a bit late tonight, but if you like, when I get home tomorrow I'll pop round and give you some lessons. There's something called Skype, it's a way of making a phone call using the computer with a video screen, so you can see the person you're talking to. Would you like me to do that?" Fiona put both her hands up to her face and gasped.

"Would you? We'd love that. Arnie said something about, what was it, oh yes, internet phone calls. He wrote it in the letter, how to call him and that. But we wrote and told him we didn't know how, and of course normal calls to New Zealand and to here are so expensive." Derby smiled at the couple.

"Definitely. Tomorrow then."

She said as she headed back to her own front gate and path.

The evening was still so wonderfully warm, that Derby once again ate her dinner on the patio. She was feeling a little low and longed to hear Geoff's voice. She desperately wanted to phone him, but didn't want to interrupt if he was still busy. Mulling over her decision, she turned her phone over and over in her hand, nearly dropping it when it rang. She answered excitedly, the ringtone telling her it was Geoff.

"Hi."

His deep voice soothed and warmed her, immediately lifting her mood.

"Hi back."

She said.

"How has your day been?"

He asked. Derby went on to describe the day, happily announcing the return of her car.

"I had to get a taxi to the gym last night."

She told him.

"Bet that was a bit of a pain then."

He replied.

"The driver was very chatty, made the journey easier. And it was the same one coming back."

"Not too bad then. Hope the staff looked after you properly."

Geoff said, a hint of a question in his statement.

"Yes, a coach called Molly took me through my routine…she…"

Derby was about to say the girl had told her he was the boss, but she wanted to ask him about that when she saw him.

"She what?"

Geoff asked casually.

"She was very nice…said I was doing well."

She heard Geoff give a little laugh.

"I'll check you know."

He laughed again.

"Mr Stone, what exactly are you going to check?"

She tried a haughty voice, but ended up giggling instead. It was so easy and comfortable talking to him. Any conversation between her and David was dull and mostly consisted of monosyllabic words.

"I'll be checking you out little Derby."
He told her, his voice sexy and inviting. Derby felt her insides liquefy. Felt a deep throbbing between her legs and her heartbeat quicken. Her voice became husky as she replied.

"I can't wait for you to get back…to check me out."
"Me too."
He told her gently.

They spent nearly an hour on the phone talking about all sorts do things. Geoff told her the girls all looked set to pass, but two of the boys would definitely need to re-take the course. He explained that their teenage arrogance got in the way. They didn't listen very well, assuming they knew what to do before it had been fully explained. Because of that, they missed some vital instructions and so made silly mistakes. Derby had never thought about the seriousness of the training a gym coach needed until now. Again she realised how much of a bubble she had been living in.

Finally Geoff had to go. But the conversation ended with his promise to phone her as soon as he was back. They said goodnight, Derby longing to add the words 'I love you' but afraid of how he would react. She might just scare the bejoobers out of him and that she didn't want to do.

For the rest of the evening Derby pottered about the house. Nothing really needed doing except loading the dishwasher. She re-arranged a few things in the food cupboard and tidied the bottles under the sink. But she felt restless, the high talking to Geoff having dropped off, the low mood returning. She sat at her laptop and explored Skype, so she would know how to set it up for Bob and Fiona, and she spent a little time on Facebook. Nothing really occupied her though. Finally feeling completely fed up, Derby powered down the computer and stood up to make a cup of tea. She felt warm dampness between her legs and a dull throb in her lower abdomen. Knowing what was happening, she quickly headed for the bathroom. She felt a mild relief that her period had started. Even though Liam had used a condom and Geoff hadn't she didn't want that sort of complication.

Derby spent a restless night, dreams of Geoff intermingled with dreams of Liam. So much so, it was a relief to get up and prepare for work. Outside the sky was dull and cloudy, the temperature cool enough for a jacket, it looked like the summer was breaking, and this made Derby a little sad. Just as she arrived at the nursery a few drops of rain began to fall. By the time the children got there it had turned into a downpour. Toddlers dressed in a variety of waterproof coats and wellington boots huddled in the entrance. Parents and carers with dripping umbrellas, struggled to remove outdoor wear from wriggling children, whilst trying to hang up bags and backpacks. Finally, the little ones skipped, hopped and danced into the main nursery saying their goodbyes to the adults.

Wet days at the nursery were far more challenging than dry ones. Even though Derby had plans for organised activities for each day, it was still better when the children could go outside and run around. There was a small covered courtyard with sand and water tables, but the breeze had picked up so much that even using that space was out of the question. Still, all of Derby's staff were well trained and the nursery day went smoothly. Derby did hope though that the day would be fine for the inspection the week after.

Geoff called Derby during the middle of the afternoon to tell her he was on the way home. He told her he expected to be back by six and asked if she wanted to come over to his house. Excitedly she agreed, the day becoming sunnier despite the persistent rain. Angela noticed an uplift in her friend's countenance.

"Good news?"

She asked quietly.

"Oh yes. Geoff's on his way back."

She all but whispered back. Angela grinned and wiggled her eyebrows, making Derby laugh. But with a carpet full of very active children, Derby decided it wasn't the right place to discuss it.

As derby left the nursery for the evening she suddenly remembered her promise to Bob and Fiona. She didn't want to let the couple down, nor did she want to miss an evening with Geoff. She pulled out her phone and sent Geoff a message.

Just remembered I promised my neighbours some help with their Skype. But I really want to see you too. Can I come over still only later?xxx

She hit send and with her phone held tightly in her hand walked quickly towards home.

Derby was just unlocking the front door when her phone chirped. She slipped into the hallway dropping her bag on the floor. She opened the message at the same time as closing the door.

Little Derby I won't mind if it's midnight when you get here just as long as I see you. Xxxx

Derby leaned against the wall hugging her phone to her chest and feeling very happy.

After a hasty sandwich and a cup of tea, Derby headed next door. Bob opened the door to her and welcomed her in. He led her to the sitting room, where Fiona was waiting with the laptop open on a coffee table. It wasn't switched on. She looked up at Derby and smiled, then patted the sofa next to her. Derby sat down, the cushion giving a little underneath her, but still very squashy and comfortable. Bob had disappeared into the kitchen, but soon returned with a tray of tea and biscuits.

"Fiona made these this morning, especially for you."

He told Derby, as he lowered the tray onto the table and sat in an armchair. Derby smiled at the older woman.

"That was very nice of you."

Fiona handed Derby a china cup on a saucer and offered her the plate of biscuits. Derby took one and bit into it. It melted on her tongue, buttery and sweet.

"Mmmm…delicious."

She said. Fiona grinned, a little blush forming on her cheeks.

"Oh…they're nothing special."

She said, waving off the compliment, but Derby could tell she was pleased.

Despite their age, Bob and Fiona were fast learners. All they had needed was some instruction, and as they were both very keen, it didn't take Derby long to teach them how to navigate around the laptop and check their internet connection. She set up their Skype account and taught them how to send emails, so they could arrange with their son when to call.

"You know, you should have been a teacher."

Bob told her when they were finished. Derby shook her head, feeling a little sad.

"Didn't stay in school long enough to get the qualifications."

She said resignedly. Fiona patted her hand.

"Yes I remember you were very young when you came here."

Derby gave her a tiny smile, but didn't feel ready to share, or burden, as she thought of it, this lovely couple with her troubles. So instead she said.

"Well I love the nursery. I've never regretted choosing that career, and I've worked my way up to managing it, so it's all worked out well."

Bob looked at his wife and she looked back. Derby felt that between them they had silently agreed that they didn't fully believe her. She thought that maybe one day, she would tell them her life story. But in some ways, seeing the happiness between the old couple, she felt embarrassed about her own failed years, for that's how she now thought of the time as being.

To put an end to any further discussion, Derby made sure Bob and Fiona were happy with how to use the computer. Then she stood up, smiled, and told them she should be getting home. They both saw her to the door and waited until she entered her own front door.

Derby headed straight upstairs and stripped off her work clothes. She chose jeans and vest, and because it was still dull and cool outside, pulled on a chunky cardigan over the top. Glancing at the clock she saw it was seven thirty. She had spent quite a long time next door. Carefully but quickly, she applied light makeup and fluffed her hair. She blew a little kiss to her reflection, then giggled, she didn't think she looked too bad.

Before leaving the house, Derby sent Geoff a quick message to say she was on her way. She also asked him to text her his postcode, she wasn't sure she could find his house without using her SatNav. He replied immediately. Checking she had her house keys, her phone chirped again. She glanced at the screen and saw the message was from David. She felt a little twinge of disappointment, but opened it.

Be home tomorrow.

She took a deep breath and let it out on a long sigh, then began tapping a reply.

Ok

Then had to think about what else to say.

Glad you are better.

Left it at that and pressed send.

As she climbed into her car, she wondered what time David would come back. She had barely thought about him all week but couldn't, and wouldn't feel guilty. To her, his return was just going to complicate things, but she refused to let it get in the way of her new life. Somehow, she knew she would live her double life, and if he noticed anything different, well to hell with him, it would be his problem, not hers.

Feeling better about her decision she pulled away from the kerb. The rain had stopped, but dark clouds raced across the sky, collided, became bigger, then swirled apart, thinning. The wind was still strong, and Derby felt it buffeting her little car, her mind now fully on driving. Even though she had passed her driving test years ago, she had little experience driving. This was the most challenging time on the road ever, and she needed to concentrate. For the first time she wondered what winter driving would be like, and knew she would face it like everything else.

Finally, Derby pulled into Geoff's driveway and turned off the ignition. As she reached for the door, it was opened for her. Geoff leaned in and smiled, offering his hand to help her out. Derby's heart did a little flip and her pulse quickened. She took his hand and he pulled her out of the car, straight into his arms. For a second his smiling face hovered close to hers, then he pressed his lips to hers and kissed her. Derby wrapped her arms around his neck, and threaded her fingers through the hair at his nape. He pulled her closer and kissed her deeply, lingeringly, while leaves danced around their feet, lifted by the wind.

After what seemed like forever, Geoff leaned back but still held her tightly.

"Hello."

He said, a wide smile on his face. Derby grinned back.

"Hi."

She said, breathless from his kiss and his gorgeous face. Still holding her hand, he pulled her towards the porch way.

Stepping over his threshold felt like coming home. None of the oppression that existed in her own hallway was present. Despite the age of this house, it felt fresh and airy, whereas her own house seemed much older, tired and lacking in atmosphere. Her house had no love in its walls, Geoff's felt full of it. She was sure this old place had seen years of happiness.

Derby followed Geoff into the kitchen chatting comfortably on the way. She felt so completely at ease it was weird. How could someone she had known for such a short time, make her feel like she had known him for years.

Geoff flipped the switch on the kettle and held up a packet of tea. Derby nodded and watched him deftly spoon leaves into the pot. She didn't know anyone who made real tea, but found she liked it. In fact, so far she liked everything about the tall, muscular man before her.

The tea made, Geoff put the pot, cups and saucers onto a tray and led the way into the sitting room. Although he had shown her the room during her previous visit, her mind had been elsewhere, specifically on his body. Now she took in every feature. There was a beautifully tiled fireplace, which she imagined burning brightly on a cold winter day. The décor was pure Victorian, lovingly restored, reminding her of period dramas she had occasionally seen advertised on the television, but never watched.

Geoff put the tray on a table and Derby settled herself on a large soft sofa. He sat next to her and began pouring tea. Handing her the cup and saucer, he smiled.

"It's so good to see you."

He told her, his eyes bright. Derby sipped the hot drink, careful not to scald her tongue, and failing.

"Ouch."

She said, putting the drink down. Geoff put an arm around her and pulled her against his shoulder.

"It's hot."

He stated and she giggled.

"Let me make it better."

He said as he tilted her chin up to his face. Willingly, she let him take her lips, gently pushing his tongue into her open mouth. He tickled the tip of her tongue with his, then traced the inside of her mouth sensuously. Her insides flamed as she pulled his head nearer to intensify the kiss. To soon for her, the kiss ended.

"Better?"

He asked. Derby nodded.

"More than better."

"I've really missed you Derby."

Geoff told her sincerely. She opened her mouth to say the same, but he continued.

"More than I thought I would. More than anyone ever before."

Derby blushed, pleased with his words, but uncertain of how to reply. She knew how she felt, but didn't know how to communicate her feelings without scaring him off. He sensed her hesitation.

"I'm going too fast. I'm sorry."

He said. Derby put her hand on his chest.

"Oh no. I…it's not that at all. I just…oh hell…I missed you very much Geoff."

She finished hurriedly.

Geoff picked up her tea and handed it back to her. She took it, thinking how she had blown her chance to tell him how she felt. He sipped his own drink, looking at her over the top of his teacup.

"Did I scare you?"

He asked after a moment. Derby felt relief wash over her.

"No…no definitely not. I thought it was me, going to scare you off."

They laughed together, the easiness between them returned.

Geoff cooked them dinner, Derby declining his offer of wine. She wanted to be completely alert for the drive home. The rain had begun again, the wind lashing it against the windows. Derby watched the weather as she stood in the kitchen handing Geoff their dinner things which he loaded into the dishwasher. The trees and shrubs were almost bent double from the force of the wind. It really did look like the summer had broken.

"Penny for them."

Geoff said making her jump a little. She turned to him.

"Just thinking about the weather. I hope the summer isn't over."

Geoff laughed and tickled her side, making her giggle.

"Oh the weather. Forgotten me already have you?"
He joked. Derby moved into his arms, taking the lead for the first time.

"Never going to happen."
She whispered as she reached up on tiptoes and kissed him. He folded her into his arms and the kiss deepened. What seemed like minutes later, they moved apart slightly.

"I want you Derby."
Geoff stated.

Derby's face flushed hot at the same time her blood ran cold, her thoughts racing. Was this then all it was about? Was Geoff really only interested in her for the sex? She stepped back a little and looked into his eyes. His dark brows had come together ever so slightly, a puzzled expression on his face. Her heart beat hard against the walls of her chest. How would she handle this if she was right?

"Derby, what's wrong?"
Geoff asked, bending at the knees to look directly into her eyes. Derby lowered her lids, sighed and then opened them again.

"I…well…it's the time of the month…you know."
She mumbled shyly.

Geoff rubbed her shoulders gently and kissed her forehead. A soft chaste kiss that said more than words. He then pulled her to him and tucked her head into his shoulder. Derby felt tears begin and tried to hold in a sob, and failed. Geoff stroked her hair as she shuddered, tears flowing freely. For a while neither spoke. They just stood in the kitchen, Geoff giving her comfort as the rain and wind whipped about the old house.

Eventually Derby's tears subsided. She was reluctant to move and show her tear stained face, sure it would be blotchy and puffy. Geoff sensed her crying had slowed and leaned back to look at her. Derby covered her face with her hands.

"Oh don't. I must look a right mess. I'm sorry."
She gabbled all at once. Geoff laughed gently.

"It's fine little Derby. And you look cute."
Derby laughed, pressing her hands to his chest, damp from her tears.

"Never been called cute before."

She said as she rubbed her thumbs under her eyes and looked at them.

"My mascara has run."
She told him as she showed him the black smudges.

"Well you still look lovely. So…are you going to tell me what started it?"
He asked her in a soft voice.

Derby felt embarrassed and uncertain of what to say. She wanted to be truthful but didn't want to hurt him. Geoff sensed her hesitation and pulled her into a hug, patting her back, no sexual connotation in it. Derby buried her head in his chest, took a deep breath and mumbled her explanation.

"I had a horrible thought that maybe this is all just about sex."
There, she had said what she most feared. She scrunched her eyes shut, waiting for his reaction.

Geoff stopped patting and began rubbing her back soothing the tension in her shoulders. He dropped a little kiss on the top of her head and held her, comfortingly. Then he whispered close to her ear.

"Derby, this has never been about sex. I saw something in you the first time we met. Sex is easy to get, anywhere."
He stopped and Derby leaned back to look at him. There was a frown on his face, as though he was having difficulty saying what he wanted to say.

"Geoff?"
Geoff took Derby by the hand and led her to the kitchen table. They sat down and he took her hands in his. He cleared his throat and for the first time, Derby felt he looked nervous.

"Umm…women have sort of thrown themselves at me most of my life. But like I told you, since my divorce, there have only been two, until now that is. I mean, I like sex, of course I do, and years ago, before I got married, well…that was what it was about…But…you…Derby,…there's…something…much…mo…I …umm….it's….I'm falling for you."
He lowered his head as his cheeks turned bright red.

Derby knew she felt the same way. She had admitted it to Angela, but she also knew she wasn't ready to admit it to Geoff. She was certain she loved him, but everything felt so fragile still.

She had only just emerged from her old life, she wanted to experience more of the new. She thought life with Geoff could be wonderful and fulfilling, maybe enough, but just then she wasn't sure. Now she had to convey that to him without sounding like she didn't care.

"Geoff…"

He looked at her.

"You don't feel the same do you?"

He asked, misery in his voice, and Derby felt like the harshest bitch on the planet.

"Please Geoff."

She gave his hands a little shake.

"I have to sort out my feelings. All of this has happened so fast. I haven't experienced life like normal people."

She knew she was making a bad job of explaining.

"It's ok Derby, really, I'm pushing you. Please tell me though that I'm not just a stepping stone."

"Oh Geoff, no, no…never. It's just my head. I'm confused about my life, not about my feelings for you. Do you get that? I don't think I'm making much sense."

Geoff squeezed her hands.

"I'm sorry. I'm rushing. I shouldn't have said anything. Can we go back a few minutes please?"

Derby giggled.

"Not a chance Mr Stone. You can't take it back. Look I promise I will sort my head out soon and I promise…" her voice took on a serious note, "promise that you will be a part of my life."

He lifted her hands to his lips and kissed them.

The drive home was better than Derby thought. The rain still lashed the car, but the wind had dropped quite a lot. She pulled up outside her house and frowned when she saw lights on inside. She was sure she hadn't left them on, hadn't put them on. She locked the car and dashed to the front door, holding her cardigan over her head. Nervously she opened the door, but didn't go inside immediately. She didn't think burglars would turn on the lights, but she wasn't taking any chances.

Quietly she stepped into the hallway leaving the door wide open in case she needed to make a quick escape. She looked about for something to use as a weapon and saw her large umbrella. Just as she went to pick it up, she heard voices, recognising her husband's and his mother's. Derby groaned inwardly. He had come home early. She closed the front door and stepped into the sitting room.

David was stretched out on the sofa, a large fur throw she didn't recognise covering his legs. His mother sat in an armchair holding a mug. They both looked up as she walked in, Irene giving her a very disapproving look.

"Oh you're home then."

She said as though talking to a disobedient teenager. Derby felt her skin prickle with nerves.

"I've been....at a friend's house….from work."

She all but stammered. Irene sat up straight. David hadn't spoken at all.

"Well you should have been here like a proper wife."

Irene said haughtily.

"David said he'd be back tomorrow."

Derby answered back, finally finding her confidence. Irene looked at her son, then back at her daughter-in-law.

"Humph. Still not good enough."

Derby took a deep breath and decided it was not worth arguing. She turned to her husband and said.

"So are you all better now?"

She looked at the fur throw and thought it was far too over the top. It must belong to Irene, or David's sister. Even though it was wet and windy outside, the temperature hadn't dropped too much, it was still summer. David put on a face that demanded sympathy.

"Mostly. I'm pretty drained out though. Mum brought me back tonight so I could get some rest in my own bed. I'll probably just chill out here tomorrow, then go back to work Saturday."

"Yes, rest is what he needs."

Irene piped up, before Derby could speak. Derby lifted a hand in resignation.

"Well I'll be at work, so he'll get all the rest he needs. Now I've got some things to do…so…"

She indicated towards the front door. Irene bristled.

"I'd better get home then."

She stood and leaned over her son, kissing the cheek he offered.

"I'll call you tomorrow, see how you are."

Then as she stepped through the front door that Derby held open, she lowered her voice and said.

"You've developed an attitude I don't like my girl. Be warned, I'm keeping an eye on you."

Derby couldn't be bothered to answer, but made it clear she didn't like her comment by closing the door with a bang.

David was huddled on the sofa under the throw when she went back into the sitting room. He was flipping channels on the television. Derby stood for a moment watching him, comparing him to Geoff. She felt nothing for the man in front of her, and felt nothing coming back from him. Even when she and Geoff were not touching, there was electricity between them. She felt love emanating from him, enveloping her, making her feel warm and content. David was like a robot, emotionless and cold.

"Any chance of a cuppa?"

He asked without looking away from the TV. Derby sighed, nothing had changed.

After a very restless night, Derby climbed out of bed relieved the morning had arrived. David was as usual snoring loudly, and as she went into the bathroom, Derby almost believed the last week had been one long dream. She showered quickly and tiptoed back into the bedroom to get dressed. Her husband lay cocooned in the duvet, fast asleep and didn't stir.

A hasty cup of tea and slice of toast later, Derby quietly pulled the front door closed and let out a breath. The sun was shining again, the sky was clear and it was very warm. David being home depressed her, but once away from the house, she found a spring in her step, and a smile curving her lips.

Throughout the day Derby managed to tell Angela what Geoff had said. Managed to explain to her friend her own feelings, and was able to text Geoff. By the time the nursery day ended, Derby was in a much better frame of mind. She was determined not to let David's presence back in the house affect her, or interfere with her new life. She didn't know exactly how she was going to organise things, but she resolved to do it somehow.

David was lying on the sofa watching TV, the fur throw over him, when she got home from work. It was stuffy and smelled sweaty inside the house. None of the windows were open, and the back door was still locked. The dishwasher was still full of clean crockery but there were dirty plates and cups heaped in the sink. The kitchen showed no signs of any cooking, and Derby assumed David had eaten only food that he didn't have to prepare. This was confirmed by the open loaf of bread on the side, and empty crisp packets in the bin. Angrily, she threw open the window and back door, shoved the bread in the fridge and sprayed the sides with anti-bacterial fluid.

As she put the bottle back under the sink, David appeared behind her, stretching, yawning and rubbing his belly.

"What's for dinner. I'm starving. Thought you might have made me something proper to eat before you went to work."

Derby straightened and gripped the edge of the sink, taking deep breaths to calm her anger. It didn't work. Fury bubbled up from inside and spilled from her lips.

"For fuck sake David. You're forty one years old. Can't you get yourself something to eat!"

David stood stock still and Derby suddenly felt like laughing. He looked like he had suddenly been frozen, his mouth wide from another yawn, his hands flat on his belly. Then he came back to life.

"There's no need for that language."

He said moodily. Derby threw her hands in the air in despair.

"Fine, I'll get you some dinner."

She bit out. David simply turned and headed back to the sitting room, throwing over his shoulder.

"Sausage and chips."

Muttering oaths under her breath, Derby prepared sausage and chips and added frozen peas. She had no appetite herself. When the meal was ready she plonked it onto a tray and stomped into the lounge.

"Sit up!"

She all but barked out at David. He was too engrossed in some sport on the television to notice the abruptness in her voice as he swung his feet to the floor. Derby handed him the tray, grabbed her laptop and headed back to the kitchen.

Derby booted up the computer and checked emails and Facebook. There was nothing very interesting in either of them, but it helped calm her temper. Then she made a sandwich and went out to the patio. Thankfully, the evening was warm. She nibbled her sandwich and sent Geoff a message saying she missed him. When he didn't reply she began to worry. Eventually she heard back from him and sighed with relief. He had been in the gym, coaching and couldn't message her back. She then remembered she hadn't asked him the 'boss' thing, but still didn't want to bring it up in a text.

Several messages later, some very flirtatious, Derby decided it was time for bed. She had a very busy day ahead of her and wanted to be as fresh as possible. She wasn't sure she would be. David's return had unsettled her more than she had anticipated. His presence in the bed, his snoring, had disturbed her far more than usual. She had spent most of the night wishing she was tucked up close to Geoff.

When Derby went through to the sitting room, she found it empty, the TV still on. She went quietly upstairs, in case David was in the bathroom, but found him stretched out in bed. Sighing, she returned to the lounge and went through the normal routine of switching off and locking up. Back in the bedroom she made sure her alarm was on, and settled down for what she hoped would be a good night's sleep.

Derby had a better night than she expected. She slept mostly through, just a couple of dreams waking her. After the normal routine with David, she smiled with joy when he left, closing the door behind him. Derby flew around the house, vacuuming and dusting, setting the dishwasher and washing machine and finally locking the front door as she headed for her car. She lowered the roof and gave the accelerator an extra push as she revved the engine, delighting in its sound. Then she pulled away from the kerb and headed for the city.

Derby stood on the balcony of the flat watching the shops open at the side of the marina. The boats bobbed on the water, a few owners on board. A waft of bacon drifted up and she realised she was hungry, but there was nothing in the flat. Making a quick decision, she left the flat and headed to the main entrance. The young security officer was on duty. He wasn't as friendly as the older man, just nodding. However, plucking up a bit of courage, she smiled in a friendly way.

"Hi. I'm expecting a furniture delivery but don't have a specific time. Would you mind keeping an eye out if I just pop to the café?" adding "I'll get take out."

The security officer looked down at her. He was taller than Geoff. A tiny smile broke his stern expression.

"No problem. Do you want me to show them up if they get here before you get back?"

Derby accepted his offer, handing over her key.

Derby set off at a quick pace around the marina to the opposite side. The sun was shining brightly, tiny diamonds of light bouncing off the water. A few boat owners sat on their decks, waved and called goodmorning. She greeted them back and felt she was in another world.

Inside the first café she reached, she ordered a bacon roll and black coffee. The aromas from the small kitchen were wonderful she thought, maybe more intense because of the outdoor atmosphere around her. She imagined camping might have the same effect, and thought about asking Geoff, maybe they could arrange a trip together.

The furniture hadn't arrived when she returned. She thanked the security officer, who now told her his name was Alfie, and who looked longingly at her bacon roll. Back in the flat, she again stood on the balcony, relishing her breakfast. She heard a shout from below and saw the two men from before, waving at her from their boat. She laughed and waved back.

"Is it going?"

She asked. One of the men held up crossed fingers.

"Just about to find out."

"Good luck."

She called back. Then watched as the other man turned something and the engine chugged to life. At first it miss fired, but a few revs later it smoothed out and ran evenly.

"Well done."

Derby called. Both men grinned up at her, obviously pleased with their success.

Just then the internal phone buzzed indicating she had a visitor. She went inside and lifted it, her insides wobbly with excitement. Alfie was on the other end, the furniture men were waiting. She asked him to send them up and then went to wait in the hallway.

Soon after, Derby stood and gazed around her lounge. The sofas and coffee table were exactly where she wanted them, and made the flat look just how she imagined. She went into the bedroom and with a little squeal of excitement, flung herself onto the bed. She lay face down, and giggling, beat her closed fists and feet against the mattress.

Chapter 14

Leather And Lace

Reluctant to leave, but knowing it was necessary, Derby locked up her apartment. Even though she had some furniture, there were still many things she needed. So she headed into the city on a shopping spree.

After parking the car in a multi-story close to the shopping centre, she took out her phone and tapped a message to Geoff.

Are you free some time today. I have a surprise for you. Xxx

She didn't expect to get a reply immediately, and was stepping out of the car when her phone chirped.

At the gym this morning but will be finished by twelve. Do you want to meet up? Xxx

Derby hugged the phone to her chest, then did some quick time calculations.

Actually I was thinking I would pick you up. How about four? Xxx

Geoff messaged her straight back.

Sounds exciting I'll be ready. Xxx

With a lightness to her step, Derby descended the stairs from the car park to the shops below. It was busy, people bustling about, but she felt excitement rather than annoyance as she dodged other shoppers.

By two o'clock, she had made several trips back to her car to store her purchases. She had bought so many things, it was impossible to carry them about. As she sat in a coffee shop eating a Panini and drinking a cool fruit juice, she reflected on what she had bought. She had shopped by room, starting with the kitchen and dining area. Stainless steel saucepans, which she planned to hang on hooks, shiny cutlery and cooking utensils were stashed in the boot of the car. Placemats, tablecloths, tea towels and crockery were stacked on top. In the passenger foot well, bags of towels, embroidered bed sets, sheets and pillows filled the space. She knew she had more to get, but at least had all of the necessary items.

Back at the flat, Derby took two trips to unload the car. She placed everything in its respective room and checked the time. It was nearly three thirty, not enough time to go to the supermarket. She would just have to go with Geoff and buy essentials. She giggled to herself, imagining the look on his face, when she told him where they were going, imagined his comment about the supermarket being the surprise.

At two minutes to four, after a quick detour home to put the washing in the tumble dryer, Derby pulled into Geoff's driveway. He was at the door waiting for her. She jumped out of the car and met him on the steps, leaping into his open arms. They kissed and held one another for a long time.

"You look happy."
Geoff said, when they moved apart.

"I am. It's been a great day so far."
Geoff gave her a quizzical look.

"What have you been up to little Derby?"
He asked with a grin.

"Wait and see."
She told him, giving nothing away.

"One thing though. David's back home. Well he's gone into work today. But I'm not going home tonight. I'll think something up. He won't be happy, will have to fend for himself."
Geoff squeezed her hand.

"I'm making things difficult for you."
He stated. Derby started shaking her head right away.

"No, no, you're not. Don't ever think that. This is not about you and me. It's about how I want my life to be now after all the years I've wasted. I've just got to work out the best way to deal with it."
Geoff smiled.

"Ok."
Then swinging her hand.

"What's this surprise?"
Derby giggled as she thought about his reaction to the supermarket.

"Come with me."

She said, tugging him towards her car.

"Got to lock up first."

He said, laughing at her impatience. So Derby waited in the car whilst he went back inside. A minute later, he emerged, stuffing his wallet in his pocket and jangling his keys. He slid into the passenger seat, buckled his seatbelt and turned to face her.

"Ready."

The supermarket car park was jammed but Derby found a space and pulled in. She glanced at Geoff and giggled at the surprised look on his face.

"This is my surprise?"

He asked, humour in his voice.

"For now."

Then unable to hold back her laughter she continued.

"You should see your face."

He gave her a little poke in the side.

"You are a devil. What is going on?"

Grabbing his fingers she replied.

"Wait and find out. But we have to get supplies first."

On the way into the shop, Geoff tried to coax more information from her. However, Derby refused to be drawn. He dropped 'picnic' and 'beach' into the conversation, but she avoided confirming or denying anything. In the end he gave up as he saw her filling the trolley with milk, bread, a selection of food for the fridge and freezer, fruit, vegetables, toiletries and wine. At the check out he threw in one last comment.

"Just doing your weekly shop then."

She laughed as she packed the goods.

"Mmhmm…something like that."

Was her reply, and heard him sigh.

With the shopping loaded into the boot, they settled back in the car. The roof was down, the hot sun beating on their faces. Derby drove out of the car park, now sure of the route to the flat. Feeling relaxed and confident she headed towards the city, her hair blowing about her, Geoff sitting by her side.

Alfie was still on duty when Derby led Geoff into the building. He gave them a smile and an afternoon greeting, but his expression was all professional. Once inside the lift Geoff turned to Derby.

"Going to tell me now?"

She giggled and shook her head.

"Told you. Wait and see."

Derby unlocked the door to her 'apartment' and all but bounced into the hallway. Shedding her sandals, she turned on the balls of her feet beckoning Geoff. He stepped out of his shoes too, and without a word, followed her through to the lounge. Derby unlocked the patio doors and stood back allowing him to take in the scene.

"Welcome to my place."

She said, excitement evident in her voice. Geoff stepped out onto the balcony and she joined him. He appeared to have lost his voice, and for a moment Derby was worried.

"Is...is...something wrong?"

She asked him uncertainly. Geoff pulled her too him.

"Derby, angel, nothing is wrong. It's just...this is a complete surprise. Not at all what I was expecting."

Derby sighed with relief.

"Phew. Thought I'd made the biggest mistake ever just then."

Geoff hugged her.

"When did you get it?"

He asked. Derby paused, suddenly aware of how fast everything had happened. She looked up into his deep blue eyes, her own shining, an immense and almost overwhelming feeling of love for the man before her.

"Just a week ago, today. I can't believe it was only last Saturday that I decided to get a place of my own."

"Why don't we get all your shopping in from the car, then you can tell me all about it."

Shortly after, they sat on the balcony, a bottle of wine open in front of them. Derby related her story of how and why she had decided to rent the flat. Geoff listened attentively, letting her explain all of the details without comment. When she finished, he leaned back in his chair sipping from his glass.

"You are an amazing woman Derby."

He told her. She gave a self deprecating laugh.

"No I'm not. I'm stupid for having put up with all that I have for so long."

Geoff reached out and took her hand.

"No Derby you are not. Other women in your position would just go on putting up with it. You realised you could change your life, and took steps independently to do it. That makes you a very strong woman."

He squeezed her hand encouragingly. She took the praise without comment but still felt foolish for the wasted years.

Noises from the marina drifted up to them as they sat and chatted about nothing in particular. Derby had already given him a tour of the flat, his eyes widening when she showed him the bedroom. She was just disappointed knowing they would have to wait a few days to make full use of it. Now though, they sat, completely comfortable with one another's company. So much so, it felt to Derby like she had known Geoff for years.

They cooked dinner together, Derby conscious of the fact that she hadn't used the cooker before, and that she had only ever cooked for David. Her husband wasn't very ambitious about food, so with him she stuck to plain meat and vegetables, most of which he didn't like, so usually consisted of carrots and peas. But she herself had always wanted to be more adventurous, just never had. By the time she got home from work, it was always too much bother to cook two different meals. Now with Geoff by her side, they put together salmon steaks, rice and salad.

Derby laid the dining table with one of her new cloths, set placemats and coasters, cutlery and wine glasses. She had forgotten candles, but decided that as it was still light outside, it didn't matter too much. She told Geoff to open more wine whilst she went and freshened up. In the en-suite bathroom, she quickly applied light makeup, then in the bedroom, pulled one of her new dresses from the wardrobe. She had brought some of her new clothes with her especially for the occasion.

Back in the dining area, Geoff was already seated. He stood up as she walked over to him. Derby glowed with pleasure at his gentlemanliness, so unlike David who waited for his food to be put in front of him, and didn't even thank her for it. Geoff placed his hands on her shoulders, and gave her a light kiss on the lips. Then together, they brought the food to the table and ate, talking and enjoying their time together.

After dinner they cleared away together, and then Geoff suggested a stroll along the marina. Derby loved the idea. She had so far only briefly been down there. Now as the light began to fade they walked hand in hand to the opposite side of the flat. The shops were all closed, but there was a small bar with tables outside which Derby hadn't noticed before. They ordered their drinks and then went out to one of the tables overlooking the marina. The evening was very warm and still. Lights from some of the boats reflected off the gently lapping water, and they heard the occasional ding of a bell from the mast of one of the yachts. It was the most romantic scene Derby had ever experienced.

Time was irrelevant as Derby relaxed and enjoyed everything around her. A group at a nearby table laughed and clinked glasses, obviously celebrating something. An older couple sat close, his arm around her shoulders, sipping their drinks without speaking, comfortable in their silence. Geoff slid his hand across the table and took hers, rubbing his thumb across her palm. Soft music floated out from the bar creating a surreal atmosphere and making Derby feel truly alive.

"Derby, did you let David know you won't be home?"

Derby bit her lip.

"Damn."

She said softly.

"I forgot. Better text him now."

She took her phone and opened messages.

David. Out with a friend. Won't be home.

She tapped send before she could change what she had written, knowing the message was abrupt and not caring. She laid the phone next to her and smiled at Geoff.

"All done."

Geoff continued stroking her hand.

"Will he be mad?"

He asked in a low voice. Derby shrugged.

"Really don't care. I'm sick of running around after him, getting disapproving looks from his mummy."

Geoff laughed, deep and sexy. Just then Derby's phone chirped. Pressing her lips together, she raised it and read the message.

Fine I'm still at work.

She offered the phone to Geoff so he could read it too. His brows came together.

"Doesn't seem too concerned does he?"

He said. Derby shrugged again.

"You know. I think he's about as interested in our marriage as I am."

Geoff handed back the phone but didn't comment. The phone bleeped startling Derby. The text alert wasn't one of the personal ones, so she had no idea who was messaging her. She opened the message, anger crossing her face.

To Derby

David has told me you are not coming home tonight. How dare you. You are, unfortunately, his wife. You should be at home waiting for him. And where are you anyway?

Irene

Geoff leaned forward.

"Derby what is it?"

Derby felt like throwing the phone, but it was too precious to her to do that. So she plonked it down on the table instead. She picked up her drink and took a large swallow.

"Bloody interfering old cow."

She mumbled, so Geoff could only just hear her, but the other tables couldn't.

"His mother."

He stated, knowingly. Derby nodded, still angry but not wanting to display it publicly.

"I didn't even know she had a mobile phone."

She said, indignation in her voice. Geoff leaned back and laughed, instantly lightening her mood. She took another mouthful from her glass and then laughed with him.

"So what did she say?"

He asked, humour in his voice. Derby re-opened the message and handed it to him to read.

"Mmmm, she's not happy."

"What makes me so bloody furious, is that he went straight and told her. I mean, he's forty one years old, and he still has to run to mummy when bad Derby upsets him."

"What are you going to do?"

Geoff asked her in a more serious tone. Derby took her phone back and began tapping a reply. After she had sent it, she showed Geoff who gave a little whistle.

"No holding you back is there."

"It's about time I told her to mind her own business. And that her little boy should bloody well grow up."
Derby emptied her glass, then giggled. Geoff raised an eyebrow questioningly.

"I can imagine him sitting in his office, the manager of a big store, whining to mummy that his wife isn't going to be at home to cook his dinner."
Geoff nodded.

"Bit of an image I must say."

"Bet she trots round to our house to feed, bathe and tuck him in."
Derby added.

"Urgh, that sounds wrong on so many levels."
Geoff exclaimed. She grinned.

"It does doesn't it. Well I don't give a damn. They are not going to ruin my perfectly good evening."
Her phone bleeped again. This time the message was blunt, no formal 'To Derby' included.

Everything about my son is my business. What I do not like is your attitude. In fact I really don't like you. He should never have married you. You trapped him and ruined his life. He could be with a nice woman now and I could have grandchildren.

The last part of the message got to her, and tears slid from her eyes and down her cheeks. Geoff was by her side in an instant. He took her hands and pulled her to her feet, guiding her away from the bar towards a quiet part of the marina. There he wrapped her in his arms and let her cry, without questions.

Once the tears had subsided, Derby rubbed her face with her hands, knowing she would have black streaks of mascara on her cheeks. With a deep breath she relayed the contents of the message, and in the light from the lamps surrounding the walkways of the marina, saw anger cross Geoff's face. She put her hands on his shoulders and felt the tension in his muscles.

"It's alright Geoff. I shouldn't let her get to me. Especially when I know it's not my fault we have no children. To be honest, as much as I would loved to have had a baby, I'm actually glad it never happened. David's just too selfish, too much a mummy's boy to be a father, and she would have probably taken over anyway. I wouldn't have had any say in its upbringing, and I definitely wouldn't be here with you now."

The light from one of the street lamps edging the marina cast a soft glow across her face, making the tears glisten on her cheeks. Geoff cupped her face in his hands and smoothed away the remaining drops with his thumbs. He looked into her eyes.

"But you would have liked to be a mother?"
He asked in a low voice.

"Yes."
She whispered back.

Geoff tilted her face up and pressed a gentle kiss to her lips. She closed her eyes, taking comfort from his touch. Nothing else mattered, not David, not Irene, her marriage, or the pain she felt from the text message. Geoff was with her, holding her, and she would grab every moment she could, for she had no idea how long it would last.

Geoff put his arm around Derby's shoulder and led her to the flat side of the marina. As they neared the entrance, Derby veered off towards the end of the walkway where the marina exited to the river. She leaned her elbows on the railing and gazed at the water and the fields beyond. Geoff stood behind her, his arms linked across her waist, his face resting on her shoulder.

"I'm sorry for the tears, I'm rather emotional at the moment. Time of the month thing."
She whispered. Geoff squeezed her gently.

"Don't be sorry little Derby. I have very big shoulders and they're yours to cry on anytime you want. Besides, I think you have very good reason to be upset. That message was brutal, evil. You don't deserve that."

Derby covered his hands with her own, holding her against him. She knew he was right. She also knew that she loved him very much, but was still afraid to voice it. She had never thought about love at first sight, let alone believed it could happen. Her lonely childhood, and even lonelier adulthood had shrouded her life, entombed her will and emotions. She had existed, day after day, on the outside edge of a world that was full of people living, loving and laughing. Now, here, with Geoff, listening to the water below, flowing to the sea, she felt all of those years of nothing flowing away too, and behind, pushing them out, all of her new found feelings.

Back in the flat Derby opened the patio doors in the lounge and the bedroom, giving the night access inside. She stepped out onto the balcony and Geoff followed. They stood side by side looking across the marina, a warm breeze wafting around them. It was peaceful, beautiful, and Derby felt that she could stay there forever. Geoff covered her hand with his. She turned to him and smiled.

"It's getting late. We should go to bed."

They moved together, no need for words, the new bed inviting them. The breeze gently lifted and dropped the new voiles Derby had hung earlier as they slowly undressed one another. Without having to tell him, Geoff made no attempt at removing her undies, understanding her need to keep them on. He however, stood before her, fully naked, his tanned body gleaming from the clear starlit sky outside, hard and muscular. She ran her hands up his chest and over his taut shoulders. He closed his eyes and a small groan escaped his lips. Very gently he pushed her to the bed, settling himself alongside her. She pressed close to him and felt his erection. She wriggled to get closer, wanting him, but knowing it wasn't practical. But she didn't want to deny him release.

Derby let her hands trail down his back, her nails digging into his skin. She heard him gasp, so knowing she was giving him pleasure, she moved one hand to the front. She cupped his balls and squeezed gently. He pushed towards her and took her lips in his, his tongue probing hers as his hands massaged her hard nipples. Encouraged by his arousal, she stroked the full length of his penis, then closed her hand around him and slowly slid it up and down. He took one hand from her breasts and brushed his fingers on the inside of her legs, moving closer to the juncture of her thighs and coming to rest against the soft material of her panties.

Derby pushed her pelvis towards his hand, inviting him to stroke and massage her through the cloth, which he did, pressing his thumb and rotating it around her clitoris. She gripped him more tightly, and slid her hand more quickly, hearing his breath quicken.

His pelvis moved in time with her hand and so did hers. She felt the tension inside her build, felt Geoff become rigid. His kiss deepened, and she took his tongue as her orgasm pounded through her, and his warm fluid spilled into her palm.

For a moment time seemed suspended, both breathing fast, hearts beating together. As each came out of their orgasm, they relaxed, folded in each other's arms.

"That was amazing. Was it alright for you?"
Geoff whispered in her ear.

"Mmmm, perfect."
She said drowsily. She heard him laugh tenderly.

"Sleep little Derby."

Derby awoke spooned up against Geoff, his arm resting across her. Sunshine and warmth filled the room through the open patio doors, sounds from the marina floating up. As gently as she could, she slid from the bed and headed for the bathroom. After a quick shower, she stepped back into the bedroom, a towel wrapped around her. Geoff was awake. He held out a hand and she went to him, perching on the edge of the bed.

"You should have woken me."
He told her, kissing her lightly.

"You looked so peaceful, I didn't want to disturb you."
She said, kissing him back.

"You could never disturb me little Derby."
He told her sincerely. A huge smile spread across her face.

"Thank you Geoff. You make me feel…wanted."
A twinkle came into his eyes.

"Oh I want you."
He said. She giggled and stood up.

"Mr Stone!"
He reached for her, but she dodged him, laughing.

"Breakfast. So go and get showered."
She said in a mock stern voice. He gave a dramatic sigh and threw back the duvet.

"Ok, if I must."

Derby had cooked scrambled eggs and toast, and made a pot of tea by the time Geoff emerged from the shower. He came into the kitchen just in jeans, his hair tousled from drying it with a towel, his chest tanned and burly. He planted a kiss on her lips as she placed the food and tea on the table. Over breakfast they chatted and Geoff suggested going to the beach for the day. Derby was excited at the prospect and pleased he had thought of it, for she had intended to ask him sometime. She felt a little guilty about spending another day enjoying herself, especially with the impending inspection. But she told herself the nursery was well organised and everything was in place. She didn't really have to worry.

"I have to be at the gym for six tonight."
Geoff said, breaking into her thoughts.
"Oh, sorry, was miles away. That's fine."
Then before she lost her nerve.
"Molly said you're the boss."
Geoff looked at her.
"Is that your way of asking me?"
She lowered her eyelashes and nodded shyly.
"Derby, look at me please."
She did and was happy to see him smiling. She had wondered that he might be cross.
"I am the boss, though I don't really like that word."
He hesitated for a moment.
"Actually, I own the gym."
Derby gasped with surprise.
"You…you…own it!"
Geoff reached across the table and took her hand.
"Hey, I'm not some secret billionaire."
Derby giggled nervously.
"What are you then, millionaire?"
She asked. He rubbed her hand with his thumb.
"Let's go to the beach and I'll tell you all about it."
Derby was a little frustrated as she took two large towels from the cupboard in the bathroom. Partly because she wanted to know right then what Geoff meant, and partly because she realised her new wardrobe did not consist of beachwear. She had a swimsuit at home, but that was for the gym. What she wanted then was a cute frilly bikini. It hadn't occurred to her to buy one when she had shopped. She had never before had a use for one.

Her holidays were always separate from David's, and she spent them at home. David did the same with extra visits to his mother and sister included. Sighing, she took the towels back to the kitchen where Geoff was waiting. He had checked the footpath on his phone and told her it would take about fifteen minutes to walk to the beach. He saw her expression and was immediately concerned.

"What's wrong?"

He asked. She laid the towels on the counter.

"I don't have a bikini."

She told him sulkily. He took her shoulders and led her onto the balcony. Standing behind her, he pointed across the marina.

"See that shop there, the one with the blue and white flag. That's an outdoor shop. They'll have a bikini, and for me a backpack to carry our stuff to the beach. We can get some cold drinks from one of the other shops. Ok?"

Forty five minutes later, they were sitting on their towels on soft white sand. Derby was surprised at how quiet the beach was given that it was the start of peak season. Geoff told her it was because this part of the coastline had limited access, so families tended to go to the beaches further up where there were public car parks, and the beaches were monitored. Derby was relieved this was so, the peace was very welcome. Also it had given her a chance to change into her new turquoise bikini, without having to attempt doing it with a towel wrapped around her. The low whistle Geoff had given her once she had donned it brought a blush to her face, and fire between her thighs. It crossed her mind that everything he did and said made her want to jump on him and have sex. To take her mind off his body, she brought up the subject of the gym.

"So Mr Hotshot Businessman. Tell me all."

Geoff burst out laughing. He reached into the new backpack and pulled out a can of coke, pulled the tab and handed it to her. She sipped and waited patiently whilst he opened another for himself.

"I'm an only child too."

He began. Derby was surprised, expecting something completely different. But she let him continue without comment.

"My mother brought me up with the help of her mother. I've never met my father and even now, mum has no idea where he is. He was a sales rep, and they met when he turned up at the vet where she worked as a nurse, with samples for the surgery. They began dating and he fed her a load of bull about being in love and wanting to settle down. Anyway, she was on the pill, but it didn't work. When he found out she was pregnant he went nuts. That's when it came out he was married. He'd told her he lived in London, but that was a lie too. Turns out he lived in Norwich, and not only had a wife, but two kids as well."

Geoff paused and took a drink from his can, gazing out at the sea. Derby could tell from his far away expression that the memories hurt. Sipping her own drink, she waited silently for him to continue with the story.

"So not only do I have a father somewhere that I don't know, I also have two siblings that I don't know. I don't care, never have. My childhood was wonderful. Nan helped mum get over the shock and hurt. Then mum moved back home, and when I was born, Nan looked after me whilst mum went back to work part-time. Gramps was still alive then too, and though he was disappointed in mum getting pregnant, he put it aside and helped as much as he could."

Geoff stopped speaking and a grin spread across his face. Derby sipped her coke and pinged the tab on the can, waiting for him to continue. He gave a little laugh, remembering something from his past.

"Gramps was a real card. He had a shed, said it was his escape pod from the girls. He would go in there and try all these craft things. He wasn't very good at any of them. But Nan and mum would lovingly accept his gifts. He made me a toy train once, only it was so wonky it barely stood up. But that train was one of my favourite toys, I still have it in the attic.."

His voice had gone wistful as he paused in his memories, and Derby felt a lump in her throat. Their childhoods couldn't have been more different. She sifted sand between her fingers as she wished hers had been more like Geoff's. But she refused to allow her own miserable memories to spoil his happy ones.

"Go on."

She said softly, bringing him back to her. He tilted his can and emptied it, then tucked it into the backpack.

"Although Gramps wasn't good at arts and crafts, he was very astute with the finances. He invested wisely and so when he died he left Gran and mum very secure, and me of course. Well to cut a long story short, when Gran passed away everything was divided between mum and me. Gramps' shares had grown well, are still doing well. So I bought the gym. It wasn't much then, but I built it to what it is now, and I'm pleased to say it's making me a profit. And then I bought the house."

Geoff looked at Derby and she could see the pride shining from his eyes.

"The divorce, coming out of the Navy...I couldn't see where my life was going. I drifted for a bit doing various jobs. That's when I did the charity photos. The organisers made calendars, mugs and other stuff."

He blushed and Derby found it delightful.

"Have you got any left?"

She teased. He laughed.

"Noooo... heaven forbid...I didn't keep any of it."

Derby snapped her fingers.

"Damn..."

She said, then giggled. Geoff tickled her lightly and dropped a kiss on her lips. She longed to pull his head towards her and turn the kiss into something more, but she was keen to hear the rest of his story. So instead, she moved back and with a smile said.

"As much as I would very much like more of your kisses, I really want to hear more about you."

Geoff barked out a laugh and threw himself back onto his towel. He shielded his eyes with his hand and looked up at her. She leaned over blocking the light, so he could look into her face.

"Ok...I give in."

He raised himself onto an elbow, and she settled herself into the same position facing him.

"Mum saw I was heading nowhere. She asked me to come home, help her look after Gran. I was relieved actually, home was solid, somewhere to get a grip on my life. Gran had a heart condition, so there was no question really. Once home I happened to be watching a television programme about fitness, and that's when I decided to train as a gym coach. I got a job at a place near home and worked my way up to management.

Then three years ago, Gran had another heart attack and didn't come out of it. Mum and me were devastated but we propped each other up. She also had Ken, a guy she'd been seeing for quite some time. He was really great, and when they decided to go on a three month holiday, I decided it was time to move my own life along. That's when I found the gym and then the house. And the rest, my sweet little Derby as they say, is history."

A history that was full of life, Derby thought as she stared at the beautiful hunk by her side. Yes there had been highs and lows, pain and disruption. But at least Geoff's life had been a combination of many things. Hers had been one long single road of monotony, a straight direction, with no twists and turns, no choices beyond what to make for dinner. She placed a hand on his chest, and stroked the hair that stood out from his tan.

"Unlike my life, yours has been an adventure."
She whispered. He covered her hand with his.

"Your adventure has just begun."

He pulled her on top of him and kissed her deeply. Fire spread through her body in an instant, and thankful that the beach was so quiet, she pressed hard against the ridge she felt beneath her. She heard him groan as he gripped her buttocks tight. Hoping no one was watching, Derby wriggled into him, desperate to get as close as possible. He massaged her bottom, squeezing to increase the closeness. Derby broke from the kiss, only long enough to glance around and see if anyone was nearby. The beach was empty, so she took back his lips and slid herself up and down his body. He rubbed and pressed against her. They came together, Derby holding in the squeal that threatened to erupt from her lips, Geoff exhaling as he gripped her tight.

He rolled them onto their sides and held her. The sun was hot on their skin, the sand sticking to their lotioned bodies. He dropped tiny kisses on her face, neck and shoulders, as their breathing and heartbeats slowed to normal. Then he pushed her hair from her face and smiled lovingly into her eyes.

"Did you enjoy that?"
He asked. She nodded.

"Oh yes."
"Want to go in the sea?"
"Definitely."

She replied eagerly. Geoff stood up and pulled her to her feet. The beach was still deserted and Derby felt like it was there just for them.

The sea was cold and made her gasp as she tentatively stepped in. Geoff had dived straight into the waves, emerging like Poseidon, powerful and handsome, water streaming from his bronze body.

"It's better if you duck under right away."
He told her, shaking water from his face and hair. She shook her head, holding her arms high, taking one tiny step at a time.

"No, it's so cold."
Geoff roared with laughter and splashed her. She screamed and laughed at the same time, scooped up two handfuls of water and threw it at him.

"Right, you're in trouble for that."
He said playfully.

Derby knew what was coming, tried to turn and run, but he was too quick. He scooped her up in is arms and dunked her in the sea. She clung to his neck, gasping at the cold water. He held onto her and gently swayed her about in the waves. To her relief, the water quickly felt a lot warmer as her body acclimatised to the change in temperature. Before long she was happily swimming along beside him, enjoying the sea for the first time in her forty year life.

Later Derby drove into Geoff's driveway to drop him off. Just as she switched off the engine her phone chirped. She took it from her bag frowning at the unknown number.

"David's mother, sister?"
Geoff queried. Derby shook her head and opened the message.

Hi Derby, it's Caroline the estate agent. Just wondering if you wanted to meet up for drink this evening.
Derby sighed with relief. She had wondered the same as Geoff. She offered the phone to him and he read the message.

"Does that mean back in the city?"
He asked. She nodded.

"You should have made me follow you in my car, instead of you having to drive back here."
He said considerately.

"No, no it's fine, honest. I wanted to take you to the flat. I should say no and go home, but I don't want to. I don't have many friends and Caroline seems very nice. So, to hell with David and his family, I'm going for a drink in the city."
She gripped the steering wheel hard.

"Good for you. But please will you text me where you are and when you get home?"
Derby knew he didn't ask in a possessive way, but out of genuine concern for her safety and wellbeing. She agreed and they kissed, long and lovingly, then he hopped out of the car and watched her pull out into the road.

Derby waited until she got back to the flat, deciding to call Caroline instead of texting. She thought it would be a lot easier to make the arrangements that way. Caroline suggested getting a taxi, so they could both have a drink without worrying about driving, and gave her the name of the pub she wanted to meet Derby at.

At eight o'clock, the taxi pulled to the side of the road outside The Admiral. She saw Caroline waiting for her near the entrance and the two women briefly embraced in greeting. Before entering Derby tapped out a quick message to Geoff telling him where she was, as she promised. Inside, the pub was busy and noisy, but they managed to find a space at the bar and order drinks. Caroline then led them to the back of the pub where a door opened onto a small courtyard garden. It was cooler than inside. There were no free tables, but other patrons were perched on the stone wall surrounding a water feature, and there was just enough space for them to squeeze on too.

They chatted as they drank, Caroline asking about the flat, Derby happily describing the things she had bought. Three drinks later, Derby knew Caroline was forty five, divorced and for the last two months had been single. She had two sons, one travelling around Australia, the other repping for a holiday company in Spain.

The reason for her recent status was fifty one year old 'Fuck Head Frank', as she called him. They had had a four year relationship, which Caroline thought was monogamous, until she found out that he had been sleeping with both his ex-wife and his secretary at the same time, neither of which knew about the other, but which she rectified. Laughing and sipping her fourth vodka and coke, Caroline explained how she had arranged a lunch which would ensure they all met up.

"They all turned up at the restaurant, me waiting. So I held up my glass of cabernet and said, 'Fuck Head here has been fucking us all. Now I think he's fucked.' You should have seen their faces. I mean the ex-wife knew about me and probably thought she was getting one over on me, even though I had nothing to do with their split. I didn't even know him when that happened. Same thing for the secretary, but well their faces were a picture, not knowing about each other. And Fuck Head, he went white as a sheet. Anyway, I got up and left, leaving them to argue it out. He turned up at my door later, begging me to forgive him. I didn't."

Caroline drained her glass and sat back, a reminiscent smile on her face. Derby didn't quite know what to say. Then the two women looked at each other and burst out laughing, Derby deciding that her first judgement of Caroline was correct, she was right to like her.

Derby felt encouraged by Caroline's honesty and decided to give her an edited version of her life. She briefly explained about her marriage and David's lack of interest, but was hesitant to talk about Geoff, worrying that Caroline would object to her infidelity, given her recent experience. However, Caroline seemed to sense Derby was holding back.

"You've met someone else?"
She asked, gently covering one of Derby's hands with her own.

"Yes, I was a bit reluctant to say, you know, because of what you've been through."
Derby told her. Caroline smiled.

"It's fine Derby. I don't condemn every person who has an extramarital relationship. Each situation is different, and by what you have told me, it sounds like you have perfect justification."
Derby sighed with relief. She didn't have many friends and didn't want to alienate the ones she did have. She relaxed, feeling confident enough to tell Caroline more about Geoff. Caroline murmured the odd encouraging word, and commented on how lucky she was finding a guy so nice.

The courtyard had become even more crowded, the two women glad they had found the space on the wall earlier. A group of men were so close they loomed over them. One in particular, a bear of a man with thick dark hair. He turned, looked down at Derby and Caroline and smiled, a wide wolfish grin completely unattractive. Then his eyes widened as they settled on Derby.

"I know you. At least I've seen you."

Derby felt instantly threatened. She shook her head.

"No, no…you must have me mistaken for someone else. I've never seen you."

She mumbled. The man grinned even wider and leaned down, Derby leaning backward away from his beer breath.

"At the gym. You're Stone's little pet. Bet your old hubby don't know about that eh?"

Derby felt herself blanch. Caroline quickly intervened.

"Excuse me."

She said in an authoritative voice. The man glanced her way.

"Just who are you?"

He laughed and held out a beefy hand.

"Evan Thaniopoulos. At your service ladies."

He gave them both a sleazy wink.

"Well what can we do for you Mr Thani…whatever you said."

Caroline asked, none too politely.

"Mmmm….the Greek in me tells me one thing, the Welsh something else."

He replied. Derby and Caroline looked at each other completely puzzled.

"I don't follow."

Caroline said.

"Well this little lady here." He pointed to Derby. "Quite takes my fancy, proper hot in her slick little gym outfits, and I don't think Stone would want her husband to know he's dipping into her soft spots."

Derby felt sick, unable to speak, but Caroline came to her rescue.

"So what do you want us to do about that then?"

He leaned even closer and in a low voice said.

"Both of you? Sounds good to me, just say where and I won't say anything about her and Stone."

Derby felt her world crumble beneath her. She wasn't bothered about David, didn't care now if he found out about Geoff. What worried her was the impact it might have on Geoff's business. What his staff and clients would say about him having an affair with a gym member. She had no idea if there were any rules about it, hadn't given it a thought. Now here she was being blackmailed by this ogre, sex with him, or he would make sure her relationship with Geoff was broadcast. She couldn't speak, could barely breathe. Caroline again covered her hand with her own and squeezed reassuringly.

"Well, Evan, wasn't it? I think we can arrange something. Why don't you go and get us a drink, let us have a little chat about it."

Evan looked suspiciously at them.

"We won't go anywhere. After all, you know where my friend spends her time."

With a click of his fingers and a wink, he turned towards the bar entrance. Derby was in a state of near panic.

"What…Jesus…what am I going to do?"

She gabbled to Caroline. Still holding her hand, Caroline smiled.

"Leave it to me. I have a plan. Just follow my lead and I promise he won't give you any trouble. But we have to take him to my house. Don't be scared, I know what I'm doing."

Despite barely knowing Caroline, Derby felt safe and reassured that she would get her out of this awful situation. There was something about her, a confidence and maturity that made Derby feel protected. So when Evan returned with the drinks, Caroline put them on the wall, stood up and told him they were all going back to her place for some fun. Evan, who was obviously quite drunk, didn't notice he had bought two drinks that were going untouched. His excitement at what was ahead was enough to get him moving.

Caroline hailed a taxi outside and the three climbed in, Caroline making sure Evan didn't sit next to Derby. She gave her address and the driver pulled away. Thankfully for Derby, it only took fifteen minutes to get to Caroline's house, she hated being in the car with the huge beer breathing man.

The street where Caroline lived was quiet, which Derby felt was a bonus. Her house was detached, and no one saw them go inside. Caroline led them into the lounge and told Evan to sit down, telling him she had beer in the fridge. She took Derby into the kitchen and whispering, briefed her on the 'plan'. Derby had to grin when she found out what Caroline had in mind. They returned to the lounge, and Caroline handed Evan a can.

"Now relax, we have to pop up to the bedroom and get changed. You're going to love this."
Caroline said, taking Derby's hand and stroking her palm. Evan's eyes widened as he popped open the beer can.

"Cool, girl on girl. This is getting better by the minute."

Derby could barely contain the giggles as she followed Caroline up the stairs. The moron was completely sucked in by Caroline. In her spare room, she opened a wardrobe and slid hangers along the rails looking for something in particular. She located what she wanted and pulled two outfits out.

"I go to quite a few fancy dress parties and these are a couple of the costumes I've worn. I'd say we are the same size"
She held them up. One was a dominatrix, faux leather, plastic spikes and a whip. The other was a maid's outfit, pvc and frothy white lace.

"I've got fishnet stockings and boots to go with them, and I've got these."
She lifted a box from the bottom of the wardrobe and opened it. She took out black fur covered handcuffs, a couple of silk scarves and a huge dildo.

"It's ok. It hasn't been used." She pointed to the dildo. "Frank used to like me to cuff him to the bed, tie his ankles with the scarves and then rub the dildo with my hands. For some reason it used to turn him on. Anyway, it's going to come in very useful now."

Caroline suggested Derby wear the dominatrix outfit, since the obnoxious article sitting downstairs had a thing for her. Derby felt very conscious putting it on, this was quite different to her own sexual fantasies and her toys. But she knew she had to get rid of Evan, and Caroline's plan was a brilliant way to do it. Especially since Caroline had also noticed that the man wore a wedding band, and obviously didn't think about his own marriage.

Caroline donned the maid's costume and then took Derby into her bedroom. The bed had railed head and footboards, ideal for what they intended to do. Caroline pulled the stool from the dressing table and had Derby sit on it, positioning her in a dominant pose, knees apart, leaning forward holding the whip in both hands. She then trotted downstairs to fetch Evan.

The man filled the doorway as he entered the bedroom, and Derby could see he was much older than he'd first appeared. Caroline slipped in past him, wriggling her behind as she trotted over to Derby.

"Where would you like him Mistress?"
She asked Derby in a high girlie voice. Derby had to hold in the laughter, but managed to put on a strong harsh voice in reply.

"On the bed. Strip him to his pants."
Evan went willingly, his eyes glued to Derby, practically salivating like a huge dog.

He laid down on the duvet relaxing against the pillows. Caroline unbuttoned his shirt and threw it to the floor. Then unzipped his trousers tossing them aside too. Quickly he was left with just his pants. Caroline turned to Derby, who could see her friend was finding it hard not to laugh too. The Y-fronts, once white, were now grey and enormous. His belly, large and flabby hung over the waistband and flopped to his sides. He was really repulsive, but Derby continued the act.

"Cuff his wrists and tie his ankles."
She barked out to Caroline, who gave a tiny curtsey and bobbed about doing as demanded. Evan grinned, lapping up what he expected to be his fantasy.

Once the man was restrained and completely in their power, Derby stood up and sidled to the edge of the bed. She took the whip and trailed it from just under his chin all the way down his body. Evan squirmed under its touch but couldn't move away from it. The cuffs, though covered in fur, were locked securely in place. Derby then flicked it, not too hard, but enough for it to connect across his pelvis, but high enough up to not touch his crotch. Evan's eyes widened, fear evident, making Derby laugh, delighted that she had this awful person in her control.

Derby stepped around the bed to the other side, dragging the whip across his torso on the way. She saw him cringe, twisting to escape what he thought was going to be a lashing, but laughing, she let the whip lay still. Caroline came over to her, holding the dildo.

"Mistress, here you are."

She said, again in the high voice, handing Derby the toy. Derby let her imagination take over, beginning to enjoy the acting. She dragged the whip away and cracked it against the floor. Then she took Caroline by the hand and positioned them both at the foot of the bed. She wrapped the whip around Caroline as though holding her bound. Then she slid the dildo under her chin and down between her breasts. Caroline feigned pleasure, moaning and writhing against it. Derby then took the dildo in both hands and squeezed and massaged it as though it were real. She glanced at Evan and saw his body reacting as hoped, his erection straining against his old underwear.

Derby turned and faced him full on, her legs wide, her hands on her hips. Caroline walked around her, stroking and touching her arms and hair, whilst she stood firm and dominant. Evan began to pant, obviously desperate for the two women to indulge in the promised girl on girl, and then for them to deal with him.

"Oh girls. More, please show me more. How about removing some of the clothes, show a bit of skin."
Caroline stopped in front of Derby, her rear facing Evan. She leaned forward a little and wriggled her bottom, showing him her cheeks through the frilly panties and they heard him gasp.

"Oh we've got something far more exciting for you than taking our clothes off."
Derby told him. He licked his lips and waited.

Derby went to her bag on the dresser and pulled out her phone. She returned to the bottom of the bed and Caroline stood beside her. Then she began taking photos of Evan, from various angles. She made sure she got good shots of the cuffs, his erection and his grimy looking underwear. Then she stood back and held up the phone.

"This is all the action you're getting. Now I'm going to put these all over Facebook."
Evan blanched and then began blubbering.

"Nooooo....nooo...please...I'll...be...my...wife...my..... mates....please, please. I won't say anything about you and Stone. Don't do it. Let me go and I'll never say a word, honest."

"First though I'm sending them to my email. You're a big man and we are two quite small women."

Derby said as she forwarded the pictures.

"I'm not like that."

Evan said sulkily.

Half an hour later, Caroline and Derby were in the kitchen roaring with laughter. They had untied Evan, who had grabbed his clothes, hopping out the bedroom in a desperate bid to get out. They heard the front door slam before they had time to follow him.

"So what are you going to do with the photos?"

Caroline asked Derby.

"I'm going to speak to Geoff and then show him. He doesn't need people like that at his gym."

Chapter 15

Love And Hate

Derby took a taxi back to the flat, and as soon as she was inside, pulled out her phone and sent a message to Geoff.

Home safe and sound. Xxx

She had already decided not to mention Evan Thaniopoulos by phone, she wanted to see Geoff in person to explain about him. As she pondered over when and how, her phone indicated a message.

Good to know. Will I see you tomorrow? Xxx

Derby longed to see him, wanted to right then and there. She also knew it wasn't practical, and that in the morning she would have to leave early, go home, and get ready for work. But she knew she desperately wanted to tell him about the obnoxious man who had tried to threaten their happiness. So she tapped back a reply.

If it's ok can I come and see you on my way home in the morning. It will be early. Xxx

Geoff replied within seconds.

Of course anytime is a good time. Xxx

Derby smiled to herself and hugged the phone to her chest. She then tapped back.

Night night xxxx

Again his reply came quickly.

Night night little Derby sleep well. Xxx

Derby set her alarm for four and climbed into bed. She left the patio door open to let in the warm summer air, and the sound of the water below. At home, bedtime was a mundane routine that had to be done. Here at the flat, she felt relaxed, glad to be stretched out in the new king size bed. But she missed Geoff. At home, she had been happy to sleep alone when David had been away. She knew it was because there were no feelings between them, that his being there just made her feel cramped and stressed.

Derby settled in the middle of the big bed, spread her arms and imagined Geoff standing in front of her naked and ready. She let her hands trail down her body, closing her eyes and pretending it was Geoff. She reached her pubis and stroked the soft flesh, instantly arousing herself. Not wanting to rush, she threw back the duvet, slid off the bed and went to her wardrobe. At the bottom she lifted her box of toys and took out the vibrator.

She wouldn't be able to insert it, but she knew it would give her satisfaction. Back in bed she nestled the vibrator between her legs and switched it on low speed. Holding it, she slowly moved it over her clitoris, pushing her pelvis up to meet it. Her breath quickened as her arousal rose and she pressed it harder against her. She came on a squeal of delight, Geoff's face flashing in front of her closed eyes. As her body relaxed, she turned off the vibrator and gently dropped it to the floor. Then she pulled the duvet back over herself and completely gratified, let sleep take her.

Derby slept soundly and when the alarm went off, she awoke feeling fresh and alert. She would have loved to linger at the flat, but knew she couldn't indulge. So, she had a quick look at the boats, messaged Geoff she was just leaving, then locked up and headed for her car.

Geoff was waiting on the porch way as she pulled into the drive. He was wearing just a pair of track bottoms, his tanned torso gleaming as the sun rose. Derby leapt from her car and dived into his arms. He kissed her and pressed against her body, igniting her desire. She kissed him back, deep and satisfying, longing to drag him to bed then and there, knowing she couldn't.

"Good morning little Derby."
He said when the kiss ended. She smiled into his bright eyes.

"Good morning to you too."
Geoff led her into the kitchen and poured coffee from a pot on the counter. He handed her a mug and she sipped, breathing in the aroma.

"Mmmm, lovely."
She said. Then sobering, she put the mug down and took her phone from her bag.

"There's something I have to tell you."
Geoff leaned towards her and looked into her serious eyes.

"What's happened Derby?"
He asked gently, his voice full of concern. Derby picked up her coffee and took a swallow.

"Last night when I went out with Caroline."
She paused and Geoff frowned.

"A group of men came into the bar. One, a really horrible, disgusting pig…"

Geoff stood up straight, his eyes dark.

"He didn't hurt you did he?"

Derby quickly shook her head, and saw his tense muscles relax.

"No…oh no…nothing like that."

Then she giggled and Geoff looked at her completely puzzled.

"What?"

He asked. Derby got her laughter under control and continued.

"His name is Evan Thaniopoulos."

She waited for him to recognise the name. Geoff pressed his lips together and frowned, thinking.

"Oh I know. He comes to the gym on an hourly basis, not membership. He has no commitment and very little stamina."

Derby nodded.

"Mmhmm. That sounds about right."

"So what did he do?"

Geoff asked.

Derby explained the events of the previous evening, watching Geoff's eyes darken again when she told him about Evan's threats.

"But Caroline hatched a plan to deal with him."

She went on, and told him about the set up. By the time she finished, Geoff was leaning against the counter, his mug held tightly, laughing loudly.

"And I took these."

She said, holding out her phone. Geoff swiped the screen, laughing more and more with each picture.

"Derby, you are a devil."

Geoff managed to say. Derby stood straight, proud of her actions.

"He deserved it."

She said in a strong voice. Geoff handed back her phone and pulled her towards him.

"He definitely did."

He dropped his head into her neck and nuzzled her throat, murmuring.

"But wow! Did you look hot in that outfit."

Derby giggled as his lips tickled her neck. Then reluctantly, she pushed out of his arms and in a mock stern voice said.

"Mr Stone, I'm just not that sort of girl!"

They laughed together as he pulled her back into his arms, and she wriggled out again.

"Seriously though. I wanted you to know as soon as possible. And now I have to get home and get ready for work."

Geoff kissed her lightly, acknowledging her need to leave. He walked her to her car, and as she settled into the driver's seat and buckled her belt, he leaned on the open door.

"I'm glad you came round, and not just because of what you told me. I can't get enough of you Derby. And I will be sorting Mr Thaniopoulos out, believe me, I don't want his sort in my gym at all."

Derby reached out her hand and he took it, stroking the back lovingly.

"I love being with you too Geoff. But the next couple of days are going to be difficult. I have to see what's happening at home, and I've got the nursery inspection. So I might only be able to see you at the gym. Is that ok?"

Geoff stooped down.

"Derby, of course it's ok. I know things are awkward, and busy. I will be happy with any moment I get to see you."

He then leaned in and kissed her.

"Go home, get sorted and I'll speak to you later. I'm not going anywhere Derby. I promise."

Derby pulled to the edge of the pavement outside her house just as her alarm would have normally gone off. The street was quiet and thankfully deserted. She dashed into the house and straight upstairs, a quick glance in the bedroom showing David flat out under the duvet. The room was hot and stuffy and smelt of sweat. Leaving him there, she went into the bathroom and quickly showered.

Wrapped in a towel, she went into the bedroom and shook her husband awake. He came out of sleep reluctantly, sitting up and rubbing his eyes with his fists. Then he looked at her, his thinning hair sticking up.

"What time did you get home?"

He asked in a voice totally lacking interest. Derby frowned, unsure if his question was a trap.

"You were asleep."

She said. After all that was the truth. He yawned and stretched.

"Mmmm…I crashed about eight. Must still be worn out from that bug. Mum came round and cooked dinner yesterday afternoon."

He yawned again, threw the duvet off and clambered out of bed. Derby was taken aback. They barely spoke at any time of the day, especially the morning. She shrugged it off and got herself dressed for work.

Derby had the table laid out as normal when David came down. He sat down, waited as usual for her to fill his teacup and as usual said nothing. Derby felt a little out of sync with his behaviour, but didn't comment. She didn't want to take the chance that if she questioned him, he would do the same back. So she allowed the morning routine to pass, and breathed a deep sigh of relief when he left for work.

Angela arrived at the nursery five minutes after Derby unlocked the door. As soon as she saw Derby she questioned her about her weekend. Derby gave her a brief account, leaving out the flat completely. She still didn't want anyone else to know about it. But she went into detail when she told her about Evan Thaniopoulos, Angela laughing heartily.

"Let's hope Geoff throws his arse right out of the gym."

She said, making Derby giggle.

"I think he plans to."

Derby replied.

"But what about your weekend. What did you get up to?"

She asked, realising she had been so consumed with her own life that she hadn't asked after Angela's.

"We had a great weekend. Jake's parents arranged a family barbeque. What that boils down to is fifteen adults drinking too much, ten children eating too much, and the whole thing ending in a massive water fight."

Derby smiled, wishing she had family to have fun with.

"Do you have family Angela?"

She asked wistfully. Angela nodded.

"Yep, two sisters and a brother. I'm the youngest. My eldest sister lives in Spain, so we don't see her that often. My other sister lives in the city and my brother up the road from mum and dad, they're getting on a bit now. We all get together as often as we can, sometimes we even manage both families, which makes for quite a party, I can tell you."

Derby could tell from her tone that she was close to both her own and her husband's family, again making her feel so very alone. But she pushed the feelings aside, not wanting Angela to sense her loneliness.

Kelsey bustled in at the usual time, Chardonnay balanced on her hip. She headed for Derby and the toddler reached out to be taken. Derby lifted the little girl from her mother's arms, as Kelsey went through the normal routine of transferring care of her child to the nursery.

"Oh and guess what?"

Kelsey bubbled. Derby and Angela looked at her quizzically.

"I have the best team sales this week."

Both women beamed at the young woman, pleased she was making a success.

"And, I've only been out two nights, so mum hasn't had to sit with Chardonnay too much."

She continued. Derby lowered the wriggling Chardonnay to the floor, where she toddled off towards a table of toys.

"Kelsey I'm so glad things are looking up for you."

She said and Kelsey grinned.

"I reckon it's because you two came to my trial party. You gave me confidence. Now when I do a party, I just go for it. I think I have a knack."

Angela laughed.

"You had it all inside you sweetheart, credit goes to you."

Kelsey blushed with joy, then went over to her little girl to say goodbye.

"I'm so glad she's happy and more secure."

Derby told Angela.

"Mmm me too. She's a good mother and a lovely girl. Hope she finds a really nice lad one day."

Angela replied.

Derby was worn out by the end of the day. She had checked all her paperwork was up to date ready for Wednesday, checked supplies, the kitchen, staff area and children's toilets. She knew everything was in order and had confidence in her staff, but she was as ever nervous. Just as she locked up, her phone chirped.

She pulled it from her bag and saw the beginning of the message on the screen.

I expect you to be…

She opened the phone and read the rest of the message.

…home tonight and looking after my son as you should be. I will not tolerate your behaviour.

Irene.

Derby laughed.

"Bloody cheek."

She said to herself. Angela who was waiting whilst Derby finished locking up, looked up.

"What?"

She asked. Derby showed her the message, Angela's jaw dropping open.

"Who does she think she is?"

Derby shrugged.

"Don't care. As it happens I am going home tonight, but only because I'm so knackered from the weekend."

The two women laughed together as Derby walked Angela to her car.

Bob and Fiona were both in their front garden when Derby got home. Their smile brought pleasure to Derby and pushed Irene's message from her mind.

"We talked to Arnold, you know on the computer."

Derby beamed with genuine delight.

"I'm so glad about that. How did you find it?"

"Easy since you showed us how. We've even found our way round the internet and booked a little break in Wales."

Bob told her proudly.

"Well I knew you could do it, you just needed a little hand to get started."

A noise from her own garden startled her. Derby looked up and saw her front door opening, Irene standing, arms folded, a stern expression on her face. Derby frowned and so did Bob.

"What are you doing here?"

Derby asked in a none too friendly voice. Fiona stepped close to the fence and put a soft hand on Derby's shoulder, a motherly protective touch.

"Waiting for you."

Irene replied haughtily. Fiona leaned closer and whispered.

"Sweetie do you want me to come in with you?"

Derby patted Fiona's old hand and shook her head.

"Thank you, but believe me I will be fine."

She heard Bob smirk and say under his breath.

"Put my money on you anytime."

Derby giggled, relaxing as she said goodbye to her neighbours and headed up her pathway.

Irene stepped aside as she stepped over the threshold. Her arms were clasped tightly across her chest, her lips pursed. Derby was reminded of an irate parent waiting for a teenager, who had come home late. She felt laughter bubbling up and very nearly spilling over, containing it in fury. She ignored her mother-in-law as she walked down the hallway to the kitchen, unlocked the back door and opened it wide, letting in the summer. She heard footsteps behind her but didn't turn round. Instead she turned on the hob, checked there was water in the kettle and spooned coffee into a mug, not offering any to Irene.

Derby heard the older woman stop inside the kitchen doorway, but kept her back to her. She knew a confrontation was coming, but refused to initiate it. So she simply set about doing the things she would normally do. But when she opened the dishwasher to empty it, it had already been done. Straightening she glanced at Irene and saw a contemptuous smile on her lips. The kettle whistled and Derby made her drink, taking it out onto the patio. Then she saw the washing line full. Her clothes, David's, towels and bedding wafting in the gentle breeze.

"I don't think I like your choice of underwear. It's tarty."

A voice came from behind her. Fury filled Derby. She turned to Irene, took a step towards her and keeping her voice low said.

"Get out of my house."

Irene didn't move.

"Now!"

Derby said raising her voice. Irene shook her head.

"I will not. This is David's house. He pays the mortgage. You just…just…lodge here."

Derby set her mug down on the table so hard coffee spilled over. Anger clouded her vision, her hands balled into fists. For a moment she was speechless. Then she found her voice, still low and threatening.

"I said get out, now, or believe me I will throw you out!"
Something in Derby's voice must have shaken the older woman, for she stepped back and dropped her indignant pose. Then regaining a little of her haughtiness, she lifted her nose in the air.

"For now I will. But I will be speaking to my son about your attitude. Don't be surprised if he sends you packing."
She swung round, collected her bag from the little table in the hall and stomped out of the house.

Derby leaned on the patio table for a moment taking deep breaths. Her anger began to subside but left her shaking, causing the table to rattle and her mug to spill more coffee. She grabbed it up and took a large swallow, hoping to settle her nerves. She knew Irene disliked her, but had never dreamed she hated her so much. Straightening, she took her mug further into the garden, breathing in the scent of the roses. The smell soothed and calmed her. She shed no tears, just felt a deep sense of regret, not for David or her marriage, but for herself, for never opening her eyes to the life she had allowed herself to be cocooned in. Finishing her coffee she made a decision and turned back to the kitchen. Once inside she took her phone and tapped out a message.

Got a very nasty surprise when I got home. Your mother was in the house. She's probably already phoned you. She was vicious. I will not be spoken to like that. This is our house despite what she might think. And you for that matter. Neither of you will push me out.
She pressed send before she changed her mind and set the phone on the counter. Surprisingly, she got a quick reply.

Derby I didn't ask her to come round. She worries about me.
Frowning, she re-read the message, not able to make head nor tail of its meaning, and not really caring. She had vented her anger, got it off her chest, now she put it aside, determined not to let David or his mother ruin a perfectly good day.

Opening the freezer, she pulled out salmon fillets and placed them in foil on a baking tray. She cut new potatoes and set them in water, checked there was a bag of salad in the fridge. She knew it was David's least favourite food, healthy and tasty. She grinned to herself as she switched on the oven to heat. She would cook the meal, eat hers and leave his on a plate for when he got home. See what mummy had to say about that.

Once she had eaten her own meal and cleared away, Derby settled herself on the patio with her laptop. She browsed the net, checked emails and Facebook and sipped from a can of coke. Her phone indicated a message, the tone telling her it was from Geoff.

Hi how was your day. When can I see you? Xxxx
Her heart began to beat faster as she read.

Lots to tell you too much by text. Can't tonight are you at the gym tomorrow. Can't be out late inspection starts Wednesday. Xxxx
She sent the message and waited.

Missing you so much but will just have to be patient I suppose. Yes to gym have news for you too. Xxxx
Derby hugged the phone, feeling like a teenager.

Can't wait. Xxx
She sent. Then she heard a noise from inside the house.

Got to go David's home. Tomorrow then xxxx
Derby made her way into the kitchen without rushing. David was drinking juice from the carton, the fridge door wide open. She felt a little twinge of anger, she hated the fridge being exposed to summer bugs. David finished drinking, emptying the carton and replacing it in the slot in the door, shoving it closed. Derby sighed and re-opened the fridge, removed the carton and threw it away. David wiped his mouth with the back of his hand but didn't speak.

"Your dinner is in the fridge."
Derby stated. Her husband shrugged. She took out the plate and placed it in front of him, then left him to either eat it or leave it.

After spending an hour on the patio with her laptop, Derby ventured into the kitchen. David's plate was on the counter. He had eaten the potatoes, some of the fish and none of the salad. She smirked to herself as she cleared the kitchen. She went back outside and pulled the laundry from the line, thinking that she would have been grateful to any other person for doing the washing for her. But Irene wasn't a person to be grateful too, especially after the acid remarks about her underwear. She folded everything into the big basket, wondering when she would get the time to iron it all. Usually she staggered her washing so as not to have that problem. A thought flashed through her mind, a vision of coming home tomorrow and finding the whole pile done, well anything that belonged to David that was. She grinned, an idea forming to prevent it from happening.

David was flopped across the sofa when Derby peeked into the lounge. She didn't make a sound, leaving him to whatever he was watching on television. Quietly she went out of the front door, down her path and up Fiona and Bob's. She knocked and after a short wait, Bob opened the door with a huge smile on his face.

"Derby, come in, come in."
He said brightly, standing back to give her access.

Bob led her down the hallway and outside to the garden. Fiona was sitting on a padded garden seat and looked up smiling warmly. Bob pulled an identical chair away from the table and offered it to Derby. He waited until she sat down before taking his place next to his wife.

"Everything ok?"
Fiona questioned gently. Derby smiled, her eyes alight.

"Absolutely."

"We were worried when she spoke to you like that."
Bob said, his old bushy brows drawn together.

"He was all set to come knocking."
Fiona responded, pointing at her husband.

Derby felt a warmth spread through her, a sudden feeling of love for this old couple who she had known for years, but barely knew. Alongside that feeling was a deep hatred for Irene and her own parents. She hadn't even realised until then, that she could feel such animosity towards the people who had given her nothing over the years. But for David, she just felt pity. Her husband of twenty four years, spoilt by his mother and sister, lacked any fire, had no passion for anything, couldn't and wouldn't stand up for himself.

"That's so sweet and kind, but really I can handle that woman."
She told the couple, watching their faces as they pondered her words.

"Mmmm…I'll accept that."
Said Bob, Fiona nodding in agreement.

Fiona stood up and went to the kitchen to make tea for them all. Bob laid one of his old wrinkled hands on top of one of Derby's. He patted it in a fatherly way.

"She's worried about you for years, you know."
Derby was taken aback. She had hardly spoken to these lovely people in the years she had lived next door. She looked at Bob through lowered lashes, guilt flooding her cheeks.

"I...I...had no idea."
She mumbled. Bob patted her hand again.

"It's alright love, not your fault. We watched you move in, so young and so sad looking. Fiona wanted to come right round then, but you seemed shy and barely raised your eyes to us. We decided to wait and see if you came out of your shell, but you didn't."
Derby covered Bob's hand, sandwiching it between both of hers.

"I'm so sorry. I just didn't think."
Fiona came back with a tray of tea and biscuits.

"Just saying what we thought when she first moved here."
Bob said to his wife. Fiona sighed deeply as she sat back down. She pressed her lips together and frowned.

"Mmm, you were like...well a little robot. At first I have to admit, being nosey, but only because I was worried. I used to..."
She blushed. "...used to put a glass up against the wall to listen. I thought he might be hurting you."
She finished hurriedly.

Derby sat back in her chair. This lovely couple had watched over her and worried over her for all these years, and she had no idea. She was ashamed of herself. She was totally to blame for locking herself inside a loveless marriage, and life without love and friendship. If she had only opened her eyes years ago, so much would have been different. She let her shoulders sag.

"I've been so stupid. I've let others walk all over me and haven't even noticed. I'm so sorry for worrying you."
She gave a derisive laugh.

"David has never laid a finger on me. Never hurt me. I should...have...seen...straight...away...that...we...wouldn't......work....but...well, my parents were....are...not loving in any way."

She stopped, unsure of how to explain an entire lifetime. Again Bob patted her hand, and that so very small action opened up the flood gates and she began to talk, to tell them everything about her life.

It was getting dark by the time Derby finished her life story. Bob and Fiona had listened without interruption. She left out her relationship with Geoff and the sex because she didn't want the couple to think badly of her, but when she finally stopped talking, Fiona sat back with a sigh and said.

"You should have gone off and found someone else."
Derby looked at her, not sure of how to respond.

"I mean, I don't agree with affairs and all that, marriage is for life. But there are certain circumstances when that doesn't count, yours being one. Women or men even, shouldn't stay in a relationship just because they made their vows if there's no love."
Bob was nodding in agreement.

"Well...I have met someone, only just recently so very early days."
Derby told them. Fiona grinned.

"Good for you."

Derby then went on to tell them about how she met Geoff. She explained that it was his house she was returning from when they saw her come home in the early morning, and hoped she wasn't shocking the old couple. She really didn't want them to think she was some sort of tart. But both their reactions indicated they thought she was well overdue a proper life.

By the time Derby got round to asking Fiona and Bob the favour that would put her plan into play, it was ten o'clock. The couple held hands and laughed gleefully, eyes twinkling.

"I'd like to see her face though."
Fiona said with a cheeky smile on her face.

"Mmm me too. So I'll just pop back home and get it sorted."

Chapter 16

Two Faces

The following morning Derby did everything the way she had before she had discovered her new life, not wanting to give David any excuse to call his mother. He left for work as usual and once he was gone, she dashed about the house, getting it ready for Irene. With a smile, she locked up, jogged to Bob and Fiona's and tapped on their door. Fiona answered and the two women chatted briefly before Derby made her way to work.

By lunchtime Derby felt the nursery was as ready as it could be for the next day. She had managed to send a message to Geoff, just to say she would come by the gym that evening, but wouldn't be able to stay long. His reply made her heart flutter.

Can't wait even a minute with you is precious xxxxx

Angela noticed the glow on her face, and Derby showed her the message. Angela squeezed her arm gently.

"Good on you girl. Don't let anything or anyone get in your way."

Derby knew she was referring to Irene, having told her about the previous evening.

By the time Derby locked up the nursery she was a bag of nerves. There wasn't anything else she could do to prepare for the inspection, knew all was in order, knew they would pass as usual, but was still terrified she had missed something. On the way home she mentally ticked off a list in her head, sure she and her staff were ready.

As she approached her home, her nerves increased, but they had nothing to do with the inspection and everything to do with her mother-in-law. She had no idea if Irene would be inside waiting for her. But her fears were set aside when she saw Bob and Fiona leaning on their fence waiting for her, big smiles on their faces. They waved as she approached.

"She went in like you thought."

Fiona blurted out just as Derby stopped.

"And came back out pretty quickly."

Bob added laughing. Derby smiled.

"Was she angry?"

Derby enquired with a smile of her own. The couple nodded gleefully.

"Oh yes."

Bob told her.

"Especially when we stopped her and gave her your message."

Derby pressed her lips together and nodded to herself.

"Best go in then and see if she's left me anything. I haven't had any phone calls or texts."

"Come and let us know."

Fiona told her as she started up her path.

Derby went into her home. Nothing was out of place in the hallway, so she made her way to the kitchen. Again everything was in order, her washing basket where she had left it, the laundry still folded. So she went through the house room by room. Each one was as it should be. She went back into the kitchen and checked more thoroughly. The edge of a piece of paper was sticking out of the bin, making Derby grin widely. She opened the lid and saw it full of the little post its she had left around the house that morning. All were screwed up into small balls. Derby leaned against the work surface and laughed, pleased she had accomplished her goal.

When David came in from work, he didn't mention anything about his mother, so Derby assumed she hadn't spoken to him. This pleased her even more. She made his dinner, his favourite this time, sausage, chips and beans, placed the meal on a tray and handed it to him.

"I'm going to the gym."

She said. David, a fork of chips already on its way to his mouth, glanced up and nodded. She didn't bother telling him she wouldn't be long because of the inspection, he had never been interested before, so knew he wouldn't be now. So she turned and headed for the door. Fiona answered her knock and was delighted to know Irene hadn't left anything nasty for Derby.

With the roof down, the sun shining brightly into the car, and the wind whipping her hair, Derby felt tension flowing from her body the further away from home she got. By the time she pulled into the car park of the gym, she felt fresh and alive.

Excitement at the thought of seeing Geoff giving her a bounce to her step.

At the reception desk one of the girls smiled brightly, welcoming her with a personal "Hello Derby". She was a little startled by this.

"Geoff said to give him a shout when you get here."
The girl told her in a very friendly manner. She then spoke into her headset.

"He's on his way."
She said as she tapped keys on her computer professionally.

Barely a minute had gone by when Geoff came through the glass doors from the main gym. Derby's breath caught in her throat. He looked so handsome in his shorts and T-shirt, the muscles on his arms and legs taut, his tanned skin lustrous. His smile turned her insides to liquid, heat flushing her face.

"Hello Derby."
He said, his voice deep and thrilling. Then he placed a hand on the small of her back and steered her towards a door to the side of the desk, one she had never noticed before.

Inside was a large very comfortable office. A big antique desk dominated the room, two old leather armchairs, and a wooden coffee table set in a corner. It was totally contradictory to the rest of the shiny modern gym, but completely in character with what Derby now knew about Geoff.

As soon as she was inside and the door closed, Geoff took her in his arms. He pulled her tight to him and she lifted her face to his. His lips closed on hers and her arms came up around his neck, grasping the hair at his nape. The kiss was filled with passion, deep and long, and when it was over, Derby felt full and satisfied.

"Hello Geoff."
She said as they moved apart slightly. He grinned at her boyishly, his face lighting up with pleasure.

"I am so very glad you are here."
He told her, swaying her gently from side to side.

"So am I."
She replied, running her finger tips up and down his arms, a little groan coming from his mouth.

"God, do you know what that's doing to me?"
He murmured. Derby nodded mischievously.

"Mmm I think so."

Geoff stepped back a little.

"Little Demon."

He said with laugher in his voice.

Even though she longed to pull his clothes from his body and have him inside her, Derby thought it was neither the time nor place to do so. To make it easier for both of them to contain their desire, she stepped away from his arms.

"So, is this your office?"

She asked. Geoff nodded.

"Do your staff know about us now?"

Geoff grinned.

"Yep. I've got nothing to hide."

"Is that the news you mentioned?"

Geoff led her to the armchairs, indicating she should sit. He then went to another antique table and poured coffee into mugs from a pot, returning and placing one in front of her.

"Partly."

He said, sitting down and sipping his own drink. Derby reached for her mug then settled comfortably in the chair, waiting for him to continue.

"When I came in yesterday, I spoke to my staff and told them I was in a relationship with you."

Derby felt warmth spread through her. A relationship, not an affair.

"I have good people here. They all know I'm not married, that you are, but they don't judge and they don't gossip. I didn't go into detail, just let them know things are not right for you at home."

He paused. Derby pondered his words for a moment, then she nodded and he carried on.

"Well I also told them about Thaniopoulos."

Derby gasped. Geoff was by her side in an instant. He kneeled and took the mug from her now shaking hand.

"It's ok Derby. Some of the girls have had run ins with him, you know, him being a bit too flirty at times, but nothing serious. So they are all on your side. Anyway, like I told you he's not committed and doesn't come in frequently. I've given instructions that the next time he books a session, I'm to be told, even if I'm not on duty at that time. I will deal with him."

Derby sighed, miserable that she had caused him trouble.

"Maybe he won't come back. He was pretty ruffled when I told him I was posting the photos on Facebook, and probably worked out that I would tell you all about it."
Geoff leaned towards her, his forehead touching hers.

"Perhaps, but even if he doesn't I know where he lives. I will be speaking to him."

For the first time in her life, Derby felt fully protected and loved. This man before her, whom she had known for such a short time, was going out of his way to keep her safe. She cupped his face in her small palms and kissed his lips.

"Thank you Geoff."
She whispered. He kissed her back.

"Nothing to thank me for Derby, you're mine and I would go to the ends of the earth to make sure no one harms you."
His words sent tingles down her spine and love through every fibre of her body, but she was still too shy to say it out loud. He sensed she was holding back but didn't push her. Instead, he stood up and went back to his armchair.

They chatted about the upcoming inspection. Geoff asking all of the questions she had asked herself, reinforcing her certainty that everything was ready. She then went on to tell him about Irene and her acid remarks, watching his eyes darken with anger. She giggled, wondering how her mother-in-law would react if she were confronted by him.

"So what did you do?"
He asked. Derby giggled again.

"I left post its all over the house with messages on. In every room, on drawers, doors the laundry basket."
Geoff grinned.

"What did they say?"

"Well mostly 'hello nosey Irene'. But a few had longer messages like 'I've set traps, so if you open this drawer, I will know.' And 'Keep you paws off my things.' A couple specifically mentioned David with 'You're welcome to clear this up, it's your baby boy's mess' I left his dinner things from last night and breakfast dishes out on the counter."
Geoff leaned across the table and took her hand.

"You have a very devilish streak in you little Derby."

She shrugged, but smiled.

"It's about time I stood up for myself. And my lovely neighbours helped too."

"Oh, in what way?"

"They were watching. I had a feeling she would be round not long after I went to work and I was right. They saw her go in and when she came out gave her a message from me. I asked them to tell her that Fiona was going to be looking after the house when I was at work. That she would be doing the laundry and housework, of course she won't be, and that she, Irene wasn't allowed inside the house when I wasn't there."

Geoff frowned slightly.

"But how are you going to police that? I mean your neighbours won't be able to watch the place every minute."

Derby shrugged.

"Hopefully she will get the hint and stay away, be too wary to walk in just in case Fiona is there. She won't give me the key she has, no good changing the lock because David will just give her a spare anyway, so it's all I can think of."

Geoff took both her hands and tugged her across the table a little.

"One day, I hope none of this will matter."

Derby didn't know how to respond. She wasn't quite sure what he meant, hoped it was his way of saying he wanted a future with her, but too afraid to believe it.

"I know, too soon."

He said quietly.

"But Derby, why don't you leave him? You have the flat, your job, car, your independence."

Tears began to trickle from her eyes and down her cheeks. She pulled a hand from Geoff's and swiped them away. She didn't even know why she was crying, self-pity she thought. A box of tissues appeared in front of her. She grabbed a handful and dabbed at her wet face.

"Sorry...I'm a wreck."

She murmured. Geoff again came and kneeled by her side, pulling her into a comfortable hug.

"No you're not. A lot has happened to you recently, you have a right to be confused."

Derby sat up straight.

"No…not confused."
Geoff leaned back on his heels.

"I know how I feel…about everything…but just now it also feels like I have two faces. One you see, the other David and his mother. Oh I don't think I'm making sense at all."
Geoff waited whilst she took a breath.

"Why don't I leave him? To be honest it's all about finances. I know how callous that sounds. But you see, all these years, I haven't had to worry about money. All I have to take care of is the shopping. David's responsible for everything else. I mean the house is in both our names and it will be paid off soon, but he's always just paid all of the bills. So most of my own money is in the bank. My salary is good and I don't spend hardly any of it. That's why I was able to pay six month's rent up front for the flat, and buy new clothes and the car."

She paused on a deep sigh. Geoff stood up and went to a small fridge Derby hadn't noticed. He took out a bottle of water and handed it to her, settling himself back on the floor beside her chair. As ever considerate, he had unscrewed the lid. Derby took a long swallow of the chilled water. She shifted her position in the chair so she was full on facing him.

"I'm a bitch, right?"
She whispered. Geoff kneeled up and cupped her face with his huge hands.

"No Derby, don't say that, ever. You were young, had no support from anyone. You lived how you believed you were expected to live."

"But now I know different, yet I'm still too scared to really do something about it."
Geoff smiled warmly.

"But you are doing something about it. It takes time to change a whole lifetime, but you've made a start. Don't be so hard on yourself."
Derby giggled, suddenly feeling a weight lifting from her.

"Yes I am, and I promise I will do more."
She turned her face into his palm and kissed it.

"Now what was it you were saying about it being hard?"
Geoff laughed heartily.

"Bad, bad, bad, that's what you are."

Then he leaned up and took her lips fully, igniting her body deep and low.

The kiss lasted a long time. Derby gave her mouth and tongue to him, relishing in the feel of his hands that were now on her breasts. He stood up without releasing her, bringing her to a stand too. She turned into his strong arms and let desire overcome every other thought. He lifted her against him, pulling her body close to his and she felt his hardness pushing at the cleft between her thighs. She moaned, wriggling to get closer. He dropped one hand to her buttocks and squeezed, pressing her into him further, his erection straining at his shorts.

Derby pushed down on his shoulders, and he understanding lowered them to the floor, where she laid on top of him. She knew the office was not really the right place for this, but she wanted him so much. Straddling him, she sat up, her hands resting on the floor.

"We shouldn't, not here in your office."
She whispered. Geoff ran a finger down her throat.

"No one will come in, I promise."
His words released her hesitancy, and she leaned down and kissed him. He held her head, his fingers tangling in her long hair, the wetness between her legs spreading deep to her core.

Geoff trailed his hands down her body and up under her dress. He stroked the soft curves of her hips and insides of her thighs. Derby lifted up on her knees as his fingers slipped under the edge of her panties and touched the soft wetness beneath. she raised herself to her feet and let him pull her undies from her, stepping out of them quickly. Then she knelt over him again, and pulled down the waistband of his shorts, unleashing his straining manhood. She lowered herself onto his hardness and heard him gasp. Her warm, slick haven clasped around him as she began to slowly move up and down.

His hands resting on her hips, gripped and squeezed with each rhythmic plunge. She pressed her hands against his chest and curled her nails into the fabric of his T-shirt, eyes closed and face flushed with desire. Derby began to increase the speed of her movements, and felt him meet each thrust. Her orgasm began deep within, erupting and flowing over her, heat flooding her veins. Her body became taut, then small jagged jolts like electricity pulsated through every fibre as she pressed down on him. He thrust hard and deep, faster and faster until his body went rigid and he spilled his hot fluid into her.

Together they came down from their orgasms, Geoff softly stroking her thighs, Derby massaging his chest. He sat up and wrapped his arms around her, kissing her lovingly. Derby held his head and stroked the hair at his nape. He was still inside her, and though their desire was sated, the feeling was warm and intense and she was in no rush to move.

"That was amazing."
Geoff whispered as he lifted his lips from hers.

"It was for me too."
She whispered back.

Once they had rearranged their clothing, Geoff poured more coffee. There was an easiness between them, as though they had been together for a long time. Over the rim of her mug, Derby looked at Geoff.

"What?"
He asked.

"Oh nothing really."

"Come on."
He grinned. She sipped her coffee then lowered the cup.

"It feels so right, you know….sex between us."
She blushed.

"That's because it is right Derby."
He replied.

"I know, but it's more than that. Like we've known each other for years, like we know each other's body, what we like, what works best."
Her blush deepened, but she refused to let it get in the way of what she wanted to convey to him. He put his mug down on the table and leaned his elbows on his knees.

"It seems like that to me too."
Then he laughed a little.

"Maybe we were together in another life."
Derby scrunched her face, hoping he wasn't being serious. She had never been able to accept theories of resurrection.

"Do you believe in that stuff?"
Geoff shook his head.

"No. Not at all."

His laughter increasing at the look of relief on Derby's face.

"Phew...I know I shouldn't judge, but...well...all that hypnotism and regression stuff freaks me out a bit. I mean, however you look at it, there's no proof, and I know that doesn't mean it's not real, but well...I just find it weird."

Geoff nodded in understanding.

"I get you. Some of the Marines I knew believed, gave them hope if they got killed that they would come back as someone else. Me, I believe there's something beyond, I just don't know what."

Derby hoped he was right. After having taken a lifetime to find this man, the thought of never seeing him again sent waves of fear through her. She finally realised that she wanted Geoff for the rest of her life, and sometime very soon she would be able to tell him that.

The phone on Geoff's desk bleeped. He stood up and answered it, a smile forming on his lips. After telling his receptionist he would be straight out, he turned to Derby, his smile widening into a huge grin.

"Guess who just walked through the door."

He said.

"Thani what's his name?"

Derby questioned. Geoff nodded.

"This is going to be fun."

The big man had already gone through to the changing rooms when Geoff and Derby emerged from the office. The receptionist explained that he had arrived without pre-booking, taking a chance there would be room. Geoff told Derby to stay at the desk for the time being and the receptionist smiled in a friendly manner, offering her a coffee. Derby declined the drink and waited anxiously for Geoff to reappear.

He was back in minutes carrying a sports holdall, Evan Thaniopoulos plodding alongside him, a very sheepish expression on his face. As the two men came through the door, Evan saw Derby and blanched. Geoff obviously hadn't told him she was there. He tried to head straight for the door, but Geoff took him by the upper arm and guided him towards the reception desk. He didn't resist. Despite being a lot bigger than Geoff, he was so fat and flabby he was no match. Geoff stopped them by Derby's side.

"I think you have something to say."

Geoff said in a low but very firm voice. Evan looked around, his eyes flicking nervously, and never once settling on Derby.

"Sorry."

He mumbled. Geoff still holding his arm, gave him a little shake.

"Not good enough."

Evan winced as though hurt, but raised his eyes to Derby.

"I am very sorry."

The fear on his face brought a giggle to her lips, which she was only just able to suppress.

"Mmm…will that do Derby?"

Geoff asked. She nodded, afraid if she spoke she would burst out laughing. Geoff turned to Evan.

"Now get out of my gym. Don't ever come back. We can do without your sort. And don't be stupid and go around spreading nasty rumours about my gym. Remember, I know where you live. We still have the photos, and I don't think you would like your wife to see them."

Derby saw a tiny shudder go through Evan's body, and knew Geoff had hit home with his threat.

Geoff shoved the gym bag into Evan's hands. He wasn't expecting it and dropped it, scrabbling to retrieve it from the floor. Once he had scooped it up, he turned quickly and headed for the door, without looking back. Geoff, Derby and the receptionist laughed as he rushed out, sure they would have no more trouble from him.

"Thank you Geoff."

Derby said sincerely. And before he could reply.

"And I'm sorry you have lost a client, it's my fault."

Geoff took her hand.

"No it's not your fault. Like I said, he's annoyed some of my coaches so it was coming anyway, and clients like him, we don't need."

Derby felt reassured, loved and cared for. She noticed the receptionist glance her way, but the smile on the girl's face was warm and friendly.

"Ok, I'll accept that."

The big digital clock over the door to the gym read nine thirty. Derby was surprised at how fast the evening had gone by, and felt herself blushing when she thought about how it passed. Geoff spotted her flushed cheeks but made no comment. The receptionist was busy on her headset and computer, so didn't notice.

"I should be getting home. Try and get some rest before tomorrow."
Derby said to Geoff. He nodded, put an arm around her waist and led her towards the door. The receptionist called out "Goodbye" as she continued with her work and Derby looked over her shoulder, smiled and said "Night."

At her car Geoff took her in his arms and kissed her. She kissed him back, no longer afraid someone would see and judge. She felt free and alive. Even though she was several miles from home, and no one here was likely to know her or David, she didn't care if they did. Geoff's words earlier had set her mind ticking over the next steps. Soon she would have to speak to David. She knew she couldn't let things go on the way they had been for so many years.

Derby climbed into her car, Geoff leaning on the roof as she buckled her belt. He bent in and kissed her lightly as she started the engine.

"Text me when you're home please."
He whispered. She nodded.

"And good luck for tomorrow. I know everything will be fine, but good luck anyway."
Derby smiled.

"Thank you, and I will text."
She frowned a little.

"Don't know when I can get to see you though. The inspection will be tomorrow and Thursday, so probably won't be until after that."

"Derby, it's fine. I know you're not going to disappear. Just text me or call when you can. Of course I'll miss you, but I'll just have to keep busy, mostly to keep my mind off your body."
She laughed, delighted and girlishly.

"Mmmm, somehow I don't think this inspection will help me do that. The inspectors are usually sixty plus and dull as dish water."

Geoff laughed too as he closed her door and stood back, waving her off.

The house was quiet when Derby went in. It was past ten and Derby suspected her husband was already in bed. On tiptoe, she went upstairs and peeped into the bedroom. He was there, all bundled up in the duvet as usual, even though the night was still very warm. Barely making a sound, Derby opened the window wide, allowing fresh summer air in. She didn't linger, but went back downstairs and through to the kitchen. The remains of David's meal were on the counter, the tray still underneath the plate. Bread and butter were again left open causing Derby to huff in frustration. She tidied the kitchen, poured herself a glass of juice and went out to the patio. She knew she had to go to bed, try at least to get a good night's rest, but was reluctant to lay next to her husband. She tapped a message to Geoff as promised and felt her heartbeat increase when he replied.

Glad you are home safely. Miss you already. Night night little Derby. Xxx

As she held her phone close to her heart, she thought about what she had said to Geoff. Her two faces. A tiny thread of fear took hold of her. Which one was the real Derby? Suppose, just suppose, her birthday, her one grey hair, her need for sex, were all part of some mental breakdown. Was she coming apart? What if she couldn't control the two faces? She gave herself a mental shake and drained her juice. No, she told herself. She was one person who had been suffocated for years. One person who had always believed through her upbringing, that the life she lived was normal. One person blinkered by circumstance, her true feelings and personality buried in a life lacking love and understanding. Now, one person who had broken free from the chains of that life, had swum through the mire of that life, and emerged not gasping for breath, but filling her lungs with freshness and hope and love.

Derby, relieved that she had pushed aside her fears, concluded she wasn't going crazy, locked up the house and headed for bed. She went through her bathroom routines, put on pyjamas, which felt strange for she had slept at the flat naked, and quietly climbed in next to her husband. David stirred a little, grunted but didn't wake. Derby settled down and with her thoughts on Geoff, drifted into a sleep filled with dreams of them, limbs tangled in passion.

Chapter 17

Band Of Gold

Derby arrived at the nursery much earlier than usual. She felt fresh and ready, even though her dreams the night before had been erotic. She had woken several times, her knees pressed together, her womanly centre contracted with mini orgasms. Each time, she had glanced at David who slept soundly, snoring loudly.

Angela arrived soon after Derby, and over coffee the two women chatted as they prepared the tables. Derby told her all about how Geoff had dealt with Evan, making her laugh and declare she wished she'd been there to see it. The other nursery nurses came in, and Derby gave them a final briefing before the inspectors arrived.

Before the nursery opened, the door buzzed. Derby took a deep breath and went through to the entrance. Two men stood on the other side of the glass doors. One looked to be in his fifties, the other much younger. They held up identification cards and Derby unlocked the door allowing them access. The older man introduced himself as Robert Jenkins and his colleague, Jay Larratey. They both shook hands with Derby who showed them into the nursery, offering coffee.

As the day began and the children arrived, the two inspectors wandered around from room to room making notes. Derby, used to it, didn't feel the intrusion, but she saw some of her younger staff members were nervous. For that reason she was relieved when Robert asked her for time in the office to look through the paperwork. She had already laid out all of the essential folders that she knew he would want first, then leaving him to it, told him to ask if he needed anything else. He gave her a professional smile, nodded and opened a folder, his notes by his side.

By midday the nursery was running as smoothly as usual. Robert was still ensconced in the office and Derby hoped he would remain there for the rest of the day, the rest of the inspection even. The other inspector, Jay Larratey took over inspecting the actual nursery. After their initial quick look at each room, he explained to Derby that he would be observing individual staff members. Derby knowing the routines nodded and smiled.

"I'll also be inspecting you."

He said with a wide smile and a cheeky wink. Derby thought he was being very unprofessional, but resisted saying anything. She did however whisper to Angela what he had said.

"Huh…I know he's well fit, but come on who does he think he is?"

Angela whispered back. Derby shrugged.

"Well I've got your back if he tries anything."

Angela told her, making her giggle.

On a normal day, Derby would nibble lunch with the children, rotating with her staff the different age groups. But the inspection demanded her time, so she took a quick break in the kitchen, knowing the inspectors would want to talk to her for at least part of their lunch break. However, Robert came out of the office at twelve thirty and announced he and Jay would be out of the building for forty minutes. Jay joined him and together they disappeared. But thirty minutes later, Jay returned alone. He buzzed the door and Derby let him in.

"You're early."

She said. Jay nodded.

"Yes, he does my head in a bit. I mean he's very good at his job, but…a little too intense."

He blushed as though he'd said too much. Derby didn't comment, wanting to remain completely professional, and definitely not wanting to give them any excuse to mark her down.

"I know, I shouldn't have said that. Look…I'm sorry for the comment earlier. I'm not the arrogant cock I must have come across as. I…this is my first inspection…I'm a bit nervous."

He held out his hand. Derby took it and they shook politely.

"Forgiven."

She said. He let out a nervous breath, and Derby genuinely believed he had been worried.

When Robert returned ten minutes later, he took himself straight back to the office. This surprised Derby. Previous inspections had always included a period of one to one communication with her and the senior inspector. Maybe, she thought it would take place on the second day of the inspection, and decided not to let it bother her today.

Nothing out of the ordinary happened on the first day, much to the relief of Derby and her staff. The two inspectors stayed until the last child had been collected, said polite goodbyes and left. What Derby did notice, was the frequent glances Jay Larratey gave Kelsey when she came to collect Chardonnay. A lot of people often looked at the young woman, even those who knew her. She had a bright bubbly voice and infectious giggle. She was very pretty, and even though at times she appeared somewhat dizzy, she was intelligent and a brilliant mother. But the looks she saw Jay giving her was of a man attracted to a girl, and despite his earlier mishap, during the rest of the day he had come across as nice. Derby decided then that she would introduce the two tomorrow.

Derby strolled home. She was in no rush. The weather had remained bright, hot and sunny and she felt the day had gone well. Trees lined the few streets she had to walk along to get to home, their branches thick with green leaves. Children played in some of the gardens, and some played on the pavements, safe as traffic was minimal. A few mothers waved to her as she passed, used to seeing her but still unknown to them. She waved back and smiled, pushing back the little prick of sadness that she had never experienced what they had.

Fiona and Bob were in their front garden waiting for her. They opened the gate and with delight Derby entered. The old couple greeted her like she was their own daughter, smiling and offering her a cold drink. Derby accepted gratefully. Even though the walk was short, she was thirsty. Fiona disappeared inside and soon emerged carrying a tray of glasses.

"How was the inspection?"
Bob asked, sipping his juice. Derby took a long swallow of hers and answered.

"It went very well I'm pleased to say. Hopefully tomorrow will too and then it will be all over, for a while that is."

"I'm sure you have nothing to worry about."
Fiona added, patting Derby's arm.

"Any visitors?"

Derby asked, nodding in the direction of her own house. Both of them shook their heads, smiling.

"Nah…think she got the hint."
Bob said finishing his drink. They all laughed together, comfortably, like a family sharing.

Derby chatted for a while longer then went to her own home. She wanted to message Geoff, tell him about her day. She also decided that she should probably stay home at least until the weekend, be the normal dutiful wife that she had been for so many years. That way, David would have no excuse to run to his mother, and Irene would have no excuse to admonish her. But she missed her flat and she missed Geoff. She checked the time and quickly decided she could drive to the flat, check everything was alright and come straight home before David got in. She wouldn't be able to see Geoff, but at least she had seen him the night before.

The house didn't need much attention since Irene had gone over it so thoroughly, so Derby grabbed her keys and bag and jogged to her car. Not wanting to be delayed, she didn't stop to put the roof down, settling for opening both windows instead. She pulled away from the kerb and drove off up the street.

Thankfully traffic was light going towards the city, but she was glad that she had chosen the flat at the marina and not the one in the centre. It meant she didn't have to get into the increasing lines of vehicles building up on the ring road, as the road to the marina veered off before.

George was on duty when she went into the building. She stopped just long enough to say hello, and with a quick wave dashed up the stairs, not wanting to delay by waiting for the lift. She paused outside the door to her flat, taking a deep breath before unlocking it. As she stepped inside, she felt like a different person. Even though the first day of the inspection had gone well, it had made her tense. Now here in the flat, as she slid the patio doors open and stepped onto the balcony, her tension released, flew away over the water. She could almost see it, imagined it was a huge winged creature, launching itself from her shoulders and taking flight towards the sea.

Derby stayed at the flat only long enough to drink a cup of coffee, text Geoff and take a breather on the balcony. The marina was quiet below, boats bobbing peacefully and sending her a wave of calm. It was enough to refresh her. She washed up her cup, locked up and headed back to the car park. This time she dawdled, lowered the roof and opened the windows. She put on her seat belt, fiddled with the radio and made sure she was comfortable. Then she drove towards home at a lower speed than was necessary, enjoying the wind in her hair and the sun on her face.

Derby spent the evening in the garden. Once David was fed and she had cleared away, she took herself outside with her laptop, checked emails and updated her Facebook status. David as was usual, didn't notice where she was. They had shared a few words since his arrival home, then after he had eaten he settled in front of the computer. She had ventured back inside a couple of times to get a drink, but didn't seek her husband. By the time she felt ready for bed, David was already tucked up sleeping deeply.

The second day of the inspection went as smoothly as the first. Derby had not been able to introduce Jay to Kelsey in the morning, but was determined to make sure they met. She had though, been able to point him out to Kelsey when she dropped Chardonnay off, and the young woman's eyes had told Derby a lot. So when Robert told Derby they were finished, just before the parents and carers arrived, she managed to delay their departure.

"So how did we do?"

She asked. She knew they would receive a full written report, but also knew he would give her a verbal brief.

"Very well Mrs Waite."

Then he smiled, something he hadn't done during the past two days.

"You run a very well organised establishment. I don't think I have ever inspected a nursery as good as this one. I can tell you, you achieved outstanding in all areas."

Derby beamed.

"Thank you Mr Jenkins. That is good news."

"Credit goes where it's due."

He said as he checked the clasps on his briefcase.

Kelsey walked through the door just as Robert held out his hand to Derby. She shook it and then turned to Jay.

"Mr Larratey, do you have just a teeny moment?"

Jay hesitated.

"I'll be in the car."

Robert said, exiting the building.

"There's someone I'd like you to meet."

Derby said to Jay, guiding him towards Kelsey who was kneeling and busy hugging Chardonnay.

"Kelsey."

The young woman looked up.

"This is Jay Larratey, one of the inspectors."

Lifting Chardonnay into her arms, Kelsey stood. She was about a head shorter than Jay who was looking down into her face smiling brightly. He held out a hand.

"Pleased to meet you, Kelsey."

Kelsey jiggled Chardonnay to her hip to free up a hand.

"You too."

She said and Derby could see she was rather nervous.

"Why don't I take Chardonnay and get her a drink, whilst you two have a chat."

Derby offered holding her arms out to the toddler. Chardonnay launched herself at Derby giggling, and so she took the tiny girl to the kitchen.

Derby didn't want to delay Jay's leaving too long, worried that Robert would get annoyed. But she did want to give the couple time to at least see if they wanted to exchange numbers. So she gave Chardonnay some juice in a plastic cup, mentally counted five minutes and returned to the main nursery. As she approached, she could see Kelsey and Jay had their phones out. Pleased with herself, she gave Chardonnay a tickle, the little girl's squeal notifying her mother of their return.

Jay said goodbye to both women and smiled warmly at Kelsey, waving to Chardonnay as he made his way to the door. As soon as he went through it, Derby burst out.

"Well?"

Kelsey feigned ignorance.

"What do you mean?"

Derby laughed.

"You know what I mean. Are you going to see him?"

Kelsey beamed.

"Well he asked for my number, and asked what I was doing Saturday night. So I would say yes to that question."

Derby put an arm around her shoulder.

"Good for you. I hope it goes well."

Kelsey gave a little shrug.

"Me too, but you know, well Chardonnay comes first, so we'll see."

Derby nodded in understanding. She knew Kelsey well enough to know that no matter how nice a man might be, unless he fully accepted that Chardonnay was part of the package, he wouldn't stand a chance. Unfortunately, Derby had worked with children long enough to know that didn't always happen with other single parents. Many times over the years, her heart had broken over a child neglected and rejected, when a parent had concentrated all of their attention on a new partner. Derby pushed those memories into the deep recesses of her mind, and turned her attention back to Kelsey.

"Hopefully this guy will be exactly how he appears. I mean it's not like he doesn't know you have a daughter, and his line of work is all about children."

Kelsey gave a tiny shrug.

"Like I said, we'll see. It would be nice to have someone to share things with, go out occasionally, but we do ok, the two of us."

She joggled Chardonnay, pressing her nose up against the toddlers and laughing with her child.

As the nursery emptied of children and adults, Derby flitted about tidying. Angela had stayed as well, the other nursery nurses having left on a high, as Derby passed the good news onto each of them. Finally when it was just the two of them, they sat on the child size bench in the outdoor play area sipping juice. Derby took a deep breath and let it out slowly.

"So glad that's over."

She said.

"Oh me too. Even though I never thought we would be in trouble, it's still a great feeling when it's over."

Angela replied. Derby looked at her friend.

"You've been doing this nearly as long as me."

Angela nodded.

"Yep. In between having the children. There's nothing else I would want to do."

Derby knew exactly how she felt, the only difference being not having her own children.

"How did you find it, being a working mother?"

She asked. Angela pondered for a moment, twirling her glass.

"Hmm. Hard, even though they were here at the nursery with me. I still had to let the other staff look after them, that was difficult, but at least I got to see them, didn't miss things, like first word and step. Jake's great. He's a very hands on father, so between us we manage well."

Derby could see contentment on her friend's face and hoped one day, someone would see that look on hers.

Once home, Derby sent Geoff a message telling him about the inspection. He messaged back congratulations, and how much he was looking forward to seeing her again.

It's going to be the weekend. Best stay home for a few days. xxx

Derby texted back.

Can't wait. Missing you so much already. Xxxx

Derby held her phone clasped in both hands and bobbed about the kitchen, her heart bursting with love.

David came home at the usual time and went through his same routine of getting changed. Derby made his dinner and when she handed it to him tried to engage him in a conversation.

"We passed the inspection with flying colours."

David, already tucking into his food, pressed a button on the television remote, bringing it to life.

"Uh…what?"

He said, scanning the menu.

"I said, we passed the inspection."

She replied trying to keep anger out of her voice.

"What inspection?"

He mumbled, settling on a news channel. Derby took a deep breath.

"I told you, the nursery had an inspection."

"Oh did you? And it went well?"

Derby threw her hands up in the air.

"I give up."

She mumbled to herself and swung around towards the lounge door. As she exited, she glanced back over her shoulder. David was so engrossed in both his food and programme, he didn't notice her leaving the room.

Grabbing her laptop, Derby stomped out to the garden. She booted it up and opened Facebook. A few of her friends were online, but she didn't feel like chatting. She was angry and frustrated. She put the laptop to one side and wandered onto the lawn, but even the garden, the flowers and the beautiful blue sky couldn't distract her from her mood. She went back to her computer and powered it down, put it in his skin and made a decision.

Ten minutes later she was on the road and heading for Geoff's house. She had no idea if he would be home, hadn't waited to text him and find out. It didn't matter if he wasn't there, just being out of her house, away from David was enough. If Geoff wasn't home she would go to the flat, anywhere. Being alone was far better than being with someone who ignored you.

Derby pulled into Geoff's driveway and a peace came over her. His car wasn't there, but just sitting outside his house drove all of the anger and irritation from her. She leaned back in her seat and looked up at the sky. Small fluffy white clouds drifted across her vision. The trees along the perimeter of the house rustled, their thick leaf- ridden branches swaying and sighing poetically. She closed her eyes for a moment, drinking in her surroundings. The she took her phone and sent Geoff a message.

At your house. Is that alright? Needed to get out of mine. Xxxx

A few seconds passed and she received a reply.

Of course. There's a key in a key safe next to the front door. The code is 1981.

I'll be home about nine. Can you wait? Xxxx

Derby beamed.

Definitely. All night if you want. Don't care anymore. Xxxx

Geoff texted back immediately.

Like the sound of that. Make yourself comfortable. Will try and get away sooner. Xxxx

Derby unlocked the house and stood for a moment before entering. Then she went inside and made her way through to the kitchen. She turned the key to the back door and stepped out, the garden immediately bringing back the memories of sex with Geoff. She breathed in deeply, the scents of the shrubs and flowers making her feel alive and fresh.

She strolled through the trees to the little clearing, trailing her hand along soft petals on the way. She stopped at the bench, closed her eyes and lifted her face to the warm sun shining through the trees. She didn't linger, headed back to the house and back inside. She wandered slowly from room to room, noticing the improvements Geoff had done since her last visit. Each space was filled with his aura and Derby felt her heart filling with love.

Derby was curled up on a sun lounger reading a book she had chosen from Geoff's huge collection, when he arrived home. He came straight across the patio, leaned down and kissed her long and lovingly.

"You have no idea what seeing you here means to me."
He whispered. Derby smiled up into his handsome face.

"Tell me."
She murmured back.

"Everything."
That one word gave her all the encouragement she needed. She stood, the book falling from her knees and wrapped her arms around his neck. He lifted her off her feet and held her in his strong warm arms, pressing his lips to hers, delving into her moist mouth and finding her tongue. She moaned with pleasure and gripped the hair at his nape. Eventually the kiss ended and Geoff settled her to her feet again.

"Hello little Derby"
She giggled.

"Are you alright?"
He asked.

"I am now."
She sighed and leaned into him.

"Are you hungry?"
He said stroking her hair.

"Only for you."
She felt his chest vibrate with his deep laugh.

"Minx. And as much as I would very much like to strip you right here and make love to you, I do need some food."
She stepped back a little but still in the circle of his arms.

"Have I put you out, disrupted your evening?"
Geoff smiled down at her.

"Derby, you could never put me out."

"Would you like me to get you something to eat?"
She asked, still afraid she had disturbed his evening.

"I'm only going to have a sandwich. Sure you don't want something, I have strawberries?"
She laughed and turned towards the kitchen, pulling him by the hand.

"In that case…."

Derby stood by Geoff's side nibbling on a bowl of strawberries as he made himself a sandwich. She was as ever awed by him. A sandwich to her husband consisted of sliced white bread, butter and cheese or ham. Geoff's sandwich was hand cut from rich wholemeal bread, sliced chicken and salad. Even though she had already eaten, it made her mouth water.

Holding his plate, Geoff led them back to the patio, waiting for Derby to sit down before he did. He bit into his food and saw Derby watching. With a grin he held out the sandwich and she leaned towards him and took a bite. Never in her life had she shared food with another human being, and it was another experience to relish, especially with Geoff.

"Mmmm, that is so tasty."
She mumbled. Geoff laughed and offered her more. She shook her head.

"No, you need it. I've already eaten. I'll just stick to the strawberries."
She picked up one of the soft sweet fruit, bit into it, and licked her lips as the juice spread across them.

"As soon as I've finished this…"
Geoff said, the desire in his eyes very evident.

Geoff kept to his words. He swallowed the last bite of his sandwich, came around the table and pulled her to her feet. She came willingly. Lifting the bowl of strawberries, he led her inside the house and without a word up the stairs and into the big bathroom. He placed the bowl on a little stand next to the tub and turned on the taps. Steaming water flowed into the bath. Derby waited. He added scented bubble bath and big frothy foam bubbles began to form in the water. He turned to Derby.

"Need a relaxing soak?"

"Only if you are too."

She said with a cheeky grin.

"Absolutely. You're not getting all of the strawberries."

He checked the water, turned off the taps, stepped over to her and slowly lifted the hem of her dress. Derby raised her arms as he pulled it over her head and laid it on a chair. She stood before him in bra and panties. He ran his hands over her bare shoulders, down her neck and took her breasts gently. She pushed against his palms her mouth opening slightly.

His hands continued down the sides of her body, over her hips and rested on her thighs. Her breath quickened and she brought her hands up and tangled her fingers in his hair. He moved back up her body and unclasped her bra, the light lacy garment floating to the floor. He stood back for a moment, his eyes burning as he took in the sight of her near naked body.

Derby slid her fingertips into the waistband of her undies and heard him gasp. She stopped briefly, enjoying teasing him. She moved her hands closer together and her fingers further inside the delicate fabric. Geoff stepped back and watched.

"Take off your clothes please."

She said, pausing her hands. He quickly obliged, shedding his shorts, T-shirt and trunks. That he wanted her was very obvious.

Derby spread her legs just a little, and pulling her shoulders in tight, let her hands glide back and forth inside her panties. Geoff licked his lips, his penis twitching in readiness. She looked into his eyes, a small smile on her lips, confident in the knowledge of what she was doing to him.

"Oh God Derby. You're sending me crazy."

He murmured. She nodded.

"I know, there's more."

He gasped as she eased the lace down her hips and let it slide to the floor. She stepped out and came towards him, one hand still stroking just above her pubis. Taking a strawberry from the dish, she bit into it, trailed the fruit down between her breasts and stopped just short of her other hand.

Inches from his erection she stopped and pushed his shoulder down. He lowered himself to the floor and knelt in front of her. She offered the strawberry and he took it. Then he watched, as she moved her fingers between her thighs and stroked her labia. He groaned as she slid her middle finger up and down and stroked her own clitoris, little moans of pleasure coming from her lips. Then she took his head in her hands and pulled him towards her sweet, wet, waiting centre.

Geoff closed his lips on her labia and sucked. Derby, hands tangling in his hair moaned and writhed against him. She opened her legs wider and his tongue explored deeper, sending spikes of desire up through her whole body. Slowly she moved up and down, as his tongue flicked and licked and his lips sucked, each movement penetrating deeper.

Inside she felt her orgasm build, gripped his hair and pushed her pelvis harder towards his mouth. Then she exploded, jolting against him, a small scream coming from her lips. She held on to him as she came, then as his tongue flicked her clitoris, came again sending waves of pure pleasure flooding through her veins. He held her hips, his mouth still pressed into her, his tongue still delving and she came again for the third time. She gasped for breath, and finally her body let go and relaxed. Her fingers loosened in his hair and he moved his head away from her.

Derby inhaled deeply and let it out slowly through pursed lips. She rested her hands on Geoff's shoulders, and pushed him backwards until he was on his back on the floor, his erection proud and big. Derby straddled him, and sensuously lowered her hips, taking him deep inside her. He gripped her hips and pushed up, filling her. She clenched her inner muscles around his girth and heard him gasp. Slowly she lifted up, and just before he came out of her, she jigged up and down in short bursts, tickling the tip of his manhood before plunging back hard onto him.

She heard his breath quicken, felt his finger tips hold tightly to her flesh. She leaned forward, so he could penetrate more deeply, moving with him, rolling her pelvis to meet each thrust. She looked into his face, watched his climax come. His eyes were shut, his jaw clenched, and as his orgasm mounted she watched his lips open, his teeth clamp together.

Then he threw his head back against the floor, took in a deep breath, held it as his body shuddered around hers and let it out in a whoosh. His hands stilled on her hips, holding tight, and as his warmth flooded her insides she came again, her nails digging into his chest. Together their breathing slowed and Geoff opened his eyes, sat up and held her. Tears seeped from her eyes and trickled down her face, such was the depth of her emotions. He felt them on his skin and kissed them away gently.

With his arms still around her he raised them both from the floor. He placed one arm under her knees and lifted, gently lowering her into the still warm bubbly water. He stepped in with her and sat behind her, his legs either side of her body. She leaned back into him and he softly massaged her shoulders in the scented water. Nuzzling her neck he whispered.

"It gets better every time."

She slid around to face him, placing her palms against his cheeks.

"I…know…what…you…mean…You…make…me…feel so…so…uninhibited."

He laughed, the sound resonating around the high ceilinged room.

"It's wonderful to watch you like that. I used to think of you as an emerging butterfly. But really you're a kitten turned into a tigress."

She giggled and held out her hands making claws of them.

"Grrrr Mr Stone."

They laughed together as he took her small hands in his large ones kneading her fingers.

"Why do you wear it?"

He asked gently, as he rubbed a thumb across her wedding ring. Derby looked down at the band of gold that had not been removed from her finger for over twenty four years. She pressed her lips together, thought about his words and spoke.

"Habit mostly. Partly, because up until now I believed marriage was sacred, that it should only happen once no matter what. But now…now I've met you, well I know different. This…" She slipped the band from her finger. "is nothing but a physical reminder that I am married. It holds no power, is no bond. There was no love in it when David put it on my finger, of that I'm sure, and there's definitely no love in it now."

She dropped the ring over the side of the tub, and heard it clink and roll across the floor.

"I love you Geoff."

She said as she leaned into him and kissed him in the warm softly scented bath.

"I love you too Derby. You can't know what it means to me to hear you say it."

Chapter 18

Secrets Uncovered Part 1

Geoff kissed her back knotting his hands in her hair, the ends of which trailed in the water. The kiss was full of deep love for both of them. The sex had been amazing, powerful and sensual. But her declaration of love to him had set them on a new course.

Once the water cooled, Geoff stepped out and held her hand, helping her out too. He took a bath sheet from the rail and wrapped it around her, gently drying off her skin and hair. She stood, luxuriating in his touch. When she was thoroughly dry, he took another towel and dried himself. Then he glanced around the room, bent and retrieved her ring from the floor. He held it out to her in the palm of his hand.

"I don't want it."

She said firmly.

"Are you sure?"

He asked. She nodded vigorously. He closed his fist around the band and nodded back.

"Ok. I'll find an envelope to put it in."

She agreed and followed him out of the bathroom.

Downstairs, Geoff lifted a small white envelope from an antique writing desk in the lounge. He dropped the ring inside and closed the flap. He held it out to Derby. Holding the towel around her with one hand, she reached and took the envelope in the other. Without a word she turned for the kitchen, found her bag and dropped the envelope into it. Then she swung round, smiling at Geoff who had followed her through the door.

"You alright?"

He asked softly.

"Mmhmm. Absolutely."

She said, but there was a falseness to her cheeriness. Geoff sensed it in her voice and crossed the room, resting big warm hands on her bare shoulders.

"What is it really Derby?"

Her shoulders shook and tears flowed from her eyes. Geoff pulled her into his arms and held her whilst she sobbed. He stroked her back and smoothed her hair, not speaking, knowing she would when she was ready. Eventually the tears subsided and Derby lifted her face to his. Her nose was stuffed up from crying, her cheeks red and her eyes puffy. Geoff brushed away the remaining tears with his thumbs and pressed a light kiss to her lips.

"I bet I look a right mess."
She mumbled. Geoff shook his head.

"Not at all."
She frowned, not believing him. He laughed.

"Honest. A bit red that's all."
She giggled, her breath still catching from crying. Geoff bent at the knees and looked into her eyes.

"So what brought it on?"
Derby sighed deeply. She hated crying, had done a lot of it recently. But mostly she didn't want Geoff to think she was some weird woman who flipped from one mood to another. So, placing her hands against his hard chest and twiddling her fingers through the hair she said.

"It's stupid really."
She paused, trying to voice her thoughts and struggling. Geoff waited patiently then said.

"Let's go outside. I'll make us a drink and you can gather your thoughts."

Geoff settled her in a chair at the patio table and went back to the kitchen. Derby unwrapped herself from the damp towel and leaned back in the comfort of the lounger. A warm breeze brushed her skin, soft as tissue. She looked up into the dark sky, stars twinkling, gems on a cushion of velvet. Geoff returned with two mugs of coffee. He handed one to Derby, pulled a chair close to her side and sat down. She took a sip, put the mug down and spoke.

"My wedding day wasn't how I had imagined it to be. There was David, of course. His mother and sister and my parents. But it wasn't a day for celebration. The families were there only to make sure it actually happened, or rather my parents were. His were opposed to it, but even they were ashamed of having an illegitimate child in the family. So they came to witness the event.

There was no reception, no toasts and no congratulations. After, David and I went back to our bedsit, and they all went home. I haven't seen or spoken to my parents since. I think his mother may have told them that I wasn't pregnant after all, but I don't know for sure, they've never been in touch."

Derby stopped, picked up her mug and sipped her coffee. Geoff covered her empty hand with one of his and squeezed lovingly. His towel had slipped from his hips, but even though both were naked in a warm dark garden, comfort and love was what he wanted to give her then.

"That must have been awful for you."
He told her, his voice low and gentle. She nodded.

"Yes, it was. Not surprising since my parents had never been there for me anyway, but still pretty hard. His mother and sister disliked me from the off, I tried, did everything a dutiful little wife should, but it was never good enough."

Derby emptied her cup and sat holding it in both hands. For a moment her thoughts were back in time, on the day of her wedding. The day every woman should hold in her heart as the most precious memory ever. But for Derby it had only added to the years of disappointment before, and then those up until the morning of her fortieth birthday.

Geoff quietly took the mug from her hands and rested it on the table. He held her hands in his and stroked her fingers softly. Derby came back to him, a tiny smile on her lips, eyes dark with emotion.

"I'm done Geoff. With all of them. I've wasted too much of my life, let them bully me into submission. I'll have to do some checking, you know solicitors and all that, but soon I will be free."

Geoff raised her hands to his lips and kissed them lovingly. Then he pressed them against his heart.

"I'll be right by your side Derby. It's taken me a lifetime to find you."
Derby breathed deeply. Even though they had both said 'I love you' there was a little thread of fear inside her that was still unsure of how serious Geoff was.

"Sure?"
She asked tentatively. Geoff held her hands even tighter.

"More than anything, anytime in my life."

He told her, conviction in his voice, as he pulled her to her feet and settled her on his lap. Derby felt a happiness deep inside she had never realised had been missing. It blossomed and bloomed, its petals spreading open, releasing a scent of pure contentment. She nestled into his shoulder and he cradled her in his arms. Neither had thoughts of sex, just deep profound love.

Derby had very much wanted to stay all night. But she knew she had to get home, be there when David woke up, and to get ready for work. As they kissed goodbye in Geoff's driveway, she promised him the whole weekend. They arranged to meet at the flat the next evening and decided to make plans from there. So, with the top down, Derby drove towards her house, the stars winking at her from above.

David came down for breakfast the same as he did every day. His cereal was ready, his tea poured and as usual any conversation non-existent. Derby desperately wanted to tell him then and there about her plans for the weekend, about Geoff, but didn't have the nerve. Instead she resolved to be tactical, think it through and set a time that suited her, especially as she suspected Irene and Brenda would be heavily involved, once it all came out. So she let David leave for work, oblivious to her thoughts.

Mid-morning Derby popped out of the nursery and along to the bakery nearby. She bought a selection of cream cakes and three sponge cakes. The cream cakes for the staff, and the sponges to be cut into small pieces for the children, as a celebration for passing the inspection. The day had a far more relaxed feel about it now the inspection was complete.

Derby made sure she spoke to and thanked each of her nursery nurses personally, and gave them a cake to eat during their break. She and Angela nibbled on theirs in the kitchen at lunchtime, as they cut the sponge cakes into slices.

"So what's been happening lately?"
Angela asked.

"Phew, where to begin."
Derby replied.

"How about a drink after work and you bring me up to date."
Angela suggested. Derby agreed, mentally working out times. She could meet Geoff a bit later, she knew he wouldn't mind, would in

fact encourage her interaction with her friend. So licking cream from her fingers, Angela took a plate of sponge to hand out to the children.

Derby and Angela went to the same place after work they had visited the first time. Derby bought the drinks, delighting in her new confidence. She leaned casually against the bar and ordered two glasses of wine, smiling her thanks to the barman. Angela had found a table and was waiting for Derby, watching her friend, happy for her change.

The atmosphere was the same as before, but now Derby felt comfortable with it. Where the music and adult voices had seemed too loud and intrusive before, Derby now listened, tapping her foot lightly to a tune she didn't know, but found she was enjoying. She no longer felt alien. It was all still very new, but now she felt like she fit. Angela looked at the difference she could detect on her friend's face.

"Who would think it was just three weeks ago."
She said. Derby drinking in the atmosphere along with her wine replied absentmindedly.

"Mmm....sorry, what?"
Angela giggled.

"What?"
Derby asked again, having no idea what she had missed.

"Three weeks Derby."
Angela told her.

"Three weeks? You've lost me."
Derby said, swirling her wine a little.

"Three weeks ago, we sat here and you opened up for the first time. Remember?"

Derby took a very deep breath and let it out slowly. She gazed into her glass, just three weeks and so much had happened.

"Phew…seems like a lifetime ago."
She said, barely above a whisper. Angela reached across the table and covered Derby's hand.

"Chick, for you it has been a lifetime. So much of what the rest of us take for granted has been new and fresh to you, and it's all happened in that short space of time. I mean, in some ways, I sort of envy you…skipping a lot of the tough stuff…I'm sorry, that sounded harsh and I didn't mean it the way it came out."

Angela paused, hoping she hadn't upset her friend. But Derby looked up, a smile breaking across her lips.

"It's fine Ang' I know what you mean. I mean no one could say I've had it hard…"

She burst into giggles and Angela joined in.

"…actually the last three weeks I have."

She finished, still giggling. Angela laughing so much, she slopped wine over the rim of her glass onto her own hand.

"Ooops, don't want to waste that."

She said, as she licked the liquid from her fingers. Slowly their laughter abated and the two women settled back into their previous conversation.

"My life with David has been dull, but compared to some women, I've had it easy."

Angela nodded in agreement.

"I see what you mean. But still, many wasted years."

The bar had filled up considerably, young and older clientele mingling, chatting and drinking, watched by Derby as she slowly sipped her drink. She wanted to make it last as she had no intention of having any more, she would be driving later to meet Geoff.

"Yep, definitely that, but at least no abuse, no having to put up with affairs…except my own recent one…"

She smirked and Angela gave her a devilish look.

"…and, well, when I think of Kelsey struggling as a single mother, I wonder how she does it."

Angela pressed her lips together and nodded again.

"I know. She's brilliant, and I suppose if you have to, you do it. But if I didn't have Jake, I don't know how I'd cope."

"Wonder what sort of mother I would've been."

Derby said wistfully.

"A very good one."

Angela told her.

"So you were going to tell me what's been going on."

Angela prompted.

Derby took another deep breath, and holding her glass between her hands began telling Angela her news. There were snippets of it she already knew, like the time on the beach with Geoff, and how he had dealt with Evan, but Derby realised there was a lot she hadn't told her friend. So she told her all about Irene, her next door neighbours, Bob and Fiona, and the decision she had made to herself about Geoff. Angela listened without interruption until she finished.

"I see what you mean about phew."
She said. Derby pressed her lips together.
"Oh yes."
"Do you have a plan?"
Angela asked. Derby shook her head and took a deep breath, holding it for a few seconds.

"No, not really. Not at all actually. I just know I can't go on like I have. Even if things go bottoms up with Geoff, and I so hope they won't, well, I can't go back to life before him. I've grown, taken a very long time I know, but I have. I can see all the mistakes I've made over the years, like flipping through a photo album, and I won't be making them again. Even if I have to be on my own."

She finished by lifting her wine glass and draining it, placing it firmly on the table. Angela sat back and grinned.

"Go Derby, go Derby."
She mimicked an American school girl's voice, her hands fisted and rotating in front of her. Derby laughed at her friend.

"I know."
Angela said, now jiggling her shoulders in time to the music.

"How about you come to our house on Sunday, and bring Geoff? We can barbeque."

Derby hesitated just a fraction of a second before agreeing. She had no idea if Geoff would want to socialise with her friend but hoped he would. She herself was suddenly looking forward to it, and she thought Geoff would too, had the feeling he would want to see her happy and enjoying herself. She also had the sneaky feeling that he would want to show off their relationship a little bit, and she definitely wanted to show him off.

"I'm going to say yes."
Derby said. Angela squealed like a child and bounced up and down in her seat.

"So the fun begins."
Angela said, draining her glass too.

The two women left the bar, making arrangements for Sunday. Angela suggested the couple come round about midday, meet Jake and the children, and then have a relaxing afternoon eating and drinking. Derby laughed at her enthusiasm and agreed to everything she said.

"Then next time, we'll make it a real party."

Angela dropped in, just as Derby was about to head for home.

"What?"

Derby halted. She saw the smirk on her friend's face.

"Haha…got you."

Derby pressed her lips together and feigned a swipe at Angela who ducked out of the way giggling.

"Seriously though."

Angela said, straightening.

"When you get sorted we'll have a party, introduce you and Geoff to some of our friends."

Derby felt a little lump in the back of her throat, happy and relieved that she had finally come out of the grey and into this new world of colour and light.

As Derby rounded the corner at the end of her street, she saw a familiar but unwelcome car parked outside her home. With a big sigh and a frown, she quickened her pace. As she approached, she hoped Bob and Fiona would be in their garden. She needed the warmth of their smiles and the sense of security the old couple gave her. But with disappointment, she saw their garden was empty.

As Derby levelled with the car, the driver's door opened. Brenda, David's sister stepped out. Derby hadn't seen the woman in a long time and was surprised at how large she had got. Brenda was a tall woman, and had always towered ominously over Derby, but her width had increased a great deal over the years. Now she stared angrily down at Derby, whose first instinct was to turn and run. But Derby's new confidence won through and she stood her ground.

"Brenda."

Was all she said. David's sister sneered.

"Well?"

Derby frowned, completely puzzled.

"Well what Brenda?"

The other woman folded her arms across her enormous chest, and leaned into Derby's face.

"You know what. You…you BITCH!"

Derby gasped at the hatred that emanated from her, and took a defensive step backwards.

"Oi! You…"

Both women swung towards the strong voice that came from behind them. Derby felt relief wash over her as Bob threw open his gate and stomped towards them, Fiona close behind. He lifted an old hand and pointed a finger at Brenda.

"Don't you dare speak to her like that!"

He said furiously, his bushy silver brows coming together.

Brenda pulled herself up to her considerable height, pushing her huge bosoms forward. Derby had forgotten how big the woman was and how haughty she could come across, but Bob didn't appear to notice, wasn't in the least perturbed by her size.

"And who are you? What's more, what business is this of yours?"

She said, looking down her nose at him. Bob stepped right up to her, and though she loomed over him, he wasn't intimidated.

"We are Derby's friends and we look out for her. That makes this our business."

He told her, a forcefulness to his voice that Derby was surprised of but glad of too. Brenda seemed lost for words at his reply. Then she glanced sideways at Derby and a flush came to her cheeks. She unfolded her arms and jabbed a finger at Derby.

"Mum might not be able to defend herself, but I can."

Derby wanted to giggle, felt it bubble up, tried to contain it and failed. It burst from her lips. She covered her mouth, but couldn't stop and hitching managed to say.

"Not…not…be…able…to…to…de…fend herself."

Her laughter made Bob and Fiona laugh too. This encouraged her, and in a more steady voice was able to say to Brenda.

"Your mother…is more than capable of defending herself. Now…say what you came to say and then…shove off."

Brenda stood stock still. Even though Derby had had little contact with the woman over the years, when she had, Brenda had always put her down. Many times she had made snide remarks to her, side comments about not having children and digs about her having trapped David. Derby had taken the lot, never once having the confidence or will to retaliate. So now that she had, Brenda was shocked into silence. However, she soon recovered.

"We, that is mum and me, don't think you are treating David the way a wife should. And we are not going to put up with it. This is David's house and we want you out."

Derby stepped forward, the expression on her face making Brenda step back nervously, despite her size. Encouraged by this and the gentle hand that Fiona rested on her shoulder, Derby looked up at the big woman.

"You and mummy can say what you like. But, this house is in my name as well. Nothing will change that unless David and I decide to. You don't get to be a part of it. Go back and tell mummy that the both of you can keep your interfering noses out of my business. Oh and tell mummy I pity her son, my husband, she's brought him up to be a complete arsehole sap. Now get out of my face."

Derby turned her back on Brenda, but glanced over her shoulder when she heard Fiona laugh. Brenda stood frozen, her mouth forming a perfect 'O'. Her hands were clasped under her flabby double chin, and she was taking short breaths.

"Need a hand?"

Derby heard Bob ask, and turned back to see him holding Brenda's car door open like a chauffeur. Brenda huffed and clambered into the seat, knowing that despite wielding her size at Derby, it was Derby who had taken control.

Derby stood with Bob and Fiona flanking her as Brenda drove off down the street. The old couple linked arms with her and the three laughed together.

"Tea?"

Fiona asked. Derby nodded and they separated and walked up the garden path.

"Mmmm…just what I needed."

Derby said, sipping hot tea from a china cup.

"That woman is horrible."

Fiona exclaimed, Bob nodding in agreement.

"She is. They're both like it. I really do pity David, but it's not really an excuse for the way he is. I mean people have to take responsibility for their own behaviour, they can't keep blaming their upbringing. Actually, that's not really fair. I don't think

David even realises how he's been over the years. Maybe we have both just been victims of circumstance, I don't know, we never talk, so I honestly don't know how he feels about anything."

Derby sighed. The last three weeks had been a whirlwind of change for her. She had discovered herself, sex, enjoyment and pleasure, and most of all Geoff. But she hadn't stopped to think that David might have gone through the same things as her over the years. That her husband of twenty four years, had also lived a dull and loveless life, because they had been forced together, and neither knew or up until now cared enough to do anything about it. Derby emptied her cup and stood up.

"That was lovely, and thank you both so much for coming out and supporting me. Sometime, and soon I think, David and I need to have a conversation, but, I have a weekend planned and I don't want that spoilt, so I think later rather than sooner."
Bob placed his old hand over hers.

"Don't rush it Derby. Do it when you feel ready and not because his mother and sister have forced your hand."

Derby leaned forward and kissed his cheek, making him blush. She then did the same to Fiona, who pulled her into a motherly hug. Then she left the old couple to their evening and went home. Closing the front door Derby leaned back on it for a moment. The familiarity of the house washed over her, oppressive rather than comforting. She hoped that when all the complications were done and dusted, they would sell it, let it go to a family who could enjoy it and love it.

Pushing away from the door, Derby trotted upstairs. David would be home soon and she wanted to be out of the house before that. However, she took time putting together the things she wanted for the weekend. Her new bikini was still at the flat, though she wasn't sure she would need it, but most of her other new clothes were still here in the wardrobe. She selected underwear, all matching sets, sexy and lacy. She chose a soft, mostly pink, printed dress for Sunday and various other garments for the rest of the time. Satisfied she had everything she needed she headed back downstairs.

The kitchen clock showed five to seven, nearly time for David's return. Derby panicked a little, but as she swung around to the fridge to get some juice, she stopped and looked at the printout stuck to the door with a magnet. It was David's weekly schedule, and something Derby hadn't looked at in the last three weeks. Every week, David would put his schedule on the fridge showing which two nights he had to stay late at the supermarket. With relief Derby saw tonight was one of those nights, she had more time than she had thought.

Taking a deep breath, Derby took juice from the fridge and poured a glass. She sipped as she leaned against the sink looking out into the garden. She was still keen to get away, go to the flat and meet Geoff, but her sudden revelation that David was in the same boat as herself, gave her a little flash of guilt. So, she rummaged in the freezer and found a plastic tub of lasagne that she had made weeks ago, pulled it out and left it on the side to defrost for David when he got home. Even if he chose takeaway, at least she had tried, given him a choice.

Feeling a lot better about the overall situation between herself and her husband, Derby finished her juice, put the glass in the dishwasher and tapped a message to Geoff.

Just leaving meet you at the flat. Love you xxxx
She felt a blush creep up her cheeks, not embarrassment for her words, but a little shyness. Saying 'I love you' to anyone was new and fresh, and she felt like a teenager saying it to her first boyfriend. She supposed somewhere back in time, she might have said it to David, but she couldn't remember it. She recalled the first, and now she believed the only time he had said it, and it made her sad, so much waste for both of them. Her phone chirped in her hand, startling her out of her reverie.

Can't wait see you there. Love you too xxxx
Derby hugged her phone as though it was actually Geoff and headed out of the door.

Derby was on the balcony looking at the boats when the buzzer sounded. Excitedly she answered, and pressed the button giving Geoff access. She was at the door when he emerged from the stairwell and flung herself into his open arms. He lifted her form her feet kissing her at the same time, and carried her into the flat, nudging the door shut with his foot.

Her hands tangled in his hair, her body instantly reacting to his kiss. Within seconds, Geoff was stripping her clothes from her body and pushing her down onto the leather sofa. She wriggled beneath him, pulling at his jeans and then he was inside her. A warm breeze wafted through the open patio doors, soft against her skin as she writhed beneath him, wanting him deeper. She drew up her knees and linked her ankles around his thighs, his thrusts becoming more rapid, her hips bucking to meet him. She came with a force that shook every inch of her, her scream muted as she bit down on his shoulder. He arched above her, eyes closed as his body became taut, then he exploded inside her and she came again.

"Hello."

Derby whispered and together they laughed.

Later, they stood side by side on the balcony looking down at the boats sipping wine. Derby told Geoff all about Brenda's visit and how Bob and Fiona had come to her rescue. She also told him the conclusion she had come to about David.

"Sad for both of you really."

Geoff said. Derby nodded, twirling her wine glass.

"Yes it is. We should have seen it though. I realise that now."

"Sometimes life itself can be a buffer. Neither of you had any experience outside of your marriage so it was the norm. Your parents, David's family, they never gave you any support, you had no one to turn to for advice, so you drifted along. I'm just glad you came to my gym that day."

Derby pressed up against him.

"Mmmm, me too."

They went to bed early but didn't spend much of it sleeping. However, when morning came, Derby felt fresh and rested. She quietly slipped out from under the duvet and stood for a moment watching Geoff sleep. He was laid on his stomach, his head turned towards her pillow. His dark lashes rested on his tanned cheeks, his hair was tousled, and she could just see the stubble on his chin. He looked beautiful.

Derby was brewing coffee and warming croissants when Geoff came up behind her in the kitchen. He nuzzled her neck, she turning her head to steal a kiss.

"Breakfast is ready."

She announced cheerily. Geoff smiled and took the mug of coffee she held out to him.

"Let's go onto the balcony. Make the most of this weather whilst it lasts."

She said, taking the plate of croissants and leading the way.

The sky was blue and clear, promising yet another perfect summer day. They sat at the small table and chairs that came with the flat, eating, chatting and sipping coffee.

"Angela, that's my friend from work, if I haven't already told you that, has invited us to her house for a barbeque tomorrow. Is that alright?"

Geoff smiled, his brilliant beaming smile.

"Little Derby, my darling, that's great. I'm pleased as punch. It will be really good to meet your friend."

He pressed his lips together and frowned slightly.

"She doesn't mind about us does she?"

Derby held his hand.

"No. She's chuffed for me actually. And she can't wait to meet you."

She wriggled her eyebrows at him.

"Uh oh, what have you said?"

He asked, grinning. Derby bit one side of her lip.

"Oh, only that you are the most gorgeous, beefed up guy any woman would die for."

Geoff laughed, his face reddening.

"Devil Derby at it again."

A noise from below made Derby stand and look over the rail. She had an idea what she was hearing and beckoned Geoff to her side. As she thought, the two men from before were again on their boat.

"Hi, how's it going?"

She called down. Both men looked up.

"Brilliant!"

One called.

"Superb!"

The other said.

"Come down and have a look!"

The first one said. He had obviously seen Geoff and didn't seem put out about his presence. Derby looked at Geoff who smiled and nodded.

"Ok. See you in a bit!"

She called back.

"Do you know them?"

Geoff asked. Derby frowned slightly, suddenly nervous that Geoff would think badly of her. But his expression was soft and gentle.

"No. They've been here a couple of times when I have, working on their boat. I've only spoken to them over the balcony…but I would like to see the boat."

Geoff put his hands on her shoulders and stroked her bare skin. He bent at the knees and looked into her eyes.

"Derby, don't look so worried. I'm not annoyed, or jealous, and actually I'd love to see their boat too. It's been years since I've been anywhere near one."

Derby relaxed against him. She had no experience with men, she didn't count David, other than Geoff, had no idea how to read their minds. But instinct told her Geoff was a good man. One she could trust and be herself with. One who would trust her.

She felt heat flood her cheeks as she recalled the sex with the car salesman, for that's how she thought of him, not by his name. And sex was what it had been, nothing more, something she had needed to do, a test for herself, a way of assessing her feelings for Geoff. And it would never happen again with another man, not whilst she was with Geoff. She had proved something to herself then. No one other than Angela knew about it and never would. That was a secret that would never be uncovered.

Pushing her secret to the back of her mind she took Geoff by the hand and headed down to the marina. The two men greeted them brightly, holding their hands out to be shaken.

"I'm Charlie and this is my brother Aaron."

Derby and Geoff introduced themselves and stepped onto the deck of the boat. The brothers showed them around, and Derby thought it looked very nice. She had no idea if the boat was a particularly good one, but from what she heard Geoff saying to Aaron concluded that it was.

"We bought it two months ago. The engine needed quite a bit of work, but now it goes like a dream."

She overheard Aaron telling Geoff. Charlie looked at her and grinned.

"He's more techy than me. I just love being out on the sea. Now she's ready."

Derby smiled back.

"Hey, our wives are coming down this afternoon and we're taking her out. Would you two like to come?"

Geoff swung round at Charlie's words, a beaming smile on his face. He looked at Derby waiting for her to make the decision. Derby could see the excitement and enthusiasm shining from his eyes, and even though she felt a little trepidation at the prospect of her very first boat trip, she couldn't deny him.

"That would be lovely."

She said, watching Geoff's smile get bigger.

"I've never been on a boat before though, so I hope I don't get seasick or anything."

Geoff came over to her and put his arms around her, hugging her tight. Charlie and Aaron glanced at one another, a knowing look crossing their faces. But neither man made any comment.

"Try not to be nervous, that helps. And if you do get queasy, it's best to stay on deck." Geoff told her gently.

She smiled at him and turned to the brothers.

"What time, and what do I wear?"

All three men laughed.

"Only a woman would think about her outfit first."

Aaron said with raised eyebrows.

"Better not let Cassie hear you say that."

Charlie responded, ducking away from his brother and answering Derby's question.

"About two, and anything you feel comfortable in really. Might be a good idea to bring a jacket or cardy though 'cos it can get a bit chilly out on the water, even on a hot day like this. Well, when we're moving anyway. And this baby can really chew up the waves I can tell you."

Aaron saw a flicker of fear pass across Derby's face.

"Hey, it's ok. Don't worry, we know what we're doing."

Geoff looked down at her.

"I'll look after you Derby. You'll enjoy it, I promise."

And Derby knew she would.

Back in the flat, Derby flicked through her wardrobe at the clothes she had brought with her. None of them seemed suitable for a day out on the sea. She sighed and Geoff came up behind her and turned her to face him.

"Come on. We're going down to the outdoor shop. There's bound to be something there."

Ten minutes later they were browsing the rails in the shop. Derby already held a pair of white linen trousers. Geoff lifted a T-shirt and cotton jacket from the rail and held them up for Derby's approval. She liked his choice. Next he found soft soled shoes and matching cap. He took everything to the counter and added shorts, T-shirt and cap for himself and bought it all.

Derby and Geoff strolled down to the marina just before two. Derby had put her bikini under her new outfit, a suggestion made by Geoff. Luckily she had decided to get changed much earlier than needed, because the minute she took off her clothes, Geoff was obviously ready for more than just a ride out to sea. Finally, when she did put on her new things, she felt full of life and energy, and eager for the experience that awaited her.

Charlie and Aaron were waiting as the couple stepped onto the deck. Two women were sitting on the leather seats, each holding a tall glass of something that had fruit bobbing about in it. They smiled at them as Charlie introduced them.

"My wife Mel, and Aaron's wife Cassie, Derby and Geoff." The women gave them friendly smiles. Aaron held out a bottle of beer to Geoff and a glass of the same drink as the wives to Derby. She took a small sip and tasted a fruity vodka mix. It wasn't too strong and very refreshing. Geoff put his arm around her and sipped his beer.

"Ok."
He murmured softly. She nodded, relaxing.

The group chatted for a while. The men mostly about the boat, but Mel and Cassie asking more about Derby. At first she was a little reluctant, only telling them she was a nursery nurse and not mentioning her marriage. But like their husbands, they seemed to guess.

"You're married, but not to Geoff aren't you?"
Cassie said, but in a nice way. Derby sighed.

"That obvious?"
Cassie and Mel grinned.

"Oh yes."

Mel said. Derby sighed again and gave the two women a very edited version of her marriage and her relationship with Geoff.

"Oh don't worry Derby. From what you've said, and I don't think it's all of it, but, good on you. This is my second marriage. I met Charlie when I was still married. My first marriage was hell. He was a brute, arrogant and plain bloody nasty. Charlie saved me. I mean, I was stuck, had nowhere to go, two little children to look after, and well, Charlie took us all in. Gave me the confidence to get out and get divorced. We married six months after, that was ten years ago and I've never looked back."

Derby felt a little ashamed of herself. Yes her marriage to David had leached the life out her, but nothing bad had ever happened. This brave woman in front of her, had obviously had a very traumatic time in the past. And even though she had only just met her, warmed to her, she was pleased that she had found happiness.

Not too long after, Charlie and Aaron prepped the boat and began manoeuvring them out of the marina. Geoff stood by Charlie as he steered, and Derby could see the excitement on his face. He looked comfortable and at ease, and Derby thought oh so sexy, his legs slightly apart and his feet planted firmly. She switched off from the women for a second as she heard him speak.

"It's been a long time since I've been on a boat. But being back on the water, it feels like it was just yesterday"

Derby smiled to herself, switching back to Mel and Cassie as she heard Geoff ask some technical questions about the boat and its engine.

Some time later, Derby stood next to Geoff as the boat sped over the waves. True to his word, Aaron and Charlie did know what they were doing. Mel and Cassie seemed to be as much at ease as their husbands and Derby was pleased that she wasn't at all seasick. Aaron glanced over his shoulder to Geoff.

"Want to take her?"

Geoff stepped eagerly forward, pulling Derby with him. Aaron and Charlie settled next to their wives, confident in Geoff's ability.

"Go for it."

Charlie called. Geoff looked at Derby and grinned.

"Don't be scared."

She wasn't.

Geoff gradually increased the speed and steered the boat in a wide sweeping arc across the water. Derby felt salt air on her face and her hair was whipped about, but she was exhilarated. The rush of the sea as they flew over the waves, the dip and rise of the boat, and Geoff by her side in complete control, filled her with love and excitement. Geoff briefly looked at her, and leaned in closer.

"We'll have to get one."

He told her over the sound of the waves and the roar of the engine. Derby gasped with pleasure. He had said 'we' not 'I' and that one tiny word meant more than anything.

What seemed like hours later, but wasn't that long at all, Charlie slowed the boat, and brought it into a tiny bay, where cliffs rose on all sides. Aaron hopped overboard and together the brothers brought the boat to a stop. Mel and Cassie jumped out into water thigh deep and waded to shore. Derby hesitated. Geoff grinning, jumped into the sea and held his arms out to her. She dropped into them and he carried her onto the sand.

"What a gentleman."

Cassie called.

"Yeah, our boys don't do that."

Mel answered. Both women were laughing, not mockingly, just easy banter towards their husbands.

"Huh, you two spend more time in the sea than we do."

Charlie called back. He was still on deck handing a cool box and various bits down to his brother.

"Yeah, you should carry us."

Aaron added.

Derby laughed along with the wives as Geoff went back to help Aaron carry some of the stuff. Not long after, the group were settled on rugs with cold drinks. The smell of barbequed meat wafted up from a small pit Charlie had dug, lined with flat rocks and covered with a wire grill. Derby didn't think life could get any better at that moment. She was with a wonderful man, new friends and enjoying herself more than she ever thought possible.

The sun was just beginning to set as they returned to the marina, a beautiful red glow over the horizon which turned the sea a deep dark blue. Geoff stepped off the boat and held his hand out to Derby. The couple turned and thanked their friends for a wonderful day. Mel and Cassie hopped onto the pontoon and hugged Derby, Aaron and Charlie joining them, hugging her too and shaking Geoff's hands. The six swapped numbers and agreed to meet up again soon, and then Geoff and Derby made their way back to the flat.

The day had worn them out, but once inside they both found it had also increased their desire. Geoff took her into his arms as soon as the door was closed and kissed her deeply.

"Mmmm, I've been waiting to do that all day."
He murmured. They had shared little kisses and touches throughout the day, but kept them brief, not wanting to embarrass the two couples who had welcomed them.

"Me too."
Derby whispered back.

That was all it took. Clothes heaped on the floor as Geoff pulled her against him, his erection ready. Derby pressed into him, but again the difference in their height prevented what she wanted. She groaned. Geoff took her buttocks in both his hands, kneading them. Then he lifted her from her feet. She wrapped her legs around him, opening herself to him, and he was inside her, deep and fast.

Derby held onto his neck as he kissed her, his hands gripping her bottom, pulling her onto him with each thrust. She linked her ankles around his waist and moved rhythmically, driving him deeper the faster he plunged. Her orgasm started low and began to build. She dug her nails into his shoulder, felt his teeth nip her neck and then she came, squealing "More" as she felt his hot fluid spill into her.

Still inside her and still holding her, Geoff walked them both to the bedroom. He eased them onto the bed, laying back so Derby was on top of him. She sat up and wriggled her pelvis. He was still firm and she enjoyed the sticky wet sensation moving around him gave her. Geoff stroked her breasts, smiling up at her.

"I love you so much Derby."
Her eyes shone as she leaned towards him.

"I love you very much too Geoff. You're all I want."
She kissed him gently, his still erect penis feeling warm inside her. He cupped her face and kissed her back, and she came again.

Sleep came easily to both of them. Geoff held her spooned against him, one arm resting over her thigh. She was comfortable, didn't feel in the least bit restricted, slept deeply, and awoke refreshed. She stretched languidly, arched her back like a cat, and relaxed back against the pillows. The bedroom door was open and she heard whistling coming from the kitchen. It got louder and Geoff appeared in the doorway with a mug of tea for her. He kissed her as he handed her the drink.

"Breakfast awaits you on the balcony."
He was dressed in just shorts, his hair damp, his face clear of stubble.

"I didn't hear you shower."
Derby said as she sipped her tea.

"You looked so lovely and peaceful asleep, I went into the main bathroom."
He told her as he stroked her cheek with one finger. Derby planted a tiny kiss on his hand.

"I'm going to have a quick shower too, is that ok? Breakfast won't spoil?"
He shook his head.

"I'll be waiting."
They spent a lazy morning around the flat and the marina. Derby had thoroughly enjoyed breakfast, hot croissants, fresh fruit and steaming coffee. Except for the coffee, she knew she didn't have the rest in the kitchen. Quizzing Geoff, he told her he had popped out to the shops below. She beamed at this information. They cleared the kitchen together and then wandered down onto the walkway.

A few light clouds flitted across the sky, in no way threatening. Hand in hand with Geoff, Derby was excited that the weather was again going to hold for Angela's barbeque. The boats swayed slightly on the water, several owners breakfasting on their decks, waving and calling hello as they passed. Geoff paused several times to lean on the rails and point out various makes and models to Derby, enthusiasm evident in his voice.

On the opposite side to Derby's flat, the line of shops were already busy. They took their time exploring them, Derby surprised at the choice. Geoff pointed out the one where he had bought their breakfast, and Derby pulled him in, wanting to see what else they sold. Inside she discovered a deli counter full of delicious cold meats and various cheeses. The shop also had a small bakery and fridges with milk, butter and spreads. Along one side were baskets of fresh fruit, most locally sourced. The smells were wonderful, and Derby couldn't resist the tasty looking Danish pastries. Before she had a chance to get her money out, Geoff had already handed over change from his pocket, taking the bag with two pastries from the assistant.

Back on the walkway they nibbled on their sweet confection and continued strolling. Towards the far corner of the marina, Geoff stopped them at the window of a business advertising boat sales and sailing instruction courses. There were several cards in the window, similar to an estate agents. Geoff pointed at one.

"I like that."

Derby looked. There was a photo of a sleek white boat with details written underneath. She had no idea what any of it meant, but thought it was probably a good boat if Geoff was keen, and it did look very nice.

"Oh, that's even better."

He told her excitedly, pointing out another boat.

"I haven't got a clue about any of them, but they do look lovely."

Derby admitted. Geoff laughed, squeezing her hand.

"I'll teach you if you want."

"I'd like that."

She said, looking up at him. He planted a light kiss on her lips.

"When we do buy one, I'll make sure you know all about it first, so you can make an informed choice with me."

Derby felt herself trembling, inside and out. Geoff was talking about the future, their future. She had hoped, and longed that they would have one, but hadn't dared accept it was a foregone conclusion. Geoff looked into her eyes.

"You ok?"

He asked seriously. She pulled him to her and snuggled into his arms.

"I so want us to be together, always."

She murmured, and before he could answer.

"I've dreamt about it, but didn't dare believe it could be true."

Geoff tilted her chin and looked into her face. She was blushing, her cheeks rosy. He kissed each one lightly, then the end of her nose.

"You're so beautiful when you blush."
He told her huskily, making her flush deepen.

"I can't read the future little Derby, but I do believe we, together, can make it happen. It's what I want too"
Derby held onto him and silently vowed to never let him go.

At just after twelve, Derby knocked on Angela's front door. She opened it and with a huge smile, beckoned them in.

"Jake's in the garden getting the barbeque started."
She said, as she led them down the hallway to the back of the house. Childish squeals were coming from that direction, and Derby assumed the children were with their father. She smiled wistfully at the sounds, so normal, yet so alien to her own life.

Angela stepped out of the back door onto a flagged patio that edged a fairly large garden. Jake, her husband looked up from his task of lighting the well used barbeque, smiled, wiped his hands on a cloth and strolled over. He was a tall, handsome, wiry man with thick dark curls speckled with grey. Angela introduced Derby and Geoff, Jake shaking Geoff's hand, but giving a little kiss to Derby on her cheek.

"At last. I get to meet 'The Derby'"
He said with a wide easygoing grin.

Derby blushed and gave Angela a sideways look. Angela shrugged with a smile. But before any further comments could be made, two boys, one chasing the other flew towards Angela, ducking around her, using her as a post.

"Can't catch me!"
One squealed, giggling.

"Can!"
Said the other, trying to grab his brother.

"Whoa you two. Slow down, look we have guests."
The boys stopped their game and politely said hello to Derby and Geoff. However, seconds later they were off again running around the lawn. A girl, obviously younger than the boys,

sauntered towards them, her arms folded. She approached her mother with pursed lips.

"Those two."

She said, trying to sound grown up. Angela draped and arm over her shoulder.

"Hello Poppy. I'd like you to meet friends of mine."

Poppy looked at Derby and then at Geoff, who was now chatting to Jake.

"You work with mummy don't you?"

She said. Derby nodded down at the girl.

"And he's not your husband is he?"

Everything seemed to freeze for a second as Angela gasped, the two men's conversation stopped and Derby stood rooted to the spot.

"Poppy! That's rude."

Angela finally found her voice. Derby shook her head.

"It's alright Ang'."

Then she stooped down so she was nearer the girl's height.

"No Poppy, Geoff's not my husband, but he is my boyfriend."

Poppy looked into Derby's eyes, a serious expression on her young face. Then she looked up at Geoff who was still standing next to Jake.

"Hmmm, I suppose that's ok then."

She said. The adults looked at one another and burst out laughing. Poppy frowned a little, not sure what she had said to make them laugh. Then she gave a tiny shrug, spun round and headed for a swing at the back of the garden.

"Little madam."

Angela said to them.

"How old is she?"

Geoff asked.

"Seven going on sixteen."

Jake answered with a resigned sigh.

"She must have overheard me telling Jake about you and Geoff."

Angela said apologetically.

"We usually try not to let any of them hear adult stuff, but I bet Poppy had her ears on alert, she does that sometimes."

Derby touched her friend's arm.

"It's fine Ang' really. I'm not ashamed."

Geoff held out his hand and she took it, a knowing look between them.

"Um…sorry…I'm a terrible host. How about a drink?"

Jake piped up.

The afternoon flew by. The barbeque was smoking, a light breeze wafting delicious scents of cooking meat across the garden. Angela had been able to calm her sons long enough to properly introduce them, eleven year old Ben and nine year old Will, before they declared they were starving to death. Jake handed them paper plates of sausages in rolls and burgers in buns, and they plonked down at the bench table, and bit into their food just as though they were starving.

Poppy had given up on the swing, instead bringing two dolls to the table, where she sat having a conversation with them and pretending to feed them from her plate. Angela looked at her daughter lovingly, and a little stab of pain again went through Derby's heart.

"You have a beautiful family."

She told Jake and Angela when the four of them sat down to eat. Smiling at their offspring, they both agreed.

"Bloody hard work at times."

Jake said with a look that told them he wouldn't have it any other way. Angela nodded her agreement.

By eight o'clock, Poppy was drooping, and Ben and Will had quietened to playing some sort of game only they seemed to know the rules to. Jake stood and lifted his daughter from the rug on the grass and brought her to Derby and Geoff to say goodnight. As Derby smiled up at the little girl, she leaned out of her father's arms, her own reaching for Derby. Surprised, Derby took her as little arms wrapped around her neck and Poppy hugged her hard.

"Night night Derby. I like you and your boyfriend."

She then gave Derby a kiss on the cheek. Then she leaned towards Geoff who had an arm around Derby.

"Night night Geoff."

She said before turning back to her father.

Jake and Angela took their child up to bed, explaining they would be as quick as they could, that story would be short tonight.

Ben and Will had decided to go indoors to continue their game, Will knowing it wouldn't be long before it was his bedtime too. Derby and Geoff sat quietly waiting, enjoying the peace of the evening.

Just as Jake and Angela returned, Geoff's phone trilled. He pulled it from his pocket and looked at the screen. He sighed.

"Sorry I have to take this."

He stood up and moved away politely. Derby heard a couple of words, "No one else", and "Ok" then he came back and sat down.

"I have to go to Edinburgh tomorrow."

He told them all, but mainly Derby. She looked at him, guessing there was more.

"How long?"

Geoff took her hand and kissed it.

"Two weeks."

She sighed, she would miss him and didn't know how she would fill the time. All the years she had spent in her dull lonely marriage, she had got by, not thinking about what to do day after day. But Geoff had changed that. Now every day was about him. She got on with her normal life, her work, and she was happy with that, but she now knew that her life was much happier and fulfilled because he was there.

"I'd rather not go. But there's a group of us independent gym owners. We have an agreement to help each other out. If something happens to someone and they have to be away from their gym for more than two weeks, we step in and do it for them. It's not fair to leave our other staff members to cope for a longer period, so we cover two weeks each. A guy called Christopher Hibbert has broken his femur and I'm on the list for first rotation. I'd much rather stay at home with you."

Derby squeezed his hand.

"I'll be ok Geoff. I promise. I'll miss you, very much, but this is who you are, what you do. Please, I don't want that to change. You have to go, I understand."

He lifted her hand to his lips and kissed it lovingly.

"I'll call every day."

"And I'll look after her Geoff."

Angela piped up.

"When do you have to leave?"

Derby asked. Geoff pressed his lips firmly together, his face scrunched up.

"In the next hour."

He said. Derby felt her heart drop with disappointment. She had hoped they would spend the rest of the night together.

"I'm so sorry. It's a long drive and I have to be there for the morning."

Derby tried a smile and found it worked.

"It's fine Geoff. I'll still be here when you get back."

"What sitting on Jake and Angela's patio."

He said to lighten the mood, and it worked, the four of them laughing.

Derby decided to stay at the flat even after Geoff had kissed her long and lovingly before he left. He called her when he got home and again as he set off for Scotland, promising to call her when he arrived safely.

There hadn't even been time for the sex that usually followed the deep sensual delving of her mouth that his tongue gave. Now she stood naked on the balcony, feeling desire pumping through her, the evening air brushing her skin, feather soft. The marina below was quiet and dark, the dimmed light coming from the street lamps and the bars on the opposite side. Her corner was peaceful, the sky was clear and the glistening ball of moon turning the river into a snaking silver thread, winding silently towards the sea.

Thoughts of Geoff, the warmth of the evening, moonlight and soft warm air on her naked skin, ignited every nerve in her body. She trailed her hands over her breasts, down her stomach and let them come to a rest at the juncture of her thighs. She slid her fingers down, feeling wetness and stroking the inside of her labia. She stopped briefly, remembering her toys. She quickly returned to her bedroom and pulled out the dildo and a clitoral stimulator, she hadn't tried either yet.

Returning to the balcony she began again, letting her fingers find their way into the moist depth of her vagina. She slid back and forth, her pelvis moving in time with her hand. She pressed her thumb against her clitoris and bit her lip at the pleasure. Then leaning against the balcony rail, she eased the dildo into her waiting wet portal of her deepest centre. She writhed against the rubber hardness, spreading her legs wider. She pushed with her hand and pressed down with her hips, her head thrown back to the dark velvet sky. Each thrust with the dildo bringing her nearer to climax. Faster and faster she moved, one hand holding the dildo, the other rubbing the tiny hard bud of her clitoris with the stimulator. She came, shuddering and jerking, her heart pounding and her breath fast.

She slumped forward slightly, still holding the dildo inside her, moving it slowly, rotating it. Gradually her body returned to normal and she slid the toy out, letting the tip tickle every sensitive part of her womanhood, and giving herself another quick orgasm at the same time.

Feeling satisfied, Derby went into the bedroom and climbed under the duvet. She laid her phone on the bedside cabinet so she would hear it when Geoff phoned. He had said it would take about six to seven hours to get to Edinburgh, and she had told him to call her as soon as he got there, even if it was the early hours of the morning. She snuggled down, closed her eyes and fell into a deep sleep.

At four thirty, Derby's phone rang. She awoke immediately, knew it was Geoff from the ringtone. He had arrived at his destination. He sounded tired and her heart went out to him. She wanted so much to rub his huge shoulders, smooth his hair and kiss away his fatigue.

"I'm going to get a few hours sleep. I'll call you later. I love you and miss you already."
He said.

"I miss you too. Take care, I love you."
Saying it came so easy now, felt comfortable, felt right.

A Brief Interlude

For two whole weeks, Derby struggled to fill her time. Geoff, true to his word phoned every day, but there were still many hours to occupy and the weather didn't help her mood, flipping between hot sunshine, showers and fierce storms. The nursery took care of the week days, but the evenings were the worst. Even her sex toys remained in her wardrobe at the flat, some still in their packaging, no substitute for the deep longing in her heart and body.

Derby almost believed the twenty four days before Geoff left for Edinburgh had been a dream, perfect and pure, but just a dream. Work, home, the old unending mundane life of being a dutiful wife to David, who didn't notice one way or another, that seemed like reality. She had to keep prodding herself, make her believe that life with Geoff was real.

Her only relief came on the odd occasion she went to the gym, the flat or Geoff's house. He had told her to use it whenever she wanted. But his absence was so palpable it made her profoundly lonely, so much so she couldn't stay where he wasn't. At least at home there were no reminders, no smells, no him, just a gap in her heart. One that could only be filled when he returned.

Chapter 18

Secrets Uncovered Part 2

Derby awoke with her heart racing. The dream she came too from, still flooded through her body, turning her insides to liquid. She quickly glanced to one side and sighed, David was curled up sound asleep next to her. The dream had been so real, she expected to see Geoff's beautiful face smiling lovingly at her, but it had only been a dream. Very real and very powerful, she could still feel the feather like touch of his fingers probing her soft wet centre, but only a dream.

Quietly pushing aside the duvet, she tiptoed out of the bedroom to the bathroom. She knew David wouldn't wake yet, but she didn't want to chance that he might. She needed to be alone for a little while longer, needed to shower away the memories her subconscious pounded her with.

She looked in the mirror whilst the water heated, threaded her fingers through her long dark hair and was relieved to see there were no more grey hairs. She brushed her teeth and stepped under the shower, the force of the water tingling her nipples, and running softly down her stomach and over her already sensitive pubis. She imagined the water was Geoff's hands, stroking her inner thighs, reigniting the arousal left over from her dream.

Derby squeezed soft silky body wash into her palms and began to slowly lather her body. Her hands moved in circles, starting at the top of her body and moving lower and lower with each rotation. She reached the mound of her pubis and opened her legs a little wider, sliding her hands between them. She closed her eyes, her face turned up to the water. It felt so good, Geoff's face clear in her imagination, his eyes hot and wanting.

She let her fingers begin a gentle exploration of her labia, teasing herself. She lightly pinched the little hard nub of her clitoris and bit down on her own lip as pleasure erupted. Still massaging with one finger, Derby inserted another inside herself and bending her knees, she moved it in and out, slowly at first, then as her climax began, more quickly. All the while, she saw

Geoff, her hands were his hands, and she came, her body shuddering and jerking, saw his smile, saw his lips move telling her today was the day he would be home.

Wrapped in a bath sheet, Derby went back to the bedroom, not bothering to be quiet anymore. David was still buried under the covers, his eyes shut tight. Derby leaned over him and shook him unceremoniously.

"Come on, wake up."

She said, her voice firm. David stirred, stretched and opened his eyes.

"Awww is it morning already?"

He grumbled. Derby responded with a nod, and turned to the dressing table. She heard her husband lift himself from the bed and closed her eyes. She didn't want to see his belly stretch across his pyjamas, didn't want to see his thinning hair stand up in wisps. What she wanted was to saviour the memory of Geoff's face as she showered and pleasured herself.

The table was laid, the tea made, and everything set for a normal day before work. David sat, waiting for Derby to do what she did every morning.

"I'm going to be late tonight."

Derby casually stated as she poured David's tea and handed it to him. David took the mug, nodded once then tucked into his breakfast. Derby only just managed to resist an impatient huff, biting hard into her toast instead.

David, as ever a stickler for routine, left exactly on time. Derby, filled with excitement and anticipation, rushed around clearing the breakfast things and then darted out the door for work. She saw Bob and Fiona at their front window and waved joyfully to the old couple. Fiona popped open the window calling cheerily.

"Morning love, have a good day."

"Oh I will."

Derby called back gleefully.

Angela noticed Derby's happy mood as soon as she walked into work. She stood in the doorway and watched her friend, not wanting to intrude, for Derby looked as though she was having a good time. The CD player was switched on, emitting the children's songs they used for group singing. Derby was humming along to the tunes and dancing as she prepared the room. What made

Angela bite back a loud laugh, was Derby's style of dance. It was in direct contrast to the music. As 'The Wheels On The Bus' burst from the CD player, Derby shimmied and wiggled as though dancing to the latest chart hit.

One little spin brought Derby face to face with Angela. She stopped, her arms over her head and a shocked almost guilty expression on her face. Angela couldn't prevent the giggle then.

"Coffee?"

She asked. Derby recovered and burst out laughing.

"Please."

She said, a little breathless.

Holding mugs of coffee, the music still playing but turned down low, the two women prepared the nursery together.

"Geoff home today then?"

Angela asked. Derby, sipping her drink, grinned and nearly spilt her coffee.

The day seemed to go so slowly for Derby. Even Geoff's texts that he was on the road and expected to be home by eight, couldn't gee it up. Kelsey noticed her agitation when she came to collect Chardonnay.

"What's up Derby?"

She whispered. Derby smiled, and Kelsey could see in her eyes that there was nothing wrong.

"Just…"

Derby didn't know how to finish. Only Angela knew about Geoff, she wasn't ready to go public yet, but Kelsey as ever intuitive grinned back, leaned in close and again whispered.

"I think I can guess. If I'm right, good on you girl. Hope he's amazing."

Derby gave a little gasp, the flush appearing on her cheeks completely giving her away. Kelsey patted her shoulder.

"S'alright. I won't say anything."

"Thanks Kelsey. I'll tell you about it soon, I promise."

She would, she knew, as she now thought of Kelsey as a trusting friend.

Finally the nursery was quiet, tidy and ready to be locked up. Derby checked the windows, the back door and headed for the front. She set the alarm and pulled the front door closed, locked it and double checked. As she turned she froze. Standing in front of her was both Irene and Brenda. Both women stood with their arms folded. Derby recovered quickly, and hoped they hadn't noticed the fearful jolt their presence had given her.

"What do you want?"

She asked. Irene stepped forward slightly.

"What I have always wanted. You out of my son's home and life."

Derby sighed, thinking, this is getting a bit old now. What she said was.

"And I told you, my house too, so not happening."

Brenda pointed a finger.

"I don't know what you're up to madam, but I won't stand by and let you get your sticky little fingers on what my brother has worked his whole life for."

Derby felt a bubble of laughter start deep within her chest. It rose and popped out of her mouth before she could stop it, obviously angering the two women in front of her, indicated by their frowns.

"Don't you dare laugh."

"How dare you laugh."

They both burst out at the same time, fury on their faces making them look like twins. A flicker of thought passed through Derby. At least David looks like his father, and not his crow faced mother and sister. This brought more giggles and confidence.

"Go to hell, the pair of you."

She swung towards the street, leaving them huffing and gasping out incoherent replies.

Derby reached home in record time. Anger had replaced the laughter, as she virtually power walked her way to her house. She couldn't believe the nerve of them, ambushing her outside her place of work, confronting her and trying to intimidate her. She was tiny compared to them, and she believed they had hoped to use both their considerable size to bully her into submission. But she had stood her ground, and after all the years of acquiescing to their dominance, had shown them she wasn't a walkover anymore.

Derby stayed home for only as long as it took her to change from her work clothes and grab an overnight bag. She pulled on fresh matching, very lacy and very sexy underwear, a soft print dress in a stretchy fabric, and light sandals. Then she headed for the door and her car. Nothing was bringing her home tonight, and in the morning she would go straight from Geoff's to work.

With the top down, Derby breathed in the hot summer air as her car ate up the miles between her house and Geoff's. He wouldn't be home yet, but she didn't care. She wanted to be where he would soon be. As she drove, she thought about what Irene had said, and knew that she too wanted to be out of David's life. But she was damned if she was going to let his mother and sister have any control over when and how it happened.

"My decision in my time!"

She yelled, her hair whipping about her face, as the distance to the centre of her heart grew smaller.

Geoff's driveway was cool and quiet, the trees blocking some of the evening sun, and buffering what little noise there was from the surrounding road and houses. Derby turned off her engine, and for a moment just sat looking up at the beautiful old building. She felt so comfortable, like this was home. Peace washed over her, David, his mother and sister, all forgotten. She stepped out of her car, leaves crunching underfoot in the quietness, and breathed deeply, absorbing all of the scents around her.

Inside the house, Derby bent and retrieved Geoff's mail that had piled up, placing it on the hall table. It felt so natural. She stepped into the front rooms and unlatched the windows, letting fresh summer air in. Little specks of dust flitted and glimmered in the sunlight, disturbed by the gentle breeze. Derby then made her way through the rest of the house, doing the same in each room.

When she came to Geoff's bedroom, she stopped inside the doorway and closed her eyes. She breathed deeply. She could smell him, longing for his arms and lips, pressing hard against the walls of her chest. A brief moment of dizziness washed over her, and she held onto the door frame until she recovered. Then she went into the bathroom and splashed cold water on her face. Feeling better, she headed down stairs to the kitchen. There she ran a glass of water and drank thirstily, realising it had been some time since she had drunk anything.

With the back door open, Derby made a pot of tea and thought about preparing dinner for when Geoff got home. She then sighed, admonishing herself for not thinking to stop at the supermarket on the way for supplies. Geoff had been away for two weeks, the fridge would be empty and everything in the freezer would take too long to defrost. She knew nothing about the area around the house, so didn't know if there was a shop nearby. Sighing again, she pulled her phone from her bag, about to do a search, when the doorbell chimed.

Derby jumped a little, the sound totally unexpected. Laying her phone to one side, she trotted down the hallway to the front door. On opening it she found a smiling Molly, a box in her hands.

"Hi."

The young coach said. Derby smiled back.

"Hi back."

"Geoff asked me to bring this over."

She passed the box to Derby. Inside was milk, bread, cereal, eggs and croissants.

"Geoff said to tell you that you're absolutely not to worry about dinner, he's got it covered."

"How did you know I would be here?"

Derby asked.

"Geoff said you would. He asked me to get a few things, thought you wouldn't have time, and asked me to bring them round, not before seven."

She glanced at her watch.

"It's ten after seven."

She stated, a broad smile showing her satisfaction that she had delivered the box efficiently. Derby grinned at her.

"Thank you Molly. It's not time I was lacking, more like, didn't think."

Molly put a finger to her lips.

"Sh, I won't tell if you don't."

Then giggling she spun round and jogged toward the street.

"Thanks again, and bye."

Derby called, Molly waving over her head.

Derby carried the box into the kitchen and unpacked it, putting the milk into the fridge. She felt like she was glowing, emitting light from deep within. Once again Geoff had shown her how much he cared, how much he loved her, and she couldn't wait for him to come home, see his face, feel his lips on hers and his arms wrapped around her.

A CD player standing on the counter caught Derby's eye. She popped open the drive and saw a disc inside. Its label told her it was a collection of pop tunes from when she was in her late teens. Grinning she switched it on and turned up the volume. The first track was one she remembered well, had enjoyed during her youth. She increased the volume and listened, the words coming back to her. She began to sing along, letting her hips pick up the rhythm. Soon she was hopping and bopping about the kitchen, letting her hair fly around her face.

Geoff unlocked his front door and heard loud music coming from the back of the house. He smiled to himself. Quietly he lowered his bag to the floor and made his way towards the kitchen. He stopped just inside the doorway and watched, his heart filling with joy and love. Derby was shimmying about the kitchen. She had her back to him and the sight of her swinging hips sent blood rushing to his loins.

As she spun round, she saw him and came to a stop, one hand on her heart. Her face was flushed and her hair was all over the place, but she was grinning, her eyes alight. She squealed with delight and flung herself into his arms.

"You're early and you made me jump."
She said as she grabbed his shirt in both hands. Geoff smiled down at her.

"Couldn't resist the show."
He told her. Derby blushed.

"It was very sexy."
He said, his voice husky, his body giving way just how sexy she had appeared to him. Derby pressed close, feeling his desire. She wrapped her arms around his neck and lifted her face to his. She raised herself on tiptoes, the tip of her tongue protruding from her slightly parted lips. Slowly she leaned towards him, lightly pressing her mouth against his. She let her tongue touch his lips, her teeth nip gently and heard him take in a breath. Geoff stood still, holding her, letting her take control, which she did.

Derby pressed her lips to Geoff's, pushing her tongue between them and tangling her fingers in his hair. She felt his hardness and tilted her pelvis towards him, wanting more. She could feel her own wetness as she lifted one knee and wrapped her leg around his thigh, rotating her hips and shuddering with pleasure. Geoff shifted slightly, grasping her buttocks and pulling her in close, but still allowing her to retain control.

Derby trailed her fingers up and down his back, bringing soft murmurs from deep within his throat, as she pushed her tongue further into his mouth. She tucked a finger into the waistband of his jeans, sliding it to the front. Then she began to undo his button and zip, easing the denim and snug trunks down his thighs, baring his erection. She then lifted the hem of her dress and removed her own underwear, stretching up as far as her height would allow.

Geoff lifted her from her feet and she wrapped both legs around him, linking her ankles. Bracing her hands on his shoulders, she lowered herself onto him. She took her mouth from his and bit down on his shoulder, as she moved him in and out, slow at first, then faster has their joint desire mounted. Geoff held her buttocks tight, squeezing as he pumped in rhythm with her movements. Derby came with a power she couldn't define, and as she did, Geoff came too, bucking and jolting.

As their orgasms subsided, Geoff still held her wrapped around him, still deep inside her. He rained tiny kisses all over her face and neck and she stroked the hair at the nape of his neck.

"Did you miss me?"

She whispered, and felt his laugh rumble from inside his chest.

"Oh yes. Most definitely. What about you?"

Derby giggled.

"No, not at all."

Geoff shook her gently, sliding out of her.

"Minx."

Was all he said as she lowered her feet to the floor. She still had her arms around his neck and the smile she gave him was full of love.

"More than I can say."

She told him on a more serious note.

"I love you Derby. More than I can say."

He held her tight and for a while they simply stood, clinging to each other, loving each other.

As good as his word, Geoff had organised dinner. He'd brought it all home and cooked it while they chatted and told each other about their respective two weeks. Shyly, Derby divulged the enormous gap and emptiness she had felt without him there, and several times during the meal preparation, Geoff had stopped and kissed her, touched her and caressed her.

"There will be times when I have to be away."

He told her. She covered his hand with her own, as he shook potatoes in a colander.

"I'll cope."

She told him sincerely.

"It won't stop me missing you, but I will cope knowing you will come home to me."

"Always."

He told her, and she knew he meant it.

Derby went from Geoff's to work the next morning, dropping her car home first. Parking was so tight at the nursery and she lived so close, she didn't think it was fair on the other staff who had to drive to work. She didn't bother contacting David, had no inclination to. She didn't know if his mother and sister had spoken to him and didn't care. Each confrontation she had with them recently strengthened rather than weakened her. Over the years, they had been able to intimidate and control her. Not anymore. She was free, she was in love, and there was nothing they could do to hurt her anymore.

The morning passed with the usual bustle of nursery life. Angela had managed a few words with Derby, who had given her a brief recount of Geoff's return. Kelsey has again noticed Derby's happiness and this time, Derby promised to have a word at the end of the day.

Lunchtime came, and as usual Derby sat with some of the children supervising their meal. Today it was the two to three year olds. Most were quite capable of feeding themselves, but a few still needed help. She was just spooning yogurt into a toddler's mouth, when a wave of nausea went through her. She took a deep slow breath and gradually it passed.

"You ok?"

One of the other nursery nurses asked. Derby looked up at the frowning girl.

"Mmm think so. Just felt a bit queasy."

She replied.

"You do look a bit pale. Want me to take over whilst you get a cold drink?"

Derby nodded and stood up feeling slightly dizzy. She went into the kitchen, poured a glass of water and stood sipping it. The dizziness passed, but she still felt a little sick. Angela came into the kitchen.

"Kerry said you weren't feeling well."

"I'm alright, I think. Just felt a bit sick and dizzy. Hope I haven't finally picked up that bug."

Angela gave her a tiny frown.

"Well if it gets worse, you go home. Right?"

Derby smiled.

"Yes mum."

Angela grinned and went back to the main nursery. Derby stood for a bit longer sipping her water, the sick feeling subsiding. Once it was completely gone, she went back as well.

By the end of the day, Derby had forgotten about feeling ill. Once it had disappeared, she felt fresh and energetic again. Kelsey arrived to collect Chardonnay and as promised, Derby chatted and told her a little about Geoff. Kelsey smiled and patted her arm.

"I'm not going to judge you Derby. For all the time you've looked after my angel, I've had a funny feeling that you've been living a very sad life. I haven't asked and you've never spoken of it. I didn't want you to think I was being nosey, you know, some people really don't like others to know about their life.

So, I just watched. When you had your birthday and came to my house, it was like you were a different person, like something had happened."

"It had. But then I hadn't even met Geoff. I just woke up on my birthday and realised things had to change. Then, I had no idea what it would be, and now, well I wonder how I have managed to get through the past twenty odd years, no more, and stayed sane. Everything is different now. I've woken from a very long sleep and I'm not going back."

Derby said the last part with a very firm set to her face. Kelsey gave her a brief hug.

"Good to hear. We girls have to take control of our lives."

She closed her hand into a fist and gave a little air punch making Derby giggle.

Derby decided to go home, but only because she wanted to see Bob and Fiona. The old couple had made her feel so welcome she didn't want to abandon them, even though she really didn't want to be anywhere near her house. As she walked, she thought about what Irene and Brenda had said the day before. They were in no way right, and she would defend her entitlement to the house, but she didn't want it. She knew that very soon, her and David were going to have to talk about it.

Bob was in the front garden when she arrived. He raised himself slowly from a bend, pressing his hands into the small of his back. Beaming at her he said.

"Hello love. How are you?"

Derby opened the gate and stepped into the garden.

"I'm fine. How about you two?"

Bob stretched a little, rubbing his back.

"We're alright for our age."

Then he grinned.

"Plenty of life left in us yet."

He lifted a hand and waved towards the house.

"Come on in. Fiona's baking, has been all afternoon. I know she'll love to see you."

Derby smiled and followed him up the path.

"Fiona! Got to trade you in for a really cute younger model."

Derby burst out laughing.

As they entered the house, Fiona was coming from the kitchen wiping her hands on a tea towel. She lightly flicked the flour covered cloth towards her husband, her aim true, cuffing him around the head, flour floating down onto his already grey hair.

"As if."

She said with a cheerful giggle. Bob rubbed his hands across his face, then cupped his wife's cheeks, planting a kiss on the end of her nose.

"She wouldn't have me."

He said in a mock sad voice.

"Never mind old fella. You'll always have me."

Fiona told her husband, love shining from her aging eyes.

Derby felt a little lump in the back of her throat. The couple were so attuned to one another, and obviously still so very much in love. She longed for a relationship like that, hoped and prayed that Geoff would give it to her.

"Derby, come and have some of my Victoria sponge."

Fiona urged her. Derby smiled and let the older woman lead her into the kitchen, which smelt of heaven.

Fiona continued on through the kitchen and out the back door. The patio table was laid with a lace cloth, tea pot and china.

"Would you fetch another cup and plate please Bob!"

She called back over her shoulder.

"Now you sit there."

Fiona told Derby as she pulled out a chair.

Bob joined them, and Fiona poured tea into china cups and cut thick slices of delicious looking sponge cake. Derby took a bite and felt the cake melt in her mouth.

"Mmmm, this is gorgeous."

She told Fiona, who grinned, obviously pleased with the compliment.

"My wife does know how to bake. For that reason alone I'll keep her."

Bob said, giving Derby a wicked wink.

"Do you want to see your next birthday husband dear?"

Fiona said in a soft voice. Bob grinned at her, then took a huge bite from his slice of sponge.

The three chatted and ate, and Derby felt relaxed and content. She sipped hot strong tea, and watched and listened to the banter between the old couple. The evening was warm, bees buzzing amongst the lavender that edged the patio.

"Derby."

Fiona called gently. Derby looked up, not realising she had been miles away, absorbed in the comfort of her surroundings and company.

"Oh I'm sorry."

She said. Fiona leaned across the table and patted her hand.

"You weren't quite with us there love. I was just saying, we were a bit worried last night."

Derby sat up, a frown of concern on her face.

"Oh, why?"

"Well…we saw those two…"

Fiona paused, her lips pursed.

"Bitches."

She continued in a hushed voice, and Derby had to stop herself from smiling at the way she spoke.

"They let themselves in."

Now her voice had become indignant.

"Was David home?"

Derby asked gently, keeping concern out of her voice. Fiona nodded.

"And at first we thought you were too. We heard raised voices. I can tell you, Bob was about to go round and make sure you were ok, but when he opened the front door he saw your little car wasn't there."

Fiona stopped, sipped her tea and looked up over the cup, a sparkle in her eyes.

"Well, when we realised you weren't there, we...we listened."

Bob leaned towards Derby.

"She turned off the telly so we could hear better."

Derby grinned.

"And they were arguing."

Fiona said, her voice now little more than a whisper. Derby raised her brows, keen to find out more.

"Did you by any chance catch what about?"

Fiona sat back nodding, a look of satisfaction across her face.

"You."

Derby took a deep breath, held it and let it out slowly. She had never heard her husband argue with anyone, let alone his mother and sister. She was eager to learn more, and Fiona didn't disappoint her.

"Well, what we heard anyway. She, that is the mother was ranting something about you not getting your hands on his house. It went on for a while, the other one piping up every now and then. At first he said nothing, then he yelled at them. It was funny really.

They were gabbling like a pair of old geese, then they...just shut up. What we could make out, was that he told them to. We also heard him say that no matter what, you were his wife and the house belonged to both of you. Then he...and get this...he told them to leave. We heard the door slam then."

Bob was nodding.

"And, we peeked out the front window and both of them were stomping down the path."

Derby didn't quite know what to make of it. In all the years before and after her marriage, she had never known David say boo to his mother and sister, never mind actually defend her. It made her sad, and a little guilty. She knew without a doubt that she didn't love him, never had, and she was sure he felt the same. It was just such a waste for both of them.

"I think it's about time David and I sorted things out."
She told the old couple.

Derby unlocked the front door and entered the hallway. The house was the same as ever, dull and lifeless. David wouldn't be home for a while yet, and she really didn't want to be there when he did, but knew she should. She went into the kitchen and to her surprise found it clean and tidy. She opened the dishwasher. The only things inside were a bowl, mug and a few pieces of cutlery. Derby frowned, uncertain of what to make of it. She looked in the fridge and found fresh milk and bread. That was even more strange, as she hadn't bought any recently.

Derby was about to head upstairs when her phone chirped a message. She looked at the screen and saw it was from David. Her heart gave a little flutter of panic. David never texted her unless she sent him a message first. With fumbling fingers, she opened the text.

Going to be very late if you're in don't wait up.
Derby was shocked. Why would he tell her this? Something had obviously changed and it worried her, but not enough to affect the plans she had for her own life. It was far too late for that. She tapped a short reply.

Ok staying at a friend's.

Derby knocked on Bob and Fiona's door. Fiona answered and Derby briefly told her about David's message. Bob came up behind his wife and listened too. Derby went on to say that she was going to stay at Geoff's and Fiona beamed, gently squeezing her arm.

"When you finally move away from here, you'll come and visit us won't you?"
Fiona asked. Derby felt a little jolt inside. She hadn't actually thought that far ahead. But by bringing it up, Fiona had unwittingly

pushed her into realising that she would indeed be doing just that. She took the old woman's hand.

"Whatever happens, you two are like family to me now. Nothing could keep me away."

Fiona pulled her into a hug, patting her back as though she were a little girl. Derby felt tears prick her eyes, and held onto Fiona, determined not to let them fall and only just succeeding.

As she drove away from the kerb, Bob and Fiona stood side by side at their gate waving to her. She watched them in her mirror as she neared the end of the road. They were still waving as she turned. The tears that had threatened slid over her cheeks and she swiped at them, she didn't want blurred vision whilst she drove.

Geoff greeted her with a kiss, lifting her from her toes and wrapping his arms around her. Still holding her, he spun her round in the hallway making her squeal. Then lowering her to the floor he took her by the hand and led her to the kitchen. A wonderful aroma filled the room, and Derby realised that despite the cake she had eaten, she was very hungry.

"I just knew you would be here."

Geoff told her brightly. She pressed against him, laying her head on his shoulder.

"Something is going on with David, something weird."

She felt his muscles tense under her cheek, his fingers tighten slightly on her hand. He tilted her face up to his and she saw fear in his eyes. Immediately she felt guilty for worrying him. Raising her hand to his cheek, she softly stroked his skin, it was slightly rough and bristly.

"Oh I'm sorry. Whatever is going on with him will not affect us, I promise."

She felt him relax, the frown smoothing out across his brow and his smile radiant.

"God, my heart stopped for a minute. So…what do you think it is then?"

Derby shrugged.

"No idea, and frankly I don't really care."

Geoff pulled her into his arms and held her tight.

Over dinner, which they ate on the patio, Derby relayed all that had happened. He listened attentively. When she was finished he sat for a moment, chewing thoughtfully.

"Well…sounds like maybe he's finally come to his senses about his mother and sister then."

He then laid his knife and fork down and reached across the table for her hand.

"About you too. But, and I know I don't really have the right to say this, I'm not letting you go. He's had years to realise what he's had. I realised almost the moment I met you."

Derby clung to his hand, more tears threatening to fall.

"You have every right, and oh my God, hearing you say that, I have no words to tell you how it makes me feel. It's so big. Do you know what I mean?"

Geoff nodded. He stood up and pulled her up with him. He wrapped her in his arms and kissed her deeply. The meal was instantly forgotten as fire ignited within. She pulled his head closer, wanting more than just a kiss, which Geoff gave her willingly, right there on the patio.

Derby again left for work from Geoff's house, kissing him goodbye on the porch. He wasn't due into the gym until ten, and she was close to being late. She had started off getting ready with plenty of time to spare, but Geoff had decided to join her in the shower. Despite telling him she had no time for frolicking, his very large erection had her own body reacting immediately. The shower ended with both of them wet and slick on the bed, Geoff deep inside her.

He then insisted she eat something before she set off, which she actually realised she needed. So after tea, toast and fresh fruit, she finally stood on the porch kissing him goodbye. He leaned against the door frame in just a pair of trunks, his feet bare and his face tanned and smiling. She wanted to jump out of her car and throw herself back in his arms, but her job was too important. So she resisted temptation and drove away waving. She took her car home and just made it to the nursery on time.

Mid-morning Derby was helping Angela hand out milk and snacks to the children. As she leaned down towards a tot she felt light headed and suddenly queasy. She took a deep breath and stood up straight. The dizziness passed but her stomach flipped. She turned to Angela, who immediately noticed something was wrong.

"Derby?"

Was all she said as Derby fled from the room to the bathroom. She only just made it. Angela came in after her.

"You ok?"

She asked worriedly. Derby sat back on her heels.

"Phew. That was horrible. I'm never sick. Looks like I've got the damned bug after all."

"You do look really pale. Go home, get some rest, I'll sort things here."

Reluctantly Derby agreed and gathered her things. Once outside in the warm fresh air, she felt a lot better. In fact she thought, more than better. She slowed her pace as she neared home, a sudden but exciting thought flitting across her mind. One which she would not, dare not acknowledge. By the time she reached her house, she had her car keys in her hand.

Derby entered her flat carrying a small bag. She placed it and her handbag on the kitchen table. Staring at the little bag she began to shake. She left it unopened and went through to the lounge, unlocking the patio doors and stepping out onto the balcony.

She leaned on the railing looking down at the boats. It was fairly quiet, most of the owners at work. She saw a couple sitting on the deck of their boat reading newspapers and sipping from mugs. It was such a normal domestic scene, but it brought tears to her eyes. She rested her head on her folded arms and let them flow, not even sure why she was crying.

Eventually the tears subsided and Derby stood straight taking a deep breath. She wiped at her face and did a quick mental calculation. She shook her head very slightly.

"Get a grip girl. It won't be, you know."

She whispered to herself. Then taking a very deep breath she turned and went back inside.

Ten minutes later Derby sat on the balcony, a glass of water in front of her. Her insides were churning, her mind in a whirl. Excitement bubbled up and she let out a little giggle, quickly replaced by a hitch of fear. She lifted the glass with a shaky hand and sipped, some of the water slopping over the side. She didn't know what to do. She had to tell Geoff and was terrified of his reaction. She had to tell David that their marriage was over, that would be easier. She had to, she thought, but she didn't know what else she had to do. Get a bigger flat flitted through her mind. What she decided, was to go home and collect the rest of her new things and move into the flat. Then later, she would go back and talk to her husband.

With the top down and the summer air filling her lungs, Derby drove home. All the way she kept thinking about the secret deep within her, her precious most wanted secret. At times she thought about just keeping it to herself, not telling anyone. But she knew at least one person deserved and needed to be told. She just hoped that he would be pleased. But she resolved, if he wasn't, well then she would deal with it by herself. After all she had been pretty much by herself all her life, not anymore, she thought, not ever again.

For once, Derby was glad Bob and Fiona were not in their front garden. She quickly trotted up her path and unlocked the front door. She dropped her bag in the hallway and darted up the stairs, planning on staying only long enough to gather her clothes.

She pushed her bedroom door open, a noise registering at the same time as the sight that had her frozen to the spot. David was kneeling on the floor leaning over one side of the bed. His face was turned towards her, his eyes closed in ecstasy, hands fisted in the duvet, gripping tightly. A huge man was kneeling behind him. His black glistening skin stretched taut across muscles that rippled in his arms as he braced himself either side of David, supporting his weight as he pumped back and forth. His neck was stretched up, his eyes closed too, his teeth white and gleaming. Both men were breathing hard and fast, oblivious to her presence.

David scrunched his face up, and a noise began in his throat as his lover pumped and pushed harder and faster. Derby stood and watched her husband in the throes of what looked to be a very powerful orgasm, not wanting to see, but too shocked to move. She watched as the two men came at once, both almost growling out their pleasure. Watched as David's lover's body went taut above him. Watched as they both gasped out breaths of delight, their bodies shuddering in passion.

Derby must have made a noise of some sort, for David's eyes flew open and bulged, his mouth forming a perfect 'O'. His lover, still unaware had his eyes still closed. He was moving slowly now, undulating his hips, obviously still inside David.

"Oh God."

David moaned, his tone telling his lover something was wrong. The man opened his eyes and saw Derby too. Quickly he pulled out of David and sat on the carpet, thereby preventing Derby from seeing his nakedness.

Derby turned and spun from the room. She fled downstairs and into the kitchen. She heard her husband call her name and waited. David appeared in the doorway, pulling his dressing gown close over his naked body. Derby was leaning forward, her arms folded across her chest, holding herself. David stepped towards her.

"Derby…God…I'm so sorry. I never wanted you to find out like this. Never wanted you to find out at all."

He reached out a hand and touched her shoulder. Derby straightened, tears pouring from her eyes, streaming down her cheeks. David stepped closer and stopped. His expression changed from concern to surprise. Derby wasn't crying. She was laughing. She was holding her stomach as her body shook with silent laughter.

David stood motionless. Then a movement behind him made Derby glance beyond her husband. She lifted one hand from her stomach and pointed, her laughter taking her breath away. David's huge lover filled the doorway. But what made Derby laugh even more uncontrollably, was that he was wearing her old faded pink dressing gown. It was far too small for the man's physique. The sleeves stretched at the seams where his biceps bulged, came only to the middle of his thighs in length, and was being held together at the front by his enormous hands.

"David are you ok?"

He asked in a voice that sounded as though it came from the throat of a bear. Derby had to lean against the counter, trying to take great gasping breaths.

"I'm fine Ed. Could you wait in the other room please?"

For some reason, the man's name sent a fresh wave of laughter through Derby, weakening her legs. She lowered herself to the kitchen floor and slowly the giggles began to subside. David came over and sat down next to her. She looked sideways at her husband, the frown on his face wiping out anymore laughter.

"I thought you would be angry."

He mumbled. His eyes began to well up, and suddenly Derby saw her husband in a completely different light.

In front of her was a man she didn't know at all. A man who had lived his whole life, most of it with her, with a secret buried deep within. A tear slipped over his lashes onto his cheek and Derby saw how tortured he was. She reached for him and he came into her arms like a child. He leaned his head against her shoulder and she felt his body shudder as his tears flowed.

"Sh…come on. David, it'll be fine."
She soothed in a motherly voice, stroking his head.

Eventually David's crying stopped and he lifted his head from her shoulder. He sat back rubbing his face with his hands.

"Shall I make some coffee?"
She asked gently.

"Please."

Derby pulled herself to her feet and turned to the hob. She lifted the kettle and as it was already filled, switched on the burner.

"Would you mind if I called Ed in now?"
Derby, her back to her husband, pressed her lips tight together, the name still gave her the giggles. Setting her face to serious, she glanced over her shoulder.

"Of course."
She said.

She heard David move and let out a breath, relaxing her shoulders. She then busied herself lifting mugs and spooning coffee into them. She had the milk out of the fridge when the two men returned. She was relieved to see, both were now wearing track bottoms and T-shirts, although she couldn't ever remember David ever wearing that attire before. Holding the milk bottle up, she smiled.

"How do you take your coffee Ed?"

"Milk two sugars please."
He told her, his voice sounding even deeper. She made the drinks and handed them to the two men.

"Can we sit down?"
David asked tentatively. Derby nodded and he led them into the lounge.

Derby took the armchair letting her husband and his boyfriend sit together on the sofa. For a minute the only sound was the three sipping form their mugs. Then David put his down and leaned forward, his hands resting on his knees.

"Derby, I'd like you to meet Ed, my…partner."

Derby had to bite back the giggles again. Here was the David she did know, all formal and serious.

"Nice to meet you."

She replied holding out her hand. Ed's huge one engulfed hers, but the shake was light.

"I know this must be a shock for you."

He stopped at Derby's raised brows.

"But, you laughed."

He stated.

"I thought you were upset, angry."

Derby shook her head.

"Admittedly, it was a shock. More I think seeing you two like…well having sex. But that you're gay? Hmm it explains a lot."

David sat nodding his head, his hands clasped in front of him. Ed put a hand on the back of his neck and massaged gently. Derby felt a little lump in her throat, the man obviously cared deeply for her husband.

"Why haven't you….you know, come out?"

Derby asked. David sighed.

"My mother, my sister."

Was all he needed to say. Derby nodded, knowing how difficult it must have been for him. She opened her mouth to ask another question, but David began to speak again.

"When we first met I thought you were the prettiest girl I had ever known, and I was attracted to you. We started hanging out, and I could tell you were mad about me. When I first felt…something for another man, I pushed it away, refused to let myself feel like that. Then we, you know, had sex and it did feel good.

So I thought, made myself believe, that I was 'normal'. I so needed to be. Mum and Brenda, they always sneered upon any mention of homosexuality. Back then, everyone sort of used to take the piss out of gays, were downright nasty about them sometimes. I was a good looking bloke, girls fluttered their lashes at me, flirted with me. I wanted to be part of the little crowd we were in."

Derby nodded.

"I remember the girls. I felt so excited that you chose me."

"I'm so sorry Derby. I was a coward, still am."

Derby left the chair and knelt in front of her husband. She took his hands and squeezed them in her own small ones. She felt both had been victims of their families' prejudices and lack of care.

"It's alright David."

She said soothingly. Without moving David continued.

"When we were forced into getting married I made myself think things would be ok. Made myself not gay, if that makes sense. I thought having a baby would do that. Then of course you weren't pregnant, and I couldn't bear it. I realised I couldn't bury my sexuality, but I also knew I couldn't do anything about it, tell anyone, least of all you. You had gone through a rough time with your parents, they had disowned you, and that was my fault. I had to keep up the pretence, and if my mother and sister had found out, well they would have ignored me forever.

I know how selfish that all sounds. I mean I've been plain bloody cruel to you. Sex maybe once, twice a year. No children. I even told you to come off the pill and start trying, and when it didn't happen, you begged me to get checked, but…and…oh God Derby, I am so sorry."

David stopped. He pulled his hands from hers and covered his face as fresh tears gushed from his eyes. Ed put his arm around him and pulled him close, giving him comfort where Derby couldn't. A tiny thread of dread pierced her heart. She wanted to hear what David had to say, but was fearful of what was coming next. Ed patted David's back, and in his deep voice encouraged him to go on with his story. So with breath hitching, David looked at Derby.

"I knew then that I wanted men. I would see them and think about their hair, their eyes, their figure. I didn't do anything about it at that point, but what I knew was that I couldn't risk being a father. So I had…I had…a…vasectomy."

Derby gasped, more shocked at that news than finding out her husband of twenty four years was gay. She felt herself pale and had to take a deep breath. Then a flush began to creep into her cheeks as anger replaced shock. She flipped to her feet and saw David flinch.

"You…did…that! How could you? Damn it David, all these years…"

She couldn't finish. Had no idea what to say. Instead she whirled from the room, heading for the back door. She needed air, wanted to be out of the house, but she also knew she needed to calm down.

Outside, she flung herself into a garden chair. He hands were fisted into balls and she was breathing deeply. Calm down, calm down, she recited silently to herself. This can't be good for you. Slowly she got her breath under control.

David and Ed appeared in the doorway, David carrying a glass of water. Without a word he handed it to her and she sipped. He slid onto the chair opposite and leaned his elbows on the table. Ed came and stood behind him.

"You have every right to be angry, and I have no excuse. Please let me finish?"

Derby just nodded.

"As the years went by, I did try and be a normal husband. But I had no idea what that meant. I didn't go with anyone for a long time, five years after we got married actually. He was a sales rep and we had a lunch meeting. It was instant attraction, and we…ended up in a hotel."

Derby squirmed. She wasn't sure she wanted to hear what he was telling her. David didn't notice and carried on.

"That first time, it felt like it was my first time ever. I'm sorry that sounds so harsh."

Derby leaned back in her chair and gave a short mirthless laugh. All the years she had put up with his lack of love, the uneventful sex, he had been getting full satisfaction elsewhere. She looked into his eyes, and with a voice dripping with sarcasm said.

"Not at all David. You did what you had to…to keep you sane and keep it from mummy and sister."

David sat back and put his hand over his face. Ed stood behind him massaging his shoulders, his black skin shining in the bright sunlight. Derby watched them, longing for Geoff to be by her side, giving her comfort. She sighed.

"I'm sorry. That wasn't really fair."

"No, you're right. Selfish is me. Mum and Brenda mollycoddled me. Treated me like china. I could never do anything wrong. I was spoilt rotten and I couldn't bear the thought of them thinking badly of me. I'm still like that. Over the years, I haven't had a lot of lovers, but enough, and I've got very good at hiding it. Ed and I have been together for two years, and I know we are meant to be together for good.

Things would have gone on the way they have always. But just lately you've been different. I don't know why, but you have. Then when mum and Brenda started hassling me about the house, and how it's mine and that you're not a proper wife, well I started thinking that maybe it's time for things to change. But I swear Derby, I wouldn't have wanted you to find out the way you did."

David's last few words brought the smile back to her face. She leaned back in the chair and turned her face up to the sun. Warmth flooded across her skin and Geoff's face came into her mind. She placed a hand across her stomach, her secret nestled deep within, protected and already loved more than anything else in the world.

"I've met someone too."
Derby said. She heard him gasp and looked at him. Ed's hands had stilled on David's shoulder.

"Only a few weeks ago. The rest of the time I've been totally faithful."
David realised his shock appeared like reprimand and quickly replied.

"Derby, I'm sorry. I have no right to judge. What are you going to do?"
Derby stared at her husband for a while, chewing her lip lightly.

"I'm leaving. Do what you want with the house."
David started to speak, but Derby cut him off.

"Not because of what I've seen today. I…I'm…had already decided. I came back home, I felt unwell at work and thought, I might as well get my things and make the break now. I had no idea you would be home. I think your family, what they've been saying to me recently, especially your mother, was the last straw. And, well, it's not just because I've met someone, I mean I knew something had to give on the day of my birthday."
David grimaced.

"Jesus. I'm a real shit aren't I. I don't think I've ever bought you anything for your birthday, taken you out. I didn't even notice the day."

He groaned and placed a hand over Ed's.

"Worse still, it's our wedding anniversary, on the same day as Derby's birthday."

Ed squeezed his shoulders and leaned in close. When he spoke his voice vibrated through the plastic patio table.

"David that's pretty awful. Don't you ever forget special dates of ours."

Derby felt like bursting into laughter again. Ed had the deepest most masculine voice she had ever heard, more so than Geoff's. Yet his words were so domestic and wifely. And David's expression and reaction was like that of a husband being admonished. What she also noted was the love that radiated between the two men.

Derby knew that neither she nor David were to blame for the wasted years. That they both had after all this time found what they needed. She stood up and looked at her husband and his lover.

"I'm going to get my things, then I'm leaving."

She said it gently. David stood up too, a question hovering in his eyes.

"It's alright David. I'm not going to tell your mother and Brenda. That's up to you. Please just do me a favour. Whatever you say to them, keep them away from me. I've had enough."

David stepped forward and put his arms around her. It was the most loving and sincere hug she could ever remember receiving from him. She hugged him back, and it felt like they were old friends rather than husband and wife.

"I'm going to tell them the truth Derby. I didn't think I could, but I will. They have to know, because they will keep on blaming you if they don't, and I've hurt you enough over the years. That's not going to happen anymore. I do love you Derby, in my own way."

"Thank you David."

She stepped out of his arms.

"Good luck to you both."

She told them as she twirled back towards the kitchen, a lightness to her step as relief washed over her.

Epilogue

Derby was curled up next to Geoff on a soft rug spread on the lawn of his garden. The night was warm and clear. Stars twinkled and shone, a bright moon hanging against a backdrop of darkest velvet. Geoff was stroking her back lightly.

"So there they were, completely in the throes of passion, and there am I standing in the doorway."
Derby told him. She felt his chest vibrate under her hand and knew he was laughing silently.

Derby mock slapped him and sat up. In the moonlight she could see his beautiful gleaming smile, bright against his tan. He made a grab for her and she landed on top of him.

"It wasn't funny. I had a shock."
She tried to sound indignant, but her own giggles gave her away.

"Alright, it was hilarious, in a sick sort of way. I mean, I should be scarred for life. Walking in on anyone having sex is embarrassing, but your own husband with another man…"
She stopped. Geoff leaned up and planted a kiss on her lips.

"We'll have to get you counselling."
He teased. Then seriously.

"So what happened then?"
Derby rolled off of him and sat with her knees drawn up. She looked sideways at Geoff, a cheeky expression gleaming from her eyes.

"It might take a while to tell."
She said. Geoff sighed and raised himself to his feet.

"Ok, snacks and a drink."
Derby giggled as he jogged to the kitchen. He soon came back with a bottle of wine, two glasses and a tray of cheese and crackers. Derby bit her lip. She hadn't yet told him her own secret, was too nervous to bring it up.

After leaving home, she had gone back to the flat and double checked the results with the second test. Then she had waited until Geoff called her, telling her he was home. She drove to his house, longing to tell him but not knowing how. She did tell him her marriage was over, but waited until after dinner to explain.

Geoff kneeled back down on the rug and poured Derby a glass of wine. He handed it to her and busied himself with the cheese and crackers. Derby held the glass and when he looked up at her, smiled and took a tiny sip.

"So, tell all."

He said, grinning and drinking his own wine.

It took some time for Derby to relay all that was said. In between mouthfuls of food, she disguised very small sips of wine, and because Geoff was engrossed in what she had to say, was sure she had pulled it off.

"Well that explains a lot."

Geoff stated when she finished. She nodded, putting her almost full glass down next to her on the grass. Geoff looked at it but didn't comment.

"Yes. I sort of feel sorry for him. I mean I know his mother and sister are complete bitches, but for him to be so afraid of telling them something so big."

"What about his father?"

Geoff asked. Derby shrugged.

"Left long before I knew David. He always said he ran off with another woman. Makes you wonder why. Doesn't excuse the fact that he had a son though, who might need him."

Geoff shifted closer to her and kissed her gently on the lips.

"Sounds like you both had it rough. You neglected, David over protected. But, and this is going to sound really bad, I'm glad, because I wouldn't have you now otherwise."

Derby felt tears prick the corners of her eyes. She tried to hide them, but a tiny sob escaped her lips. Instantly Geoff had his arms around her.

"Hey, what is it?"

Derby leaned into him, her voice muffled by his shoulder.

"I didn't get that."

He said, his voice soft and soothing.

Derby pulled back a little and looked into his eyes. Eyes that were full of love and concern, and knew no matter how he reacted he had to know.

"Geoff…I need…Oh…I have to tell you something."

Geoff put his hands on her shoulders, fear now in his eyes.

"What Derby?"

And before she could speak.

"Please don't tell me you've changed your mind about us. You seem edgy, and you've hardly touched your wine. Are you driving, leaving?"

Derby let out a deep breath. One she hadn't realised she'd been holding. She took his face in her cupped hands and kissed him hard on the lips.

"Nothing on any planet, in any universe would make me change my mind."

"Then what is it, please Derby?"

She stroked his cheeks with her thumbs and looked into his eyes.

"I'm…pregnant."

Geoff went still beneath her hands. For a moment he didn't breathe, and for that moment she couldn't. Then a smile, broad and wide broke across his face. Next Derby knew, she was in his arms and he was raining kisses all over her face and neck. She giggled and felt him laugh too. Breathlessly she managed to mutter.

"You don't mind then?"

Geoff leaned back a little.

"Mind? Oh my God, Derby, this is the best, the very best thing you could say."

He stood up and pulled her to her feet, hugging her again.

"You're sure?"

He mumbled. His voice full of emotion. She nodded.

"Did the test twice. I was sick at work, thought it was that bug. Then on my way home thought about dates. I have an on the dot twenty six day cycle. Always have had, right from the beginning, except when I thought I was pregnant and got married. So I hoped, and the tests popped up positive straight away. It's early, very early, but…"

"Positive, still positive."

Geoff finished for her.

Derby took his hand and drew him back down onto the rug. She had a million questions to ask him about their future, but was still afraid to voice them. Geoff sensed her turmoil and covered her cheek with his warm big hand.

"This is right Derby. It was meant to be. This is our beginning of forever."

She pulled his head towards her and kissed him. He responded, his tongue gently parting her lips, igniting the fire that started as a spark and rapidly turned to flame. She kneeled up against him, pushing him backward until he was flat on the rug. Through the kiss he mumbled.

"Can we still do this?"

"You bet."

Derby replied huskily, tugging at the waistband of his jeans. In an instant they were both naked. She straddled him, pressing hard down onto his shoulders as she took him inside her, revelling, that they were consummating this wonderful moment. She threw her head back, moving up and down, his hands holding her hips, matching each plunge with his thrusts. The stars and moon audience to their passion, witnesses to the future that lay ahead of them.

Made in the USA
Charleston, SC
20 November 2013